THE TROUBLE WITH
GOATS AND SHEEP

THE TROUBLE WITH GOATS AND SHEEP

Joanna Cannon

THE BOROUGH PRESS

The Borough Press
An imprint of HarperCollins*Publishers*
1 London Bridge Street
London SE1 9GF

www.harpercollins.co.uk

Published by HarperCollins*Publishers* 2016

6

Lyrics from 'Bye Bye Baby' © Bob Gaudio, Bob Crewe
Lyrics from 'Knock Three Times' © Irwin Levine, L. Russell Brown
Lyrics from 'Crazy' © Willie Nelson
Lyrics from 'Save all your kisses for me' © Tony Hiller, Lee Sheriden, Martin Lee

Joanna Cannon asserts the moral right to
be identified as the author of this work

A catalogue record for this book
is available from the British Library

ISBN: 978-0-00-813219-4

This novel is entirely a work of fiction.
The names, characters and incidents portrayed in it, while at times based on
historical events and figures, are the work of the author's imagination.

Set in Perpetua Std by Palimpsest Book Production Limited,
Falkirk, Stirlingshire

Printed and bound in Great Britain by
Clays Ltd, St Ives plc

MIX
Paper from
responsible sources
FSC™ C007454

FSC™ is a non-profit international organisation established to promote
the responsible management of the world's forests. Products carrying the
FSC label are independently certified to assure consumers that they come
from forests that are managed to meet the social, economic and
ecological needs of present and future generations,
and other controlled sources.

Find out more about HarperCollins and the environment at
www.harpercollins.co.uk/green

For Arthur and Janice

Number Four, The Avenue

21 June 1976

Mrs Creasy disappeared on a Monday.

I know it was a Monday, because it was the day the dustbin men came, and the avenue was filled with a smell of scraped plates.

'What's he up to?' My father nodded at the lace in the kitchen window. Mr Creasy was wandering the pavement in his shirtsleeves. Every few minutes, he stopped wandering and stood quite still, peering around his Hillman Hunter and leaning into the air as though he were listening.

'He's lost his wife.' I took another slice of toast, because everyone was distracted. 'Although she's probably just finally buggered off.'

'Grace Elizabeth!' My mother turned from the stove so quickly, flecks of porridge turned with her and escaped on to the floor.

'I'm only quoting Mr Forbes,' I said, 'Margaret Creasy never came home last night. Perhaps she's finally buggered off.'

We all watched Mr Creasy. He stared into people's gardens, as though Mrs Creasy might be camping out in someone else's herbaceous border.

My father lost interest and spoke into his newspaper. 'Do you listen in on all our neighbours?' he said.

'Mr Forbes was in his garden, talking to his wife. My window was open. It was accidental listening, which is allowed.' I spoke to my father, but addressed Harold Wilson and his pipe, who stared back at me from the front page.

'He won't find a woman wandering up and down the avenue,' my father said, 'although he might have more luck if he tried at number twelve.'

I watched my mother's face argue with a smile. They assumed I didn't understand the conversation, and it was much easier to let them think it. My mother said I was at an *awkward age*. I didn't feel especially awkward, so I presumed she meant that it was awkward for them.

'Perhaps she's been abducted,' I said. 'Perhaps it's not safe for me to go to school today.'

'It's perfectly safe,' my mother said, 'nothing will happen to you. I won't allow it.'

'How can someone just disappear?' I watched Mr Creasy, who was marching up and down the pavement. He had heavy shoulders and stared at his shoes as he walked.

'Sometimes people need their own space,' my mother spoke to the stove, 'they get confused.'

'Margaret Creasy was confused all right.' My father turned to the sports section and snapped at the pages until they were straight. 'She asked far too many questions. You couldn't get away for her rabbiting on.'

'She was just interested in people, Derek. You can feel lonely, even if you're married. And they had no children.'

My mother looked over at me as though she were considering whether the last bit made any difference at all, and then she spooned porridge into a large bowl that had purple hearts all around the rim.

'Why are you talking about Mrs Creasy in the past tense?' I said. 'Is she dead?'

'No, of course not.' My mother put the bowl on the floor. 'Remington,' she shouted, 'Mummy's made your breakfast.'

Remington padded into the kitchen. He used to be a Labrador, but he'd become so fat, it was difficult to tell.

'She'll turn up,' said my father.

He'd said the same thing about next door's cat. It disappeared years ago, and no one has seen it since.

*

Tilly was waiting by the front gate, in a jumper which had been hand-washed and stretched to her knees. She'd taken the bobbles out of her hair, but it stayed in exactly the same position as if they were still there.

3

'The lady from number eight has been murdered,' I said.

We walked in silence down the avenue, until we reached the main road. We were side by side, although Tilly had to take more steps to keep up.

'Who lives at number eight?' she said, as we waited for the traffic.

'Mrs Creasy.'

I whispered, in case Mr Creasy had extended his search.

'I liked Mrs Creasy. She was teaching me to knit. We did like her, Grace, didn't we?'

'Oh yes,' I said, 'very much.'

We crossed the road opposite the alley next to Woolworth's. It wasn't yet nine o'clock, but the pavements were dusty hot, and I could feel material stick to the bones in my back. People drove their cars with the windows down, and fragments of music littered the street. When Tilly stopped to change her school bag to the other shoulder, I stared into the shop window. It was filled with stainless-steel pans.

'Who murdered her?' A hundred Tillys spoke to me from the display.

'No one knows.'

'Where were the police?'

I watched Tilly speak through the saucepans. 'I expect they'll be along later,' I said, 'they're probably very busy.'

We climbed the cobbles in sandals which flapped on the stones and made us sound like an army of feet. In winter ice, we clung to the rail and to each other, but now the alley stretched before us, a riverbed of crisp packets and thirsty weeds, and floury soil which dirtied our toes.

'Why are you wearing a jumper?' I said.

Tilly always wore a jumper. Even in scorched heat, she would pull it over her fists and make gloves from the sleeves. Her face was magnolia, like the walls in our living room, and sweat had pulled slippery, brown curls on to her forehead.

'My mother says I can't afford to catch anything.'

'When is she going to stop worrying?' It made me angry, and I didn't know why, which made me even angrier, and my sandals became very loud.

'I doubt she ever will,' said Tilly, 'I think it's because there's only one of her. She has to do twice the worrying, to keep up with everyone else.'

'It's not going to happen again.' I stopped and lifted the bag from her shoulder. 'You can take your jumper off. It's safe now.'

She stared at me. It was difficult to see Tilly's thoughts. Her eyes hid behind thick, dark-rimmed glasses and the rest of her gave very little away.

'Okay,' she said, and took off her glasses. She pulled the jumper over her head, and when she appeared on the other side of the wool, her face was red and blotchy. She handed me the jumper, and I turned it the right way, like my mother did, and folded it over my arm.

'See,' I said, 'it's perfectly safe. Nothing will happen to you. I won't allow it.'

The jumper smelt of linctus and unfamiliar soap. I carried it all the way to school, where we dissolved into a spill of other children.

*

I have known Tilly Albert for a fifth of my life.

She arrived two summers ago in the back of a large, white van, and they unloaded her along with a sideboard and three easy chairs. I watched from Mrs Morton's kitchen, whilst I ate a cheese scone and listened to a weather forecast for the Norfolk Broads. We didn't live on the Norfolk Broads, but Mrs Morton had been there on holiday, and she liked to keep in touch.

Mrs Morton was sitting with me.

Will you just sit with Grace while I have a little lie-down, my mother would say, although Mrs Morton didn't sit very much at all, she dusted and baked and looked through windows instead. My mother spent most of 1974 having a little lie-down, and so I sat with Mrs Morton quite a lot.

I stared at the white van. 'Who's that then?' I said, through a mouthful of scone.

Mrs Morton pressed on the lace curtain, which hung halfway down the window on a piece of wire. It dipped in the middle, exhausted from all the pressing. 'That'll be the new lot,' she said.

'Who are the new lot?'

'I don't know.' She dipped the lace down a little further. 'But I don't see a man, do you?'

I peered over the lace. There were two men, but they wore overalls and were busy. The girl who had appeared from the back of the van continued to stand on the pavement. She was small and round and very pale, like a giant white pebble, and was buttoned into a raincoat right up to her neck, even though we hadn't had rain for three weeks. She pulled a face, as though she were about to cry, and then leant forwards and was sick all over her shoes.

'Disgusting,' I said, and took another scone.

*

By four o'clock, she was next to me at the kitchen table.

I had fetched her over because she had sat on the wall outside her house, looking as though she'd been misplaced. Mrs Morton got the Dandelion and Burdock out, and a new packet of Penguins. I didn't know then that Tilly didn't like eating in front of people, and she held on to the bar of chocolate until it leaked between her fingers.

Mrs Morton spat on a tissue and wiped Tilly's hands, even though there was a tap three feet away. Tilly bit her lip and looked out of the window.

'Who are you looking for?' I said.

'My mother.' Tilly turned back and stared at Mrs Morton, who was spitting again. 'I just wanted to check she's not watching.'

'You're not looking for your father?' said Mrs Morton, who was nothing if not an opportunist.

'I wouldn't know where to look.' Tilly wiped her hands very discreetly on her skirt. 'I think he lives in Bristol.'

'Bristol?' Mrs Morton put the tissue back into her cardigan sleeve. 'I have a cousin who lives in Bristol.'

'Actually, I think it might be Bournemouth,' said Tilly.

'Oh,' Mrs Morton frowned, 'I don't know anyone who lives there.'

'No,' Tilly said, 'neither do I.'

*

We spent our summer holiday at Mrs Morton's kitchen table. After a while, Tilly became comfortable enough to eat with us. She would spoon mashed potato into her mouth very slowly, and steal peas as we squeezed them from their shells, sitting over sheets of newspaper on the front-room carpet.

'Don't you want a Penguin or a Club?' Mrs Morton was always trying to force chocolate on to us. She had a tin-full in the pantry and no children of her own. The pantry was cavernous and heaved with custard creams and fingers of fudge, and I often had wild fantasies in which I would find myself trapped in there overnight and be forced to gorge myself to death on Angel Delight.

'No, thank you,' Tilly said through a very small mouth, as if she were afraid that Mrs Morton might sneak something in there when no one was looking. 'My mother said I shouldn't eat chocolate.'

'She must eat something,' Mrs Morton said later, as we

watched Tilly disappear behind her front door, 'she's like a little barrel.'

*

Mrs Creasy was still missing on Tuesday, and she was even more missing on Wednesday, when she'd arranged to sell raffle tickets for the British Legion. By Thursday, her name was being passed over garden fences and threaded along the queue at shop counters.

What about Margaret Creasy, then? someone would say. And it was like firing a starting pistol.

My father spent his time stored away in an office on the other side of the town, and always had to have the day explained to him when he got home. Yet each evening, my mother still asked my father if he had heard any news about Mrs Creasy, and each evening he would sigh from the bottom of his lungs, shake his head, and go and sit with a bottle of pale ale and Kenneth Kendall.

*

On Saturday morning, Tilly and I sat on the wall outside my house and swung our legs like pendulums against the bricks. We stared over at the Creasys' house. The front door was ajar, and all the windows were open, as if to make it easier for Mrs Creasy to find her way back inside. Mr Creasy was in his garage, pulling boxes from towers of cardboard, and examining their contents one by one.

'Do you think he murdered her?' said Tilly.

'I expect so,' I said.

I paused for a moment, before I allowed the latest bulletin to be released. 'She disappeared without taking any shoes.'

Tilly's eyes bulged like a haddock. 'How do you know that?'

'The woman in the Post Office told my mother.'

'Your mother doesn't like the woman in the Post Office.'

'She does now,' I said.

Mr Creasy began on another box. With each one, he was becoming more chaotic, scattering the contents at his feet and whispering an uncertain dialogue to himself.

'He doesn't look like a murderer,' said Tilly.

'What does a murderer look like?'

'They usually have moustaches,' she said, 'and are much fatter.'

The smell of hot tarmac pinched at my nose and I shifted my legs against the warmth of the bricks. There was nowhere to escape the heat. It was there every day when we awoke, persistent and unbroken, and hanging in the air like an unfinished argument. It leaked people's days on to pavements and patios and, no longer able to contain ourselves within brick and cement, we melted into the outside, bringing our lives along with us. Meals, conversations, discussions were all woken and untethered and allowed outdoors. Even the avenue had changed. Giant fissures opened on yellowed lawns and paths felt soft and unsteady. Things which had been solid and reliable were now pliant and uncertain. Nothing felt sure any more. The bonds which held things together were destroyed by the temperature – this is what my father said – but it felt more sinister than that. It felt as though the whole avenue was shifting and stretching, and trying to escape itself.

A fat housefly danced a figure of eight around Tilly's face. 'My mum says Mrs Creasy disappeared because of the heat.' She brushed the fly away with the back of her hand. 'My mum says the heat makes people do strange things.'

I watched Mr Creasy. He had run out of boxes and was crouched on the floor of his garage, still and silent, and surrounded by debris from the past.

'I think it probably does,' I said.

'My mum says it needs to rain.'

'I think she's probably right.'

I looked at the sky, which sat like an ocean above our heads. It wouldn't rain for another fifty-six days.

St Anthony's

27 June 1976

On Sunday, we went to church and asked God to find Mrs Creasy.

My parents didn't ask, because they were having a lie-in, but Mrs Morton and I sat near the front so God could hear us better.

'Do you think it will work?' I whispered to her, as we knelt on the slippery cushions.

'Well, it won't do any harm,' she said.

I didn't understand much of what the vicar was talking about, but he smiled at me from time to time, and I tried to look sinless and interested. The church smelt of wax and old paper, and gave us shelter from a fat sun. The wooden ribs in the roof arched over the congregation, soaking heat and sweat into cool, dry stone, and I shivered under a cotton dress. We had divided ourselves out in the pews, to make it look full, but I edged towards Mrs Morton and the warmth of her cardigan. She held out her hand and I took it, even though I was too old.

The vicar's words rumbled on the stone like distant thunder.

'I will be found by you,' declared the Lord, *'and I will bring you back from captivity.'*

I watched a bead of sweat make a path down Mrs Morton's temple. It was easy to drift off in church if you angled yourself properly.

'I will pursue them with the sword, famine and plague. For they have not listened to my words.'

That caught my attention.

'Those who love me, I will deliver; I will protect those who know my name and when they call to me, I will answer them.'

I stared at the thick, gold cross on the altar. It reflected every one of us: the pious and the ungodly; the opportunist and the devout. Each of us had our reasons for being there, quiet and expectant, and secreted between the pages of a hymn book. How would God manage to answer us all?

'Lamb of God,' said the vicar, 'who taketh away the sins of the world, have mercy upon us.'

And I wondered if we were asking God to find Mrs Creasy, or just asking Him to forgive her for disappearing in the first place.

*

We walked outside into buttery sunshine. It had spread itself over the graves, bleaching the stones and picking out the names of the dead. I watched it creep up the walls of the church until it reached the stained-glass windows, where it threw splinters of scarlet and purple into a cloudless sky. Mrs Morton and her hand had been absorbed by a clutch of efficient women in hats, and so I wandered around the churchyard in careful, horizontal lines, in case anyone was to be accidentally stepped upon.

I liked the feel of the ground beneath my shoes. It seemed safe and experienced, as though all the bones that were buried there had made wisdom grow in the soil. I walked past Ernests and Mauds and Mabels, now beloved and remembered only by the dandelions which grew across their names, until a neat gravel path brought me to the chancel. The graves here were so old, lichen had eaten into who they used to be, and rows of forgotten people stared back at me from headstones that stooped and stumbled like drunks in the earth.

I sat on newly mown grass, behind a grave which was patterned with whorls of green and white. I knew the women in hats were inclined to be time-consuming and I began to make a daisy chain. I had arrived at my fifth daisy when the chancel door opened and the vicar appeared. The breeze caught the edge of his surplice, and he billowed like sheets on a washing line. I watched him march across the graveyard to retrieve an empty crisp packet, and when he returned to the doorway, he took off his shoe and banged it on the church door to get rid of the grass cuttings.

I didn't realize something like that would be allowed.

'Why do people disappear?' I said to him, from behind the gravestone. He didn't stop banging, but slowed down and looked over his shoulder.

I realized he couldn't see me. I stood up.

'Why do people disappear?' I said again.

The vicar replaced his shoe and walked over to me. He was taller than he had been in church and very earnest. The lines on his forehead were carved and heavy, as though his face had spent its entire time trying to sort out a really big problem. He didn't look at me, but stared out over the gravestones instead.

'Many reasons,' he said eventually.

It was a rubbish answer. I'd found that answer all by myself and I didn't even have God to ask.

'Such as?'

'They wander from the path. They drift off-course.' He looked at me and I squinted up at him through the sunshine. 'They become lost.'

I thought about the Ernests and the Mauds and the Mabels. 'Or they die,' I said.

He frowned and repeated my words. 'Or they die,' he said.

The vicar smelt exactly the same as the church. Faith had been trapped within the folds of his clothes, and my lungs were filled with the scent of tapestry and candles.

'How do you stop people from disappearing?' I said.

'You help them to find God.' He shifted his weight and

gravel crunched around his shoes. 'If God exists in a community, no one will be lost.'

I thought about our estate. The unwashed children who spilled from houses and the drunken arguments that tumbled through windows. I couldn't imagine God spent very much time there at all.

'How do you find God?' I said, 'where is He?'

'He's everywhere. Everywhere.' He waved his arms around to show me. 'You just have to look.'

'And if we find God, everyone will be safe?' I said.

'Of course.'

'Even Mrs Creasy?'

'Naturally.'

A crow unfolded itself from the roof of the church, and a murderous cry filled the silence.

'I don't know how God can do that,' I said. 'How can He keep us from disappearing?'

'You know that the Lord is our shepherd, Grace. We are just sheep. Only sheep. If we wander off the path, we need God to find us and bring us home.'

I looked down at my feet whilst I thought about it. Grass had buried itself in the weave of my socks and dug sharp, red lines into my flesh.

'Why do people have to die?' I said, but when I looked up, the vicar was back at the chancel door.

'Are you coming for tea at the church hall?' he shouted.

I didn't really want to. I would rather have gone back to Tilly. Her mother didn't believe in organized religion and was worried we'd all be brainwashed by the vicar, but I had to agree, or it would have been a bit like turning down Jesus.

'Okay,' I said, and picked the blades of grass from my knees.

*

I walked behind Mrs Morton, along the lane between the church and the hall. The verge was thick with summer: stitchwort and buttercups, and towering foxgloves which blew clouds of pollen from rich, purple bells. The breeze had dropped, leaving us in a razor of heat which cut into the skin at the tops of my arms and made speaking too much of an effort. We trudged in a single line; silent pilgrims drawn towards a shrine of tea and digestives, all strapped into Sunday clothes and decorated with sweat.

When we reached the car park, Tilly was sitting on the wall. She was basted in sun cream and wore a sou'wester.

'It was the only hat I could find,' she said.

'I thought your mother didn't want you to be religious?' I held out my hand.

'She's gone to stack shelves in the Co-op,' Tilly said, and heaved herself down from the bricks.

The church hall was a low, white building, which squatted at the end of the lane and looked as though it had been put there whilst someone made their mind up about what to do with it. Inside, it rattled with teacups and efficiency.

Sunday heels clicked on a parquet floor and giant, stainless-steel urns spat and hissed to us from the corner.

'I'm going to have Bovril,' said Tilly.

I studied Mrs Morton, as she ordered our drinks on the other side of the room. Early widowhood had forced her to weave a life from other people's remnants, and she had baked and minded and knitted herself into a glow of indispensability. I wondered who Mrs Morton would be if she still had a husband – if Mr Morton hadn't been searching for The New Seekers in the footwell of his car and driven himself head-first into the central reservation of the M4. There had been a female passenger (people whispered), who appeared at the funeral in ankle-length black and crimson lipstick, and who sobbed with such violence she had to be escorted from the church by an anxious sexton. I remembered none of this. I was too young. I had only ever known Mrs Morton as she was now; tweeded and scrubbed, and rattling like a pebble in a life made for two.

'Bovril.' Mrs Morton handed a cup to Tilly. We all knew she wouldn't drink it, but we kept up the pretence, even Tilly, who held it to her face until steam crept over her glasses.

'Do you believe in God, Mrs Morton?' I looked up at her.

Tilly and I both waited.

She didn't reply immediately, but her eyes searched for an answer in the beams of the ceiling. 'I believe in not asking people daft questions on a Sunday morning,' she said eventually, and went to find the toilet.

The hall filled with people. It was far more crowded than the church had been, and pairs of jeans mixed with Sunday best. It appeared that Jesus pulled a much bigger crowd if He provided garibaldis. There were people from our avenue – the Forbeses and the man who was always mowing his lawn, and the woman from the corner house, who was surrounded by a clutter of children. They clung to her hips and her legs, and I watched as she slipped biscuits into her pocket. Everyone stood with newspapers in their armpits and sunglasses on their foreheads and, in the corner, some-one's Pomeranian was having an argument with a Border Collie. People were talking about the water shortage and James Callaghan, and whether Mrs Creasy had turned up yet. She hadn't.

No one mentioned Jesus.

In fact, I didn't think anyone would have noticed if Jesus had walked into the room, unless He happened to be accom-panied by an Arctic roll.

*

'Do you believe in God?' I asked Tilly.

We sat in a corner of the hall, on blue plastic chairs which pulled the sweat from our skin, Tilly sniffing her Bovril and me drawing my knees to my chest, like a shield. I could see Mrs Morton in the distance, trapped by a trestle table and two large women in flowered aprons.

'Probably,' she said. 'I think God saved me when I was in hospital.'

'How do you know that?'

'My mum asked Him to every day.' She frowned into her cup. 'She went off Him after I got better.'

'You've never told me. You always said you were too young to remember.'

'I remember that,' she said, 'and I remember it was Christmas and the nurses wore tinsel in their hair. I don't remember anything else.'

She didn't. I had asked – many times. It was better for children if they didn't know all the facts, she'd said, and the words always left her mouth in italics.

When she first told me, it was thrown into the conversation with complete indifference, like a playing card. I had never met anyone who had nearly died, and in the beginning the subject was attacked with violent curiosity. Then it became more than fascination. I needed to know everything, so that all the details might be stitched together for protection. As if hearing the truth would somehow save us from it. If I had almost died, I would have an entire speech to use at a moment's notice, but Tilly only remembered the tinsel and something being wrong with her blood. It wasn't enough – even when I connected all the words together, like a prayer.

After she told me, I had joined her mother in a silent conspiracy of watchfulness. Tilly was watched as we ran under a seamless August sky; a breathless look over my shoulder, waiting for her legs to catch up with mine. She was protected from a baked summer by my father's golfing umbrella, a life lived far from the edges of kerbs and the cracks in pavements, and when September carried in mist and rain, she was placed so close to the gas fire, her legs became tartanned in red.

I watched her without end, inspecting her life for the slightest vibration of change, and yet she knew none of this. My worries were noiseless; a silent obsession that the only friend I had ever made would be taken from me, just because I hadn't concentrated hard enough.

*

The noise in the hall drifted into a slur of voices. It was a machine, ticking over in the heat, fuelled by rumour and judgement, and we stared into an engine of cooked flesh and other people's feet. Mr Forbes stood in front of us, sailing a cherry Bakewell through the air and giving out his opinion, as warmth crept into the material of his shirt.

'He woke up on Monday morning and she'd gone. Vanished.'

'Beggars belief,' said Eric Lamb, who still had grass cuttings on the bottom of his trousers.

'Live for the moment, that's what I say.' I watched Mr Forbes sail another cherry Bakewell around, as if to demonstrate his point.

Mrs Forbes didn't speak. Instead, she shuffled her sandals

on the herringbone floor, and twisted a teacup around in its saucer. Her face had worried itself into a pinch.

Mr Forbes studied her, as he disappeared his cherry Bakewell. 'Stop whittling about it, Dorothy. It's got nothing to do with that.'

'It's got everything to do with that,' she said, 'I just know it.'

Mr Forbes shook his head. 'Tell her, Eric,' he said, 'she won't listen to me.'

'That's all in the past. This will be about something else. A bit of a tiff, that's what it'll be,' said Eric Lamb. I thought his voice was softer, and edged with comfort, but Mrs Forbes continued to shuffle, and she trapped her thoughts behind a frown.

'Or the heat,' said Mr Forbes, patting his belly to ensure the cherry Bakewells had safely arrived at their destination. 'People do strange things in this kind of weather.'

'That's it,' said Eric Lamb, 'it'll be the heat.'

Mrs Forbes looked up from her twisting teacup. Her smile was very thin. 'We're a bit buggered if it isn't, though, aren't we?' she said.

The three stood in silence. I saw a stare pass between them, and Mr Forbes dragged the crumbs from his mouth with the back of a hand. Eric Lamb didn't speak. When the stare reached his eyes, he looked at the floor to avoid taking it.

After a while, Mrs Forbes said, 'this tea needs more milk,' and she disappeared into a wall of sunburned flesh.

I tapped Tilly on the arm, and a spill of Bovril escaped on to blue plastic.

'Did you hear that?' I said. 'Mrs Forbes said they're all buggered.'

'That's not very church hall-ey, is it?' said Tilly, who still wore her sou'wester. She wiped the Bovril with the edge of her jumper. 'Mrs Forbes has been a little unusual lately.'

This was true. Only the day before, I'd seen her wandering around the front garden in a nightdress, having a long conversation with the flower beds.

It's the heat, Mr Forbes had said, as he took her back inside with a cup of tea and the *Radio Times*.

'Why do people blame everything on the heat?' said Tilly.

'It's easier,' I said.

'Easier than what?'

'Easier than telling everyone the real reasons.'

*

The vicar appeared.

We knew he had arrived even before we saw him, because all around the room, conversations began to cough and falter. He cut through the crowd, leaving it to re-form behind him, like the surface of the Red Sea. He appeared to glide beneath his cassock, and there was an air of stillness about him, which made everyone he approached seem overactive and slightly hysterical. People stood a little straighter as they shook his hand, and I saw Mrs Forbes do what appeared to be a small curtsy.

23

'What did he say in church then?' said Tilly, as we watched him edge around the room.

'He said that God runs after people with knives if they don't listen to Him properly.'

Tilly sniffed her Bovril again. 'I never knew He did that,' she said eventually.

Sometimes I struggled to take my gaze from her. She was almost transparent, as fragile as glass. 'He said that if we find God, He'll keep us all safe.'

Tilly looked up. There was a streak of sun cream on the very tip of her nose. 'Do you think someone else is going to disappear, Gracie?'

I thought about the gravestones and Mrs Creasy, and the fractured, yellow lawns.

'Do we need God to keep us safe? Are we not safe just as we are?' she said.

'I'm not sure that I know any more.'

I watched her, and threaded my worries like beads.

*

The vicar completed his circuit of the room and disappeared, as if he were a magician's assistant, behind a curtain next to the stage. The engine of conversation started again, small at first, and uncertain, then powering up to its previous level, as the air filled with hosepipe bans and stories of vanishing neighbours.

It probably would have stayed that way. It probably would have run its course, and continued until people wandered home to fill themselves with Brussels sprouts, had Mr Creasy not burst through the double doors and marched the length of the hall past a startled audience. Silence followed him around the room, leaving only the click of a cup on a saucer, and the sound of elbows nudging each other.

He stopped in front of Mr Forbes and Eric Lamb, his face stretched with anger. Tilly said afterwards that she thought he was going to hit someone, but to me he looked as though all the hitting had been frightened out of him.

The words stayed in his eyes for a few seconds, then he said, 'You told her, didn't you?'

It was a whisper that wanted to be a shout, and it left his mouth wrapped in spit and fury.

Mr Forbes turned from their audience, and guided Mr Creasy towards a wall. I heard him say *Christ* and *calm down* and *for heaven's sake*, and then I heard him say, 'We haven't told her anything.'

'Why else would she up and leave?' said Mr Creasy. The rage seemed to immobilize him, and he became a furious effigy, fixed and motionless, except for the flush which crept from beneath his shirt and into his neck.

'I don't know,' said Mr Forbes, 'but if she's found out, it's not come from us.'

'We're not that stupid,' said Eric Lamb. He looked over his shoulder at a sea of teacups and curiosity. 'Let's get you out of here, let's get you a drink.'

'I don't want a bloody drink.' Mr Creasy hissed at them, like a snake. 'I want my wife back.'

He had no choice. They escorted him out of the hall, like prison guards.

I watched Mrs Forbes.

She stared at the door long after it had closed behind them.

Number Four, The Avenue

27 June 1976

The roads on our estate were all named after trees, and Tilly and I walked home from the church hall along an alley which separated Sycamore from Cedar. On either side of us, lines of washing stretched like bunting across deserted gardens, waiting for the whisper of a breeze, and as we walked, drips of water smacked a tune on to concrete paths.

No one realized then that, in many years to come, people would still speak of this summer; that every other heatwave would be compared to this one, and those who lived through it would shake their heads and smile whenever anyone complained of the temperature. It was a summer of deliverance. A summer of Space Hoppers and dancing queens, when Dolly Parton begged Jolene not to take her man, and we all stared at the surface of Mars and felt small. We had to share bathwater and half-fill the kettle, and we were only allowed to flush the toilet after what Mrs Morton described as a *special occasion*. The only problem was, it meant that everyone knew when you'd had a special occasion, which was a bit awkward. Mrs Morton said we'd end up with buckets and standpipes if we weren't careful, and she was part of a vigilante group, who reported anyone for watering their gardens in the dark (Mrs Morton used washing-up water, which was allowed). *It will only work if we all pull together*, she said. I knew this wasn't true, mind you, because, unlike the brittle yellow of everyone else's, Mr Forbes' lawn remained a strangely suspicious shade of green.

*

I could hear Tilly's voice behind me. It drummed on the parched, wooden slats of the fences either side, which were beaten into white by the heat.

What do you think? she was saying.

She had been turning Mr Creasy's words over since Pine Crescent, trying to fit them into an opinion.

'I think Mr and Mrs Forbes are in on it,' I shouted back.

She caught up with me, her legs fighting with the sentence. 'Do you think they were the ones who murdered her?'

'I think they all murdered her together.'

'I'm not sure they look the type,' she said. 'My mum thinks the Forbeses are old-fashioned.'

'No, they're very modern.' I found a stick and drew it along the fence. 'They have a SodaStream.'

Tilly's mum thought everyone was old-fashioned. Tilly's mum owned long earrings and drank Campari, and only ever wore cheesecloth. In cold weather, she just wore more cheesecloth, layering it around herself like a shroud.

'My mum says Mr and Mrs Forbes are curious people.'

'Well, she'd know,' I said.

Back doors were propped open in the heat, and the smell of batter and roasting tins escaped from other people's lives. Even in ninety degrees, Brussels sprouts still simmered on stoves, and gravy still dripped and pooled on heavy plates.

'I hate Sundays,' I said.

'Why?' Tilly found another stick and dragged it alongside mine.

Tilly didn't hate anything.

'It's just the day before Monday,' I said. 'It's always too empty.'

'We break up soon. We'll have six weeks of nothing but Sundays.'

'I know.' The stick hammered my boredom into the wood.

'What shall we do with our holidays?'

We reached the end of the fence, and the alley became silent.

'I haven't quite decided yet,' I said, and let the stick fall from my hand.

*

We walked on to Lime Crescent , our sandals sending loose chippings dancing along the road. I looked up, but sunlight shot back from cars and windows and punished my eyes. I squinted and tried again.

Tilly didn't notice, but I saw them straight away. A tribe of girls, a uniform of Quatro flicks and lip gloss, with hands stuffed into pockets, making denim wings. They stood on the opposite corner, doing nothing except being older than me. I saw them weigh out our presence, as they measured the pavement with scuffed market boots and chewed gum. They were a bookmark, a page I had yet to read, and I wanted to stretch myself out to get there.

I knew them all. I had watched for so long from the margins of their lives, their faces were as familiar as my own. I looked over for a thread of acknowledgement, but there was none. Even when I willed it with my eyes. Even when I slowed my steps to almost nothing. Tilly walked ahead, and I grew the distance between us, as stares filled with opinion reflected back at me. I couldn't find anything to do with my arms, and so I folded them around my waist and tried to make my sandals sound more rebellious.

Tilly waited for me around the corner.

'What shall we do now?' she said.

'Dunno.'

'Shall we go to your house?'

'S'pose.'

'Why are you talking like that?'

I unfolded my arms. 'I don't know.'

She smiled, and I smiled back, even though the smiling felt unquiet.

'Here,' I said, and took the sou'wester from her head and put it on my own.

Her laughter was instant, and she reached for it back. 'Some people just can't wear hats, Gracie,' she said. 'It should stay where it belongs.'

My arm linked through hers and we walked towards home. Past matched lawns and carbon-papered lives, and rows of terraced houses, which handcuffed families together through chance and coincidence.

And I tried to make it enough.

*

When we got home, my mother was peeling potatoes and talking to Jimmy Young. He sat on the shelf above her head, and she nodded and smiled at him as she filled the sink with soil.

'You've been gone a while.'

I wasn't sure if she was talking to me or to Jimmy.

'We were at church,' I said.

'Did you enjoy it?'

'Not really.'

'That's nice,' she said, and fished another potato from the mud.

Tilly's laughter hid inside her jumper.

'Where's Dad?' I took two cheese triangles from the fridge and emptied a packet of Quavers on to a plate.

'He's gone to get a paper,' said my mother, and she drowned the potatoes with a little more certainty. 'He'll be back soon.'

Pub, I mouthed at Tilly.

I unwrapped a triangle and Tilly took off her sou'wester, and we listened to Brotherhood of Man and watched my mother fashion potatoes.

Save all your kisses for me, said the radio, and Tilly and I did the dance with our arms.

'Do you believe in God?' I said to my mother, when the record had finished.

'Now, do I believe in God?' Her peeling slowed, and she stared at the ceiling.

I couldn't understand why everyone looked towards the sky when I asked the question. As though they were expecting God to appear in the clouds and give them the right answer. If so, God let my mother down, and we were still waiting for her reply when my father appeared at the back door with no newspaper, and the British Legion still smeared in his eyes.

He draped himself around my mother, like a sheet. 'How is my beautiful wife?' he said.

'There's no time for that nonsense, Derek.' She drowned another potato.

'And my two favourite girls.' He ruffled our hair, which was a bit of a mistake, as neither Tilly nor I had the kind of hair that could be ruffled very successfully. Mine was too blonde and opinionated, and Tilly's refused to be separated from its bobbles.

'Are you staying for some lunch, Tilly?' my father said.

He leaned over to speak and ruffled her hair again. Whenever Tilly was there, he became a cartoon parent, a surrogate father. He swooped down to fill a gap in Tilly's life that she never realized existed, until he highlighted it so exquisitely.

She started to answer, but he had his head in the fridge.

'I saw Thin Brian in the Legion,' he was saying to my mother. 'Guess what he told me.'

My mother remained silent.

'That old woman who lives at the end of Mulberry Drive, you know the one?'

My mother nodded into the peelings.

'They found her dead last Monday.'

'She was quite old, Derek.'

'The point is,' he said, unwrapping a cheese triangle of his own, 'they reckon she'd been dead for a week and no one noticed.'

My mother looked over, and Tilly and I stared at the plate of Quavers in an effort to be unremembered.

'They wouldn't have discovered her even then,' my father said, 'if it hadn't been for the sme—'

'Why don't you girls go outside?' my mother said. 'I'll shout when your dinner's ready.'

*

We sat on the patio, our backs pressed into the bricks to keep us in a ribbon of shade.

'Fancy dying and no one misses you,' Tilly said. 'That's not very Godly, is it?'

'The vicar says God is everywhere,' I said.

Tilly frowned at me.

'Everywhere.' I waved my arms around to show her.

'So why wasn't He on Mulberry Drive?'

I stared at the row of sunflowers on the far side of the garden. My mother had planted them last spring, and now they stretched above the wall and peered into the Forbes' garden, like floral spies.

'I'm not sure,' I said. 'Perhaps He was somewhere else.'

'I hope someone misses me when I die,' she said.

'You're not going to die. Neither of us are. Not until we're old. Not until people expect it of us. God will keep us safe until then.'

'He didn't keep Mrs Creasy safe, though, did he?'

I watched bumble bees drift between the sunflowers. They explored each one, dipping into the centre, searching and inspecting, until they reappeared in the daylight, dusted in yellow and drunk with achievement.

And it all became so obvious. 'I know what we're going to do with the summer holidays,' I said, and got to my feet.

Tilly looked up. She squinted at me and shielded her eyes from the sun. 'What?'

'We're going to make sure everyone is safe. We're going to bring Mrs Creasy back.'

'How are we going to do that?'

'We're going to look for God,' I said.

'We are?'

'Yes,' I said, 'we are. Right here on this avenue. And I'm not giving up until we find Him.'

I held out my hand. She took it and I pulled her up next to me.

'Okay, Gracie,' she said.

And she put her sou'wester back on and smiled.

Number Six, The Avenue

27 June 1976

It was *Are You Being Served?* on a Monday, *The Good Life* on a Tuesday, and *The Generation Game* on a Saturday. Although for the life of her, Dorothy couldn't see what people found funny about Bruce Forsyth.

She tried to remember them, like a test, as she did the washing-up. It took her mind off the church hall, and the look on John Creasy's face, and the spidery feeling in her chest.

Monday, Tuesday, Saturday. She usually liked washing up. She liked to watch the garden and idle her mind, but today the weight of the heat pressed against the glass and made her feel as though she were looking out from a giant oven.

Monday, Tuesday, Saturday.

She could still remember, although she wasn't taking any chances. They were all circled in the *Radio Times*.

Harold became very irritable if she asked him something more than once.

Try to keep it in your head, Dorothy, he told her.

When Harold became angry, he could fill a room with his own annoyance. He could fill their sitting room, and the doctor's surgery. He could even fill an entire supermarket.

She tried very hard to keep things in her head.

Sometimes, though, the words escaped her. They hid behind other words, or they showed a little of themselves, and then disappeared back into her mind before she had a chance to catch them.

I can't find my . . . she would say, and Harold would throw choices at her like bullets. *Keys? Gloves? Purse? Glasses?* and it would make the word she wanted disappear even more.

Cuddly toy, she said one day, to make him laugh.

But Harold didn't laugh. Instead, he stared at her as though she had walked into the conversation uninvited, and then he had closed the back door very quietly and started mowing the lawn. And somehow the quietness filled a room even more than the anger.

She folded the tea towel and put it on the edge of the draining board.

Harold had been quiet since they'd got back from church. He and Eric had deposited John Creasy some- where, although Lord knows where, she hadn't even dared ask, and he had sat down and read his newspaper in silence. He had eaten his dinner in silence, and dropped gravy down his shirt front in silence, and when she asked him if he wanted mandarin segments with Ideal milk for afterwards, he had only nodded at her.

When she put it down in front of him, he said the only sentence to come out of his mouth all afternoon. *These are peaches, Dorothy.*

It was happening all over again. It ran in families, she'd read it somewhere. Her mother ended up the same way, kept being found wandering the streets at six in the morning (postman, nightdress) and putting everything where it didn't belong (slippers, breadbin). *Mad as a box of frogs*, Harold had called her. She was around Dorothy's age when she first started to lose her mind, although Dorothy always thought losing your mind was such a strange phrase. As if your mind could be misplaced, like a set of house keys, or a Jack Russell terrier, as if it was more than likely your own fault for being so bloody careless.

They'd put her mother in a home within weeks. It was all very quick.

It's for the best, Harold had said.

He'd said it each time they went to visit.

After he'd eaten his peaches, Harold had settled himself on the settee and fallen asleep, although how anyone could sleep in this heat was beyond her. He was still there now, his stomach rising and falling as he shifted in between dreams, his snoring keeping time with the kitchen clock, and plotting out the afternoon for them both.

Dorothy took the remains of their silent meal and emptied it into the pedal bin. The only problem with losing your mind was that you never lost the memories you wanted to lose. The memories you really needed left first. Her foot rested on the pedal, and she looked into the waste. No matter how many lists you wrote, and how many circles you made in the *Radio Times*, and no matter how much you practised the words over and over again, and tried to fool people, the only memories that didn't leave were the ones you wish you'd never made in the first place.

She reached into the rubbish and lifted a tin out of the potato peelings. She stared at it.

'These are peaches, Dorothy,' she said to an empty kitchen. '*Peaches.*'

She felt the tears before she even knew they had happened.

*

'The problem, Dorothy, is that you think too much.' Harold's gaze never left the television screen. 'It's not healthy.'

Evening had tempered the sun, and a wash of gold folded across the living room. It drew the sideboard into a rich, dark brandy and buried itself in the pleats of the curtains.

Dorothy picked imaginary fluff from the sleeve of her cardigan. 'It's difficult not to think about it, Harold, under the circumstances.'

'This is completely different. She's a grown woman. Her and John have probably just had some kind of tiff and she's cleared off for a bit to teach him a lesson.'

She looked over at her husband. The light from the window gave his face a faint blush of marzipan. 'I only hope you're right,' she said.

'Of course I'm right.' His stare was still fastened to the television screen, and she watched his eyes flicker as the images changed.

It was *Sale of the Century*. She should have known better than to speak to Harold whilst he was occupied with Nicholas Parsons. It might have been best to try and fit the conversation into an advert break, but there were too many words and she couldn't stop them climbing into her mouth.

'The only thing is, I saw her. A few days before she disappeared.' Dorothy cleared her throat, even though there was nothing to clear. 'She was going into number eleven.'

Harold looked at her for the first time. 'You never told me.'

'You never asked,' she said.

'What was she doing going in there?' He turned towards her, and his glasses fell from the arm of his chair. 'What could they possibly have to say to each other?'

'I have no idea, but it can't be a coincidence, can it? She speaks to him, and then a few days later, she vanishes. He must have said something.'

Harold stared at the floor, and she waited for his fear to catch up with hers. In the corner, the television churned the laughter of strangers out into their living room.

'What I don't understand', he said, 'is how he could stay

on the avenue, after everything that happened. He should
have moved on.'

'You can't dictate to people where they live, Harold.'

'He doesn't belong here.'

'He's lived at number eleven all his life.'

'But after what he did?'

'He didn't do anything.' Dorothy looked at the screen to
avoid Harold's eyes. 'They said so.'

'I know what they said.'

She could hear him breathing. The wheeze of warm air
moving through tired lungs. She waited. But he turned to
the television and straightened his spine.

'You're just being hysterical, Dorothy. All that's over and
done with. It was ten years ago.'

'Nine, actually,' she said.

'Nine, ten, what does it matter? It's all in the past, except
every time you start talking about it, it stops being in the
past and starts being in the present again.'

She gathered the material of her skirt into folds and let
them fall between her hands.

'Would you stop fidgeting, woman.'

'I can't help myself,' she said.

'Well, go and do something productive. Go and have a
bath.'

'I had a bath this morning.'

'Well, go and have another one,' he said, 'you're putting
me off the questions.'

'What about saving water, Harold?'

But Harold didn't reply. Instead of replying, he picked at his teeth. Dorothy could hear him. Even over Nicholas Parsons.

She smoothed down her hair and her skirt. She took a deep breath to suffocate her words, and then she stood up and walked from the room. Before she closed the door, she looked back.

He had turned away from the television, and was staring through the window – past the lace of the curtains, across the gardens and the pavements, to the front door of number eleven.

His glasses still lay at his feet.

*

Dorothy knew exactly where she'd hidden the tin.

Harold never went into the back bedroom. It was a holding place. A waiting room for all the things she no longer needed but couldn't bear to lose. He said the thought of it gave him a headache. As the years turned, the room had grown. Now the past pushed into corners and reached to the ceiling. It stretched along the window-sill and touched the skirting boards, and it allowed Dorothy to hold it in her hands. Sometimes, remembering wasn't enough. Sometimes, she needed to carry the past with her to be sure she was a part of it.

The room trapped summer within its walls. It held Dorothy in an airless museum of dust and paper, and she felt the sweat bleed into her hairline. The sound of the television crept through the floorboards, and she could picture Harold beneath her feet, answering questions and picking at his teeth.

The tin sat between a pile of blankets her mother had crocheted and some crockery left over from the caravan. She could see it from the doorway, as though it had waited for her, and she kneeled on the carpet and pulled it free. Around the edge were photographs of biscuits to tempt you inside, pink wafers and party rings and Jammie Dodgers, all joining cartoon hands and dancing with cartoon legs, and she held on to them as she lifted the lid away.

The first thing she saw was a raffle ticket from 1967 and a collection of safety pins. There were Harold's tarnished cufflinks and a few escaped buttons, and the cutting about her mother's funeral from the local paper.

Passed away peacefully, it said.

She hadn't.

But beneath the pins and the grips and the buttons was what she had come for. Kodak envelopes, fattened with time. Harold didn't believe in photographs. Mawkish, he called them. Dorothy didn't know anyone else who used the word 'mawkish'. There were very few pictures of Harold. There was an occasional elbow at a dinner table, or trouser leg on a lawn, and if anyone had managed to capture his face in the frame, he wore the expression of someone who had been the victim of trickery.

She searched through the packets. Most of the photographs were rescued from her mother's house. People she didn't know, held within white, serrated edges, sitting in gardens she didn't recognize and rooms she had never visited. There were Georges and Florries, and lots of people called Bill. They had written their names on the back, perhaps hoping that, if their identity were known, they would somehow be better remembered.

There were few photographs of her own – an infrequent Christmas gathering, a meal with the Ladies' Circle. A photograph of Whiskey fell to the carpet, and she felt her throat fill.

He had never come home.

Just get another cat, Harold had said.

It was the closest she had ever come to losing her temper.

The photograph she wanted was at the bottom, a weight of memories pressed upon it. She had to see. She had to be sure. Perhaps, over the years, the past had become misshapen. Perhaps time had stretched their part in it, and bloated her conscience. Perhaps, if she could see the faces again, she would recognize their harmlessness.

They looked up at her from a table at the British Legion. It was before everything happened, but she was sure it was the same table – the table where the decision had been made. Harold sat next to her, and they both stared into the lens with troubled eyes. The photographer had caught them by surprise, she remembered that, someone from the town paper wanting pictures for an article on *local colour*. Of course, they never used it. John Creasy stood behind them, his hands pushed into his pockets, looking out from under a Beatles fringe. Sitting in front of John was that daft clown Thin Brian, with a pint glass in his hand, and Eric Lamb was opposite Harold. Sheila Dakin was on the end – all eyelashes and Babycham.

Dorothy looked at their faces, hoping to see something else.

There was nothing. They were exactly as she had left them.

It was 1967. The year Johnson sent thousands more to die in Vietnam. The year China made a hydrogen bomb, and Israel fought a six-day war. The year people marched and shouted, and waved banners about what they believed in.

It was a year of choices.

She wished she had known then that one day she would be staring back at herself, wishing that the choice they had made had been a different one. She turned the photograph over. There were no names. After all that had happened, she was certain none of them would care to be remembered.

'Whatever are you doing?'

Harold's footsteps weren't usually so discreet. She turned away from him and tucked the photograph into her waist-band.

'I'm going over a few things.'

He leaned against the door frame. Dorothy wasn't sure when it happened, but Harold had become old. The skin on his face had thinned to a lacquer, and his posture was bowed and curved, as though he were slowly returning to the womb.

'So, why have you buried yourself in here, Dorothy?'

She looked straight into his eyes and saw his mind stumble.

'I'm making . . .' she said, 'I'm making . . .'

'Headway?' Harold peered into the room. 'A mess? A nuisance of yourself?'

'A choice.' Dorothy smiled up at him. 'I'm making a choice.'

And she watched as he wiped sweat from his temple with the sleeve of his shirt.

*

When Harold went back downstairs, Dorothy walked on to the landing and looked at the photograph again. The smell came to her first, a smell that seemed to live on the avenue for weeks afterwards, held in a bite of December frost. Sometimes she thought she could still smell it now, even after all this time. She would be walking along the pavement, wandering around in her own thoughts, and it would creep up on her again. As if it had never really disappeared, as if it had been left there on purpose to remind them all. That night, she had stood where she was standing now, and she had watched it all unfold. She had replayed that scene to herself so many times, perhaps hoping something might change, that she would be able to let it go, but it was a night that had nailed itself to her memory. And she had known even then, even as she'd watched, that there would be no going back.

21 December 1967

Sirens hammer into the road, drawing the avenue from its sleep. Lights fizz and tick, and aquariums of people look out into the night. Dorothy watches from the landing. The banister digs into her bones as she leans forward, but this is the window with the best view, and she leans a little more. As she does, the bells of the siren stop and the fire engine empties men on to the street. She tries to listen, but the glass dulls their voices, and the only sound she hears is air moving through her throat, and the stamp of a pulse in her neck.

Ferns of ice grow at the corners of the windows, and she has to peer around them to see properly. There are hoses twisting across pavements, and rivers of light shining into the black. It feels unreal, theatrical, as though someone is staging a play in the middle of the avenue. Across the road, Eric Lamb opens his front door, pulling on a jacket, shouting back before he runs on to the street, and all around her, windows catch and push, spilling breath into the darkness.

She calls to Harold. She has to call several times, because his dreams are like cement. When he does appear, he has the frayed edges of someone who has been shocked into consciousness. He wants to know what's going on, and he shouts the question at her, even though he is standing three feet away. She can see the skin of sleep in the corners of his eyes, and the journey of the pillow across his cheek.

She turns back to the window. More doors have opened, more people have appeared. Above the smell of the house, above the polished windowsills and the Fairy Liquid sink, she imagines she can sense the smoke, sliding in through the cracks and the splinters, and finding its way through the bricks.

She looks back at Harold.

'I think something very bad has happened,' she says.

*

They reach the garden. John Creasy calls across the avenue, but his voice is lost in the churn of the engine and the punch of boots on the concrete. Dorothy peers through the dark towards the bottom of the road. Sheila Dakin is standing on the lawn, feeding her hands into her face, the wind whipping at her dressing gown, smacking the material against her legs like a flag. Harold tells Dorothy to stay where she is, but it feels as though the fire has a magnetic field, and everyone is pulled closer, drawn along paths and pavements. The only one who is still is May Roper. She stands in her doorway, held there by the light and the noise and the smell. Brian catches her as he rushes past, but she barely seems to notice.

The firemen work like machinery, forming links of a chain which drags water from the earth. There is an arc of sound. An explosion. Harold is shouting to Dorothy to get back inside, but she moves a little closer instead. She watches Harold. He is too interested in what's happening to notice, and she edges her way next to the wall. She just needs to see for a moment. To find out if it's really happened.

She reaches the far end of the garden, when a fireman begins sweeping the air with his arms, forcing them back like puppets, and they collect in the middle of the avenue, knotted together against the frost.

The fireman is shouting questions. *How many people live in the house?*

They all answer at once, and their voices are smeared, taken by the wind.

The fireman scans their faces and points at Derek. 'How many?' he says again, his mouth shaping around the words.

'One,' he shouts, 'just one.' Derek looks back at his own house, and Dorothy follows his gaze. Sylvia stands at the window, Grace in her arms. Sylvia watches them, then turns away, holding the child's head against her skin. 'His mother lives in a nursing home, but he's taken her away for Christmas,' Derek says. 'So it's empty.' The fireman is already running back and Derek's words are wasted to the darkness.

A roll of smoke unfolds towards the sky. It loses itself against the black, whispering edges caught against a bank of stars before it feathers into nothing. Harold finds Eric's eyes, and Eric shakes his head, a brief movement, almost nothing. Dorothy catches it, but looks away, back to the grip of the noise and the smoke.

None of them notice him, not to begin with. They are too captured by the flames, watching the darts of orange and red that fasten and catch in the windows. It's Dorothy who sees him first. Her shock is soundless, static, but still it finds each of them. It stumbles around the group, until they all turn from number eleven and stare.

Walter Bishop.

The wind slips inside his coat and lifts the collar. It takes spirals of his hair and tries to cover his eyes. His lips are moving, but the words aren't yet ready to leave. There is a carrier bag. It falls from his hand and a tin skittles across the pavement and into the gutter. Dorothy lifts it back and tries to return it to him.

'Everyone thought you'd gone away with your mother,' she says, but Walter doesn't hear.

There are shouts from the house, carried across the avenue, and one fireman's voice lifts above the rest.

There's someone in there, it says. *There's someone in the house.*

They all turn from the fire to look at Walter.

'Who's inside?' It's the question in everyone's eyes, but it's Harold who gives it a voice.

At first, Dorothy doesn't think Walter has even heard the question. His gaze doesn't move from the slurry of black smoke, which has begun to pour from the windows of his house. When he finally replies, his voice is so soft, so whispered, they all have to lean forward to listen.

'Chicken soup,' he says.

Harold frowns. Dorothy can see all the wrinkles of the future pinch together on his forehead.

'Chicken soup?' The wrinkles become even deeper.

'Oh yes.' Walter's eyes don't move from number eleven. 'It works wonders for the flu. Terrible thing, isn't it, the flu?'

They all nod, like ghostly marionettes in the darkness.

'We'd only just got to the hotel when she took ill. I said to her, *Mother,* I said, *when you're under the weather, what you need is your own bed.* And so we turned around and came home again.'

And all the marionette eyes stare at Walter's first-floor window.

'And she's up there now?' says Harold, 'your mother?'

Walter nods. 'I couldn't take her back to the nursing home, could I? Not in that state. So I put her to bed and went to ring for the doctor.' He looks at the tin Dorothy handed back to him. 'I wanted to explain to him I was giving her the soup, as he advised. They put so many additives in these things now. You can't be too careful, can you?'

'No,' says Dorothy, 'you can't be too careful.'

The smoke creeps across the avenue. Dorothy can taste it in her mouth. It blends with the fear and the frost, and she pulls her cardigan a little closer to her chest.

*

Harold walks into the kitchen through the back door. Dorothy knows he has something to tell her, because he never uses the back door unless it's an emergency or he is wearing his wellington boots.

She looks up from her crossword and waits.

He moves around the work surfaces, lifting things up unnecessarily, opening cupboard doors, looking at the bottom of crockery, until he can't hold on to the words any longer.

'It's awful in there,' he says, as he replaces a mug on the mug tree. 'Awful.'

'You've been inside?' Dorothy puts down her pen. 'Are you allowed to go inside?'

'The police and the fire service haven't been there for days. No one said we couldn't go inside.'

'Is it safe?'

'We didn't go upstairs.' He finds a packet of bourbons she had deliberately hidden behind the self-raising flour. 'Eric didn't think it was respectful, you know, under the circumstances.'

Dorothy doesn't think it's respectful rummaging around in the downstairs either, but it's easier to say nothing. If you challenge Harold, he spends days justifying himself, like turning on a tap. She had wanted to go in there herself. She even got as far as the back door, but she'd changed her mind. It probably wouldn't be wise, under the circumstances. Harold, however, had the self-discipline of a small toddler.

'And the downstairs?' she says.

'That's the strangest thing.' He takes the top off a bourbon and makes a start on the buttercream. 'The lounge and the hallway are a mess. Completely gone. But the kitchen is almost untouched. Just a few smoke marks on the walls.'

'Nothing?'

'Not a thing,' he says. 'Clock ticking away, tea towel folded on the draining board. Ruddy miracle.'

'Not a miracle for his mother, God rest her soul.' Dorothy reaches for the tissue in her sleeve, then thinks better of it. 'Not a miracle they came back early.'

'No.' Harold looks at the next biscuit, but puts it back in the packet. 'Although she wouldn't have known a thing. The flu had made her delirious, apparently. Couldn't even get out of bed. That's why he'd gone to ring for the doctor.'

'I don't understand why he didn't take her back to the nursing home.'

'What? In the middle of the night?'

'It might have saved her life.'

Dorothy looks past Harold and the curtains, and out on to the avenue. Since the fire, it had slipped into a quiet, battleship grey. Even leftover Christmas decorations couldn't lift it. They seemed dishonest, somehow. As though they were trying too hard to jolly everyone along, to pull their eyes from the charred shell of number eleven.

'Stop over-analysing things. You know too much thinking makes you confused,' Harold says, watching her. 'It was a discarded cigarette, or a spark from the fire. That's what they've settled on.'

'But after what was said? After what we all decided?'

'A discarded cigarette.' He took the biscuit and broke it in half. 'A spark from the fire.'

'Do you really believe that?'

'Loose lips sink ships.'

'For goodness sake, we're not fighting a war, Harold.'

He turns and looks through the window. 'Aren't we?' he says.

Number Three, Rowan Tree Croft

28 June 1976

'Do you not think people might be a tad suspicious, two little girls knocking on their door and asking if God is at home?' Mrs Morton put a bowl of Angel Delight on the table.

'We're going undercover.' I carved my name in it with the edge of a spoon.

'Are we?' said Tilly. 'How exciting.'

'And how do you propose to do that?' Mrs Morton leaned over and pushed the bowl a little nearer to Tilly.

'We'll be doing our Brownie badges,' I said.

Tilly looked up and frowned. 'We're not in the Brownies, Gracie. You said it wasn't our cup of tea.'

'We're going to be temporary Brownies,' I said. 'Ones who are more casual.'

She smiled and wrote '*Tilly*' in very small letters at the edge of the bowl.

'I'm going to pretend I didn't hear any of that.' Mrs Morton wiped her hands on her apron. 'And why this sudden fascination with God?'

'We are all sheep,' I said. 'And sheep need a shepherd to keep them safe. The vicar said so.'

'Did he?' Mrs Morton folded her arms.

'So I want to make sure we've got one.'

'I see.' She leaned back against the draining board. 'You do know that this is just the vicar's opinion. Some people are able to manage quite successfully without a shepherd.'

'But it's important to listen to God.' I sank my spoon into the bowl. 'If you don't take any notice of Him, He runs after you.'

'With knives,' said Tilly.

Mrs Morton frowned all the way up her forehead. 'I expect the vicar told you that as well.'

'He did,' I said.

The clock on the wall ticked away the silence, and I watched Mrs Morton's mouth trying to choose words.

'I just don't want you to be disappointed,' she said eventually. 'God isn't always easy to spot.'

'We'll find Him, and when we do, everyone will be safe and Mrs Creasy will come home.' I slid a spoonful of Angel Delight into my mouth.

'We'll be local heroes,' said Tilly, and she smiled and licked the tip of her spoon.

'I think it might take a little more than God to bring Mrs Creasy back.' Mrs Morton leaned over and opened another window. I could hear an ice-cream van drift through the estate, drawing children from their gardens like a conjuror.

'We've decided she probably isn't dead after all,' I said.

'Well, that's something.'

'And now we need God to find her. You have to remember that God is everywhere, Mrs Morton.' I waved my arms about. 'So He can quite easily find people, and bring them back from captivity.'

'Who said that?' Mrs Morton took off her glasses and pinched at the marks they had left.

'*God*,' I replied, in a very shocked voice, and I made my eyes as wide as I could.

Mrs Morton started to speak, but then she sighed and shook her head, and decided to deal with the drying up instead.

'Just don't raise your hopes,' she said.

'It's nearly *Blue Peter*.' Tilly slid from her chair. 'I'll put the television on to warm up.'

She disappeared into the front room, and I unpeeled my legs from the seat and took my bowl to the sink.

'Where are you going to begin?' said Mrs Morton.

'We'll just work our way round until He pops up.' I handed her the bowl.

'I see.'

I had got as far as the hall when she called me back.

'Grace.'

I stood in the doorway. The ice-cream van had travelled further away, and broken notes edged into the room.

'When you go around the avenue,' she said, 'you'll make sure that you miss out number eleven.'

I frowned. 'Will I?'

'You will,' she said.

I started to speak, but her face didn't suggest that it wanted to have a conversation.

'Okay,' I said.

There was a beat before my answer. But I don't think Mrs Morton heard it.

Number Four, The Avenue

29 June 1976

The policeman was very tall, even after he took his hat off.

I had never seen a policeman close up before. He wore a thick uniform, which made him smell of material, and his buttons were so shiny I could see our whole kitchen reflected back at me as he spoke.

Routine inquiries, he said.

I thought I would like a job where inquiring about everyone else's private business was considered perfectly routine.

I watched the cooker dance around on his chest.

There had been a knock on the door in the middle of *Crossroads*. My mother was all for ignoring it, until my father looked out of the window and saw a police car parked on the other side of our wall. He said Shit, and I laughed into a cushion and my mother told my father off, and my father nearly fell over Remington on his way into the hall.

Now the policeman stood in the middle of our kitchen, and we stood around the edges, watching him. He reminded me a bit of the vicar. They both seemed to be able to make people look small and guilty.

'Well now, let me see, well,' my father said. He wiped the sweat from his top lip with a tea towel and looked at my mother. 'Can you remember when we last saw her, Sylve?'

My mother gathered the place mats up from the kitchen table. 'I can't say as I do,' she said, and put them all back again.

'It could have been Thursday,' my father said.

'Or Friday,' my mother said.

My father cornered a glance at my mother. 'Or Friday,' he said into his tea towel.

If I had been the shiny policeman, I would have taken one look at their behaviour and arrested them on the spot for being master criminals.

'Actually, it was Saturday morning.'

Three pairs of eyes and a tea towel turned towards me.

'Was it now?' The policeman crouched down and I heard the material creak around his knees.

It made him smaller than me, and I didn't want him to feel awkward, so I sat down.

'It was,' I said.

His eyes were as dark as his uniform. I stared into them for a very long time, but he didn't appear to blink.

'And how do you know that?' he said.

'Because *Tiswas* was on.'

'My kids love *Tiswas*.'

'I hate it,' I said.

My father coughed.

'So what did she say when you saw her, Grace?' the policeman creaked again and shifted his weight.

'She knocked on the door because she wanted to borrow the telephone.'

'They don't have one,' said my mother, in the kind of voice people use when they have something that someone else doesn't.

'And why did she want to do that?'

'She said she wanted to ring for a taxi, but I didn't let her in because my mother was having a lie-down.'

We all turned to my mother, who turned to her place mats.

'I've been told to never let strangers into the house,' I said.

'But Mrs Creasy wasn't a stranger, was she?' The policeman finally blinked.

'She wasn't a stranger, but she looked strange.'

'In what way?'

I leaned back in the chair and thought about it. 'You know how people look when they have really bad toothache?'

'Yes.'

'Well, a bit worse than that.'

The policeman stood up and put his hat back on. He filled the whole room.

'Will you find her?' I said.

The policeman didn't answer. Instead, he went into the hall with my father and they spoke so quietly I couldn't hear a word they said. Even when I held my breath and leaned all the way across the kitchen table.

'I don't think they will,' I said.

My mother emptied the teapot. 'No,' she said, 'neither do I.'

Then she filled the kettle very violently, because I don't think she meant the words to come out.

*

I didn't know, and it didn't matter how many times people asked me.

Even when Mr Creasy burst into our sitting room and stood between my mother and Hilda Ogden, I still didn't know. His face was so close to mine, I could taste his breath.

'She didn't tell me where she wanted to go, she only asked if she could borrow the telephone,' I said.

'She must have told you something?' Mr Creasy's words crawled across my skin and crept inside my nostrils.

'She didn't. She just wanted to ring for a taxi.'

His collar was frayed at the edges, and there was a stain on the front of his shirt. It looked like egg.

'Grace, think. Please think,' he said. He put his face even closer to mine, waiting to snatch the words as soon as they appeared.

'Come on, old man.' My father tried to edge between us. 'She's told you everything she knows.'

'I just want her home, Derek. You should understand that, surely?'

I saw my mother start to get up, and then hold the arms of the chair to keep herself still.

'Perhaps she was thinking of going back to where she used to live.' My father put a hand on Mr Creasy's shoulder. 'Walsall, was it? Or Sutton Coldfield?'

'Tamworth,' said Mr Creasy. 'She hasn't been back for six years. Not since we got married. She doesn't know anyone there now.'

His breath still fell into my face. It tasted uneasy.

*

'Where's Tamworth?' Tilly dragged her school bag along the pavement.

It was the last day of term.

'Miles away. In Scotland,' I said.

'I can't believe you were interviewed by a real policeman and I wasn't in on it. Was it like *The Sweeney*?'

Tilly's mother had recently given in to a television set.

I thought about the smell of material, and how my words were recorded in a small, black notebook by the shiny policeman, who made notes very slowly with a pencil, and licked his lips as he wrote.

'It was exactly like *The Sweeney*,' I said.

We threaded through the estate. Around us, the temperature

loosened and stirred. Milk was rushed from doorsteps, car doors were pulled wide, and people hurried dogs along pavements before the day was stolen away by the heat.

'Is the policeman going to look for her?' Tilly's bag scraped the concrete and clouds of white dust held the air. 'What did he say?'

'He said that Mrs Creasy is officially a Missing Person.'

'Missing from what?'

Thinking made my feet slower. 'Her life, I suppose.'

'How can you be missing from your own life?'

I slowed a little more. 'Missing from the life you belong in.'

Tilly stopped to pull up her socks. 'I wonder how you know which one that is.' She spoke with an upside-down head.

I realized I had stopped moving, and I turned away from Tilly so I could frown.

'You'll understand when you get older,' I said.

Tilly looked up from her socks. 'Your birthday's only a month before mine.'

'Anyway, God knows exactly where you belong.' I marched away from the questions. 'So it doesn't really matter what anyone else thinks.'

'Where do we start looking for Him?' Tilly still pulled at her socks, trying to make them the same height.

'Mr and Mrs Forbes.' My hand followed the hedge as I walked. 'When we're singing hymns, they never have to look at the words.'

'But we won't find Mrs Creasy if she's gone to Tamworth, even with God,' Tilly shouted.

A cat began following us. It padded along the top of a fence, marking its journey with careful paws. I watched it stretch to the next wooden post and, for a moment, we had matching eyes. Then it jumped to the pavement, folded itself into the hedge and disappeared.

'Was that next-door's cat?'

But Tilly was too far away. I turned back and waited for her to catch up.

'She hasn't gone to Tamworth,' I said. 'She's still here.'

Number Six, The Avenue

3 July 1976

'Go on then.' Tilly elbowed me with the edge of her jumper.

I stared at the doorbell. 'I'm working up to it,' I said.

Mr and Mrs Forbes' house was the kind of house which looked as though no one was ever at home. All the other houses on the avenue seemed bewildered by the heat. Fingers of weeds crept along garden paths, windows were dimmed by a film of dust, and long evenings lay abandoned on lawns, as if everything had forgotten what it was supposed to be doing. The Forbeses' house, however, remained smug and determined, as though it was setting an example to all the other, more slovenly, houses.

'Perhaps no one is in,' I said, 'perhaps we should try tomorrow.'

I slid the toe of my sandal along the edge of the doorstep. It was brushed smooth.

'They're definitely at home.' Tilly pressed her face against a slice of stained glass in the door. 'I can hear a television.'

I put my face next to hers. 'Perhaps they're watching a film,' I said. 'Perhaps we should come back later.'

'Do you not think we owe it to Mrs Creasy to ring the bell as soon as possible?' Tilly turned to me and adopted her most serious face. 'And to God?'

Sunlight reflected from the brilliant white of Mrs Forbes' Cotswold chippings, and I creased my eyes against the glare.

'As a Sixer, Tilly, I have decided to assign ringing the doorbell to you, while I prepare my speech.'

She looked up at me from under her sou'wester. 'But we're not actually in the Brownies, Gracie.'

I gave a small sigh. 'It's important to get into character,' I said.

Tilly frowned and stared at the front door. 'Perhaps you're right. Perhaps no one is at home.'

'Someone is very much at home.'

Mrs Forbes appeared on the path which ran down the side of the house. She wore the kind of clothes my mother saved for doctor's appointments, and under her arm was a large roll of dustbin bags. She snapped one free, and a small group of pigeons tumbled from the roof in shock.

She asked us what we wanted. Tilly stared into the chippings and I folded my arms and stood on one leg, and tried to take up a very small amount of room on the doorstep.

'We're Brownies,' I said, as soon as I remembered.

'We're Brownie Guides. We're here to lend a hand,' said Tilly, although she managed to stop herself from singing.

'You don't look like Brownies.' Mrs Forbes narrowed her eyes.

'We're being casual.' I narrowed my eyes back.

I said that we needed help from our neighbourhood, and Mrs Forbes agreed that she was, indeed, our neighbourhood, and suggested we might like to come inside, out of the heat. Behind Mrs Forbes' cardigan, Tilly waved her arms around in excitement, and I waved my arms around back again to try and calm her down.

We followed Mrs Forbes' heels down the side of the house, as they clicked a neat path on the concrete, and our sandals smacked and squabbled behind her in a tangle of keeping up. After a moment, she turned, and as Tilly and I were both still waving our arms around, we almost fell into her.

'Does your mother know you're here, Grace?' she said. She held her hands up, as though she were directing traffic.

'We told her, Mrs Forbes,' I said.

Her hands dropped back, and the tap of her heels began again.

I wondered if Mrs Forbes realized that telling my mother something and my mother knowing about it were usually two very different things, that my mother's fingers would often fly to her throat and she would strongly deny ever being told anything of the sort – even when my father presented her with witnesses (me) and a word-by-word account of the entire conversation.

'She never asked about my mum,' Tilly whispered.

Tilly's mother was usually considered too unpredictable to ask after.

I straightened the back of her jumper. 'It's all right. Asking about my mum will cover both of us. You are always welcome to borrow her.'

Tilly smiled and linked her arm through mine.

I sometimes wondered if there was ever a time when she wasn't there.

*

Mrs Forbes' carpet was the colour of cough syrup. It ran along the hall and into the sitting room, and when I looked back, I saw it climb all the way up the stairs. There were still lines where the vacuum cleaner had sailed across, and as we walked into the sitting room, there was an extra square of syrup, just in case you were to discover that a whole houseful wasn't quite enough.

Mrs Forbes asked if we'd like some cordial, and I said yes, and I wouldn't say no to a custard cream, and she'd made an *oh* shape with her mouth, and left us to sit on a dark pink sofa, which had twisty arms and its own set of dimples. I decided to balance on the edge. Tilly had sat down first. The seats were so deep, her legs didn't reach the floor, and they stretched out in front of her, like a doll.

She rolled across and peered into the gap between the sofa and the wall.

'Can you see Him yet?' she said, from near the carpet.

'Who?'

She rolled back, her face crimson with effort. 'God,' she said.

'I don't think He's simply going to pop out of the sideboard, Tilly.'

We both looked at the sideboard, just in case.

'But shouldn't we make a start?' she said. 'Mrs Creasy might be in peril.'

I stared at the room. It looked as though someone might have served it into the house with an ice-cream scoop. Even the things that weren't pink had a mention of it, as if they hadn't been allowed through the door without making a firm commitment. There were twists of salmon rope holding back the curtains, fuchsia tassels on each of the cushions, and the pot dogs guarding the mantelpiece had garlands of rosebuds around their necks. Between the pot dogs was a line of photographs: Mr and Mrs Forbes sitting on deckchairs at a beach, and Mr Forbes standing next to a motor car, and Mrs and Mrs Forbes with a group of people, having a picnic. Right in the centre was a girl with her hair pinned into waves. All the people in the other photographs looked away from the lens with serious eyes, but the girl stared straight into the camera and smiled, and it was so honest and so unprotected, it made me want to smile straight back.

'I wonder who she is,' I said.

But Tilly was examining the space behind the settee. 'Do you think He's down here somewhere?' She lifted a cushion and peered at the back of it.

I looked up at the champagne teardrops which spilled from the light fitting. 'I think it might be a bit too pink, even for Jesus,' I said.

*

Mrs Forbes returned with a tray and a selection of biscuits.

'I'm afraid I don't have any custard creams,' she said.

I took three fig rolls and a garibaldi. 'That's all right, Mrs Forbes. I'll just have to manage.'

I could hear the noise of a television in the room next door, and Mr Forbes' voice shouting instructions at it. It sounded like a football match. Even though the sounds were just the other side of the wall, they seemed very far away, and the rest of the world played itself out beyond the pink insulation, leaving us wrapped in Dralon and cushions, protected by china dogs and cellophaned in an ice-cream silence.

'You have a very nice house, Mrs Forbes,' said Tilly.

'Thank you, dear.'

I bit into my garibaldi and she rushed a paper doily on to my knee.

'The key to a tidy house is anticipation. And lists. Lots of lists.'

'Lists?' I said.

'Oh yes, lists. That way, nothing ever gets forgotten.'

She pulled a piece of paper from the pocket of her cardigan.

'This is today's list,' she said. 'I'm up to the dustbins.'

It was a long list. It crossed over two pages in loops of blue ink, which thickened and smudged where the pen had stopped to think. As well as vacuuming the hall and putting out the dustbins, it had entries like *clean teeth* and *eat breakfast*.

'Do you put everything on your list, Mrs Forbes?' I started on my first fig roll.

'Oh yes, best not to leave anything to chance. It was Harold's idea. He says it stops me being slapdash.'

'Could you not remember things without writing them down?' said Tilly.

'Heavens, no.' Mrs Forbes shrank back in her chair, and she faded into a pink landscape. 'That wouldn't do at all. Harold says I'd get in a terrible mess.'

She folded the piece of paper exactly in half, and returned it to her pocket.

'So how long have you two been in the Brownies?'

'Ages,' I said. 'Who's the girl in the photograph?'

She frowned at me and then looked over at the fireplace and frowned again. 'Oh, that's me,' she said, in a surprised voice, as though she had temporarily forgotten all about herself.

I studied Mrs Forbes and the girl in the photograph, and tried to find something that matched. There was nothing.

'Don't look so shocked,' she said, 'I wasn't born old, you know.'

My mother used this saying quite frequently. I had learned

from experience not to say one word in reply, and I sipped my cordial to avoid having to make a comment.

She walked over to the mantelpiece. I always thought of Mrs Forbes as being solid and blustery, but close up she became diluted. Her posture was a slight apology, the folds of her clothes measuring out the end of a story. Even her hands looked small, trapped by arthritis and livered with time.

She ran her finger around the frame of the picture. 'It was just before I met Harold,' she said.

'You look very happy.' I took another fig roll. 'I wonder what you were thinking about.'

'I do, don't I?' Mrs Forbes took a cloth from her waistband and began dusting herself. 'I only wish I could remember.'

On the other side of the wall, the football match ended rather abruptly. There was creaking and grumbling, and the click of a door, and then the sound of footsteps across the syrupy carpet. When I turned around, Mr Forbes was standing in the doorway, watching us. He wore a pair of shorts. His legs were pale and hairless, and they looked as though he could easily have borrowed them from someone else.

'What's going on here, then?' he said.

Mrs Forbes put herself back on the mantelpiece and spun round.

'Grace and Tilly are Brownies.' Her eyes were so bright, they were almost enamelled. 'They're here to lend . . .' she faltered.

He folded his forehead into a frown and put his hands on his hips. 'A book? Money? A cup of sugar?'

Mrs Forbes was hypnotized, and she wrapped the duster around her fingers until they became mottled with white.

'To lend . . .' Mrs Forbes repeated the words.

Mr Forbes continued to stare. I could hear his dentures click against the roof of his mouth.

'A hand,' said Tilly.

'That's right. A hand. They're here to lend a hand.'

She unwound the duster, and I heard the air leave her lungs in little pieces.

Mr Forbes grunted.

He said *as long as that's all it is*, and *does Sylve know she's here*, and Mrs Forbes nodded so vigorously the crucifix around her neck did a little dance on her collarbone.

'I'm going to post my letter,' said Mr Forbes. 'If we wait for you to do it, I'll miss the second collection. I just need to find out where you've hidden my shoes.'

Mrs Forbes nodded again, and the crucifix nodded along with her, even though Mr Forbes had long since disappeared from the doorway.

'My teachers do that to me all the time,' said Tilly.

'Do what, dear?'

'Throw words at me until I get confused.' Tilly picked garibaldi crumbs from the carpet and lifted them on to the plate. 'It always makes me feel stupid.'

'It does?' said Mrs Forbes.

'I'm not, though.' Tilly smiled.

Mrs Forbes smiled back. 'Do you enjoy school, Tilly?' she said.

'Not really. A lot of the girls don't like us very much. Sometimes we're bullied.'

'They hit you?' Mrs Forbes' hand flew to her mouth.

'Oh no, they don't hit us, Mrs Forbes.'

'You don't always have to hit people,' I said, 'to bully them.'

Mrs Forbes reached for the nearest chair and lowered herself into it. 'I expect you're right,' she said.

I was about to speak when Mr Forbes came back into the room. He was still wearing his shorts, but he had added a flat cap and a pair of sunglasses, and he was carrying a letter. He reminded me of my father. Whenever it became hot, he swapped his trousers for shorts, but everything else he kept exactly the same.

Mr Forbes placed his letter on the sideboard, and sat on the sofa with such force, the aftershock almost suspended Tilly in mid-air. He began tying his shoes, tugging at the laces until little fibres of fabric hovered in the space above his fingers. I stood up to give his legs more privacy.

'So you can cross this off your list for a start, Dorothy,' he was saying. 'Although there's plenty more to be getting on with.'

He looked over at me. 'Will you be staying long?' he said.

'Oh no, Mr Forbes. Not long at all. We'll be gone as soon as we've lent a hand.'

He looked back at his feet and grunted again. I wasn't sure if he was approving of me or the tightness of his shoelaces.

'She gets very easily distracted, you see.' He nodded at Mrs Forbes with the brim of his cap. 'It's her age. Isn't it, Dorothy?' He made a winding motion at the side of his temple.

Mrs Forbes smiled, but it sat on her mouth at half-mast.

'Can't keep a thing in her head for more than five minutes.' He spoke behind the back of his hand, like a whisper, but the volume of his voice remained exactly the same. 'Losing her marbles, I'm afraid.'

He stood, and then bent very theatrically to adjust his socks. Tilly edged to safety at the far end of the settee.

'I'm off to the post box.' He marched towards the hall. 'I shall be back in thirty minutes. Try not to get yourself in a muddle whilst I'm gone.'

He had vanished from the doorway before I realized.

'Mr Forbes.' I had to shout to make him hear.

He reappeared. He didn't look like the kind of person who was used to being shouted at.

I handed him the envelope. 'You've forgotten your letter,' I said.

Mrs Forbes waited until the front door clicked shut, and then she began to laugh. Her laughing made me and Tilly laugh as well, and the rest of the world seemed to creep back into the room again, as if it wasn't quite as far away as I thought.

Whilst we were laughing, I looked at Mrs Forbes, and I looked over at the girl on the mantelpiece, who laughed with us through a corridor of time, and I realized that they were a perfect match after all.

*

'I didn't know we'd actually have to do actual housework,' said Tilly.

Mrs Forbes had left us tied into aprons up to our armpits. Tilly stood on the far side of the room, rubbing Brasso into a sleeping West Highland white terrier.

'It's important that we don't arouse suspicion,' I said, and took the last garibaldi back to the settee.

'But do you think God is here?' Tilly peered at the dog and ran the duster over its ears. 'If God keeps everyone safe, do you think he's keeping Mrs Forbes safe as well?'

I thought about the cross around Mrs Forbes' neck. 'I hope so,' I said.

Mrs Forbes returned to the room with a new packet of garibaldis. 'What do you hope, dear?'

I watched her empty them on to the plate. 'Do you believe in God, Mrs Forbes?' I said.

'Of course.'

She didn't hesitate. She didn't look at the sky or at me, or even repeat the question back again. She just carried on rearranging biscuits.

'How can you be so sure?' said Tilly.

'Because that's what you do. God brings people together. He makes sense of everything.'

'Even the bad things?' I said.

'Of course.' She looked at me for a moment, and then returned to the plate.

I could see Tilly beyond Mrs Forbes' shoulder. Her polishing had become slow and deliberate, and she willed a whole conversation at me with her eyes.

'How can God make sense of Mrs Creasy disappearing?' I said. 'For example.'

Mrs Forbes stepped back, and a mist of crumbs fell to the carpet.

'I've no idea.' She folded the empty packet between her hands, even though it refused to become smaller. 'I've never even spoken to the woman.'

'Didn't you meet her?' I said.

'No.' Mrs Forbes twisted the packet around her ring finger. 'They only moved into the house a little while ago, after John's mother died. I never had the chance.'

'I just wonder why she vanished?' I edged the sentence towards her, like a dare.

'Well, it was nothing to do with me, I didn't say a word.' Her voice had become spiked and feverish, and the sentence rushed from her mouth in order to escape.

'What do you mean, Mrs Forbes?' I looked at Tilly, and Tilly looked at me and we both frowned.

Mrs Forbes sank on to the settee.

'Ignore me, I'm getting muddled.' She patted the back

of her neck, as if she was checking to see that her head was still firmly attached. 'It's my age.'

'We just can't understand where she's gone,' I said.

Mrs Forbes smoothed down the tassels on one of the cushions. 'I'm sure she'll return in good time,' she said, 'people usually do.'

'I hope she does.' Tilly untied the apron from under her arms. 'I liked Mrs Creasy. She was nice.'

'I'm sure she was.' Mrs Forbes fiddled at the cushion. 'But I've never spent any time in that woman's company, so I couldn't really say.'

I moved the garibaldis around on the plate. 'Perhaps someone else on the avenue might know where she's gone.'

Mrs Forbes stood up. 'I very much doubt it,' she said. 'The reason Margaret Creasy disappeared is nothing to do with any of us. God works in mysterious ways, Harold was right. Everything happens for a reason.'

I wanted to ask her what the reason was, and why God had to be so mysterious about his work, but Mrs Forbes had taken the list out of her pocket.

'Harold will be back soon. I'd better get on,' she said. And she began running her finger down the lines of blue ink.

*

We walked back along the avenue. The weight of the sky pressed down on us as we pulled our legs through the heat. I stared at the hills which overlooked the town, but it was impossible to see where they began and where the sky ended. They were welded together by the summer, and the horizon shimmered and hissed and refused to be found.

Somewhere beyond the gardens, I could hear the sound of a Wimbledon commentary drifting from a window.

Advantage, Borg. And the distant flutter of applause.

The road was deserted. The beat of an afternoon sun had hurried everyone indoors to fan themselves with newspapers and rub Soltan into their forearms. The only person who remained was Sheila Dakin. She sat on a deckchair on the front lawn of number twelve, arms and legs spread wide, her face stretched towards the heat, as though someone had pegged her out as a giant, mahogany sacrifice.

'Hello, Mrs Dakin,' I shouted across the tarmac.

Sheila Dakin lifted her head, and I saw a trail of saliva glisten at the edge of her mouth.

She waved. 'Hello, ladies.'

She always called us *ladies*, and it turned Tilly's face red and made us smile.

'So God is at Mrs Forbes' house,' said Tilly, when we had stopped smiling.

'I believe he is.' I pulled Tilly's sou'wester down at the back, to cover her neck. 'So we can say for definite that Mrs Forbes is safe, although I'm not very sure about her husband.'

'It's just a pity she never met Mrs Creasy, she could have given us some clues.' Tilly kicked at a loose chipping, and it coasted into a hedge.

I stopped walking so suddenly, my sandals skidded dust on the pavement.

Tilly looked back. 'What's the matter, Gracie?'

'The picnic,' I said.

'What picnic?'

'The photograph of the picnic on the mantelpiece.'

Tilly frowned. 'I don't understand?'

I stared at the pavement and tried to think backwards. 'The woman,' I said, 'the woman.'

'What woman?'

'The woman sitting next to Mrs Forbes at the picnic.'

'What about her?' said Tilly.

I looked up and straight into Tilly's eyes. 'It was Margaret Creasy.'

Number Two, The Avenue

4 July 1976

Brian sang to the hall mirror as he tried to find the parting in his hair. It was a little tricky, as his mother had insisted on buying a starburst design, and it was more burst than glass, but if he bent his knees slightly and angled his head to the right, he could just about fit his whole face in.

His hair was his best feature, his mother always said. Now girls seemed to like men's hair a little longer, he wasn't so sure. His only ever got as far as the bottom of his jaw and then it seemed to lose interest.

'Brian!'

Perhaps if he tucked it behind his ears.

'Brian!'

Her shouting tugged on him like a lead. He pushed his head around the sitting-room door.

'Yes, Mam?'

'Pass us that box of Milk Tray, would you? My feet are playing me up something chronic.'

His mother lay on a sea of crochet, her legs wedged on to the settee, rubbing at her bunions through a pair of tights. He could hear the static.

'It's the bloody heat.' Her face was pinched into lines, the air in her cheeks filled with concentration.

'There! There!' she stopped rubbing and pointed at the footstool, which, in the absence of her feet, had become a home for the *TV Times* and her slippers, and a spilled bag of Murray Mints. She took the Milk Tray from him and stared into the box, with the same level of concentration as someone who was trying to answer an especially difficult exam question.

She pushed an Orange Creme into her mouth and frowned at his leather jacket. 'Off out, are you?'

'I'm going for a pint with the lads, Mam.'

'The lads?' She took a Turkish Delight.

'Yes, Mam.'

'You're forty-three, Brian.'

He went to run his fingers through his hair, but remembered the Brylcreem and stopped himself.

'Do you want me to ask Val to fit you in for a trim next time she comes round?'

'No thanks, I'm growing it. The girls like it longer.'

'The girls?' She laughed and little pieces of Turkish Delight swam around on her teeth. 'You're forty-three, Brian.'

He shifted his weight and the leather jacket creaked at his shoulders. He'd bought it from the market. Probably wasn't even real leather. Probably plastic, pretending to be leather, and the only person who was fooled was the idiot wearing it. He pulled at the collar and it crackled between his fingers.

His mother's throat rose and fell with Turkish Delight, and he watched her dig her tongue around in her back teeth to make sure she'd definitely got her money's worth.

'Empty that ashtray before you go. There's a good boy.'

He picked up the ashtray and held it at arm's length, like an uncertain sculpture, a cemetery of cigarettes, each dated with a different colour of lipstick. He watched the ones at the edge tilt and waver as he carried it across the room.

'Not the fireplace! Take it to the outside bin.' She sent her instructions through a Lime Barrel. 'It'll stink the house out if you leave it in here.'

A curl of smoke twisted from somewhere deep in the mountain of fag ends. He thought he'd imagined it at first, but then the smell brushed at his nostrils.

'You want to be careful.' He nodded at the ashtray. 'This is how fires start.'

She looked over at him and looked back at the box of Milk Tray.

Neither of them spoke.

He nudged around, and found the glow of a tip in the

ash. He pinched at it until it flickered and the pleat of smoke stuttered and died. 'It's out now,' he said.

But his mother was lost to the chocolates, gripped by bunions and Orange Cremes and *the film now starting on BBC2*. He knew she would be exactly the same when he returned from the Legion. He knew she would have pulled the blanket over her legs, and the Milk Tray box would be massacred and left to the carpet, and the television would be playing out a conversation with itself in the corner. He knew that she would not have risked moving from the edges of her crocheted existence. A world within a world, a life she had embroidered for herself over the past few years, which seemed to shrink and tighten with each passing month.

The avenue was silent. He pulled the lid from the dustbin and tipped the cigarettes inside, sending a cloud of ash into his face. When he had finished coughing and swiping at the air, and trying to find his next breath, he looked up and saw Sylvia in the garden of number four. Derek wasn't with her — or Grace. She was alone. He rarely saw her alone, and he dared to watch for a moment. She hadn't looked up. She was picking at weeds, throwing them into a bucket and brushing the soil from her hands. Every so often, she straightened her back, and gathered her breath and wiped her forehead with the back of a hand. She hadn't changed. He wanted to tell her, but he knew it would only lead to more trouble.

He felt a line of sweat edge into his collar. He didn't know how long he'd been watching, but she looked up and saw him. She lifted her hand to wave, but he turned just in time and got back inside.

He put the ashtray on the footstool.

'Make sure you're home by ten,' his mother said, 'I'll need my ointment.'

The Royal British Legion

4 July 1976

The Legion was empty, apart from the two old men in the corner. Every time Brian saw them, they were sitting in the same place, and wearing the same clothes, and having the same exchange. They looked at each other as they spoke, but had two separate conversations, each man lost in his own words. Brian adjusted his eyes after the walk down. It was cooler in here, and darker. Summer soaked into the flocked walls and the polished wood. It was swallowed by the cool slate of the snooker table, and fell into the thread of the carpet, worn down by heavy conversation. The Legion didn't have a season. It could have been the middle of winter, except for the sweat that caught the edge of Brian's shirt and the pull of walking in his legs.

Clive sat on a stool at the end of the bar, feeding crisps to a black terrier, who stamped his paws and whistled at the back of his throat if he felt the gap between crisps had become too long.

'Pint, is it?' he said, and Brian nodded.

He eased from the stool. 'Another warm one,' he said, and Brian nodded again.

Brian handed his money over. There were too many coins. He lifted his pint and beer slipped from the top of the glass and on to the counter.

'Still looking for work?' Clive took a cloth and ran it across the wood.

Brian murmured something into his glass and looked away.

'Tell me about it, love. If they cut my hours any more, I'll have to go back on the game.' He turned his hand and examined his nails.

Brian stared at him over the top of his glass.

'It's a bloody joke,' said Clive, and he laughed, and Brian tried to laugh with him, but he couldn't quite get there.

*

He was on his second pint when they arrived. Harold walked in first, all shorts and shouting.

'Evening, evening,' he said, even though the bar was still empty. The men in the corner nodded and looked away.

'Clive!' Harold said, as though Clive was the last person he expected to see. They shook each other's hand and put their other hands over the top of the shake, until there was a pile of shaking and commotion.

Brian watched them.

'Double Diamond?' Harold nodded at Brian's glass.

Brian said no, he'd buy his own, thanks, and Harold said suit yourself, and he turned back to Clive and smiled, as though there was a whole other conversation going on that Brian couldn't hear. In the middle of the unheard conversation, Eric Lamb arrived with Sheila Dakin, and Clive had to disappear into the back to find a cherry for Sheila's Babycham.

By the time Brian followed them to the table, he found himself wedged against the wall, trapped between the cigarette machine and the mystery of Sheila Dakin's bosom.

She wrinkled her nose at him. 'Have you started smoking again, Brian? You smell like an old ashtray.'

'It's my mam,' he said.

'Maybe think about getting your hair cut as well,' she said, and dipped her cherry in the Babycham. 'It looks a right bloody mess.'

There was a radio on somewhere, and Brian could hear a slur of music, but he couldn't tell what it was. The Drifters, maybe, or The Platters. He wanted to ask Clive to turn it up, but Clive had been standing at the end of the bar for the last five minutes, twisting a tea towel into the same pint glass and trying to listen to their conversation. It was the last thing he'd want to do.

'Order, order.' Harold said and tapped the edge of a beer mat on the table, even though no one was speaking. 'I've called this meeting because of recent events.'

Brian realized he was nearly at the end of his pint. He swilled the glass around to try and catch the foam which patterned the sides.

'Recent events?' Sheila twisted at her earring. It was heavy and bronze, and Brian thought it looked like something you might find on a totem pole. It dragged the flesh towards her jaw, and pulled the hole in her ear into a jagged line.

'This business with Margaret Creasy.' Harold still held the beer mat between his fingers. 'John has it in his head it's something to do with number eleven. Got himself in a right state after church last weekend.'

'Did he?' said Sheila. 'I wasn't there.'

Harold looked at her. 'No,' he said, 'I don't expect you were.'

'Cheeky sod.' She began twisting at the other earring. Her laugh took up the whole table.

Harold leaned forward, even though there wasn't any space to lean into.

'We just all need to be clear,' he said, 'about what happened.'

The music had finished. Brian could hear Clive's tea towel squeak against the glass and the hum of the old men shuffling their words.

'You might as well sit down, Clive, as stand over there.' Eric Lamb nodded at the empty stool with his glass. 'You're as much a part of this as any of us.'

Clive took a step back and pulled the tea towel into his chest, and said he didn't really think it was his place, but

Brian saw Harold persuade him over with his eyes, and Clive dragged the stool across the lino and pulled himself between Harold and Sheila.

'I deliberately didn't ask John tonight.' Harold sat back and folded his arms. 'We don't need another scene.'

'What makes him think it's anything to do with number eleven?' Sheila had finished her Babycham, and was turning the stem of the glass between her fingers. It crept towards the edge of the table.

'You know John. He's always looking for something to worry about,' said Harold, 'he can't keep his mind still.'

Brian agreed, although he would never say so. When they were kids, John used to count buses. He reckoned they were lucky.

The more buses we see the better, he said, *it stops bad things happening*. It would make them late for school, walking round the long way, trying to spot as many as they could. Brian would say, *It's made us late, how can that be lucky* and laugh, but John would just gnaw at the skin around his fingers and say that they can't have seen enough.

'John doesn't think that pervert's done her in, does he?' said Sheila. The glass tipped towards the floor, and Eric guided her hand back.

'Oh no. Nothing like that, no. No.' Harold said no too many times, they came out of his mouth like a string of bunting. He looked down at the beer mat.

'Wouldn't surprise me if he has,' said Sheila, 'I still reckon he took that babbie.'

Harold looked at her for a moment, and then lowered his eyes.

'The baby turned up safe, though, Sheila.' Eric took the glass from her hand. 'That's all that matters.'

'Bloody pervert,' she said. 'I don't care what the police said. It's a normal avenue, full of normal people. He doesn't belong there.'

A silence unfolded across the table. Brian could hear the Guinness slide down Eric Lamb's throat, and the tea towel crease and pleat between Clive's fingers. He could hear the twist of Sheila's earring, and the tap of Harold's beer mat on the wood, and he heard pockets of his own breath escaping his mouth. The silence became a sound all of its own. It pushed against his ears until he could stand it no longer.

'Margaret Creasy talked to my mam a lot,' he said. He put the pint glass to his mouth. It was almost empty.

'About what?' said Harold. 'Number eleven?'

Brian shrugged behind the glass. 'I never sat with them,' he said. 'They played Gin Rummy for hours in the back-room. Good company, my mam said she was. A good listener.'

'She was always in and out of your house, Harold.' Sheila clicked open her purse and put a pound note in front of Clive.

'She was? I never saw her.'

'Probably keeping Dorothy company,' she said, 'while you were out and about.'

Brian went to put a tower of coins on the note, but Sheila brushed him away.

'Dorothy saw Margaret Creasy going into number eleven,' said Harold. 'She's just as hysterical about it as John is. She thinks someone's said something.'

Clive pulled the empty glasses together, catching each one with a finger. 'What is there to say? The police said the fire was an accident.'

'You know Dorothy,' said Harold, 'she'll tell anybody anything, she doesn't know what she's saying half of the time.'

The glasses rattled as they left the table.

'As long as the police don't change their minds and start digging everything up again.' For once, Sheila's voice was low. She still held on to the purse, and Brian watched her click at the clasp. Her hands were rough from the heat, and the polish on her nails crept away from the edges in ragged lines.

'For Christ's sake, Sheila, that's exactly what I'm talking about.' There was no one else in the bar. Even the old men had left. Still Harold scanned a room of empty chairs behind him, then turned back and edged himself nearer the table. 'Stop scaremongering. We agreed back then that we just made our feelings known, that's all. The rest of it was chance.'

Brian leaned back in his chair. He could feel the edge of the cigarette machine biting into his shoulder. 'She talked to everyone, though, didn't she? She went round the whole

93

avenue. You don't know what she found out. She was smart, Mrs Creasy. Really smart.'

Sheila pushed her purse back into her handbag. 'I hate to bloody say it, but Brian's right. Perhaps she knew more than any of us.'

'It was an accident,' said Eric Lamb. He stretched the words out, like instructions.

Now his glass was gone, Brian didn't know what to do with his hands. He pressed his thumb into the drips of beer on the table, pulling them into lines, trying to make a pattern. This was the problem when people had known you since you were a child, they could never quite let go of assuming you needed to be told what to think.

'We just need to stay calm,' said Harold. 'None of this loose talk. We did nothing wrong, understood?'

Brian shrugged his shoulders, and his jacket creaked and crackled in reply. Probably wasn't leather after all.

*

They walked back through the estate, Sheila linking her arm through Brian's to steady herself, because her shoes were bloody impossible to walk in. Brian didn't think her shoes were the problem, but he offered her his arm anyway. It was almost ten. Eric Lamb had gone on ahead, and they'd left Harold at the Legion, helping Clive to close up. It was the best part of the day, Brian thought. The heat had faded into a heavy silence, and there was even a pale breeze, pushing into the quietness and tracing a path through the highest leaves.

As they reached the garages at the end of the avenue, Sheila stopped to pull at the strap on her shoe, and she wavered and swayed, and leaned into Brian to keep her balance. 'Bloody things,' she said.

He stared at the road. Light escaped from the sky and pressed against the horizon, taking the familiar and the safe along with it. In the dusk, the houses looked different, exposed somehow, as though they had been stripped of their disguise. They faced each other, like adversaries, and right at the top, set back from the rest, was number eleven.

Still, silent, waiting.

Sheila looked up and followed his gaze. 'Makes no sense, does it?' she said. 'Why would you stay when you know you're not wanted?'

Brian shrugged. 'Perhaps he feels the same about us. Perhaps he's waiting for an apology.'

Sheila laughed. It was thin and angry. 'He'll wait a bloody long time for mine.'

'But do you really think he did it? Do you really think he took the baby?'

She stared at him. Her whole face seemed to narrow and tighten, until the whites of her eyes were lost to hatred. 'He's the type, isn't he? You've only got to look at him. You're not that thick, Brian.'

He felt colour wash across his face. He was glad she wouldn't notice.

'Strange Walter,' he said.

'Exactly. Even the kids can see it.'

He glanced at the lights in Sheila's window. 'Who's sitting with yours?' he said.

She smiled. 'They don't need no sitter. Our Lisa's old enough now. She's sharp, just like her mother. I trained her well.'

He looked over at number eleven again. It was becoming lost to the light, the edge of the roof slipping into an inky black. 'It's what kids do, though, isn't it?' he said, 'Copy their mams and dads?'

Sheila's shoes dragged on the pavement, pulling at the concrete with their heels. 'Exactly,' she said. 'And don't you go feeling sorry for Walter Bishop. People like that don't deserve sympathy. They're not like us.'

The rattle of the latch reached across an empty road.

'Do you really think the police will be interested in the fire?' he said. 'After all this time?'

She turned in the half-light. He couldn't see her face, just an outline. A shadow slipping and shifting against the darkening bricks. When she answered, it was a whisper, but he heard it creep across the silence.

'We'd better bloody hope not,' she said.

And her shoes scraped against the step, and a key twisted in a lock, and Brian watched as the last piece of daylight was stolen from the sky.

He crossed over, towards home, stuffing his hands into the pockets of his jacket. He thought he'd imagined it at first, but then he felt it again, cardboard rubbing against his knuckles. He stopped and pulled at the ripped lining until it broke free.

A library ticket.

He stood underneath the street lamp, and the name on the ticket was caught in liquid, orange light.

Mrs Margaret Creasy.

He frowned and folded it in half, and he pushed it back against the lining, until it finally disappeared.

*

Brian stood in the doorway and looked into the sitting room. The giant cave of his mother's sleeping mouth looked back at him, and it made the rest of her face seem strangely trivial. The Milk Tray was disembowelled on the footstool, and the debris of her evening decorated the carpet – knitting needles and crossword puzzles and television pages torn from a newspaper.

'Mam?' he said. Not loud enough to wake her, but loud enough to reassure himself that he'd tried.

She snored back to him. Not the violent, churning snore that you would expect, but something softer. A thoughtful snore. His father once said that his mother was delicate and graceful when they first met, and Brian wondered if her snoring was all that was left of that narrow, fragile woman.

He stared at his mother's mouth. He wondered how many words had fallen out of it and into Margaret Creasy's ears. She couldn't help herself. It was as though she used hearsay as a web to trap people's attention, that she didn't believe she was interesting enough to hold on to them any other way.

His mother's mouth widened a little more, her eyes squeezed a little more tightly, and from somewhere deep in her chest came the faint rasp of unconsciousness.

Brian wondered if she'd told Margaret Creasy about the night of the fire. About what she saw, or thought she saw, in the shadowed corners of the avenue.

And he wondered if these had been the magic words that had made Margaret Creasy disappear.

20 December 1967

Brian draws the flame of the match into his roll-up, and watches the tobacco spark and flicker in the darkness.

He can smoke indoors if he wants to. The rooms are painted with the yellow skin of his mother's cigarettes, but he prefers to stand outside, to feel a bite of winter against his face and stare into the blackness undisturbed.

The avenue is held in a frosted quiet. All the houses are buttoned up against the cold, three bars on the fire, condensation climbing high in the windows. There are Christmas trees peeping through gaps in the curtains, but Brian doesn't feel very much like Christmas. He doubts anyone does, in all honesty, after everything that's happened.

The roll-up is thin and quick. It scratches the back of his throat and tightens his chest. He decides to take one last drag and go back into the carpet warmth of the kitchen, when he sees a movement at the top of the road. Somewhere at the edge of number eleven, there is a shift in the darkness, a brief change of light which catches the corner of his attention as he's about to turn.

He shields the cigarette in his palm to cover its glow, and tries to pull the view into his eyes, but beyond the orange pool of the streetlight, the shapes die away into an inked black.

But there was definitely a movement.

And as he closes the back door, he's sure he hears the sound of disappearing footsteps.

*

'You can smoke in here, Brian.' His mother nods at a bloated ashtray. 'You could help me string these Christmas cards.'

She is pushing the cards into tiny red and green pegs, like bunting, and coming to the end of a packet of custard creams.

'I fancied a bit of fresh air, Mam.'

'As long as you don't forget your kidneys,' she says.

He walks over to the window and pulls the curtain a fraction, just enough to stare through an inch of glass.

'What are you looking at?' Her voice twitches with interest, and she rests the cards on her lap.

'Number eleven.'

'I thought you said he'd gone away with his mother. I thought we'd all agreed there was no point watching the house until he gets back.'

'There's someone in his garden.'

She is on her feet. A pile of Christmas cards somersault into the air, and three lowly mangers and a donkey fall to the carpet.

'Well, if you're going to do it, do it properly,' she says. 'Switch the big light off and pull the curtains back.'

He does as he's told, and they both stare out into the darkness.

'Do you see anything?' she says.

He doesn't. They watch in silence.

Sheila Dakin visits her dustbin, and the avenue fills with the sound of glass drumming against metal. Sylvia Bennett draws the curtains back in one of the upstairs rooms and stares into the road. It feels as though she is looking straight at them, and Brian ducks below the windowsill.

'She can't see you, you daft bugger,' his mother says. 'The light's off.'

Brian resurfaces, and when he looks up, Sylvia has disappeared.

'Perhaps it was those lads from the estate again,' says his mother. 'Perhaps they came back.'

Brian leans into the window. His legs are going dead and the back of the settee is pushing into his ribcage. 'They wouldn't dare,' he says. 'Not after what happened.'

His mother sniffs. 'Well, I can't see anything. You must have imagined it, there's no one out there.'

As she speaks, Brian sees it again. Movement behind the thin, leafless trees which stand in Walter Bishop's garden.

'There.' He taps on the glass. 'Do you see them now?'

His mother presses her face against the window and breaths of fascination travel across the view.

'Well I never,' says his mother. 'What on earth is he doing?'

'Who?' Brian joins her at the glass. 'Who is it?'

'Move your head, Brian. You always get it in the way.'

'Who is it?' he says again, moving his head.

His mother folds a pair of satisfied arms across her chest. 'Harold Forbes,' she says. 'That's definitely Harold Forbes.'

'Is it?' Brian risks putting his head near the glass again. 'How can you tell?'

'I'd know that hump anywhere. Very poor posture, that man.'

They both stare into the dark, and their reflections stare back at them from the glass, ghostly white and open-mouthed, and painted with curiosity.

'There are some very odd people about,' says his mother.

Brian's eyes adjust to the night, and after a moment he sees the figure, slightly bent and occupied with something he's holding in his hands. He is moving between the trees, making his way around the front of number eleven. It's definitely a man, but Brian has no idea how his mother can be so certain it's Harold Forbes.

'What is he carrying?' Brian wipes breath from the glass. 'Can you tell?'

'I'm not sure,' says his mother, 'but that's not what interests me the most.'

Brian turns to her and frowns. 'What do you mean?'

'What interests me the most,' says his mother, 'is who has he got there with him?'

She's right. Beyond the stooped, wandering figure in the trees, there is a second person. They're slightly taller than the first, and straighter, and they are pointing to something at the back of the house. He tries to press his face further into the glass, but the image just blurs and distorts and becomes an untidiness of shapes and shadows.

Brian puts forward a number of possibilities, all dismissed by his mother as too young, too old, too tall.

'So who do you think it is, then?' says Brian.

His mother pulls herself to her full height and presses her chin into the flesh of her neck.

'I have my suspicions,' she says, 'but of course, it would be wrong of me to speculate.'

There is only one thing his mother enjoys more than gossip, and that is withholding it from an interested party, based on her sudden unearthing of the moral high ground.

They argue. Brian never wins their arguments, his mother is far too practised and far too stubborn, and by the time he gives up and looks back into the avenue, the figures have disappeared.

'That's that then,' says his mother. The cards still lie on the carpet, and she gathers several Virgin Marys on the way back to the settee.

'What do you think they were doing?' Brian says.

She takes another biscuit, and he has to wait for an answer until she has prised off the lid of the custard cream and examined its contents.

'Well, whatever it is,' she says, 'let's hope it involves getting rid of Bishop once and for all. We've had too many incidents around here just lately.'

For once, he agrees with her. The last few weeks had seen one disruption after another. The police never used to visit the avenue at all, now it seems as though they're never away from the place.

'I know one thing.' His mother bites into her custard cream, and a spray of crumbs settle themselves down on the antimacassar. 'It's a good job you're here, Brian. I wouldn't be able to sleep in my bed, otherwise. Not as long as that man's still at the top of the road.'

Brian leans back on the windowsill, but it digs into his spine, cracking against his vertebrae. The room is too hot. His mother has always kept it too hot. As a child he would stand in this very spot, staring through the window, trying to work out a way of making the heat escape and disappear forever.

'I'm going for another cigarette,' he says.

'I don't know why you don't smoke in here, Brian. Isn't my company good enough for you?'

She has gone back to threading Christmas cards. There is a theme, Brian thinks. She is threading another Baby Jesus on to a row. There are thirteen stars of Bethlehem. Thirteen preoccupied donkeys. A queue of Baby Jesuses to hang across the mantelpiece and watch them eat their Christmas dinner in silent, paper hats.

'I just fancy a bit of fresh air,' he says.

'Well, don't be gone ages. You know with my nerves I don't like being on my own for too long. Not until all this nonsense is sorted out.'

Brian takes his tobacco tin and box of matches from the windowsill. 'I'll be as quick as I can,' he says.

And he walks back into the darkness.

Number Four, The Avenue

5 July 1976

It was Monday. The first real day of the holidays. The summer built a dusty bridge to September, and I lay in bed for as long as I could, holding on to the moment before I took the first step.

I could hear my parents in the kitchen. The noises were familiar, a sequence of cupboards and plates and doors, and I knew which sound would come next, like a piece of music. I squashed the pillow under my head and listened, and I watched a breeze press into the curtains, sending them billowing like sails. Still I knew it wouldn't rain. You could smell rain, my father said, like you could smell the seaside. All I could smell as I lay in bed was Remington's porridge and a drift of bacon climbing into the room from someone else's kitchen. I wondered if I could get away with going back to sleep, but then I remembered I needed to find God and Mrs Creasy, and my breakfast.

*

My mother was being very quiet. She was quiet when I walked into the kitchen, she was quiet for the entire time I ate my Rice Krispies, and she was still quiet when I put my bowl in the sink. Although it was strange that, even when she was quiet, she still managed to be the loudest person in the room.

My father sat in the corner, cleaning his shoes on a piece of newspaper, whilst my mother orbited the cupboards. Every so often, he said something very ordinary to see if he could tempt someone into a conversation. He had already tried the weather, but no one had joined in. He'd even spoken to Remington, but Remington just beat his tail against the lino and looked confused.

'First day of the holidays, then,' he said.

'Mmm.' I crouched in front of the fridge, and stared inside to imagine what my lunch might be.

'So how are you and Tilly spending the summer?'

'We're finding God,' I said, from inside the fridge.

'God?' he said. I could hear the brush drag across leather. 'That'll keep you occupied.'

'It shouldn't be that difficult. He is everywhere.'

'Everywhere?' said my father. 'I'm not sure He hangs around on this estate much.'

'Don't start again, Derek.' I peered above the fridge door

and watched my mother feed cutlery into the drawer from a tea towel. 'I've told you why I'm not going.'

'I didn't mean that, but now you come to mention it . . .'

I sat very still, behind a blackcurrant yoghurt and a dozen free-range eggs.

'I shouldn't need to explain myself. You go to enough funerals in your life, without going to the ones you don't have to.'

'I'm just worried no one will turn up.' My father had stopped brushing and stared at his shoes. 'I'd go myself if I wasn't at work. Two o'clock's a really bad time.'

'Thin Brian's mum will be there,' said my mother.

'She goes to everyone's funeral. It's the only time she ever leaves the house.' My father patted his brush into the tin of polish. 'They all cancel each other out.'

'I didn't even know Enid very well.' My mother held her hands to her face, and I heard her sigh escape through the gaps. 'It's awful she died on her own, but I don't see how going to her funeral will make her feel any better about it.'

The woman on Mulberry Drive. I was becoming an excellent detective.

'Suit yourself,' said my father, and the sound of my mother's silence started all over again.

*

'I can't believe Mrs Forbes fibbed to us,' said Tilly.

I had called an emergency meeting in my bedroom. It

wasn't ideal, because Tilly was very easily distracted, but Mrs Morton had gone to visit her husband's grave and stock up on Penguins, and her kitchen table had become temporarily unavailable.

I thought about my parents. They fibbed about the amount of time it would take to get somewhere and exactly how long my tea would be, and although my mother always said my presents were from both of them, when I opened each one on Christmas morning, my father always looked as surprised as I did.

'Grown-ups fib all the time,' I said. 'The most important thing is why Mrs Forbes did it.'

I wrote the date in my notebook. I knew Tilly was looking at the Whimsies on the shelf behind my head. I could see her eyes following the line. 'You have a bushbaby,' she said, 'and a giraffe. I don't have either of those.'

'Tilly, you need to concentrate.'

Her eyes reached the end of the shelf. 'You have two bushbabies,' she said. 'Two. I don't even have one.'

'They're a pair,' I said. 'They match. There are supposed to be two.'

'I didn't know they came in pairs. I suppose they can't be separated then.'

'Tilly, this isn't about Whimsies. We're supposed to be making a plan.'

'I knew she wasn't telling the truth,' said Tilly.

My pen rested on the line. 'How?'

'She had that look. The same kind of look my mum gets

when she talks about my dad. I know it's her handwriting in my Christmas cards.'

'My mother writes all my Christmas cards.'

'It's not the same, though, is it?' said Tilly.

'No,' I said, 'I don't suppose it is.'

The breeze tapped against the curtains. My mother spent all day drawing the curtains to keep the heat out, and then drawing them back to let it escape again. I climbed across the bed, and around Tilly, and pulled them open a fraction. Tilly turned and looked through the glass.

'What's Mr Creasy doing?' she said.

John Creasy stood in the middle of the avenue, staring towards the bottom of the road.

'He's waiting for the bus,' I said, 'it stops at the end of the avenue at five to eleven.'

'Shouldn't he stand at the bus stop?'

'Oh no, he doesn't want to catch it. He's waiting to see if it drops Mrs Creasy off. He waits every day,' I said.

The bus pulled up as we watched. I could hear the brakes hiss and spit, and the flat cough of the engine, but the platform stayed empty, and Mr Creasy walked towards his house with his hands deep in his pockets. We turned back to the notebook.

'Who else was in the picnic photograph?' said Tilly.

I lifted my legs on the bed. 'Mr and Mrs Forbes,' I said, 'and Mrs Creasy.'

'Yes, but who else?'

I shut my eyes and tried to see. I'd been too interested

in looking at Mrs Forbes with her hair pinned in waves, and the image swam and swayed behind my eyelids.

'Thin Brian,' I said eventually. 'Thin Brian was definitely there.'

Tilly frowned. 'Who is Thin Brian?'

'Mr Roper. He lives at number two with his mum.'

'Is there a Fat Brian?'

I thought for a moment. 'No,' I said, 'there isn't.'

'So shall we go and find out what he knows?'

'Oh yes, we will. But not this afternoon.'

Tilly looked up and scratched the end of her nose with her jumper. 'Why?'

'Because this afternoon,' I said, 'we're going to a funeral.'

*

'I'm not sure this is such a good idea, Gracie.' Tilly stood in front of my wardrobe and stared into the mirror.

'You told me you didn't have anything black,' I said.

'But it's a poncho.'

'It has black in it,' I said.

She peered at herself. 'It has lots of other colours in it as well.'

'It's important to wear black at a funeral. It's respectful.'

'What black are you wearing?'

'I was going to wear my black socks,' I said, 'but it's too hot, so I'm wearing a black watchstrap.'

I tried to hand her my spare pair of sunglasses, but then

I realized she hadn't got any arms, so I put the sunglasses on to her face. 'I still don't understand why we're going,' she said.

'Because no one else might. I heard my father telling my mother.'

'But we didn't even know the woman on Mulberry Drive.'

I looked at our reflections in the mirror. 'It's not important,' I said. 'Someone has to be there. Imagine no one going to your funeral. Imagine leaving and no one caring enough to say goodbye to you.'

There was a lump in my throat, and I had no idea where it came from. I had to squeeze the words past it to speak, and when they appeared, they sounded trembly and strange from all the squeezing.

Tilly frowned at me and tried to hold out her hand through the wool. 'Don't get upset, Gracie.'

'I'm not upset,' I said. 'I just need her to know that she mattered.'

I pulled my hand away and I tried to swallow everything back down. I was older and meant to be setting an example.

I put my sunglasses on and smoothed down my hair. 'Anyway,' I said, 'God will be there. We might uncover some clues.'

*

We weren't the only people in the church, and I was glad, because I never understood when you were supposed to sit and stand and kneel, and it was useful to have someone else to copy. Mrs Roper sat at the front, rubbing her feet, and next to her was the barman from the British Legion, although there was no sign of Thin Brian. On the second row, there were two old men who both seemed to be talking to themselves. We slid into the pews right at the back, so that we could discuss everything. As we were arranging our feet on the cushions, Mr and Mrs Forbes walked in. Mrs Forbes went towards the front, but Mr Forbes pulled her arm and jabbed his finger at some seats nearer the middle, where Eric Lamb was sitting.

'I wonder if God knows about Mrs Forbes and how much she fibs,' whispered Tilly, and smoothed down her poncho.

The vicar had met us at the door and said that he didn't know we were friends with Enid, and I told him we were like daughters to her, and he said, did we know she was ninety-eight? We'd taken a hymn book between us and nodded underneath our sunglasses. Somewhere above our heads, the organ was playing introduction music. The notes were soft and apologetic, and they soaked into the stone and the wood before they even had a chance to be heard.

'Is that Jesus?' said Tilly.

I followed her eyes to a statue. The man was wearing red and gold material, which was wrapped around him in folds, and he stood on a piece of wood halfway up to the ceiling. He held his hand out as though he was inviting us up there to join him.

'I think so,' I said. 'He has a beard.'

'They all have beards, though, don't they?'

I glanced around and realized there were lots of people standing on pieces of wood, looking down on us. It was confusing, because they all looked thoughtful and slightly disappointed, and all of a sudden it wasn't really very clear at all which one was Jesus.

'No,' I said, 'I think Jesus is this one. He looks the most religious.'

Whilst we were deciding, the vicar walked down the aisle and stood in front of Enid's coffin.

She must have been very small.

'I am the resurrection and the life,' says the Lord. 'The one who believes in me will live, even though they die.'

The vicar was very loud and convincing. Even though I could never understand what he said, I always seemed to want to agree with him.

We have come here today to remember before God our sister Enid, and to give thanks for her life. To commit her body to the ground, and to comfort one another in our grief.

I stared past the vicar to Enid's coffin, and thought of the ninety-eight years which lay inside. I wondered if she'd thought of them too, alone on her sitting-room carpet, and I hoped perhaps that she had. I thought about how she'd be carried from the church and through the grave-yard, past all the Ernests and the Mauds and the Mabels, and how ninety-eight years would be put inside the ground, for dandelions to grow across her name. I thought about the people who would forever walk past her, on their way to somewhere else. People at weddings and christenings. People taking a shortcut, having a cigarette. I wondered if they would ever stop and think about Enid and her ninety-eight years, and I wondered if the world would have a little remembering left for her.

I wiped my face before Tilly had a chance to see. But I was glad. It meant that Enid mattered. That ninety-eight years was worth crying for.

The organ started again, only more sure of itself, and all the hymn books began to rustle.

'What does *abide* mean?' Tilly pointed at the page.

I looked at the words. 'I think it means you have to behave yourself,' I said.

People sang in very quiet voices, and Tilly and I mimed a bit, but Mrs Roper made up for everyone else by putting her hymn book back on her seat and singing at the top of her voice.

When we'd sung about behaving ourselves, the vicar climbed into the pulpit and said he was going to read from the Bible.

When the Son of Man comes in his glory, he said, *and all the angels with him, he will sit on his glorious throne.*

I sat back with a Liquorice Allsort.

All the nations will be gathered before him, and he will separate the people one from another, as a shepherd separates the sheep from the goats. He will put the sheep on his right and the goats on his left.

'Sheep again,' said Tilly.

'I know,' I said. 'They're everywhere.' I offered her an Allsort, but she shook her head.

Then he will say to those on his left, 'Depart from me, you who are cursed, into the eternal fire prepared for the devil and his angels.'

Tilly nudged me with her poncho. 'Why does he hate the goats so much?'

'For I was hungry and you gave me nothing to eat, I was thirsty and you gave me nothing to drink.'

'I'm not sure,' I said. 'He only seems to like sheep.'

'I was a stranger and you did not invite me in, I needed clothes and you did not clothe me, I was sick and in prison and you did not look after me.'

'Oh, they didn't look after Him,' said Tilly. 'I suppose that makes sense.'

Then those on the left will go away to eternal punishment, and only those on the right to eternal life.

The vicar nodded his head, as though he had told us something very important, and I nodded back again, even though I wasn't very sure what it was.

'But I don't understand,' whispered Tilly. 'How does God know which people are goats and which people are sheep?'

I looked at Eric Lamb, and at Mr Forbes, who was rearranging Mrs Forbes' hymn book for her. I looked at

Mrs Roper rubbing her feet, and the barman from the British Legion, and at the two old men, who still bowed their heads and whispered to themselves. And then I looked at the vicar, who looked back at all of us from the top of his little flight of stairs.

'I think that's the trouble,' I said, 'it's not always that easy to tell the difference.'

*

When we left the church, the vicar stood in the doorway, saying goodbye to everyone. He shook my hand and said thank you for coming, and I shook his hand back and said thank you for having us. He tried to shake Tilly's hand as well, but it was lost somewhere in her poncho and she couldn't find it in time. Everyone else seemed to disappear, but Mrs Roper leant against a gravestone, pinching at her toes.

'I'm a slave to my legs,' she said to us, as she pinched a bit harder. 'I'm always under the doctor.'

'It was very good of you make it,' I said, 'when you're in such dreadful pain.'

Mrs Roper looked up and shielded her eyes from the sun, and gave us a very wide smile.

'You must be very religious, to make such an effort.' I held my hand out like Jesus, and pulled her up from the grave.

'Oh, I am,' she said, 'but it does me the world of good to get out. It really perks me up.'

I told Mrs Roper that she was a wonderful example to the next generation, and Mrs Roper said that yes, she was, and her smile became even wider.

She put the order of service into her handbag and clicked the clasp shut. 'Are you girls walking back to the avenue? Shall we walk together?'

I said that we would like that very much, and I could see Tilly smiling behind her poncho.

We'd got as far as Lime Crescent before she mentioned Mrs Creasy.

'Terrible business,' she said, pressing a handkerchief into her armpit, 'disappearing like that.'

'Did you know her very well?' I said.

'Oh yes.' She swapped armpits. 'Better than most people. She found me very easy to talk to.'

'I expect she would,' I said, 'because you know what it's like to suffer, Mrs Roper.'

Mrs Roper agreed that she did.

'But why do you think Mrs Creasy disappeared?' She walked very quickly, and I had to take more steps to keep up. Somewhere behind me, I could hear Tilly's breathing. It sounded like a little steam train.

'Well, it could be all sorts of reasons, of course.' We'd reached the end of the avenue, and it seemed to make Mrs Roper slow down. 'But I know what my money is on.'

I reached into my pocket. 'Would you like another tissue, Mrs Roper? You look positively exhausted.'

She took the tissue and smiled. 'Are you girls in any rush? Only I've just opened a new tin of Quality Street.'

We followed her along the garden path.

When I turned round, Tilly was smiling so much, I was worried that someone might hear.

Number Eight, The Avenue

5 July 1976

'Did you and your wife have an argument?'

It took PC Green six minutes and thirty-two seconds. John knew this, because he had been watching the clock on the mantelpiece. When he'd written out the list of questions he thought they would ask, he'd put this one at the top. Now, everything was out of order.

'Mr Creasy?'

'No, we hadn't had an argument.'

He was going to add that they never argued. He was going to add that in six years, he and Margaret had never disagreed about anything, but then he decided that PC Green might think it odd, that he might be one of those strange people who believed that arguing with your spouse was somehow healthy, so he stopped himself from saying anything else by watching the second hand on the clock instead.

'Mr Creasy?'

'I'm sorry, I didn't catch the question?'

The policeman was perched right on the edge of the settee, as though he didn't intend to stay for very long. As though the fewer parts of his body he committed to sitting down, the less time he'd have to spend there. His collar number was 1279.

'I was asking whether your wife might have had a disagreement with anyone else?'

Twelve months in a year, seven days in a week. What could the nine stand for? He couldn't think of any nines.

'Margaret got along with everyone,' he said. 'She was friendly with all the neighbours. Too friendly, really.'

The policeman stopped writing and looked up. 'Too friendly?' he said.

John picked at the threads on the arm of the chair. That's torn it. Policemen were like doctors. They started off with their own idea about something, and cherry-picked your words to prove themselves right.

'I mean, she spent a lot of time helping people. Trying to sort out their problems.'

The policeman looked down at his notebook. 'I see,' he said. 'Neighbourly.'

A stitch in time saves nine. That would do, although it wasn't strictly factual. John watched PC Green writing down the words. He wondered how he could wear such a thick uniform in this heat. The police force should issue them with a summer uniform. Or perhaps they did.

Perhaps this was the summer uniform, and the winter one was even thicker.

'Are you tape-recording this?' he said.

PC Green held up his hands. As though that would prove anything. 'No one's under arrest, Mr Creasy, we're just following up on a few questions.'

'Only I told all this to your colleague last week. PC Hay. Collar Number 7523. Seven days in a week, fifty-two weeks in a year, plus the Holy Trinity.'

PC Green paused his writing, and stared.

'You do know PC Hay?'

The policeman nodded. He still stared.

'Then you'll know that I've already been asked these questions. In a different order of course, but I answered all of them very thoroughly.'

'I appreciate that, Mr Creasy.' The policeman didn't seem to want to lower his eyes, but then he gathered himself and turned back a few pages in his notebook. 'We've just had a phone call, several phone calls, from . . .' he stumbled around his words, '. . . a concerned neighbour, and the sergeant felt it might be worth revisiting things.'

'A concerned neighbour?'

'I'm not at liberty to say who, Mr Creasy.'

'I'm not asking you to, PC Green. I wouldn't want you to break the rules.'

There was no air in the room. John could feel his chest tighten and pull with the effort of breathing. All his muscles were quarrelling with his mind, trying to prevent him from filling his lungs, and the ends of his fingers had begun to prickle. He knew it was happening, but he couldn't stop it.

'You told PC Hay that your wife had no family?'

'I did.'

He wanted to open a window, but he was afraid to turn his back.

'That you lived in Tamworth when you first married, and then you returned to this house after your mother died?'

'That's right.'

He wasn't even sure his legs would hold his weight. They felt watery and distant, as if someone were stretching them away from his body.

'Are you feeling all right, Mr Creasy? You've gone very pale.'

He crossed his legs to test them out. 'I'm just hot,' he said. 'There's no air.'

'Let me open a window.'

The policeman stood and tried to move around the furniture. His uniform seemed to get in the way. It made him awkward and rigid, and the edge of his jacket caught a pile of newspapers on the windowsill. They slipped on to the carpet. John wondered how policemen managed to chase criminals when they couldn't even negotiate someone's living room.

PC Green sat down again. He was even further towards the edge of the settee than he had been before. 'Is that any better?' he said.

John nodded, although it made no difference. The heat had become a gatekeeper. It refused to let anything past, holding itself up against the rest of the world, and sealing them all in an airless prison.

'Is there anything else, PC Green?' He pushed his hand into his hair, and felt a film of sweat slide across his skin.

The policeman flipped through the pages. John could hear him talking about hospitals and being positive, and railway stations and bus terminals, and how grown people sometimes needed a break from their own lives, and how they usually returned of their own volition. And the heat, lots of words about the heat. He had been given these reassurances so many times, he should start saying them to himself from now on and save them all the bother.

'Mr Creasy?'

PC Green was looking at him again. He stared into the policeman's face and tried to find a clue to the question.

'Number eleven, Mr Creasy. Did your wife ever talk to Walter Bishop?'

John Creasy could hear the sound of his own breathing. He wondered if the policeman could hear it too. He tried opening his mouth, but it seemed to make it worse. The air rattled across the roof of his mouth and sucked all the words from his throat.

'Mr Creasy?'

'I should very much doubt it, PC Green.' John could hear his own voice, but he wasn't sure how it had managed to find itself. 'Why do you ask?'

'He's just the only neighbour we haven't managed to speak to yet.' When the policeman frowned, the whites of his eyes disappeared. 'Nothing to worry about,' he said. It made him look worried.

'She left without her shoes. Did you know that, PC Green?'

The policeman shook his head. He didn't stop frowning.

'It's very dangerous, walking in slippers.' John began picking at the arm of the chair again. He could hear his nail lifting up the threads. 'It's not safe.'

'Do you have anyone who could stay with you, Mr Creasy. A family member, a friend?'

John Creasy shook his head.

'Are you sure?'

'I'm very sure, PC Green. I am never anything but very sure.'

The policeman closed his notebook and stood up. He put the pencil back into his top pocket. 'We'll be in touch if we hear anything. I'll let myself out, shall I?'

It was fifteen steps to the front door. A lot can happen in fifteen steps.

John stood with him, and rested his weight against the chair. 'I'll go with you, if you don't mind,' he said, 'you can't be too careful.'

*

The house hadn't changed much since he'd moved back. Margaret had talked about building a little conservatory, but he'd told her it would attract flies and possibly even mice if they started having their tea in there, and Margaret had smiled and patted his hand, and said it didn't matter.

He missed her reassurance. The way she stole his disquiet and diluted it, and how her unconcern would pull him through their day. She never dismissed his worries, she just disentangled them, smoothing down the edges and spreading them out until they became thin and insignificant. He missed her conversation, the ease of her words as they ate, and the sound of cutlery resting on a plate. He had tried to carve into the quiet with the television and the radio, and the sound of his own voice, but his noise just seemed to grow the silence and make it taller, and it followed him from room to room, like water pouring from a glass.

Since she'd disappeared, he'd noticed that the silence happened everywhere. People glanced at him occasionally, when they thought he couldn't see, and sometimes whole groups of them would all turn around at the same time, but no one ever spoke. They avoided him in shops. They lingered by the tinned fruit and assorted household goods, rather than join his queue at the till. They rummaged for imaginary items in their handbags and read postcards about prams for sale and evening classes, instead of walking past him in the street. He could hear them whispering. He could hear the opening statements and the expert witnesses, the rhetoric and the verdicts, and the sound of opinion being passed. Then they would edge away from him, as if disappearing people was contagious and, should they be careless enough to get too close, they might find themselves vanishing as well. Margaret always said he took too much notice of other people, but it was very difficult to avoid it, when they were making so much of an effort to be unnoticeable.

Even though he was alone, the sitting room still felt unsettled. John could see the dent on the edge of the cushion where the policeman had rested his weight, and the untouched glass of water on the coffee table, and in the silence, he could still hear the questions, hanging in the air like lengths of rope.

Did your wife ever talk to Walter Bishop?

John chewed at his nails. He needed to get out of the room.

There were twelve steps. Thirteen if you counted the one just before you reached upstairs, but that was more of a mini landing. Margaret had placed a spider plant there a few weeks ago, but there were concerns that it might be a tripping hazard, so she moved it into the spare bedroom. It was ironic, because now there were items on all of the steps. Books and letters, and cardboard boxes filled with paperwork and photographs. He had to step around gas bills and insurance policies, Margaret's secretarial work and her bookkeeping certificates. Instruction manuals and exercise books, and newspaper cuttings – it all had to be checked. Everything needed to be searched. If Margaret had left of her own free will, she had to have found something which had made her disappear. If no one had said anything to her, she must have discovered it all by herself. There was something in the house. Something that had told her his secrets, and he needed to find it.

He picked his way around the debris as he climbed. Over the past two weeks, he had checked all through the downstairs and in the garage. The kitchen had taken the longest, lifting every lid, searching between every plate. You couldn't be too careful. So much of the house was still his mother's. Towards the end, she saved everything. Receipts and coupons and old bus tickets. He'd found them in the strangest places, tucked behind the breadbin, inside a forgotten library book. Perhaps there was a newspaper clipping? A mention of it in a letter? Perhaps Margaret had tripped up on the evidence without meaning to. Perhaps the past had just fallen into her hands by mistake.

He opened their bedroom door. The room smelled scorched and static. As though layers of heat had settled themselves upon the memories and smothered them. He had tried to sleep in this room for the first few days, but it was impossible. The bed felt too light, weightless almost. He felt as though he might float away without her there beside him, and when he did manage to doze, he would wake a few minutes later and lose her all over again.

Instead of sleeping, he had walked. He walked as

the rest of the estate slept, along the avenues and the crescents, through corridors of people drifting out of awareness, and the stillness was an opiate to him, cushioning his mind and unthreading his thoughts. He walked to the park, where Margaret liked to sit by the bandstand and watch the children playing. Then he walked to the bench overlooking the pond and stared at the spines of bulrushes gathered at its banks, and the ducks, skirting the edges of the water, tucked into a feathery sleep. He chose the route she would take to do the shopping, marking her journey along the High Street. He walked past mannequins, past windows cellophaned in orange, past the cool silver trays of the fishmonger, empty of everything except growths of fraudulent parsley. He trailed the sound of his own footsteps on deserted streets, all the way to the library, and then back through the marketplace and down to the canal. He knew she liked to sit by the towpath and eat her lunch. During the day, there was a string of people to pass the time with, dog walkers and cyclists, and shoppers taking a shortcut into town, and each evening as they ate their meal, she would laugh and tell him their stories. But in the darkness, the ash trees bowed their heads towards the water, searching for their reflections, and the canal became black and limitless, stretching like a ribbon of ink into the distance. The night altered the landscape, until it became as confusing and unfamiliar as another country.

As he traced her path through the streets, he would

speak as though she were walking alongside him. Before she disappeared, he never said *I love you*. Unsure of themselves, the words had become trapped and awkward, and reluctant to leave. Instead of saying *I love you*, he said *Take care of yourself*, and *When will you be back?* Instead of saying *I love you*, he placed her umbrella at the bottom of the stairs, so it wouldn't be forgotten, and in the winter he put her gloves on the chair by the door, so she would remember to pull them on to her hands before she left. Until she disappeared, this was the only way he knew how, but since she had gone, he found that the words had become untethered. They fell from his mouth in the silence, certain and unashamed. They rattled under the bridge at the canal, and tripped across the towpath. They waltzed around the bandstand and chased along the pavements as he walked. He thought that if he said the words often enough, she would be certain to hear them, and surely if he continued to walk, they would eventually meet. Statistically, there could be only so many steps you had to take before you found someone again.

*

He pulled open the wardrobe doors, and a heave of recognition rolled through his body. Her clothes were so familiar, so intimate, he felt imprisoned by them, unable to look away. He had suggested to Margaret that she hang them in some sort of order. Colours, perhaps, or type of garment. It would make everything so much easier to find, he'd told her. But she had just laughed and kissed the top of his head, and said that he thought too much. Her outfits remained disordered and unplanned, and they looked back at him from the rail, a whole audience of Margarets, spectating on his misery. He breathed in, thinking her scent might have been waiting for him behind the doors, but the summer had stolen it away. There was only the bland smell of material, warmth pressed between its layers, and the bite of chemicals from dry-cleaning wrappers. Despite the chaos, it was well taken care of. Hems were restitched, shoes were reheeled, and tears were disappeared. Margaret liked to mend. It made her happy to see things repaired, and the repairing made John feel safe. Now she was gone, he could imagine the threads beginning to loosen and the edges beginning to lift, and all the holes that would form for his life to fall into.

He felt ashamed to search her clothes, but still his hands wandered over the jackets and the coats, looking for a way into her life. He found that sometimes the pockets weren't pockets at all, just pieces of material fastened to the front, like trickery, and the ones he did find were empty of everything except a discarded tissue or a Fisherman's Friend. Her handbags were just as meaningless. Crumpled 'To Do' lists and escaped half-pence pieces, spare glasses ready for the optician, and long-ago receipts. Fragments of an ordinary life. A life she had decided to leave.

He sat back. The litter of his search spilled on to the

carpet around him, and he glanced to and from the door, soothing himself with the fear that he still might be discovered. As he shifted his weight, knots of an unravelled life dug into his back. Soon, the house would be overpowered, the chaos would flood every room, and there would be nowhere left for him to exist. Before Margaret left, there was always something to do, something which needed folding or filing or straightening. There was an arrangement, a plan. Now he had become untethered, drifting between layers of his own thinking, surrounded by drawers and cupboards and wardrobes which vomited their contents on to the floor, as he searched for an answer to a question which might not even exist. His fingers laced the back of his head, trying to anchor his mind, covering his ears to block out the sound of his own pulse. He measured out his breaths, like Margaret had taught him. Counting, waiting. It would pass, he just needed to find a distraction, a sense of control. He reached over for one of the lists and unfolded it.

It was dated the 20th of June, the day before she vanished. He could imagine how she would have spent the week from her words: *butcher (order meat), library books, opticians, raffle tickets for Legion (Wednesday), make hair appointment.* He imagined the route she would have taken, the people she would have stopped to speak to. Everyone liked to talk to Margaret. She would walk from one end of the High Street to the other, moving from conversation to conversation. Finding something in everyone.

He wondered if he should do a job from the list. He looked over the carpet for the spectacles, and found them wedged between a packet of Polo mints and a hairbrush. There was a tiny screw missing from one of the hinges, and the arm of the glasses drooped towards the floor. He held his breath, not daring to move. Perhaps it was still in the handbag, but if it wasn't, and he reached to look, he might disturb something and it would never be found. He needed to see an example of what he was looking for, and so he turned the glasses around without moving anything except for his wrist. It was only then that he noticed the lenses. They were thick and heavy and bulged from their black frames like a cartoon. He held them to his eyes and the room became drunk and misshapen. These certainly weren't Margaret's glasses, and they definitely weren't his, yet they looked oddly familiar.

The thought found him within seconds. He stood, like a reflex. The glasses. The Polo mints. The hairbrush. Everything scattered across the carpet.

Number eleven, Mr Creasy. Did your wife ever talk to Walter Bishop?

He rushed to open a window, the breath of his fear escaping on to the glass in staccato beats. Above the roofs, a river of starlings rolled and turned, spinning out their harmony across a bleached sky, and he tried to find something familiar, something safe. But in the heat, sounds cut across the surface and distorted the picture. The bristles on Dorothy Forbes' sweeping brush, as they bit into the concrete, the creak of Sheila Dakin's deckchair, Grace and Tilly's smiles as they walked along May Roper's path. Grace's sunglasses were too big, and he watched as she pushed them back on to her face. May Roper was talking, her arms moving in the space around her head, her lips twisting and stretching and punching out the words. He watched Grace reach into her pocket and offer something up. He heard Sheila drag her deckchair through the grass and a dull tap as the wooden frame caught the edge of a glass. He watched Harold Forbes shouting something to Dorothy, miming instructions from inside the living room. He heard sounds he'd never noticed before. The avenue had become an animation, a carnival. The temperature had brought everything to a point, sharpening the volume and the contrast and the brightness, and digging them into his skull.

The view was lost to his breathing, and he wiped it with the sleeve of his shirt. When it cleared, he looked across at number eleven.

He thought he caught the glare of a reflection, as a window turned against the sun. He thought he heard the click of a catch, and he thought he saw the shadow of Walter Bishop, watching from the edge of the glass.

*

The tea made him feel a little better. It wasn't so much the tea itself, it was more the act of making it. The ritual of filling the kettle and warming the pot, of stirring the leaves until it was just the right strength. *Distract yourself*, that's what Margaret always told him. When you start getting anxious, give your mind something else to think about. He had become an expert at distracting himself. He had distracted himself so much, he found himself drowning in distractions, and all the little details in the world seemed to join up together in his head and make a whole new problem to worry about.

Margaret said he should find a hobby. He had tried, but everything came with its own set of worries. Fishing gave you far too much time to think, cricket was practically riddled with hazards, and heaven knows how many bacteria you could find in a garden. And so he did what he always did for a hobby. He went to the British Legion. The only problem was, it was the British Legion which had started all this in the first place. The irony was, he was on the verge of going home that night. It was early December, and frost had already painted itself on to the pavements. He was thinking of calling it a night, before the temperature dropped even further and the walk home became even more dangerous. Perhaps if he had, none of this would have happened. Although he knew from experience that if something bad was going to happen, it would happen regardless of how much you tried to avoid it. Bad things find you. They seek you out. No matter how you might try to ignore them or hide away, or walk in the opposite direction. They will discover you eventually.

It's only ever a question of time.

11 December 1967

Harold is talking again. John can hear him over a whine of voices.

'Do you want to know what I think?' he is saying.

No one answers, but this has never stopped Harold from divvying up his opinion and handing it around the table.

'I think that if the police won't move him on, then we need to take matters into our own hands. That's what I think.'

There are nods and murmured yeses. John sees May Roper hammer at Brian's leg under the table.

Harold is drumming his wedding ring against the edge of a glass, and Dorothy blinks with each beat. Derek Bennett turns his pint ninety degrees at a time, and the group drifts back into a silence.

John wants to leave. He can see the door from where he's standing. A few steps and he could be outside, walking away, leaving them all to it, but the whole avenue is here. Everyone except his mother, who is babysitting Grace and watching Fred Astaire tap-dance his way to a happy ending. It would look too obvious if he left. They would notice, and then they would realize that he was weak and useless, and cowardly. He has to stay. For once, he has to stand up for something. He has to find his voice, if only to make up for all the years he has existed in a silence.

'We've tried watching the house,' says Derek. 'Fat lot of good that's done. If anything it's made things worse. He never shows himself now. At least before, we knew what he was up to.'

'A man like that should never be allowed to live on a road like ours,' May Roper says.

John sees her hammer Brian's leg under the table again.

'My mam's right,' says Brian, like a tendon reflex.

'They say he has the right to live where he wants.' Dorothy is still blinking, even though Harold's wedding ring is silent.

'The world's gone rights mad,' says Sheila. 'Far too many people have rights these days.'

Everyone nods. Even Dorothy Forbes, who manages to fit it in, in between her blinking.

'What kind of a person harms a child? What kind of evil is that?' says Derek.

Sheila Dakin reaches for her Babycham, but she misjudges it and the drink spills across the table.

'I'm sorry,' she says. 'I'm so sorry.'

They find Clive and a tea towel, and everyone lifts their glasses while the mess is wiped away.

'He always says it's a mistake,' Sylvia tightens her arms around her cardigan, 'a misunderstanding.'

'There have been far too many misunderstandings.' Eric Lamb is drinking Guinness, and he wipes it from his mouth

as he speaks. 'The photographs, what happened with Lisa.
I thought taking a baby was a one-off, but it clearly wasn't.'

'A man like that shouldn't be allowed to have a camera,'
says May Roper.

'My mam's right.' Brian manages to speak just before
the hammering starts.

Sylvia's arms are still across her chest. She has a Britvic
orange, but it waits in its glass, untouched. 'The police
said photography was his hobby, that they couldn't stop
him.'

'A man like that shouldn't be allowed to have hobbies,'
says May. 'Heaven knows what other photographs he's
taken.'

Everyone looks down and takes a sip of their drink. There
is a silence. It unfolds across the table like a cloth, and no
one seems keen to disturb it. Clive moves in between them,
collecting empties. He shares a look with Harold, but
neither of them says anything. John watches Clive all the
way to the bar. There are too many glasses and not enough
fingers.

Sylvia is the one to speak first, although her voice is so
quiet, John can barely hear the words. 'The only way you'll
get him off the avenue,' she says, 'is if he hasn't got a house
to live in.'

'It's a shame he doesn't come back after Christmas
and find it gone,' says Sheila.

John frowns at her.

'He always goes away for Christmas, John. Tinsel and

turkey with his mum. Somewhere no one knows him, and no one knows what he likes to get up to.'

Sheila was right. It was the only time Walter Bishop ever left the avenue. He didn't even go away in the summer. Instead, he stayed at number eleven, baking himself within its walls, all the way through until September.

'Pity he doesn't come back in the New Year and find it bulldozed to the ground,' says Derek. 'Bloody pervert.'

Harold leans back in his chair and folds his arms. 'Of course,' he says, 'you don't always need a bulldozer to get rid of a house.'

Eric stares over his pint of Guinness. There is the edge of a smile in Derek's eyes, and under the table, May Roper begins hammering again.

'What do you mean?' says Brian.

'What I mean, lad, is that sometimes fate plays a part in these things. An electrical fault, a spark from a fire. It doesn't mean anyone will get hurt.'

Eric places his pint on the table. There is a carefulness about it. 'I hope you know what you're suggesting, Harold.'

'I'm not suggesting anything. I'm just saying – these things happen.'

'Or they're made to happen,' says Sheila.

'Jesus Christ.' Eric pulls his hands across his face.

'Never mind Jesus Christ. Jesus Christ doesn't have to live next door to him. Neither do you for that matter.'

Eric says nothing. He shakes his head very briefly, but it's enough to set Harold off again.

'I've had enough, Eric. I've had enough of living next door to that bloody weirdo. If we don't do something, then God help me, I won't be responsible for my actions. You've got to think about the children. There are kiddies on this avenue.'

John has seen Harold angry before. Harold spends his whole life being angry about something; he's like a walking argument. But this is different. This anger is darker and more brutal, and it comes from a place John thinks he recognizes. Perhaps they all feel an anger in their own way, because each face around the table has changed. They have shifted, chosen another path of thinking. He can see it in their faces, and in the way they take their opinions to the floor. Only Dorothy looks ahead. There is a brightness fixed into her eyes.

'We all feel the same, Harold. Try not to upset yourself.'

John can hear it, a brittle pacification, a faint tremor of experience in her voice.

*

The flash takes them all by surprise. It's sudden and shocking, and they all look up to find themselves staring into a lens.

There are two men. One with a camera, and one with a notepad and an air of curiosity.

'Andy Kilner, local paper,' says the notepad. 'For the Seasonal Edition. A bit of local colour. Christmas spirit, good will to all men, and all that.'

'I see,' says Harold.

'Any quotes?' says the notepad.

'I don't think so.' Harold reaches for his pint. 'We've said all there is to say.'

Number Two, The Avenue

5 July 1976

'It was a beautiful service.'

Mrs Roper took a compact from her handbag, and I watched her press powder into the sweat on her upper lip.

'If today's taught me anything,' she said, 'it's taught me that life is too short.'

Ninety-eight, Tilly mouthed to me from across the room. I bobbed my shoulders so no one else would see.

'It was a lovely send-off, Brian.' The compact clicked shut and Mrs Roper slid it back, deep into the macramé. 'You should have been there.'

Brian sat in the corner, next to a standard lamp. It had a large cream shade, which spread out like a skirt, and his head had to be angled slightly, to avoid being swallowed by the fringing.

I looked at the tin of Quality Street. It was on a footstool at the side of the settee.

'You have a beautiful singing voice, Mrs Roper,' I said.

'Thank you, dear.' She reached over. 'Toffee Finger?'

My hand crept through the twists of colour, and I saw Tilly shake her head very slightly and smile.

'The order of service is on the windowsill. You want to have a read of it, Brian. Before I put it with the rest.'

He glanced from the edge of his eyes. 'I haven't got time now,' he said. 'I'll read it later.'

There was no air in Mrs Roper's sitting room. It smelled of caramel and mint, and the sweetness hung in the air and wrapped itself around us like a bandage. The walls were a pattern of confectionery, swirls of coffee and cream, and above the fireplace was a selection of photographs in silver frames. Within the frames was a row of people who all looked the same – round and shiny, with fairground smiles, and they stretched out across the mantelpiece like Russian dolls.

'My parents,' said Mrs Roper, when she saw me looking, 'and my brother and sisters.' She unwrapped a Toffee Penny.

I smiled.

'All dead now, of course.'

I stopped smiling.

'Heart attacks,' said Brian, from the edge of his fringe.

Mrs Roper's chewing slowed down temporarily, as she looked over at Brian. 'It's true,' she said, looking back and picking up speed again. 'My mother dropped down dead in the middle of Miss World 1961. I couldn't ever look Michael Aspel straight in the eye after that.'

I took another triangle. 'Is that what happened to Mr Roper?'

'Oh no,' she said. 'He caught the ferry to Yarmouth twelve years ago and was never seen again.'

'He drowned?' said Tilly.

'No, he ran off with one of the girls from the typing pool,' said Brian.

Mrs Roper shot him a stare. Then she shrugged her shoulders and a smile folded up her face and wrinkled her nose. 'Still. Nothing's forever, is it?' she said, and passed over another Quality Street. 'It's all God's will.'

'So, you do believe in God, Mrs Roper?' I said.

'Oh God, well, yes, God.' She spoke as though I had brought up the subject of an old and dear friend. 'The Lord giveth and the Lord taketh away.'

'Do you think the Lord taketh away Mrs Creasy?'

I saw Tilly move towards the edge of her seat.

'Oh she's been taken away all right.' Mrs Roper leaned forward and fanned herself with a copy of *The People's Friend*. 'But I don't think God had anything much to do with it.'

'Mam, don't start.' Brian shifted his position, and I could hear the springs in the armchair wake up and yawn.

'Well, it wouldn't be the first time, would it?' said Mrs Roper.

Brian shifted again. 'Why don't we have a brew? I've been hoovering all afternoon.'

'What a good idea, Brian.' Mrs Roper lifted her legs on to the crochet. 'Put the kettle on. There's a good boy. Funerals always make me so thirsty.'

*

I offered to help Brian with the tea, and we waited in the strip of kitchen which stretched along the back of the house. The cupboard doors were an unhappy walnut, and it was so dark and quiet I felt as though I was sitting inside a box.

'Don't take no notice of my mam,' Brian said. He spooned tea leaves into a bright orange pot. 'She gets carried away. Spends too much time on that settee, shuffling her own thoughts.'

'Doesn't she get out very much?'

'Not since my dad went.' He opened one of the cupboards, and I could see a tangle of plates and bowls, waiting to overbalance. 'Sat herself down in the front room when he left, waiting for him to come back and apologize, and she hasn't really moved much since.'

The kettle began to boil. It was shy at first, clicking against the spout, a soft tap on the metal. Then it became louder, rattling its impatience and spreading an angry whistle of steam across the tiles.

'You must have been upset when he went. It must have been a shock.'

'Not really,' he said. 'I could smell it coming. Like rain.'

He lifted a tray down from the top of the fridge. It looked worn and tired, rings of teacups past circling out the days.

'Do you think that's what happened with Mrs Creasy?' I said. 'Do you think she planned to leave?'

Brian didn't answer for a while. Instead, he arranged the milk jug and the teapot and the sugar bowl on the tray, and then he began lifting cups from one of the cupboards. The patterns on the cups were all different, and foxgloves and daisies and hydrangeas all argued with each other about who wanted to be the loudest.

'I'm not sure,' he said, after a while. 'I don't think so.'

I waited. I had discovered that, sometimes, if you held on to the silence, people couldn't stop themselves from filling it up.

'She'd made an appointment for the next day.' He reached towards a biscuit barrel next to the kettle. It was made in the shape of a bloodhound, and he had to remove the top of its skull in order to retrieve a packet of ginger nuts. 'She wouldn't have let them down. She wasn't that kind of lady.'

'Who was the appointment with?'

Brian pulled a pink and green tea cosy over the teapot, tugging at the knitting to fit around the spout. He turned to look at me, and was about to speak when Mrs Roper's voice reached out along the hall from the sitting room.

'Have you gone to China for that tea, Brian?'

The packet of biscuits rolled towards the edge as he lifted

the tray. He looked into my eyes for just a moment, and then looked away. 'It was with me,' he said.

*

'In the middle of Sunday dinner,' Mrs Roper was saying, as we walked in. 'One minute she was dishing up the roast potatoes, and the next, she was face down in a plate of Paxo.'

'Mrs Roper was just telling me all about heart attacks,' said Tilly. She looked slightly pale. 'Although I think we might have covered everything there is to say.'

'I was explaining to Tilly how important it is to live for the moment,' said Mrs Roper. 'You never know what's going to happen next. Look at Ernest Morton, look at Margaret Creasy.'

Brian set the tray down on the coffee table. There were squares of a chessboard blocked into the wood, but no sign of any chess pieces. He leaned the packet of ginger nuts against the milk jug.

'Plate, Brian. Fetch a plate for the biscuits. We've got company.' Mrs Roper waved her arms around and clicked her tongue across her front teeth.

'He's a nice boy,' she said, as Brian left the room, 'harmless enough, but a bit simple. Like his father.'

'You spent a lot of time with Mrs Creasy, then?' I said.

Brian returned and spread the ginger nuts out on a plate, and they were sent to live with Mrs Roper on the settee.

'We spent hours playing cards,' said Mrs Roper. 'I knew her better than anyone.'

'But you don't know why she disappeared?' I worked out that it was still possible to reach a ginger nut if I moved to the very edge of my seat. 'She didn't say anything to you?'

'No, she didn't.' Mrs Roper looked deeply disappointed in herself. 'She never said a word.'

Brian poured the tea. I could see him glance at his mother in between cups.

'Although she might not have had much choice in the matter.' She spoke very quickly, whilst Brian was occupied with the sugar bowl.

'Don't fill their heads with that nonsense, Mam.'

'I'm only speaking my mind, Brian. That's why your grandfather fought in the war, so I can speak my mind.' She sank one of the biscuits into her tea and tiny crumbs of ginger floated around in the milky waves. 'There's plenty of people on this avenue who know a lot more than they're letting on.'

'What do you mean, Mrs Roper?' I said.

She sucked at the ginger nut before it disappeared into her mouth, and then she stirred more sugar into her tea. I could hear her spoon clicking against the hydrangeas as it drifted around the cup. Brian stood in front of her. He tried to rest his arm on the mantelpiece, but it was a fraction too low.

'What I mean', she said, looking at Brian before she spoke, 'is that the world is made up of all sorts of people.'

Brian still hadn't moved.

'There are decent people,' said Mrs Roper, 'and then there are the weird ones, the ones who don't belong. The ones who cause the rest of us problems.'

'Goats and sheep,' said Tilly from across the room.

Mrs Roper frowned. 'Well, I suppose so, if that's the way you want to look at it.'

'It's the way God looks at it,' said Tilly, and folded her arms beneath her poncho.

'The point is, these people don't think like the rest of us. They're misfits, oddballs. They're the ones the police should be talking to, not people like us. Normal people.'

'Have the police been to see you as well, Mrs Roper?'

She drowned another biscuit. 'Oh yes, they've been. PC something. What was his name, Brian?'

'Green.' Brian went back to sit by the window, under the fringing.

'That's it. PC Green. He doesn't know any more than the rest of us about where Margaret's gone. Although I didn't see him knocking at number eleven, did you, Brian?'

Brian shook his head. I had a feeling he might have been asked this question before.

'How do you know which people they are,' said Tilly, 'the people who don't fit in?'

Mrs Roper sucked more tea out of her ginger nut. 'It's as plain as the nose on your face. They have strange little habits, odd behaviour. They never mix with anyone else. They even look different.'

'They do?' I said.

'You'll understand as you get older. You can spot them a mile off. You'll learn to cross the street.' She pointed to the footstool. 'Pass us that ashtray, Brian, my legs are killing me, I can barely move.'

'Perhaps that's why they don't mix,' said Tilly, 'because everyone else is on the other side of the street?'

But Mrs Roper was concentrating on lighting her cigarette, and within a few seconds a blanket of Park Drive began to drift across the room.

Out in the avenue, the sound of an engine stammered to a halt, and there was a thud of car door closing.

Brian caught his head on the shade as he peered around the standard lamp. 'That's interesting,' he said.

'What?' Mrs Roper looked up from the tin of Quality Street with the instinct of a wild animal.

'It's the police again.'

She sprang from the settee like a jack-in-a-box. We all moved towards the window, and Tilly managed to squeeze under Mrs Roper's armpit. We watched PC Green replace his hat and straighten his jacket, and begin walking towards the top of the road.

'Is he going to number eleven?' said Mrs Roper.

'It doesn't look like it.' The policeman crossed the street, and Brian moved the curtain slightly to improve the view.

We looked, as PC Green walked past each of the houses, until he came to a stop outside number four.

'It looks like he's going into your house, Grace.' Brian let the curtain fall back across the glass.

Mrs Roper took a long drag on her cigarette. 'Well I never,' she said.

Number Four, The Avenue

5 July 1976

Tilly and I sat exactly halfway up the stairs.

I had worked out, through a series of experiments, that this was the most useful step. Any higher and you couldn't hear the words; any lower and you risked being discovered and sent to your room, and repeatedly told proverbs about people who listen in doorways.

'Have we missed anything?' said Tilly.

My mother had pushed the sitting-room door to, but there was just enough of a gap to see PC Green's jacket and my father's left shoulder.

'I think they're just offering him a cup of tea,' I whispered. 'I don't think they'd do that if he'd arrested them.'

I could hear my mother. Her voice was brittle. Like an egg. 'I'd rather stay, if that's all right with you,' she said.

My father's left shoulder was shrugging, presumably along

with his right one. He said, 'There's nothing I would say to you that I wouldn't say in front of my wife.'

My father never described my mother as *my wife*.

I could tell from PC Green's back that he was taking his notebook out of his pocket. Through the doorway, I could hear the pages turning over, and the sound of my father tapping his fingers against the back of a chair.

'Mr Bennett, you are the owner of Bennett Property and Management Services?' said PC Green, 'based at number 54 St John's Street?'

My father said that he was. His voice was small and insignificant. It didn't even sound like my father any more, it sounded like someone who was trying to remember how to be valuable.

'We've had a witness come forward,' said PC Green, 'who saw Mrs Creasy entering your office building at . . .' – there was the sound of another page turning – '. . . approximately two o'clock on the afternoon of the 20th of June.'

The tapping stopped and a band of silence took its place. As though no one knew who was supposed to speak next.

In the end, it was my mother. 'That was the day before she disappeared,' she said.

'It was,' said PC Green. 'It was also a Sunday.'

I heard a breath leave my mother's mouth. It sounded as though she had been holding on to it for some time. 'Well, I don't know what she'd be doing there, but it wouldn't be anything to do with Derek. He goes to his

Round Table meeting on a Sunday afternoon, don't you, Derek?'

'Mr Bennett? Could you confirm where you were on the afternoon of Sunday, the 20th of June?'

My father didn't confirm anything. Instead, he shuffled his feet on the carpet and we all listened to the sound of my mother's breathing.

'Mr Bennett?'

'I may have talked to her briefly that day,' said my father, eventually. 'In passing.'

The policeman's notebook turned again. 'Yet when I spoke to you last week, Mr Bennett, and I asked you when you last saw Mrs Creasy, you distinctly said that *it could have been Thursday, or possibly Friday*,' said PC Green.

Tilly turned to me on the staircase and made her eyes very wide. I made mine very small back again.

'It must have slipped my mind,' said my father. 'But now you come to mention it, yes. Yes, I did see her on the Sunday.'

'Is your office open on a Sunday, Mr Bennett?' said PC Green.

'No.' My mother's voice answered the question. 'His office isn't open on a Sunday.'

'Then perhaps you could explain to me why Mrs Creasy would be visiting your premises?'

'Derek?' I couldn't see my mother's face, but I could imagine it, stretched over the question like a drum.

I had never seen my father like this. He was always the

one asking questions, waiting for explanations. It felt strange, as though the light had shifted, and I realized that I had only ever read one chapter of a story. When my father eventually spoke, Tilly and I had to lean through the banisters to hear his reply.

'She wanted some advice,' he said. 'It was the only day she could make it.'

'Some advice?' said PC Green.

'That's right.'

'On . . .' I heard the pages turn again. I didn't like the pages. '. . . property and management services?'

I could see my father's left arm. It was crossing over to join his right. For a while, the only sound was the kitchen clock, eating away at the seconds.

'She was thinking of making an investment,' he said eventually.

'I see, Mr Bennett, only her husband hasn't mentioned any of this to us.'

'I don't believe she'd discussed it with her husband, PC Green. This is the 1970s. Women can make decisions all by themselves these days.'

His voice had expanded. He was almost back to being my father again.

I could see the policeman adjust his jacket and replace his notebook, and I heard him suggest to my father that he have a think about whether anything else might have slipped his mind. He said '*slipped his mind*' as though he was learning to speak a foreign language. My father said that he would, in his brand new, expanded voice. The sitting-room door was pulled open and everyone moved towards the hall. Tilly and I had to run up to the landing and be soundless all at the same time.

'What do you think that was all about, then?' Tilly said when we got to my bedroom. Her breath was stolen by stairs and excitement.

I shrugged my shoulders. 'Not sure,' I said.

'Don't you think it's strange that your dad never mentioned it before?'

'Maybe.'

'Well, I think it's really strange.' She stretched out *really* as she lifted the poncho over her head. 'It doesn't make any sense.'

We sat on the bed. The eiderdown felt slippery cool against the back of my legs. Below our feet, I could hear the swell of my mother's voice, ebbing and flowing against the ceiling.

Tilly picked up one of the bushbabies and held it to her face. 'I don't think your mum's very happy,' she said.

I brushed my hands across the material and a wave of static fizzed through my fingers. 'No,' I said.

'She's probably upset that the policeman had to come back. They're very busy, aren't they? That's probably all it is.'

'Probably,' I said.

'I don't think it's anything to worry about,' she said, with a face full of worrying.

My mother's voice continued to cut through the floor-boards. The words were splintered and incomplete, which somehow made it worse. If I could hear what was being said, I might be able to find a pocket of reassurance, because I knew my mother was sometimes perfectly capable of embroidering a whole evening of arguing out of absolutely nothing at all. I wanted this to be one of those times, and so I held my breath and tried to make sense of the pieces, but they struck the ceiling like gravel.

Beyond my mother's voice was the low, grumbling apology of my father, and in between handfuls of my mother, I heard him say 'There isn't anything else to tell' and 'Why would I lie about it?' And then he was lost again in a wave of shouting.

Tilly put the Whimsy back on the shelf. 'It's strange, though, isn't it, why he didn't mention seeing Mrs Creasy before?'

I moved the bushbaby very slightly to the left. 'It must have just slipped his mind,' I said.

The words sounded like a foreign language.

6 July 1976

We followed Mrs Morton down the High Street. She sailed, like a vessel, along the pavement, skirting around pushchairs and small dogs, and people who had stopped to wipe ice cream from their chins.

July had found its fiercest day yet. The sky was ironed into an acid blue, and even the clouds had fallen from the edges, leaving a faultless page of summer above our heads. Even so, there were those who still nurtured mistrust. We walked past cardigans draped across elbows and raincoats bundled into shopping bags, and one woman who carried an umbrella wedged into her armpit, like artillery. It seemed that people couldn't quite let go of the weather, and felt the need to carry every form of it around with them, at all times, for safekeeping.

Mrs Morton managed to speak to everyone she met without ever stopping. My mother would pause in shop doorways and at the edge of pavements, until the carrier bags ate into her fingers and my feet scraped impatience on the concrete, but Mrs Morton seemed to be able to have a conversation as she walked, giving out small samples of herself to everyone without ever being anchored by their questions. She did, however, pause outside Woolworth's to stare at a stack of deckchairs propped on the pavement near the doorway. Tilly and I pointed to things in baskets that we felt we needed – lawn darts and Stylophones and badminton racquets wrapped in cellophane. There were even towers of buckets and spades, and a chimney of sand-castle moulds, which reached all the way up to Tilly's chin. The nearest beach was fifty miles away.

I stared through the doorway at a river of Pick-n-Mix.

'Shall we stand inside for a moment, to get out of the sun?' I looked at Mrs Morton.

'We're supposed to be going to the library,' she said.

'It's important to avoid heatstroke.' I looked back at the Pick-n-Mix. 'Angela Rippon said so.'

Mrs Morton followed my gaze. 'I think we'll all survive,' she said, 'for the next three and a half minutes.'

*

The library was right at the end of the High Street, where the shops faded into accountants and solicitors and architects, with their Georgian fronts and thick brass plates. It looked over the park and the memorial gates, and last year's poppies lay bleached into a bloody pink against the railings. My mother usually took me to the library, but since PC Green had been to the house, her life seemed to have become disconnected from times and dates. My parents had the same circle of conversation every few hours, in which my mother would accuse my father of lying, and my father would accuse my mother of being ridiculous, and then they would both accuse each other of being unreasonable. The words would spin around the room for a few minutes, until they span out of energy, and then they would disappear to recharge themselves for the next time my parents met on the stairs or in the hall, or across the kitchen table.

Mrs Morton pushed the library door, and Tilly and I walked underneath her arm. After my bedroom, this was my favourite place in the world. It was carpeted, and had heavy bookcases and ticking clocks and velvet chairs, just like someone's living room. It smelled of unturned pages and unseen adventures, and on every shelf were people I had yet to meet, and places I had yet to visit. Each time, I lost myself in the corridors of books and the polished, wooden rooms, deciding which journey to go on next.

Mrs Morton took my last-time's books from her bag and placed them on the front desk.

'Grace Bennett's books are returned on time,' said the librarian. She snapped at the front cover of each one, sending little gusts of air across the counter. 'That must be a first.'

I gave her my biggest smile, and she handed over the tickets and frowned. Her hands were covered in ink and it had leaked into the creases around her nails.

I had five tickets. Five adventures to choose.

The first thing I did was visit Aslan and Mowgli, and Jo and Meg. I had read them so many times, it felt like we were friends, and I had to run my finger down the spine of each book to check it was in its proper place and make sure they were all safe, before I could even think about doing anything else. Tilly pointed at books she wanted, and I left her reading *Alice in Wonderland* on a very small chair in front of a very small table.

I wandered past Mrs Morton, who was standing in front of the Westerns.

'Aren't you staying in the children's room?' she said.

'I've outgrown it, Mrs Morton. I'm ten now.'

'But there are some very appropriate books in there for young ladies of ten.' She had a novel in her hand. It had a picture of a Stetson on the front, with a smoking bullet hole right through its centre.

'Yes, I know, I've read all of them,' I said.

'All of them?'

'Yep.'

The book was called *A Bullet for Beau Barrowclough*.

'I need to broaden my reading,' I said.

She put Beau Barrowclough back on his shelf. 'Well, make sure you don't broaden it too widely.'

*

I walked through the romances, behind cookery and travel, and past the side room full of old newspapers and posters about coffee mornings, to the non-fiction room at the back of the building. Here the shelves were wider and the corridors were longer, and the smell of the pages was even heavier. It was unfamiliar. The ripe, solid smell of learning. I'd just reached *C* when a conversation drifted across the top of the shelves.

That's exactly what I heard. Except I heard she'd had an argument with him.

Oh no, no argument. Out of the blue, it was.

One of the voices was the grumpy librarian with the inky hands.

They moved somewhere along the aisle, and for a moment I lost reception.

Well, it stands to reason, doesn't it? Who else would it be? said the other voice, when I found them again.

I always go and stand in the back when he comes in here. He gives me the creeps.

He's not right in the head, is he? You can tell by just looking at him.

I took a dictionary of quotations from the shelf, in order to make room for my ears.

She was in here, you know, a few days before she disappeared.

The other voice made a surprised noise. *What did she take out?*

Nothing. Didn't have her library card. She spent about half an hour in the side room and then left.

Wouldn't surprise me if she was under his patio.

Me neither. He's got the look of a killer, that one. You can see it in his eyes.

Oh he has, Carole. You're so right.

And the voices floated away from the dictionaries and the encyclopaedias, and disappeared somewhere beyond the solar system and local folklore.

*

'Have you chosen?' Mrs Morton stood at the front desk with Tilly.

'I have,' I said, although I was using my chin to steady the tower of books in my arms, and it wasn't easy to speak.

'Grace, however many have you got there?' said Mrs Morton. 'You only have five tickets.'

'Tilly said she'd lend me four of hers.'

'I did?' said Tilly.

Mrs Morton turned her head to look at Tilly's book. 'What did you choose?'

'*The Lion, the Witch and the Wardrobe*,' said Tilly.

'She always chooses that,' I said. 'She has a crush on Mr Tumnus.'

'I do not!' She pulled the book to her chest. 'I just like the snow.'

Mrs Morton studied my tower of books. 'Shall we have a look?' she said.

She lifted the top one from the pile. '*Inside the Mind of a Serial Killer*.' An interesting choice. And what do we have here?' She took another book. '*Secrets of the Black Museum*.' And another. '*Murders of the Twentieth Century: An Anthology*.' She raised her eyebrows and stared at me.

'For research,' I said.

She glanced at the book which now sat on the top of the pile. '*A Bullet for Beau Barrowclough*?'

'It's the cover,' I said, 'it spoke to me.'

'I think it's time we had a little rethink, don't you?'

*

When we'd revisited the shelves, and the librarian had stamped and clicked, and run inky fingers over my rethinking, we left the carpets and the cool, polished corridors and walked into a heat which shimmered the tops of the trees and made the edges of the world wave and swim.

'Gosh,' said Tilly, and I held on to Narnia whilst she took off her jumper.

'We'll walk back through the park,' said Mrs Morton, pointing towards the gates with the intrepidness of a sub-Saharan explorer. 'We'll find some shade.'

The park wasn't that shady. There were pockets of cool shadow, where the trees swept a darkness over the paths, but most of it was held in a slick of heat, and we crissed and crossed to keep ourselves hidden. There were people who didn't seem to mind. They lay on T-shirt pillows, the aerials on their radios telescoped towards the sun, forgotten novels turned into the grass. There were children paddling and squealing, the sun holding on to each kick, as their parents pulled down sunhats and rubbed cream into powdery knees.

I realized the click of Tilly's sandals had faded away, and I looked back. She was standing next to the bandstand, leaning into the rails, her jumper still knotted around her waist. Further along the path, Mrs Morton stopped too and blocked the sun with the edge of her hand.

'I'm all right, Mrs Morton,' Tilly said. 'It's just the heat. It makes your legs watery.'

I looked at Mrs Morton's face as she walked past me, and it made my mouth dry and uneasy.

She looked into Tilly's eyes and touched Tilly's forehead and frowned, and said we should all sit for a moment in the shade of the bandstand. There was no one else in there, only streaks of bird droppings on the peeled wooden rails and an old newspaper, which turned over and over on the concrete, as a breeze read through its pages.

Tilly said she was *fine, honestly, fine*, but her skin was porcelain-white and my eyes found Mrs Morton's concern and photocopied it.

'I just felt wobbly, that's all,' said Tilly.

'You shouldn't overdo it.' Mrs Morton put her hand over Tilly's. 'You need to take special care of yourself.'

'Grace said nothing bad would happen to me. She said she wouldn't let it.'

Mrs Morton found my eyes for a moment, and turned back. 'Of course nothing bad is going to happen to you. But your mother likes you to be careful, doesn't she?'

Tilly nodded, and I saw beads of sweat move across her forehead.

'So we'll just sit here for a moment. Let you get your breath back.'

I remembered the little kiosk next to the war memorial. 'Maybe an ice cream would help,' I said, 'or a Topic?'

Tilly shook her head and said perhaps a little sip of water would be nice.

Mrs Morton looked around, her hand still on Tilly's.

'I'll go,' I said. 'I'll find you some water.'

I escaped from the bandstand and welcomed scorched heat on my shoulders and the sound of people not worrying. The kiosk was beyond the coloured Frisbees and the transistor radios. It had stripes of pink and yellow all around its frame, and the canvas cracked and snapped in the breeze as I waited for the man to find a plastic cup.

I looked across to the bandstand, and I didn't want to go back. Back to the concern hidden in the edges of Mrs Morton's eyes, and to Tilly, pale and quiet and small.

Number Twelve, The Avenue

9 July 1976

Crazy, sang Patsy Cline.

'Crazy,' sang Sheila Dakin, half a second afterwards.

She sang above the hoover, and the smell of hot summer carpets and a dust bag which begged to be emptied. Patsy knew what it was to suffer. She was a casualty of life, was Patsy. You could hear it in the vibrato. She pushed the vacuum cleaner along the hall, past a chorus line of coats and a pile-up of Keithie's Matchbox cars, and took a sharp right into the living room.

'Give it a rest, Mum.' Lisa lifted her legs on to the settee.

Sheila slid into a key change as she made her entrance.

'Mum! I'm trying to read!'

The vacuum cleaner knocked against the furniture,

and its lead snaked around the room, gathering table legs and forgotten shoes, and the edge of an ashtray.

'You'll miss my singing when I'm not here any more.' Sheila pulled at the flex. 'You'll ache to hear these notes again.'

Lisa looked up from her magazine. 'Why? Where are you going?'

'Nowhere. But when I do, you'll ache, Lisa Dakin. Mark my words.'

She caught the mirror as she passed, and rubbed at the mascara under her eye, but it only sank further into the creases, and came to rest in the folds of skin which refused to unfold back to where they belonged.

The record was scratched and worn, but the brush of the guitar always edged her a little further into the misery, and she paused the hoover to make sure she didn't miss being edged.

'Why is it always the same bloody song? There must be better songs to sing than that,' Lisa said, turning pages.

'She died in a plane crash, you know.'

'You've said.'

'She was only thirty. Her whole life ahead of her.'

'I know. You've said.' Lisa looked over the back of the settee. 'You've also said about Marilyn, and Carole and Jayne.'

'It's worth remembering, Lisa. There's always someone worse off than yourself.'

'They're dead, Mum.'

'Exactly.'

Sheila flicked another switch, and the dust and the heat and the churn of the motor faded out. 'That's me done. I'm going back outside.'

Lisa turned a page. 'I really wish you wouldn't sunbathe on the front. It's not dignified.'

Her face is changing, thought Sheila. It's shaping itself, finding her father. With each year, Lisa moved a little further away. It must have happened slowly, meal by meal, conversation by conversation, but Sheila only noticed if there was an argument. Then she would realize there had been another step, and just how far she was being left behind. She could deal with her daughter becoming older. She could deal with the boys and the truanting, and the faint whisper of Silk Cut and chewing gum. It was the reflection it made which couldn't be folded up and put away.

'It's my front garden,' Sheila said. 'I'll do whatever I want in it.'

'People stare.'

'Let them bloody stare.'

'It's like going to the corner shop in your slippers, and leaving your curlers in. You just don't do it.'

'Says who?'

'Everyone else.' Lisa turned another page. 'And when everyone else says something, it's probably worth listening.'

'I see.' Sheila wound the flex around the hoover. 'So why aren't you out there looking for a summer job? Like everyone else?'

There was no reply.

'This time next year you'll be leaving school. Don't think you can sit around here all day on your arse doing nothing.'

Keithie appeared and dumped his little body on to one of the chairs. 'I can sit around on my arse, though, can't I?' he said.

Sheila looked at him. 'For now,' she said, 'for now. And don't say arse.'

Arse, arse, arse.

Lisa turned another page. 'I wish Margaret Creasy would hurry up and come back. You were a different person when she was around.'

'I was? How?'

'Less snapping. Less swearing.' She looked at Sheila over the top of the magazine. 'Not so many headaches.'

She was sharp, like her mother. Too sharp.

'She'll be back,' said Sheila. 'It's the heat. It knocks daft into people.'

'Unless Walter's had her. He likes making people disappear.'

Sheila looked over at Keithie. He was digging the end of a pen into the arm of the chair, flooded with concentration.

Arse, arse, arse.

'Careful,' she said, 'he doesn't understand.'

Lisa put her magazine down. 'He knows the crack, don't you, Keithie?'

'Strange Walter,' said Keithie. 'He's like a magician. He makes people disappear.'

He laughed. A fizzy, bubbly laugh that only children can find.

'Doesn't understand, my arse,' said Lisa.

Arse, arse, arse.

'Don't say arse!' Sheila picked up a cushion and put it back on the settee.

'I don't know why he hasn't moved on.' Lisa spoke without taking her eyes from the page. 'Someone should do something. He stares all the time.'

'Stares?'

'He gives me the creeps.' Denim shifted over denim. 'When I'm with my friends, he stands at that front window, watching everyone. Like he's trying to figure out what to do next.'

Sheila tried to twist the plug around the flex, but she couldn't manage it without taking her eyes off Lisa. 'Has he said anything to you?'

'Mum, that's the point.' There they were, those extra teenage syllables. 'He never speaks. He just watches.'

'You'd tell me – if he did?'

There was a brief nod. Lisa pulled at her hair, taking out the band, and it slipped across her shoulder unsupervised, faultless. 'Someone should do something,' she said. 'We all think someone should do something.'

Sheila was about to reply, when she heard footsteps on the path.

'Doorbell!' said Keithie, and shot out of the room before anyone could stop him.

Arse, arse, arse all the way down the hall.

'God, I hope it's not that policeman again,' said Lisa. 'Right bloody laugh a minute he was.'

'He needn't bother.' Sheila lifted a cold cup of coffee from the table. It had left rings on the wood where it had waited for her. 'We've said all there is to say.'

'You know he was at number four yesterday? Spent ages in there. I saw Derek Bennett this morning, and he looked like he'd been shot.'

'You never said.'

'I haven't seen you.' Lisa stared. 'You were still in bed when I went out. I got Keith's breakfast and I dressed him, and I put up with his bloody questions.'

Sheila gripped the cup. It had a skin of milk, yellow and tired, catching at the edges. 'I was exhausted,' she said.

'Yeah.' Lisa looked back at her magazine. 'I'd be exhausted too.'

'If you've got something to say, why don't you just bloody say it?'

'I haven't got anything to bloody say.'

There went another step, Sheila thought. Another few inches further away.

*

'Is this a bad time?'

Sheila turned to the doorway. Dorothy Forbes dressed in alternating layers of taupe and concern. Bloody typical.

'Dorothy,' she said. 'How lovely. Of course it isn't.'

Keithie stood next to Dorothy, a broken pen in his hand. He looked up at her and smiled. *Arse, arse, arse*, he said.

*

'I don't mean to be a bother.'

They sat in the kitchen. It was better there. Out of the way of Keithie and his *arses*, and Lisa's sharp eyes. She tried to keep Dorothy's attention on the conversation, instead of on last night's pots and the ashtray on the draining board, but the sunlight fell through the window and seemed to point at everything she would rather forget.

'Never a bother, Dot,' she said.

She watched Dorothy cough and smile at the same time, but neither of them was very successful, and then she remembered that Dorothy didn't like being called Dot. It made her feel like an ending, she said, like a piece of punctuation.

'Did you want a drink, Dorothy?'

'Oh no. Not for me, thank you.'

They smiled at each other through a silence.

'Is it Keithie? Has his football been annoying Harold again?'

'Oh no. Nothing like that.'

'Lisa?'

'No. Nothing to do with Lisa.'

This was Dorothy. This had always been Dorothy. Travelling all around the houses, taking a long ride to get to somewhere nearby. Yet she couldn't be rushed. If you rushed her, she would become flustered and deny everything, and no one would ever know what was waiting to be said. Sheila sometimes wondered if Dot would go to her grave with thousands of unspoken words in her mouth. Whole encyclopaedias of information that no one would ever get to hear.

She waited.

'It's Margaret Creasy,' Dorothy said eventually. 'Well, it's John Creasy, really. Well, it's everyone. I've tried talking to Harold, but you know Harold, he won't hear anyone else's opinion. And Eric Lamb isn't much better. I didn't know who to turn to. You were there, you see. You understand.'

When the words did arrive, there were busfuls of them.

Sheila reached for the ashtray. 'We were all there, Dorothy. The whole avenue was there.'

Dorothy tried to rest her hands on the table, but there were cups and newspapers and Keithie's Etch A Sketch in the way. Instead, she left them sitting on her handbag. 'I know,' she said, 'it feels like yesterday.'

'It was nine years ago, Dot. What on earth makes you think it's got anything to do with Margaret.'

'Because that's how it works, doesn't it?' she said.

Sheila took a cigarette from the packet and tapped it against the table. 'How what works?'

There was always a glaze of anxiety to Dorothy, even when she was younger. She combed the landscape for the next catastrophe, whittling at her thoughts until she'd shaped a problem out of them and then grooming herself with the satisfaction of worrying about it.

Dorothy gripped the handbag like a fairground ride. 'Fate,' she said. 'Whatever choices we make. They always come back on us.'

There was a flicker. A very small flicker.

'Now you're being daft.' She lit the cigarette. Cigarettes always calmed her down. 'You're running away with yourself again.'

'The police came back. Did you see them?'

'I heard about it.'

'They must know something. They've been asking questions, looking for Margaret, and they've found out.' Dorothy's words were sliding in a chorus from her mind to her mouth. 'Perhaps they've already found her. Perhaps she's told them everything and they're going to come back and arrest us.'

'Would you calm down! Margaret knew nothing, she wasn't even here.'

'But she talked to everyone on the avenue, Sheila. She was the kind of person you couldn't help opening up to.'

Sheila picked at the faint tracks of polish still left on her nails. 'She was a good listener.'

'Exactly.' Dorothy's fingers travelled along the straps of her handbag. 'And people like that sometimes end up listening to things you don't mean them to.'

She looked up. 'Oh God, Dot, what did you say to her?'

'Nothing. I didn't say a word.' Dorothy frowned. 'At

least, I don't think I did.' And then she blinked – far too slowly.

Sheila dragged her fingers through her hair. She could feel last night's hairspray pulling on her hands. 'Jesus, Dot.'

Sheila lit a cigarette, then saw the last one still glowing back at her from the ashtray.

'She spoke to everyone, Sheila, not just me.'

Dorothy took a breath so sharp and so unexpected, it made Sheila flinch.

'What?' she said.

'What if Margaret worked everything out? What if she confronted someone and that's why she's disappeared?'

'Would you calm the hell down!' Sheila knew she was shouting, but she couldn't stop herself. 'We don't even know why she went!'

'We need to talk to John. We need to find out what she said before she left.'

Sheila drew on the cigarette. Short, brief breaths that pulled smoke towards her lungs in tiny pieces.

Lisa pushed her head around the door. 'Everything all right?' she said.

'Everything's fine. Just fine.' Sheila still looked at Dorothy. The smoke wandered between them. It twisted lazy patterns in the sunlight and curled itself towards the ceiling.

'Only if anyone's interested, someone needs to go to the corner shop,' Lisa said. 'We've run out of milk.'

Sheila reached for her purse. 'Take Keithie with you, there's a good girl.'

Lisa started to protest, the noise of a wild animal stirring at the back of her throat.

'Don't start, Lisa, just take him.' She handed her the coins. 'I need to pop out for ten minutes. He's only six, he can't stay here on his own.'

'Nearly seven,' said a voice from the hall.

She turned back to Dorothy. 'Wait out the front for me while I get my shoes.'

*

The pantry was cool and dark. She could hear Dot pulling at the front door, and Lisa bribing Keithie to his feet.

It was behind the flour. Crouching in a tin filled with spilled rice and pasta shells.

She was supposed to have poured it away. She'd told Margaret she'd poured it away. She reached into the tin and felt it reach back to her. One more and then she would. Just one more, because right now she really needed it.

*

He didn't answer at first. Dot climbed over the flower bed and pressed her face against the glass. Sheila could hear her pointing at the mess and whittling.

She took the chewing gum out of her mouth and shouted through the letterbox. There was nothing, although she thought she heard a door open somewhere deep in the house.

'John, I know you're in there,' she shouted again.

Dorothy climbed back. 'Perhaps he's out,' she said. 'He might be looking for her.'

'He's in there.'

Sheila looked through the letterbox. She could see cardboard and paper, towered into piles, and the corner of a table filled with carrier bags. It looked like he was packing to move out, except nothing was packed. It had just spread itself out over the surfaces.

She shouted again. 'I know you're in there, and I'm not leaving, so I'll just stand out here until you decide to open the door.'

It opened.

It took a moment for her vision to adjust, the darting orange black to fade away, but then she saw John, standing at the bottom of the stairs. It looked as though the clothes he wore held a week's worth of sleeping, and his eyes were bruised and doubtful.

'For heaven's sake, John. What are you playing at?'

Sheila pushed the door further open, and it caught on yellowed newspapers and a spatter of unopened mail. He stood back, like a child, and let them walk through. Dot held her hand to her mouth, feeding on the chaos.

'What's all this about?' Sheila lifted the edge of a carrier bag, but it seemed as though it might start a chain reaction and the whole house would collapse around them, and so she let it drop again. 'What are you doing?'

He chewed at his nails, like a rodent. 'I'm trying to find it.'

'Find what?'

'Whatever made Margaret leave. She must have discovered something. The house must have told her what happened.'

She took a long breath. The air smelled of sweat and desperation, and Dorothy was slowly adding to it behind her left shoulder. She went to pick up an umbrella from the chair by the door.

'Don't touch that!' John reached forward and returned it to its place. 'I left it there. For Margaret. She might forget it otherwise.'

She watched him. She could see the fear ticking beneath his skin, his thoughts so tightly packed they had begun to warp and fracture. He had been like this before. Everyone had faltered then. What had happened had reduced them all to a silence, quietening their lives for months afterwards, but it was John who seemed to migrate even further than anyone else. Taking himself to the very edges of his life, and staying there out of harm's way.

'Let's go and sit in the kitchen,' she said, 'let's make a drink and talk about it.'

*

They drank black tea from cups Sheila had washed with a paper towel. Dorothy sat as far away as possible from hers, as though she thought it might possess some kind of toxic property, and John stared down into his every time Sheila asked him a question.

'She must have said something, John?'

'Nothing. She didn't say anything. Why do people keep asking me the same questions?'

'So you woke up, and she just wasn't there? No warning?'

'I went to bed first. When I woke up, I thought she'd nipped to the shop, or popped in to see one of you. She was always in and out of other people's houses.'

'She was,' Dorothy said, 'everyone's.'

Sheila caught Dot's eye, and then turned back. 'And she didn't say anything about anyone else on the avenue? Nothing anyone had said to her?'

'Nothing.'

'Nothing about Walter Bishop?'

Their eyes matched for a moment, and there was silence.

He looked back into his tea. At the edge of the room, she could hear Dorothy begin to hyperventilate.

'John?'

'She must have been to see him. His glasses – they're in her handbag. She was taking them to be mended.'

'I knew it.' Dorothy stood and her cup rattled against a stack of plates. 'I knew I'd seen her coming out of number eleven.'

A whimper was carried into the room from the bottom of John's throat. It sounded like there was an acceptance about it, a death rattle. Sheila felt a swell of panic, and she wasn't sure if she had caught it from everyone else, or whether it belonged somewhere inside herself.

'Let's just calm down. Let's think it through,' she said,

but the words were swallowed by the stream of panic that poured from the rest of the room.

Dorothy was still on her feet. You could tell that she wanted to pace, but the room was too small, and what little space there was left was taken up by John's searching. She twisted her hands instead, trying to free the adrenaline.

'Margaret's worked it out,' she said. 'She'll have gone to the police.'

Sheila looked at John. 'Would she? Without speaking to you?'

'I don't know.' He shook his head. 'I don't think so.'

Sheila closed her eyes and measured out the breaths. She could feel her hands start to tremble, and she put them into fists to try and make it stop.

'We'd know if she'd told the police.' She tried to make her voice steady, reasonable. 'They would have questioned us by now.'

'So if she hasn't gone to the police,' said Dorothy, 'then where has she gone?'

John looked up. 'Perhaps she found out the truth. Perhaps she confronted someone.'

'She spoke to everyone, Sheila. She knows all our secrets.' Dorothy was an endless wave of panic now. Her eyes a terrified white.

'Oh, for God's sake,' said Sheila. 'We did nothing wrong!'

'How can you say that?' John gripped the edges of the

table. 'How can you say that we did nothing wrong. We killed somebody.'

*

It was there again. The darkness.

Despite the crush of heat, despite the sunlight which needled at his skin, the avenue still seemed to be wrapped in a shadow. John stood at the front-room window and watched Sheila and Dorothy leave. They got as far as the middle of the road, when Dot started throwing her arms around and semaphoring out her anxiety with a handkerchief.

He shouldn't have said it. He shouldn't have said they'd killed someone.

But it was the truth. They had.

It didn't really matter, did it, whether anyone had intended to? Some things were so bad, so very wicked, it didn't make any difference at all whether you meant them or not. If that were not the case, then anyone could get away with anything, just by claiming they hadn't really planned to do it.

He glanced up at number eleven, and number eleven glanced back at him.

When he returned his attention to the avenue, Sheila Dakin's fingertips were pressing into her temples, and Thin Brian had wandered over from his dustbin to see what all the handkerchief-waving was about.

John was sure they couldn't see him.

He had taken refuge behind a vase of flowers Margaret had placed on the windowsill. Margaret didn't believe in artificial flowers. She said there was too much fakery in the world as it was, without putting it in a jug and introducing it into your living room as well. They were fresh then, of course, but now he could smell it, the inevitable, strange sweetness of decay that always seems to break through, no matter how much you might try to cover it up with all sorts of other smells.

He watched Dorothy's handkerchief fluttering in the afternoon sunshine, and Sheila admit defeat and lean against her garden wall.

There were forty-seven bricks in Sheila Dakin's garden wall. He knew this already, of course, but it never did any harm to double-check these things. When Margaret was here, he hadn't felt the need to double-check anything. She'd stolen his worrying from him, and packed it away and made it silent. But since she disappeared, it hadn't taken very long at all before it had unpacked itself again and returned to his life like an old friend.

There were sixty if you counted the half bricks.

Dorothy was pointing her handkerchief in the direction of his house, and Brian was staring at it and frowning.

Do something, Margaret used to say. *Don't just count things, do something purposeful instead.*

Thirteen half bricks. Thirteen. It made him uneasy.

Don't stand there, John, counting your days away.

Perhaps if he'd spoken up sooner, perhaps if he'd found

his courage in the beginning, the shape of his life would have been different.

Take action, John.

As he turned, his shirtsleeve brushed against the edge of the flowers, and the smell crept its way into his mouth. A new attitude, that's what was needed. If he altered his ways, if he stopped counting everything, perhaps Margaret would somehow sense it and come home to him.

He slammed the living-room door, and the echo jumped around the house. It sprang from the walls and the ceilings. It shook the tables and the chairs, and the little vase which sat on the windowsill began to tremble. A handful of petals quaked and shivered and let go of their stems, and a trail of decay leaked itself on to the paintwork.

*

'You took your time.' Brian stood at the edge of the pavement with his hands jammed into his pockets. 'I thought you were going to hide behind those dead flowers all afternoon.'

John looked back at the house. Sometimes Brian seemed to know things and John could never work out how he managed to do it.

'You've set her off something good and proper.' Brian nodded over at Dorothy, who was throwing her arms around in front of Sheila. John couldn't catch every word, but he heard *finished*, and *done for* and *Holloway*. 'Whatever did you say to her?'

'I just told the truth. Sometimes you need to be decisive. Sometimes, it's important to speak up.'

John stood up a little straighter, and used his new attitude to tighten his jaw.

'Is it now?' Brian tapped the side of his nose and smiled. 'And sometimes, my friend, it's important to say nothing at all.'

John untightened his jaw and stared at his shoes.

'And don't think you two will get off scot-free, either.' Dorothy stopped spinning and pointed at them. 'The police will be after all of us as soon as they cotton on to what happened, so you can take that stupid grin off your face, Brian Roper.'

Brian coughed and stared at his own shoes.

'For God's sake, Dorothy, will you quit with the bloody theatricals.' Sheila heaved herself from the wall. 'It isn't helping anybody. If the police want to come after us, they'll come after us. They can't prove a thing.'

Brian bit into his lip, Sheila dug her fingers further into her temples and Dorothy began to wail and wave her handkerchief around again. The noise made John's head ring, and he covered his ears and closed his eyes and tried to make it go away.

'Everything all right?'

None of them had heard the postman. He leaned against his pushbike and scratched the side of his head with the edge of an envelope.

Sheila looked up and folded her arms. 'Perfect,' she said.

'Fine,' said Brian.

'Perfectly fine,' said Dorothy. She tucked her handkerchief into the sleeve of her cardigan and smiled.

The postman frowned. 'Right you are, then,' he said, and began to push his bike along the avenue. The wheels squeaked in the heat, and John wondered if the Post Office gave them a little can of oil to carry around with them, or whether they were expected to provide their own.

They all watched him lean his bike against the wall of Walter Bishop's house and disappear.

'New,' said Dorothy, without taking her eyes off number eleven.

Sheila folded her arms a little more tightly and leaned into Dorothy's gaze. 'Is he?'

'*Not from round here*,' mouthed Dorothy.

'Isn't he?'

Dorothy tutted. 'You've only got to listen to his vowels.'

A few moments later, the postman appeared again and retraced his steps back down the road. He still had the envelope in his hand.

'Second delivery?' said Dorothy, when he reached them.

The postman nodded. 'No one in at number eleven, though. I'll have to take it back.'

They all stared at the envelope. It was fat and white, and Dorothy strained her neck so much to read the postmark, John became concerned it might dislocate.

'Kodak?' she said.

'Looks like photographs.' The postman squinted at the packet.

Dorothy stretched out her hand. 'I'll take them if you like?' She smiled, and the tips of her fingers wavered ever so slightly.

The postman hesitated, then he pointed to his badge. 'More than my job's worth,' he said. 'Royal Mail, you see. We're a public service. Like the police.'

'The police?' said Dorothy.

'And the fire brigade,' said the postman.

'The fire brigade?' said Sheila.

He smiled and turned his bike around. You could hear it squeaking all the way to the bottom of the avenue.

'I wonder what that was all about, then?' Brian nodded into the space where the postman had stood.

'Photographs,' said Sheila.

'Evidence!' Dorothy took her handkerchief out again. 'So much for not being able to prove anything. I bet he's got photographs of heaven knows what still hidden away in that house!'

'Oh Lord.' Sheila sank back on to her wall.

'I'm not sure how much more I can take of this,' said Dorothy. 'I can feel one of my headaches coming on.'

'What do you think, Brian?' John could feel the tingling wake at the bottom of his throat. 'Do you think we're in trouble?'

Brian stared at him. He stared so hard, John couldn't

meet his eyes, and he had to look over at Dorothy Forbes' driveway instead.

'I think that if we'd done something when we had the chance, then we wouldn't be in the mess we're in now.' Brian was still staring at him. 'I think if you'd listened to me, if you'd spoken up, then everything would be different.'

John turned to him. 'But you just said that sometimes it's important to keep quiet.'

Brian started walking, his hands still in his pockets. 'And that,' he said, 'is the most important thing of all.'

'What is?' John shouted.

'Knowing the bloody difference,' he shouted back.

John watched Brian walk across the avenue to Number Two. He stopped by Dorothy Forbes' driveway and kicked a chipping across the tarmac.

There had been one hundred and thirty-seven chippings, but now there were one hundred and thirty-six.

John knew this, because he'd just counted them.

*

Sheila closed her front door. She could still hear Dorothy wailing and waving her handkerchief, just like the night of the photographs.

Even now, Sheila could replay it all in her mind. It was like a cine film she brought out for special occasions, occasions when she needed to reassure herself that they were all blameless and well-intentioned. There were children to think about. She hadn't had Keithie then, but there was

Lisa, and you had to set an example to your kids. The days of teaching them with a belt had gone, thank Christ, and you needed to show them how to survive, show them how to avoid tempers and bruises, and men who were determined to get what they could out of you.

Men like Lisa's dad.

Men like Walter Bishop.

If she didn't show her kids, who would? It wasn't just taking the baby, either. It was everything else. It was the way he stared pieces out of you as you walked past. It was the way wisps of grey hair fell on to his shoulders, and how his jacket was threaded and shining with blackened grease. It was the very look of him. Then it was the photographs. They were the last straw. Those boys wouldn't even have been there if Walter hadn't stolen the child, so he'd brought everything on himself. It was a chain reaction. They were just being kids at the end of the day, and they meant no harm. She'd known that as soon as she saw them.

2 December 1967

The shopping bags rattle as Sheila carries them home. No matter how straight she keeps her arms, and how carefully she holds them away from her body, they chime like church bells, ringing out her failings.

Although there is no one else to hear, only Lisa. The roads are abandoned for Saturday dinners, beans on toast and tins of soup, steamy food to break the sharp frost of a December sunshine.

'What are we having for lunch?' Lisa says. She is toggled into her duffel coat. It pulls across her back and Sheila wonders if it will even last the winter.

'What's all this "lunch" business?' she says. 'What happened to "dinner" and "tea"?'

'Posh people say lunch.'

'Do they, now. And what would a six-year-old know about being posh?'

Lisa doesn't reply. Instead, she drags her feet along the pavement.

'Don't scuff your boots, they're new on.'

'I want to be posh.' A loose chipping skitters along the concrete.

'Well, we're not,' says Sheila, 'so we'll stick with "dinner", thank you very much. Or people around here will stop speaking to us.'

They cross over by the bus stop, and this is when Sheila first sees them. Two young lads, standing outside number eleven. It's nothing out of the ordinary. Since word got around about Walter, kids from the estate pass by from time to time. They shout occasionally, throw a handful of gravel and run off. Once, Sheila thought she saw one of them take a piss in Walter's garden, but she chose to turn a blind eye.

They mean no harm.

They're staring up at the windows, these two. One is tall and skinny, the other shorter, with his jumper tucked into his trousers. They can't be more than twelve, either of them.

She shouts across the road and asks them what they're up to.

'Just messing around,' shouts Tall.

Short turns around and smiles at her. He has a football, but it's not being kicked anywhere.

'Well, just watch yourselves.' She takes Lisa's hand and steers her towards the front door. 'Be careful.'

'No need to worry about us,' shouts Tall. 'We can look after ourselves.'

She didn't doubt it for one second.

*

They are still there, even after she packs away the shopping and finds a tin of oxtail soup for Lisa. There are three boys now, and as she watches from the window, another turns up to join them. The tall one goes into Walter's garden, and when he jumps back down from the wall, there is a branch in his arms. He waves it about, like the spoils of a war, and the others push and shout and try to grab at it. Short has abandoned his football on the side of the verge, and it rolls from the grass and knocks against the leaves in the gutter.

Eric Lamb is watching them too. Sheila can see him,

and they stare at each other in silence from behind the glass.

When she looks back, there are more boys. There must be nearly a dozen now, and the noise creeps into her front room. Some of them are in Walter's garden, calling up at the windows, finding encouragement in each other's faces. She can see older boys in there as well, maybe fifteen or sixteen.

Bastard, one of them shouts.

A smile traces itself around Sheila's mouth before she can think any better of it.

Lisa is pulling on her coat and pushing her feet into roller skates.

'Where do you think you're off to?' Sheila turns from the avenue.

'Out,' Lisa says, 'playing.'

She looks back at the boys. 'No, you're not,' she says. 'Not right now.'

Walter has appeared at one of the upstairs windows. He is shouting about trespassing and calling for the police. The kids are just laughing at him, mimicking his voice and finding words only their parents should know. Walter looks small and irrelevant, leaning out from the woodwork. His face is red and puffed with anger, and his arms swim into the air, achieving nothing except to make him redder and angrier. Sheila wonders, for one brief moment, if someone so weak and so bland could really be that much of a threat, and then she remembers Lisa's father, and her own father, and all the other men who came wrapped in harmless packaging.

She sets her jaw and watches. Her knuckles lie white on the windowsill.

The boys settle. A couple of them kick at the gravel on Walter's drive, but most are sitting in a line on his garden wall. Occasionally, they look up and shout, but there is a naivety about it – children who don't know why they're shouting, only that their parents have been the ones to shout first.

Walter pulls the window shut and disappears, but when he returns a few moments later, he is holding something up against the glass.

A camera. He is taking photographs of them.

The boys don't notice at first, they're too lost in their own energy. Limbs pushing against limbs. The physical conversation of adolescence.

Walter follows them with the lens. He wanders along the line. Stops. Goes back. Clicks at the shutter.

He captures all of them, taking each boy into the curve of the glass, copying their image on to the film. Stealing their childhood as they look the other way.

'Bastard,' says Sheila, 'dirty bastard.'

She is about to bang on the glass and warn them, when one of the kids looks up and sees Walter. The boy points, and it scatters them all within seconds. They leave in a commotion of bikes and jumpers, running down alleyways and along pavements, until the only sign they were ever there to begin with is a long, dead branch, resting on the end of Walter Bishop's wall.

'Bastard,' says Sheila.

'Who's a bastard?' Lisa looks up from her roller skates.

'Never you mind.' Walter is still at the window, staring down at where the boys had sat. 'And don't say "bastard". It's not a word for children.'

*

Sheila is angry all afternoon. She concentrates her anger into cupboard doors and teapot lids, but the anger chews into her thoughts and won't let go. She wants to march round to Eric's and see what he makes of it all, but Lisa trails around the house at her feet, and she knows there will be an afternoon of questions if she does.

'I'm not angry at you, Lisa,' she says for the tenth time.

'Then who are you angry at?'

'The strange man with the long hair. The man in the big house at the top of the road.'

'The one who took the baby.'

'Yes,' Sheila says, 'the one who took the baby. He's a bad man, Lisa. You're not to go near him. Ever. Do you hear me?'

Lisa nods. 'He's a bad man.'

She repeats Sheila's words and goes back to her drawing, but every so often she looks at her mother and looks out of the window, and clouds her face with thinking.

*

It's an hour later when Sheila hears the voices. There are a lot of them, dark and angry and closing in, like a storm. The December sky is slated and solemn, but it leaves just enough light to see the figures move along the avenue. It's mainly men, but there are a few women on the edge of the group, and following, a distance behind, are a crowd of children. They're the same kids from earlier. She can see Tall and Short, only there's no pushing and shouting now, just small boys and quiet steps, and worried arms folded against the cold.

'Stay here,' she says to Lisa, and she stands on the doorstep and pulls the door to behind her.

Sheila has never seen so many people on the avenue at the same time. It looks like a football crowd. These are working men, factory men. Men who claw at a pit face all week, or spend their days lifting earth and stone. They are travelling towards number eleven, their boots heavy on the tarmac, their fists closing around their tempers.

The first man reaches Walter Bishop's door and hammers into it with his knuckles.

There's not a single movement at number eleven. Just a silent, crouching darkness. It might look as though Walter isn't at home, but Sheila knows he is. Everyone knows he is. Although Walter Bishop's door remains still, each of the others on the avenue opens one by one. Eric and Sylvia and Dorothy Forbes all appear on their doorsteps. Even May Roper pulls back the curtains in her living room and peers out.

The man hammers again. His fists sound like bullets. He

steps back and yells up at the house, shouting for Walter Bishop to show himself. 'You take photographs of my kids, you come out here and you fucking answer to me.'

Sheila looks back at the door and pulls it a little closer.

The crowd circles Walter's house. The men hunger for a confrontation. The women are tighter, more controlled, but their eyes have a quiet threatening about them. It's obvious the kids have been told to stay away, because they walk at the edges of the group, trying to find a way in unnoticed. Short turns and stares at Sheila. It looks as though he's been crying.

The man is kicking at Walter's door. The others are shouting, urging the boots a little faster, a little harder. From the edge of her eyes, Sheila sees Dorothy Forbes rush along the pavement, tugging at her coat as she walks.

'I'm going to the phone box to ring the police,' she says, as she trots past Sheila's fence.

'What on earth are you doing that for?'

'It's a mob, Sheila. A mob. Heaven knows who they'll be after next.'

'They're only after Walter,' Sheila says. 'They wouldn't start on any of us. We're all respectable.'

But Dorothy has disappeared around the corner of a hedge, and Sheila stares back into the crowd and frowns.

*

The police arrive. Dorothy is standing next to Sheila on the doorstep, twisting the belt of her coat around her fingers.

She pleats the material one way, and then the other, pulling it tight against her flesh.

'Oh, do stop fidgeting, Dot.'

'I can't help myself. It's my nerves.' Dorothy lets the belt concertina from her hands, then immediately recovers it.

The police are out of the car, and it's only a moment before their uniforms are swallowed by a mass of shoulders and shouting.

'Why are they so angry?' Dorothy says. 'I was in the middle of *Emmerdale Farm*.'

'He was taking photographs. Of the children.'

She hears Dot take in a mouthful of air. 'I've seen him do that before, in the park. He sits in the bandstand with that wretched camera slung around his neck, snapping away.'

'He does?'

'Oh, not just the children, he takes pictures of every-thing,' says Dorothy. 'Flowers, clouds, bloody pigeons.'

'What kind of a man takes photographs of other people's children?'

'What kind of a man lives with his mother until he's forty-five?'

'Or doesn't ever open his front-room curtains.'

'He needs a good haircut as well.'

They both lean forward on the step and try to listen.

'Why don't you go and see what's happening, Dot?'

'Oh, I couldn't possibly,' says Dorothy, 'I might be set upon. People like that lose all sense of perspective.'

They lean a little further in silence.

'Then I'll go.' Sheila looks back at the front door. 'Just watch Lisa for me.'

*

Sheila picks her way through the crowd. She dips under elbows and around arguments, edging her way to the front, until she finds two policemen and Walter Bishop, who has been summoned to his doorstep by the sound of a uniform.

'It's quite ridiculous,' Walter is saying. 'As if I would do something like that.'

His eyes find no one. Just a damp coat of moss on the porch step and the dozens of feet which surround it.

'These gentlemen are under the impression that you've been taking photographs of their children. Are you denying that?' says the first policeman.

Walter Bishop doesn't speak. His lips move slowly around yellowed teeth, but no words appear. Sheila looks around. Short has found his father. The boy presses into the man's shadow. He looks too young. Too young to hear this kind of conversation.

'Mr Bishop?' said the second policeman.

'I do like photography, yes. I like taking pictures.'

'Of children?'

Boots catch on concrete as the crowd pushes forward. Sheila doesn't look at the men's faces. She doesn't need to.

'Amongst other things.' Walter removes his glasses and takes a handkerchief from his pocket. 'It's a hobby, Sergeant. I have a darkroom.'

'Do you, now?'

The handkerchief is grey and creased.

'We've had words about children before, haven't we, Mr Bishop?' The Sergeant's face is a mask of control, but Sheila can see a tic of irritation in the corner of his mouth. 'We discussed the appropriateness of your behaviour a few weeks ago, when a baby went missing.'

Walter's eyes meet the policeman's for the first time.

'As you very well know, those were false accusations. And as far as I'm aware, there is no law against taking pictures of people.' Walter's eyes seem to find the spark of an escape. 'Especially if you have good reason.'

The policeman's hands rest behind his back, and Sheila sees him close a fist.

'So you admit to taking photographs of these children without the consent of their parents?'

Walter replaces his glasses. He remains silent for a moment, and when he does speak, his words are framed by a tremor.

'It was evidence, Sergeant. Evidence of their wickedness.'

'Evidence?'

'Oh yes.' Walter Bishop's voice is stronger now. 'You have no idea the abuse I have to tolerate. I've telephoned you on several occasions, but you always tell me I have no evidence. Well, now I do.'

Walter has reached the end of his words, and he's gathered handfuls of self-assurance along the way. Sheila used to see it with Lisa's dad. The slow burn of arrogance, as his head caught up with his mouth.

'And what, exactly,' says the policeman, 'were these children doing that required you to gather evidence?'

'Vandalism, Sergeant.' Walter points to the rotten flower-beds and the branches of the trees, which drip with neglect. 'Trespassing. Victimization.'

The policeman turns to Short, who is still locked to his father's waist.

'Mr Bishop is suggesting that you and your friends have been trespassing on his property. Would this be a fair comment?'

Short tries to disappear into the safety of his father's shadow, but there is nowhere to go. His dad has moved back and folded his arms. The boy looks at Walter Bishop, who looks back at him with eyes full of control. It's the kind of control Sheila has seen so many times before, and it makes bile creep into the back of her throat.

'We were playing football.' Short's voice is so pale and distant, everyone has to lean in so they can hear. 'The ball bounced over the wall. We just went in his garden to get it. That's all. That's all we did.'

Short's eyes are wet and wide, and frightened. Sheila watches Short's father. He's a big man, with rough, quick hands, and a body fattened with years of being listened to. She thinks about the conceit in Walter Bishop's eyes.

'They were just playing football. They were just being kids. I saw it all from my window.'

Sheila hears her own voice before she realizes that she's

the one who is speaking. It sounds brittle. As though it might break at any second.

At the edge of the crowd, she can see Eric Lamb. He is staring right into her words.

'So you're a witness to all this?' The policeman looks at Sheila and then looks back at Walter Bishop. 'These boys were doing nothing wrong?'

'Nothing wrong at all.' Sheila watches Short as she speaks. His body is shaking, although deep within the thick of the crowd, it really doesn't feel that cold.

'I have rights,' Walter is saying. 'I can take photographs of anybody I choose. It's not a crime. You'll see when the pictures are developed just what these boys were up to.'

'Let's have a look at this camera then.'

The policeman waits while Walter disappears behind the door.

When he returns, he hands the camera over to the Sergeant.

'It's all in there. You'll find out how wicked these boys are. They need punishing. They need a good hiding, Sergeant. That's what they need.'

Words of retaliation spill from Walter Bishop's mouth, as the policeman examines the camera. The first policeman looks ahead, the strap of his helmet digging into his chin, his lips tight and deliberate.

'Would this be the same punishment you told me you'd like to give to mothers who leave their children unattended, Mr Bishop?' says the Sergeant.

Walter is silenced. Sheila can see a track of sweat crawl from his hairline.

'They shouldn't allow these kinds of people to be parents,' he says. 'Children need a firm hand. They need to be shown who's in charge.'

There's a catch of voices from the back of the crowd. A push, a hurry of boots.

The second policeman puts out his arm. It stops them. For now.

'So this has all the evidence, does it?' The Sergeant turns the camera over in his hands.

'Everything you need to arrest these people, Sergeant.'

The policeman pushes at a catch on the back of the camera.

'Oh, don't touch that!' Walter reaches out. 'If you open that it will ruin—'

The policeman flips open the catch. 'Oh dear,' he says. 'Look what I just went and did.'

'It might be salvageable. If you just give it back to me.'

Walter tries to take the camera, but the policeman tips it upside down, and its contents spills on to the concrete.

'Me and my clumsy fingers.' He grinds into the film with the edge of his boot. 'It looks like we'll never be able to see that evidence now, doesn't it, Mr Bishop?'

Walter stares at the concrete. 'What do you suggest I do?' he says.

The policeman brings his mouth so close, clouds of his breath drift into Walter Bishop's face. 'What I suggest you

do is pay a little less attention to other people's children.'
His eyes work from the ground up. The tired shoes, meal-
stained jacket, the threads of yellowed hair. 'And pay a little
more attention to yourself.'

*

The crowd is moved on. They seem hesitant. They leave behind
weighted stares and low, heavy promises. Short looks over his
shoulder as he drifts away, guided by his father's arm.

Eric Lamb walks over the road to Sheila, his hands deep
into his pockets.

'It had to be done,' she says, 'before you start.'

He says nothing.

'If the police and the council won't do anything, people
have to take matters into their own hands.' Sheila looks
back at number eleven. 'Someone has to get rid of him.'

He still says nothing.

'Someone's going to get hurt, Eric.'

'Oh, I wouldn't doubt that. I wouldn't doubt that for
one second.'

'Does it not worry you?' She pulls her cardigan around
her shoulders. 'Some weirdo on the avenue, taking photographs of other people's children?'

'Of course it does, Sheila, and I know you're still upset
about Lisa. I'm just not sure this is the best way to deal
with it.'

The cardigan is scratching the back of her neck, and she
can feel her skin start to burn against the wool.

'What other way is there?' she says. 'The rest of us need to do something.'

'A witch-hunt?'

'If needs be, Eric, yes, a bloody witch-hunt.'

She hears him draw his thoughts in with the still December air.

'There's only one problem with a witch-hunt,' he says.

'And what might that be?'

He starts to walk back towards his house as he answers her. 'It doesn't always catch the witch.'

Sheila looks over at number twelve. Lisa is waving to her through the glass, and behind Lisa is Dorothy Forbes, her expression brushed with anxiety.

Sheila twists the belt of her cardigan around her fingers. She pleats the material one way, and then the other, pulling it tight against her flesh.

Number Four, The Avenue

9 July 1976

Tilly's mum kept her in bed for three days.

I thought it was excessive, but Mrs Morton said that you couldn't be too careful. I thought you could be too careful, actually, but I decided to keep it to myself because every time Tilly was mentioned, Mrs Morton looked upset.

'It's not your fault,' I said to her. 'Although it might have been a different story if we'd listened to Angela Rippon properly.'

We played Monopoly and watched black and white films on BBC2, and ate Angel Delight, although it didn't taste as nice with just my name carved in it. One afternoon, we took the bus along the steep road out of the Market Place, and walked around in the hills that overlooked the town. Mrs Morton pointed out landmarks and I got grit in my shoes and felt miserable, and had to put lots of effort into being interested. Nothing was the same without Tilly. Everywhere we went, it felt like your house when you come back from being on holiday. It was all empty and strange.

When Tilly did reappear, she was the colour of pastry.

'You need some fresh air,' said Mrs Morton, and she put her in the shade with an extra cushion and a Wagon Wheel.

'What did you do without me?' Tilly picked out pieces of marshmallow.

'Loads,' I said.

'Did you find God?'

'I was really busy,' I said, 'I didn't have time.'

'So can we carry on looking?'

'S'pose,' I said.

And she smiled and passed me the Wagon Wheel.

Tilly had the first choice of television programmes, she didn't have to fetch her own drinks, and Mrs Morton allowed her to get away without doing any washing-up.

'I feel a bit faint,' I said, as I put another plate on the draining board, but no one took any notice.

*

After three days, we were allowed to play outside as long as it wasn't the middle of the day, and as long as Tilly wore her sou'wester. Tilly always wore her sou'wester, so I took this as meaning everything was back to normal. As it happened, it was too hot to be outside that morning, so we sat at my kitchen table trying to bend spoons like Uri Geller. We'd been at it for ages.

'It's bending, look.' Tilly held up her spoon.

It looked no different.

'It looks no different,' I said.

'There.' She pointed to a perfectly straight bit. 'There.'

My mother happened to be passing by, and she crouched down and narrowed her eyes and said that yes, it did look slightly bent. But my mother was very good at agreeing with people just to make them feel better.

'It isn't bent,' I said. 'It's straight.'

'I don't know how Uri Geller does it.' Tilly rubbed the spoon a few more times and gave up.

'It's because he's Spanish,' I said. 'Spanish people can do things like that. They can be quite clever.'

We abandoned the spoons and watched John Creasy as he waited for the bus to pull up at the end of the road, and then we watched him walk all the way back to his house by himself. He looked even more untidy than the last time I saw him. His hair stuck out in wild clumps, as though it was trying to escape from his head, and his clothes hung around his body like they weren't really a part of him. Even his shoelaces were undone, and they danced around his feet as he lumbered back up the pavement. My mother stood next to the table, watching with us.

'He doesn't look very well, does he?' I said.

'No.' She didn't take her eyes from the window. 'He really doesn't.'

Summer slid in through the curtains and drew sharp lines of sunlight across the kitchen floor. They were so definite, I could move my foot between them, and watch the yellow creep across my toes and escape on to the next tile. Remington stretched out across a series of them, like a small, Labrador-shaped tiger.

'I think it's as warm in here as it is outside,' I said. 'We might as well be sitting on the wall.'

'That's nice,' said my mother, threading a needle.

The kitchen door closed before the cotton had even found its way through.

*

We had only been sitting there a few minutes when Mrs Forbes blew past in a flurry of beige. We both leaned forward to watch her turn into Sheila Dakin's garden, and stand on the doorstep having a very theatrical conversation with Keithie.

'What do you think she's up to?' I said.

Tilly kicked at the bricks. 'I don't know,' she said, 'but I don't trust her, Gracie, do you?'

I thought about it. 'No. But everyone on this avenue is acting really strangely since Mrs Creasy disappeared.' I was thinking of my father as well, but I didn't say so, because that would have made it something which could live on its own outside my head.

After a while, Mrs Forbes reappeared with Sheila Dakin, and they crossed over towards Mr Creasy's house.

Mrs Dakin seemed to waver slightly in the middle of the road.

'I wonder if she's poorly as well,' said Tilly.

After a lot of shouting and banging, they vanished into Mr Creasy's, and as soon as they did, Sheila Dakin's door opened again and Lisa came out, dragging Keithie along by his elbow. She wore her denim jacket and the exact same mules I'd seen in the Kays catalogue.

No, you can't, my father had said, just before he started laughing.

'Come on,' I said and pulled Tilly off the wall.

Tilly always went along with stuff. It was one of the best things about her. We just made it as Lisa shut their garden gate.

'Hiya,' I said.

'Hi-ya.' She pulled the word out into two and rolled her eyes.

I scuffed my sandals on the concrete and folded my arms. 'Where are you going?'

She started walking. She still had Keithie's elbow and he was trying to claim it back.

'Cyril's. We need milk. Would you stop whining, Keith!'

'Oh, that's really funny because we're going to Cyril's as well,' I said.

'We are?' said Tilly, but she spoke so quietly, no one took any notice.

Lisa turned. Keith still twisted her arm and made a wide range of violent noises without ever opening his mouth. 'Can you get us some milk then?' she said.

'S'pose.' I scuffed my sandals a bit more. 'I thought we could all go together.'

'You'd be doing me a really big favour,' she said, and stretched out *really big favour*, so I'd know how important I was being.

I smiled.

She handed me the coins. 'And take him as well, would you. He's doing my bloody head in.'

And she walked back up the garden path, kicked off her mules and stretched herself out on the deckchair.

Keithie looked up at us. 'I always get sweets,' he said.

*

The three of us walked along Maple Road, Keithie tapping his football every few steps and then losing it over a wall or down a driveway, so we all had to wait while it was reclaimed.

'My dad likes football.' I thought I should make an effort.

'Your dad supports Man United.' Keithie didn't look up from his tapping.

'Does it matter?' I said.

'Course it does.' He stopped tapping and pointed to a patch on his jeans. 'Chelsea all the way.'

'Where's Chelsea?' Tilly stared at his badge.

'Dunno.' He started tapping again.

'Why do you wear a badge of a place you don't even know?' I said.

'Because it makes you a part of it.' He missed the last

tap, and his football drifted across the road. 'It means you fit in.'

'Only in your own head,' I had to shout, because half of him was in someone else's hedge bottom.

He reappeared, holding the ball to his chest. 'But that's the only place that matters,' he said.

*

Cyril's was on the corner of Maple Road and Pine Croft. The man who owned it now wasn't called Cyril, he was called Jim. It wasn't really a proper shop, either, it was someone's front room, made to look like a shop. Whenever the little bell rang, Jim would appear from the back in his shirtsleeves, with sleep sitting in the corners of his eyes, and each time I went in for sweets, he would fold his arms and scowl for the whole time I was making my decision.

'Hello, Cyril,' I said, because I knew it annoyed him.

He did his best scowling.

I asked him for a pint of milk, and he looked shocked because I only ever usually wanted Black Jacks and Flying Saucers. I had never bought a pint of milk before.

I put my hand on my hip. 'What about Margaret Creasy, then?' I said.

But it didn't work on Jim. He just folded his arms and asked me if I wanted anything else. Keithie pulled at my T-shirt, and Tilly and I had to scrape Tilly's pennies together to buy him a Sherbet Fountain.

When we got back to the avenue, Lisa had moved from

her deckchair and was curled into the settee, reading *Jackie*.

'I've got your milk,' I said.

'Uh-huh.'

'Shall I put it in the fridge?'

'Uh-huh.'

Sheila Dakin's kitchen was quite complicated, and you had to search for the fridge behind an ironing board and a collection of bedsheets. There were lots of dirty pots and magazines and empty cigarette packets, and the clock above the door had a picture of Elvis on it.

It's now or never, he said.

Although for someone with a complicated kitchen, Sheila Dakin's fridge was strangely quiet.

When I got back to the sitting room, Keithie was being a fire engine, and Lisa was saying, 'I can't believe you bought him sweets.'

'He told us to,' I said.

'And you do everything a six-year-old tells you to, do you?'

'Mostly,' said Tilly.

She told us we'd have to wait for our Sherbet Fountain money until her mum got home, and because all the chairs were occupied, we sat on a sheepskin rug in front of the electric fire. It was pretending to be a real fire, but because it wasn't switched on, the coal was just a sheet of cool grey plastic, like a range of mountains. There was a hole in one of the lumps, and when I looked through, I could see a tiny light bulb and three dead beetles.

'What are you doing?' Lisa said.

I lifted my face from the plastic. 'I'm taking an interest in things,' I said.

She went back to her magazine. I could hear the pages turning, and Elvis ticking away the seconds in the kitchen.

'I like your shoes,' I said.

Another page turned. I looked at Tilly, and I think she shrugged, although it was difficult to tell underneath her sou'wester.

'Tilly almost died last week,' I said.

'Uh-huh.'

'I had to resuscitate her.'

'Right.'

'I knew what I was doing, though, because I'm miles older than she is,' I said. 'Miles.'

Tilly started to speak, but I stared at her until she changed her mind.

Another page turned.

'I like your shoes,' I said.

Lisa looked up from her magazine. 'Do you want to go home, and I'll send Keithie round later with the money?'

We said no thank you, we were fine, and Lisa said *suit yourself,* and put *Jackie* in front of her face. Keithie had fire-engined himself out, and lay at right angles on the carpet, decorated in sherbet lemon and small pieces of liquorice, and so I pulled at the frizzy wool in the rug and watched Lisa as she read. I tucked my legs into my body and pushed my hair on to my shoulder, and tried to find a way to make us two chapters of the same story. By the time Sheila Dakin got back, I had pulled at the wool so much I had acquired a whole handful of sheep, and had to search very quickly for a place for it to be reattached.

I told Mrs Dakin that her milk was in the fridge and that I didn't know Keithie wasn't allowed sweets, and she looked at Lisa and raised her eyebrows without speaking.

'She said I was doing her a *really big favour*,' I said and flicked my hair.

Mrs Dakin said she was sorry we had to wait for our money, and I said it was fine, because I'd been looking at Lisa's mules and I thought I might be able to read Lisa's magazine when she'd finished with it. Lisa said she wouldn't be finished with it for ages. Probably never.

Mrs Dakin went into the kitchen to find her purse, and Lisa followed her. I could hear them talking.

She's a sweet girl, give her a bit of time, Lisa and It wouldn't kill you just to be nice and You can see how much she looks up to you. I turned to Tilly. 'Don't be embarrassed,' I said, 'they don't know you can hear them.'

When they came back, Mrs Dakin remembered something in the pantry and she disappeared for a few minutes.

'You all right, Mum?' Lisa said, when Mrs Dakin returned.

Mrs Dakin wasn't pale, because she always had a tan, but she didn't look very brown when she walked back in, just slightly yellow and uncomfortable.

'It's Dorothy Forbes,' Mrs Dakin said, 'she does my bloody head in.'

'Has she been lying to you as well?' said Tilly.

Mrs Dakin was about to light a cigarette, but she let the flame go and took the cigarette out of her mouth instead. 'Lying?' she said.

I knew Lisa was watching, and so I flicked at my hair again before I spoke. 'She lied about knowing Mrs Creasy. She said she'd never spoken to her before.'

Mrs Dakin went back to lighting her cigarette. 'Oh she's spoken to her, all right,' she said. 'She's definitely bloody spoken to her.'

'I don't think she'll ever get to heaven,' said Tilly. 'God doesn't like goats very much.'

'Goats?' Mrs Dakin's cigarette drooped very slightly in her mouth.

'What she means', I said, 'is people who fib always get discovered. God knows you've done something bad, and he'll come chasing after you with knives.'

'And swords,' said Tilly.

'Both sometimes,' I said. 'But the point is everyone gets found out eventually, and you'll never get away with it, because God is everywhere.'

Tilly and I both waved our arms about.

'Do you believe in God, Mrs Dakin?' I said.

Sheila Dakin sat down. Her cigarette had burned into a tail of ash, and it fell into her cardigan as we waited for an answer.

'I just need something from the pantry,' she said.

'You've gone really pale, Mum, do you want some water?'

'I'm just worried about Margaret Creasy,' she said. 'I'm worried she's never going to come back.'

'Course she'll come back.' Lisa sat on the arm of the settee. 'She'll just have decided she needs a break from it all.'

Mrs Dakin nodded, like a small child.

'I don't think so,' I said.

Mrs Dakin stared at me. 'Why?' she said, 'why don't you think so?'

'Because she had an appointment the next day, and she wasn't the kind of lady to let people down.'

Mrs Dakin continued to stare. She stared so hard, I could see a large company of red veins, embroidering the whites of her eyes. 'Who with?' she said.

I knew Tilly was looking at me, but I decided to answer anyway. 'Thin Brian,' I said.

'Did she,' Mrs Dakin said, 'did she now.' And she rolled up her cardigan sleeves and tried to get to her feet.

Afterwards, Tilly said we shouldn't have talked about fibbing and swords and Thin Brian, but I told her that it made Mrs Dakin think about God, and surely thinking about God can never really be a bad thing.

Number Ten, The Avenue

10 July 1976

Eric Lamb held the photograph around the edges of its frame.

It had been a cold day. Elsie had always wanted to get married in December. She'd wanted a white, furry muffler and holly at the ends of the pews, and a brush of icing-sugar snow on the paths. Even before she had known who she would marry, she had known all of this. When it was suggested, the vicar had stared at his diary and sucked air in between his teeth, and said it was his busiest time of the year. It had taken Eric three visits and a small bottle of brandy to get him to realize how important it was. As it happened, God didn't seem to realize the importance either, because their wedding day sky was a scrubbed pigeon-grey. Snowless, holly-less and with the kind of cold that whispered into your bones. Eric had left his sickbed to get married, standing in church with a temperature of 102, and shaking so much with the rigors the vicar had mistaken them for nerves and put a reassuring hand on his shoulder for most of the service. But none of it had mattered. None of it had mattered because he would have done anything for Elsie. And as long as he had Elsie, he had everything.

He replaced the photograph on the mantelpiece. When he'd said *'til death do us part*, he never really thought it would happen. It seemed so unlikely, so far-fetched. And yet here he was, sidestepping a world filled with other people's plans, walking around a shop with half a loaf of bread in a wire basket, and coming down each morning to find the house exactly the same as he had left it the night before.

He took a tin of soup from the cupboard. It was too hot for soup, but his eyes couldn't seem to find anything else. He was ashamed that he thought of Margaret Creasy now and how much he missed her, but it wasn't so much the plate of food she would carry round, it was the conversation she brought with it.

She never said that Elsie had a good innings, or it's been five years and he should pull himself together, and she never commented on Elsie's toothbrush, which still sat on the sink in the bathroom, or her coat which hung at the bottom of the stairs. She just listened. No one had ever listened to him before, they had only waited until he stopped speaking, so they could burden him their own stories. Perhaps that's why he told her.

There was a click and a whoosh of gas, and pin-pricks started at the side of the saucepan.

He had never talked to anyone about Elsie. Not properly. Not with any substance. He had murmured all the words you are expected to murmur when people offer concern, but no one really listens to the murmured words. They're like punctuation in someone else's speech, small spring-boards for another person to bounce their opinion from. Margaret Creasy was different. Margaret Creasy asked questions. The kind of questions you can only ask if you were hearing something in the first place.

He stirred the soup. The kitchen filled with a thick smell of tomatoes, and it trespassed into ninety-degree heat.

He hadn't set out to tell her, although when he went back over the conversation, it was obvious that it would happen. He had told her about the day they were given the diagnosis and how Elsie had said everything was going to be all right, and how her shoulders looked thin and worn out. He told her how Elsie paused after each sentence to give the consultant a space to put the hope, and how the consultant had stayed silent. There was no hope. The cancer was racing through her body as though it had a very impor-tant meeting to get to. He told Margaret Creasy about the hospital stays, and the long corridors he walked alone; the nurses with gentle voices and tired eyes; the doctors who circled the wards without ever stopping. He told her how Elsie seemed to disappear into the pillows, how her hands were the only thing he could recognize, how her body seemed to be leaving before she did. He told Margaret Creasy about the day Elsie decided it was enough, and the hospice they turned down, and the bag of tablets they were sent home with. The hospital bed in the front room; the people who came to clean and wash and turn. The shame, the humiliation. He told her about the pain when the cancer found Elsie's bones, how he would listen to Elsie sobbing when she thought no one could hear. He told her how Elsie said if she had a gun she would shoot herself. How they had both looked at each other. How he would have done anything for Elsie. He told Margaret Creasy everything. He'd even shown her the handful of tablets which were left in the hospital carrier bag. Margaret had told him to drop them off at the pharmacist's, but how could he, when they would want to know what happened to the rest?

He took the soup, and set it on a tray with a spoon and yesterday's bread roll, and he stared at it.

In five years, he had never told anyone about Elsie. He was good at keeping secrets, he had proved that much, but for some reason he had told Margaret Creasy. Immediately afterwards, he had felt a relief, as though saying the words out loud had leaked away some of their power. The secret had been trapped in his head, shifting to the perimeter, pushing at the sides and carpeting all the other thoughts until they became silent. He had studied Margaret Creasy's face as he'd spoken, searching for a condemnation to match to his own, looking for a reason to stop speaking, but there had been nothing.

When he'd finished, she had put her hand over his, and said, you did what you thought was right, and he had experienced an absolution so strong, it felt like a chemical reaction.

But when she left, his secret left too. It walked back with her across the avenue and went through a different front door, and wandered into a different life. He had given the secret its freedom, and a whole new set of thinking had moved into his head – thinking that kept him company at night. Thinking that made him wish he'd kept his secret to himself.

He watched a film creep over the soup.

Now Margaret had disappeared, his secret had disappeared too.

He picked up the bowl and poured its contents down the sink. It was too hot for soup anyway.

Number Four, The Avenue

11 July 1976

Should have told her that I can't linger, said the radio.

'There's a wedding ring. On. My. Fing-er,' Tilly sang back.

'How do you know the words?' I said.

Tilly was more of a Donny Osmond type of person.

She rolled on to her tummy and leaned her chin into her hands. 'Because your mum sings it every time she washes up. It's either that or "Knock Three Times".'

'Is it?'

'Twice on the pipe means the answer is no,' said Tilly.

We were sitting on the front lawn, my mother's radio playing through the kitchen window and pollen prickling our noses. I was drawing a map of the avenue and trying to chart our progress. Tilly was making helpful comments.

Mrs Forbes' flowers are taller than that and *Mr Creasy's fence isn't straight*, for example.

She reached over and drew a bird on Sheila Dakin's roof, and another one on our front lawn.

'Birds are the only thing I can draw,' she said.

We stared at the map.

'There isn't much sign of God, is there?' She traced her finger across the line of houses. 'I'm not sure we've seen even a hint of Him yet.'

I thought about Mrs Forbes' fibbing and May Roper's fondness for funerals, and the way Sheila Dakin stumbled and tripped across the avenue.

'No,' I said, 'but we've still got plenty of places to search.'

I stole a look at Tilly. 'We could go to Mrs Dakin's again.'

'We've already been there. Why do you want to go back?' said Tilly.

'No reason.'

'Is it because of Lisa?' she said.

'Nope.' I flicked my hair.

'Because you and I are best friends, aren't we, Gracie? I mean, nothing will ever change that, will it?'

'No,' I said. 'It's just Lisa and me have got so much in common.'

'You do?'

'Oh yes,' I said. 'Me and Lisa just fit together. Some people do, don't they? They just belong.'

Tilly nodded and looked back at the map. 'I suppose so,' she said.

Sometimes, Tilly didn't understand the more complicated

things in life. That is why I needed a friend like Lisa. Someone who was sophisticated and more my wavelength.

Tilly pointed at the map. 'Who lives there?'

I looked up to where she was pointing. 'No one yet.'

Number fourteen had been empty for as long as I could remember. The Pughs had moved in for a while, but they disappeared after Mr Pugh had a mid-life crisis and stole £5,000 from his accountancy firm. He had a trilby and a caravan in Llandudno. Everyone was very shocked. After they'd left, a man from the estate agent had put a 'For Sale' sign up in the garden, but Keithie knocked it over with his football on the first day, and no one had been back since.

'What about this one?' Tilly pointed to another house on the map.

'Eric Lamb,' I said. 'He does mainly gardening.'

'And there?'

Tilly was pointing to number eleven.

I didn't answer for a moment. Tilly pointed again and frowned, and said, 'Gracie?'

'Walter Bishop.' I looked across at the house. 'Walter Bishop lives there.'

'Who is Walter Bishop?'

'Someone you don't want to know,' I said.

She frowned again, and so I explained.

I explained that I had only met Walter Bishop once. Before Tilly arrived, I went to Bright's Fish Shop every Friday with Mrs Morton, and we would order battered sausage and fishcakes, whether we wanted them or not. He

223

was there one day, shifting in the queue that snaked around the shop. He was pale and shiny, like the fresh cod behind the counter, and Mrs Morton had drawn me closer into her coat. I hadn't been allowed to duck under the railing and watch the fish rise and fall in the oil, and feel the cooking on my face.

'Who was that?' I'd asked her later, as we pulled the newspaper from our tea.

'Walter Bishop.'

She didn't even need me to explain.

'Who is Walter Bishop?'

And Mrs Morton had passed the vinegar across the table and said, 'Someone you don't want to know.'

When I'd finished my story, Tilly looked over at the house as well.

'Why don't people like him?' she said.

'I'm not sure. No one ever explains. Perhaps it's some-thing to do with God?'

Tilly rubbed at the pollen on the end of her nose. 'I don't see how it can be, Gracie,' she said.

We sat in silence for a moment. Even the radio seemed to be thinking about it. I counted all the houses with my eyes, and I wondered if the vicar was right, if Mrs Creasy had disappeared because there wasn't enough God in the avenue. That He'd somehow missed some of us out, and left holes in people's faith for them to fall into and vanish.

'Perhaps we should visit Walter Bishop,' I said. 'Perhaps

we should check to see whether God is there for ourselves.'

We both looked across at number eleven. It looked back at us with quiet, dirtied windows and blistered paint. Weeds crept along its brickwork and buried themselves in its corners, and at the windows, all the curtains pulled themselves tight against the rest of the world.

'I don't think that's a good idea,' Tilly said. 'I think we'd better do what people say, and stay away.'

'Do you always do what people say?'

'Mostly,' said Tilly.

She got to her feet and said we should go and see Eric Lamb instead, and I said okay then, and folded the map up and put it in my pocket.

But as we walked across the avenue towards number ten, I looked over at Walter Bishop's house and I wondered about things.

Because I had already decided it was a secret that needed to be unwrapped.

*

It wasn't difficult to find Eric Lamb.

He was always outside, no matter what the weather, digging and pruning, and pressing seeds into the soft earth. In the rain, you could see him standing under a giant umbrella, watching over his charges, or you could find him in the shed at the bottom of his garden, with a little flask and a bobble hat. I had waited in that shed, whilst my father asked the best way to make a compost heap or when he should prune the roses, and Eric Lamb would always think over his answers very slowly, as if the words were shoots that needed to grow.

'So you're doing a gardening badge?' he said.

I stood with Tilly in the same shed. It smelled of soil and wood, dark and safe and edged in creosote.

Yes, we said, very deliberately, because speaking very slowly appeared to be catching.

He didn't look at us, but stared out of a little window, which was smeared with the effort of past summers.

After a while, he said, 'Why?'

'Because that's what Brownies do,' said Tilly, 'they earn badges.'

She looked at me for approval, and I nodded.

'Why?' he said again.

Tilly shrugged her shoulders behind Eric Lamb's back and made a ridiculous face.

'Because it shows that you can do something,' I said, trying not to look at the ridiculous face.

'Does it now?' He rested the cup from his flask on the counter. 'Do you think you need a badge to prove that you're capable of something?'

'No.' I felt as though I'd wandered into school assembly by mistake.

'Then why do it?' he said and went back to his flask.

'Because it makes you feel part of something?' said Tilly.

'It's an emblem,' I said.

'An emblem,' Tilly repeated, although it came out like bumble.

Eric Lamb smiled and screwed the cup back on the top of his flask. 'Well, we'd better go out there and earn you both an emblem then,' he said.

*

Eric Lamb's garden seemed much bigger than ours, although I knew they were exactly the same size.

Perhaps it was because his was marked out in tidy, important sections, whereas ours had old boxes thrown about and a rusty mower in the corner, and bits of grass missing, where Remington had sped around the lawn in one of his slimmer incarnations.

We stood on the edge of a border, which was marked out with string and pegs in a criss-cross of mysterious organization.

Eric Lamb folded his arms and nodded into the distance. 'What's the most important thing a garden needs?' he said.

We folded our arms as well, to help us think.

'Water?' I said.

'Sunshine?' Tilly said.

Eric Lamb smiled and shook his head.

'String?' I said, in an act of pure desperation.

When he had finished laughing, he unfolded his arms and said, 'The most important thing a garden needs is the shadow of a gardener.'

I decided then that Eric Lamb was very clever, although I hadn't yet worked out why. There was an ease about him, an unhurried wisdom that stretched like his shadow across the soil. I stared through the garden, and watched white butterflies dance across dahlias and freesias and geraniums. There was a choir of colour, singing for my attention, and it felt as though I was hearing it for the first time. Then I thought about the row of carrots I'd planted last year (carrots which had never lived, because I kept digging them up again to check they were all still alive), and I felt slightly overwhelmed.

'How do you know where to plant things?' I said. 'How do you know where they'll grow?'

Eric Lamb put his hands on his hips and stared across the garden with us, and then he nodded into the distance. I could see where the soil had eaten into his fingers and made a home within the creases of his flesh.

'You plant like with like,' he said. 'There's no point planting an anemone in a field full of sunflowers, is there?'

'No,' Tilly and I said at the same time.

'What's an amenome?' Tilly whispered.

'I have no idea,' I whispered back.

I think Eric Lamb spotted this.

'Because the anemone would die,' he said, 'it needs different things. There's a logical place for everything, and if something is where it should be, then it will flourish.'

'But how do you know,' Tilly said, 'how do you know if something is in the right place?'

'Experience.' He pointed to our silhouettes, which spilled on to the concrete. His, broad and wise, like an oak, and mine and Tilly's, spindly and slight and uncertain. 'Keep making shadows,' he said, 'if you make enough shadows, there will come a time when you will know all of the answers.'

And so he gave us trowels and a tin bucket, and sent us to the far edge of the garden to do weeding. We had gloves, too (I had the right and Tilly had the left), but they were big and clumsy and we took them off within minutes. The soil felt soft and quiet between our fingers.

After a few minutes, Keithie's head appeared on the other side of the fence, which separated Eric Lamb's garden from Sheila Dakin's.

'What are you doing?' he said.

'Weeding.' I shuffled about on the piece of newspaper Eric Lamb had given us to kneel on.

'And making shadows,' added Tilly.

Keithie wrinkled his nose. 'Why?' he said.

'Because it's interesting.' I saw Keithie look at the bucket, which had begun to fill with a collection of soil and leaves, 'And it teaches you about life.'

'What's the point?' he said.

'What's the point in bouncing a football around all day?' I said back.

'I might get discovered. I might get spotted by Brian Clough and signed up.'

Keithie bounced his football, to make a point.

'Well, if I see Brian Clough walking down Maple Road, I'll be sure to point him in your direction.'

I had no idea who Brian Clough was, but I was fairly

certain Keithie didn't realize this, and his head disappeared again. I looked across the garden at Eric Lamb. Even though he had his back to us, I could see his shoulders laughing.

We continued to weed, Tilly in her sou'wester and me in a trilby Eric Lamb had found at the back of his shed. It was strange how the weeding made your mind feel quiet. I had stopped worrying about God and Mrs Creasy, and how my mother walked out of any room my father walked into, and all I could think about was the soil tickling the spaces between my fingers.

'I like this,' I said.

Tilly just nodded and we worked in silence. After a while, she pointed to a plant which was still rooted into the soil.

'Is that a weed as well?' she said.

I leaned forward and stared at it. Its leaves were large and jagged, but it didn't look the same as the others in the bucket. There was no dandelion in the middle, and it didn't really have much of a weedy air about it.

'I'm not sure.' I stared at it a little more. 'Probably.'

'But what if I pull it up and it isn't? What if I make it die, and it was a flower after all?' she said. 'What if I make a mistake?'

Eric Lamb walked over from the other side of the garden.

'What's the problem?' He crouched beside us and we all stared at the plant.

'We can't decide if this is a weed or not,' said Tilly, 'and I don't want to pull it up if it isn't.'

'I see,' he said, but didn't come up with anything else.

We waited. My legs started to tingle, and I shifted from the newspaper. When I looked down, the previous week's headlines were printed back to front on my knee caps.

'So what shall we do?' said Tilly.

'Well, first of all,' said Eric Lamb, 'who decides if it's a weed or not?'

'People?' I said.

He laughed. 'Which people?'

'The people who are in charge. They decide if something is a weed or not,' I said.

'And who is in charge at the moment?' He looked at Tilly, and she squinted back at him in the sunshine. 'Who is holding the trowel?' he said.

Tilly scratched soil on to her nose and squinted a little more. 'Me?' she said very quietly.

'You,' repeated Eric Lamb. 'So you decide if it's a weed or not.'

We all turned and looked at the plant, which awaited its fate.

'The thing about weeds,' he said, 'is that it's very subjective.'

We looked confused.

He tried again. 'It depends very much on whose point of view it is. What's a weed to one person might be a beautiful flower to another. It depends very much on where they're growing and whose eyes it is you're seeing them through.'

We looked around at the dahlias and the freesias and the

geraniums. 'So the whole of this garden might be full of weeds to someone else?' I said.

'Exactly. If you loved dandelions, you'd think all of this was a waste of time.'

'And you'd save the dandelions instead,' Tilly said.

He nodded.

'So is it a weed or not?' he said, and we both looked at Tilly.

Her trowel hovered over the plant. She looked at each of us, and looked back at it. I thought for a second that she was about to dig it up, but then she put the trowel down and wiped her hands on her skirt.

'No,' she said, 'it's not a weed.'

'Then we shall let it live,' said Eric Lamb, 'and we will go inside and have a glass of lemonade.'

We pulled ourselves up from the newspapers and brushed down our clothes, and followed him across the garden.

'I wonder if you guessed right,' I said, as we wiped our feet on the porch mat. 'I wonder if it really was a weed.'

'I don't think that's the point, Gracie. I think the point is, everyone's allowed to think different things.'

Sometimes, you just had to humour Tilly. 'You still don't get it, do you?' I said.

She stamped her frown out into the doormat.

*

Eric Lamb reached for some glasses out of the top cupboard, and Tilly and I used the time to be curious about his kitchen.

It was strange how different people's kitchens could be. Some were shouty and confused, like Mrs Dakin's, and some kitchens, like Eric Lamb's, hardly made a sound. A clock tick-tocked above the door frame and a fridge whirred and hummed to itself in the corner. Other than that, there was silence, as we ran the taps and stared through the window and washed our hands with Fairy Liquid. Next to the stove were two easy chairs, one crumpled and sagging, the other smooth and unworn. Over the back of each were crocheted blankets, reams of multicoloured yarn, stretched together in a shout of colour, and on the dresser was a photograph of a woman with kind eyes. She watched us dry our hands and take lemonade from Eric Lamb, and I wondered if it had been her patience which had woven together the strands of wool, for a chair she could no longer sit in.

I decided to jump straight in.

'Do you believe in God?' I asked him.

I saw him glance at the photograph, but he didn't give an answer straight away. Instead, he was so quiet I could hear breath moving in and out of his lungs, until eventually he looked at the photograph again and then at me, and said, 'Of course.'

'Do you believe He keeps us where we belong?'

'Like amenomes?' said Tilly.

Eric Lamb looked through the glass and into his garden. 'I think He allows us to grow,' he said. 'We just have to find the best soil. Every plant can flourish, it just needs to find the right place, and sometimes, the right place isn't always where you think it is.'

'I wonder if goats and sheep can grow in the same soil,' said Tilly.

Eric Lamb looked at her and frowned, so we told him about the goats and the sheep, and about how God is everywhere, and we waved our arms about and drank our lemonade.

'Who is the lady in the photograph?' said Tilly.

We all turned to look at her, and she looked back.

'That was my wife,' he said. 'I took care of her until she died.'

'And now she's gone, you take care of your garden instead,' said Tilly.

He took her empty glass. 'I have a feeling you have made far more shadows than I had originally thought,' he said.

And he smiled.

*

We had just closed the front gate, when Tilly grabbed my arm. 'We didn't talk about Mrs Creasy,' she said.

I opened the bag Eric Lamb had given us. It was filled with baby tomatoes, and the smell of summer escaped from the twists of brown paper.

'Of course we did.' I put one in my mouth and felt it burst between my teeth. 'We talked about very little else.'

Tilly reached into the bag. 'Did we?'

'Tilly Albert,' I said, 'what would you do without me?'
She burst a tomato in her mouth and smiled back.

By mid-afternoon, the bag was empty. They were as sweet as sugar.

Number Three, Rowan Tree Croft

15 July 1976

'Mummy will be getting the tea ready for six o'clock tonight, Remington, so let's hope people have the good manners to be home in time to eat it.'

'If people had good manners to start with, Remington, they'd realize that the only reason we have tea on the table in the first place is because some of us go out to work.'

My parents had begun arguing through the dog.

He had been reinvented as an instrument of communication, although he still lay under the kitchen table as usual and didn't seem especially aware of his new role. He probably just thought he had suddenly become very popular and interesting.

The only time my parents spoke directly to each other was when someone else was there, or when they wanted to have an advanced argument, which involved shouting and banging cupboard doors and marching up and down the stairs. My mother had stopped asking my father questions about Mrs Creasy, and had moved on to other topics, such as why we're not going on holiday this year and whether my father would like to take a lilo to the office and just bloody well live there permanently.

Tilly and I had escaped to Mrs Morton's, where it was softer and quieter, and no one ever marched anywhere.

Mrs Morton was bottoming the pantry, and Tilly and I sat at the kitchen table.

Tilly was playing clock patience, but every time she found a King, she just put it back at the bottom of a pile.

'That's not what you do,' I said. 'It's cheating.'

'There's only me playing.'

'But they're the rules.'

'They're not my rules, though,' said Tilly. She hid another King as I was watching. 'I think people should be allowed to have their own.'

'That's the whole point of rules,' I said. 'They're there to make sure everyone does the same thing.'

'That's a bit boring, though, isn't it?' she said.

Tilly was the kind of person who sent a Christmas card in July, because she thought you might like the picture on the front. Sometimes, you just had to make allowances for her.

Mrs Morton walked past with three boxes of marshmallow teacakes.

'Do you believe in rules, Mrs Morton?' I said.

Mrs Morton and the marshmallow teacakes stopped

right in front of my face. 'Some rules are important,' she said. 'Other rules, I think, are just there to make people feel as though they're all on the same side.'

I nodded at Tilly and took a King out from the bottom of the pile.

'It doesn't work, though, does it?' said Tilly. 'Mr and Mrs Forbes never seem to be on the same side, Mr Creasy doesn't have anyone on his side now, and I'm not sure whose side Mrs Dakin is on.'

'No,' I said. I looked at the King. 'I don't suppose it always works.'

'You mum and dad definitely aren't on the same side,' Tilly said.

Mrs Morton coughed and took her marshmallows back into the pantry.

'It's because of God,' I said. 'If we could just find God, then Mrs Creasy would come home and everything else would sort itself out.'

'Perhaps she's never coming home, Gracie. Perhaps we were right in the first place. Perhaps Mr and Mrs Forbes have murdered her and buried her under the patio.'

'Mr and Mrs Forbes don't have a patio,' said Mrs Morton from the back of the pantry.

'No, I'm sure that if we find Him, then Mrs Creasy will come back,' I said. 'We just need to keep looking.'

'You said that he wasn't at Eric Lamb's house because God couldn't ever be in a place where someone is so sad, and we've looked everywhere else.'

I picked at the edge of the playing card with my nail. 'Gracie?'

'We haven't quite looked everywhere else,' I said.

Tilly stared at me, and I watched the idea find her face. 'No!' she said. 'We can't!'

I took Tilly's arm and led her out into the garden. It's amazing how much you can hear from the back of a pantry.

*

'We agreed we weren't going to visit number eleven,' she said. 'We agreed it wasn't safe.'

'No,' I said, 'you did that agreeing all by yourself.'

We sat on two giant plant pots at the back of Mr Morton's shed. You couldn't really call it Mrs Morton's shed, because even after a person has disappeared, there are still some places left in the world which will always belong to them.

'Mrs Morton said we're not to go near Walter Bishop.' Tilly shifted on her plant pot.

'Do you always do what Mrs Morton tells you?'

'Mostly,' she said.

'You said you didn't believe in rules. You said they make life too boring.'

Tilly wrapped her arms around her knees and made herself very small. 'This is different, though,' she said. 'This is a rule I think we need to keep.'

'God has to be there, Tilly. He just has to be. He isn't in any of the other houses, and number eleven is our last hope.'

'Can't we just imagine He's there, and not actually look?'

'No, we have to check. If we don't, Mrs Creasy will never come back, and any one of us could disappear next. We need to make sure we have a shepherd.'

The weight of the day pressed into my head. There was no shade behind Mr Morton's shed and the heat was angry and fierce. Its cruelty seemed to spread, reddening my skin with its temper, crawling into my hair and pulling at my flesh with a quiet, persistent rage.

'I don't really want to, Gracie.'

Tilly looked into my eyes. She never looked into my eyes.

'Well, then,' I said. 'I can do it by myself.' I tried to bury my fear in shouting. 'If you won't go with me, I'll go on my own.'

'You can't! You mustn't!'

'Then I'm going to ask someone else to go with me.' I stood up. The heat seemed even worse. I could feel it, streaming from the walls of the shed and the dusty bricks of Mrs Morton's garden wall. 'I'm going to ask Lisa Dakin.'

I still hadn't learned the power of words. How, once they have left your mouth, they have a breath and a life of their own. I had yet to realize that you no longer own them. I hadn't learned that, once you have let them go, the words can then, in fact, become the owner of you.

I looked down at Tilly. She was smaller and paler than I had ever seen her before, but the sun had begun to catch her face, and the red of its heat crept into the end of her nose.

'Why would you do that?' she said. 'I thought we were best friends. I thought we were the ones looking for God?'

'You can have more than one best friend.' My hair felt hot and bad-tempered, and I pushed it out of my face. 'And if you won't come with me, then I'm going to have to rethink the whole thing.'

Tilly didn't speak.

I made myself keep looking at her face. 'So what is it to be?' I said. 'Are you coming with me or shall I go and ask Lisa Dakin?'

She pulled at a thread on one of her buttons. 'In that case, I suppose I'll have to,' she said.

We waited in silence, Tilly, me and the argument. It didn't feel like one of my parents' arguments, where everyone stamped and slammed, and made a lot of noise. This argument was cautious and well behaved, and I wasn't sure what I was supposed to do with it next.

I started to edge my way along the little path at the back of the shed. 'But before we go, put some sun cream on,' I shouted back. 'Your nose is starting to burn.'

'Okay, Gracie.' I could hear her get up from her plant pot. 'If you say so.'

I didn't have many arguments with people. In fact, Tilly and I never had arguments. Sometimes I tried, but she would never join in. She would always say *never mind* or *okay then*, or *if you say so*.

241

This was the first real disagreement we'd ever had.

Whenever I did have an quarrel with someone, I always felt quite pleased if I was the one who won, but as I walked back into Mrs Morton's kitchen that day and listened to Tilly walking very slowly behind me, even though I'd persuaded her to do what I wanted, I really didn't feel like a winner at all.

Number Eleven, The Avenue

15 July 1976

Unlike the rest of the avenue, number eleven stood a long way back from the road. It hid behind a group of cedar trees, which gathered in a little group on the front lawn, like unhappy guests. Whilst the other houses greeted each other in a polite circle, number eleven stood hesitant and apologetic, watching the rest of the avenue and waiting to be invited in.

We stood at the edge of the garden wall.

I ran my fingers along the brickwork, and a trail of orange dust clouded into the air.

'Do you think he's in?' said Tilly.

I peered around one of the cedar trees. 'Dunno,' I said.

The house gave nothing away. It had been built decades before the rest of the estate, and this set it apart from the newcomers which had appeared around it. The bricks were dark and mossy with age, and instead of polite, squared windows, giant yawns of glass looked back at us across the grass.

'I think he's always in,' I said.

We took tightrope steps along the gravel path, all the way to the little covered porch. With each step, we looked around to see if anything had altered, to check that the trees hadn't changed position, or that the windows hadn't blinked at us as we walked past.

The front door of Walter Bishop's house was painted black, but all around the edges were whispers of cobweb, and a dead spider sat patiently in a corner, waiting for a meal which had never arrived. We stood on chessboard tiles, next to a pile of newspapers which were almost as tall as Tilly. I looked through the hall windows, and saw more newspapers. Years of headlines pressed against the yellowed glass, trying to escape.

We stared at the spider.

'I don't think anyone uses this door much,' said Tilly.

I pushed at the wooden rail, which ran around the edge of the porch. It leaned away from my hand and creaked in protest.

'Why don't we try the back?' I said.

Tilly looked at the tower of newspapers.

'I don't know, Gracie. It just doesn't feel right.'

It didn't.

Even though we were only a few steps away from the avenue, a few steps away from my front door, and Eric

Lamb and his garden shed, and Sheila Dakin's deckchair, it felt as though we had wandered a very long way from where we were meant to be.

'Don't be silly,' I said, 'come on.' Because I could never admit that to Tilly.

We walked around the side of the house, and I held on to the wall with each step, covering my hands with dusty brick-red. I could hear Tilly's sandals behind me, crunching into the gravel. It was the only sound. Even the birds seemed to be holding their breath.

I stopped by the first window and pressed my face against the glass.

Tilly peered around the corner of the house. 'Can you see Mrs Creasy?' she whispered. 'Is she tied up in there? Is she dead?'

The room looked tired and unhappy.

A stout afternoon sun beat against the glass, yet the inside of Walter Bishop's house was filled only with darkness. The dark wood of the dresser, a rusty carpet, threaded with burgundy and age, and a moss-green settee, which looked itchy and unsat upon. It was a forgotten cave of tapestry and Wilton.

Tilly's face appeared next to mine.

'It's empty,' I said. 'It doesn't even look as though there's air in there.'

I was just about to turn away when I saw it.

'Look, Tilly.' I tapped on the glass.

There was a cross. A large, brass crucifix, which stood on a shelf over the fireplace. It was all by itself. There were no photographs or ornaments, nothing to tell you anything about the person who lived there, and it made the mantelpiece look like an altar.

'I was right all along.' I stared at the cross. 'We were just searching in the wrong houses.'

'I don't think that definitely means God is here, though,' said Tilly. 'My mum has loads of recipe books, but she never actually does any cooking.'

As we watched, the sun brushed the edges of the cross and sent a splinter of light across the room. It climbed along the itchy settee, and across the tired carpet, until it reached the windowsill, where it bounced from the glass right where we were standing.

'Wow,' said Tilly. 'It looks like God is pointing at something.'

'Can I help you?'

We were so amazed with ourselves, it took a second to realize that someone else was standing there with us.

*

Walter Bishop was shorter than I remembered, or perhaps I was just taller than I had been in the chip shop. He was thinner, too, and his skin was smooth and turned to terracotta by the summer.

'Were you looking for someone?' he said.

'God,' said Tilly.

'And Mrs Creasy,' I added. In case he thought we were mental.

'I see.' He smiled very slowly, and his eyes creased at the edges.

'This is the last place to search,' Tilly said. 'We've been everywhere else.'

'I see,' he said again. 'So where have you already looked?'

'All over,' I said. 'The Bible says that God is everywhere, but we can't find Him. I'm beginning to think the vicar was making it all up.'

Walter Bishop sat on an old bench which leaned against the back wall, and gestured to a wooden seat opposite.

'God is an interesting subject to talk about,' he said. 'And what do you think has happened to Mrs Creasy?'

We sat down.

'We think she might be in Scotland,' said Tilly. 'Or perhaps murdered.'

'Do you not think there would be more policemen about, if she were murdered?'

I thought about it. 'Policemen sometimes get it wrong,' I said.

'This is true.' He looked down and began picking at the paintwork on the bench, although, to be fair, there wasn't much left of it to pick at.

Tilly took off her cardigan and folded it on to her knee. 'We liked Mrs Creasy, didn't we, Grace?'

'Very much,' I said. 'Did you know her, Mr Bishop?'

'Oh yes, she often came to visit,' Walter looked up and smiled, before he went back to the paintwork. 'I knew her very well.'

'Why do you think she left?' said Tilly.

Walter Bishop didn't speak for a while. It was so long before he answered, I was beginning to wonder if he hadn't even heard the question.

'I'm sure she'll tell us everything when she returns,' he said eventually.

'Do you think she's coming back?' I said.

'Well,' he said, 'if she does, she will certainly have a lot to say.'

It was a while before he looked up and returned his glasses to the bridge of his nose.

I felt warmth from the wood reach my legs. 'This seat is very comfortable,' I said.

'It's called a settle.'

I leaned back and felt it press into my shoulder blades. 'It's a good name for a seat.'

He smiled. 'It is.'

We sat in silence. I knew straight away that Walter Bishop was the kind of person you could sit in silence with. There were very few people like that, I had found. Most grown-ups liked to fill a silence with conversation. Not important, necessary conversation, but a spray of words that served no purpose other than to cover up the quiet. But Walter Bishop was comfortable with saying nothing, and all I could hear as we sat together on that hot July day, was the anxious cry of a wood pigeon, high up in one of the trees, calling for its mate. I looked, but although I searched all the branches, I couldn't find it.

He saw me staring.

'He's there,' Walter said, pointing to the very top of the tree, and I saw a flash of grey amongst the leaves.

'Do you think God is in that pigeon?' I said.

Walter looked up. 'Definitely.'

'And in the cedar trees,' I said.

Walter smiled again. 'I'm sure He is. I agree with your vicar. God is everywhere, or at least, someone is.'

I frowned at him. 'I've never seen you in church.'

'I don't mix very well.' He looked down and shifted his feet in the gravel.

'Us neither,' said Tilly.

'Does it bother you,' I said, 'not mixing well?'

'I think you can get used to most things if you taste them for long enough.'

Walter Bishop spoke slowly and he held the words in his mouth like pieces of food. There was a softness to his voice as well, which made his speech seem even more full of thinking.

He looked across at me. 'I don't read people very well,' he said. 'They can be very confusing.'

'Especially people on this avenue,' said Tilly.

'You mix with us all right, though, don't you?' I said. 'You can read us?'

'I have always got along very well with children.' He went back to picking at the paint.

I could see why there was so very little of it left.

We slid back into the silence. I could hear voices

somewhere beyond the trees. It sounded like Sheila Dakin or Mrs Forbes. I couldn't be sure, because the warmth of the day seemed to blanket all the sounds, until it felt as though everything was being carried away from me in the heat.

'The thing is,' I said after a while, 'no one around here seems very bothered about God.'

The picking had stopped. Walter brushed flecks of paint from underneath his nails. 'They won't be,' he said, 'until they need something.'

'Do you think God listens, even if you've not really had much of a conversation with Him before?' said Tilly.

'I wouldn't.' I pressed my legs into the settle. 'It's bad manners.'

'What is it that you want from God?' said Walter. He took off his glasses and began cleaning them with a handkerchief that didn't look particularly clean to begin with.

I thought about the question for a long time. I thought about it as I listened to the call of the pigeon in the cedar tree, and as I filled my lungs with the smell of summer and felt the warmth of the wood on my legs.

'I want Him to keep everyone on the avenue safe,' I said eventually. 'Like a shepherd.'

'Only the sheep, though,' said Tilly. 'God doesn't like goats. He sends them into the wilderness and doesn't ever speak to them again.'

Walter looked up. 'Goats?'

'Oh yes,' I said. 'The world is full of goats and sheep. You just have to try and work out which is which.'

'I see.' Walter replaced his glasses. There was a wrapping of Sellotape around one of the arms, but they still leaned far too much to one side. 'And do you think all the people on the avenue are goats,' he said, 'or sheep?'

I was about to answer, but then I stopped and thought about it, and said, 'I haven't made my mind up' instead.

Walter stood up. 'Why don't we go inside and have some lemonade. We can talk about it in there. Out of the heat.'

Tilly looked at me, and I looked up at Walter Bishop.

I wasn't sure if it was because of the missing button on his shirt, or the rash of stubble on his face. Or perhaps it was the way his hair hung in yellowed strands around his collar. Or perhaps it was none of these things. Perhaps it was just because of Mrs Morton's words, which were still marching around in my ears.

'We can drink it out here, Mr Bishop, can't we?' I said.

He walked towards the back door. 'Oh no. That wouldn't do at all. Look at the state of your hands. You need to wash them.'

I looked down. They were dirty brick-red from holding on to the wall. Even after I wiped them on my skirt, the colour was still there, eating into the lines on my fingers.

He opened the door into his kitchen. 'Do your parents know you're here?' he said.

I didn't reply at first. I stood up and looked at Tilly, and she stared back at me with uncertain eyes.

'No,' I said. 'Nobody knows we're here.'

And even as Tilly and I walked through the door, I still wasn't sure I'd given him the right answer.

Number Twelve, The Avenue

15 July 1976

'Nothing.' Brian's gaze moved between yesterday's newspaper and the tip of his left trainer.

'How could you have had an appointment with Margaret Creasy about nothing?' Sheila Dakin said.

She had summoned him to her deckchair.

He had been minding his own business, looking for some old LPs in the garage, when she'd spotted him and screeched his name out across the avenue, like a bird of prey. Now he was standing in the front garden of number twelve, with Hank Marvin and the Shadows, trying not to look her in the eye.

'Well?' she said.

He hugged the vinyl against his chest. 'It's personal,' he said.

'Don't come the high and mighty with me, Brian Roper.'

He looked at his other trainer. He couldn't tell her. He couldn't tell anyone.

If he tried to explain what happened with Margaret Creasy, no one would understand. It would only lead to more questions, and he'd tie himself up in knots trying to answer them. They'd blame him. People always did.

'Did you hear a word I said?' Sheila Dakin shifted her weight and the canvas groaned in protest.

He looked away from his trainer and pinched a glance at her. She was all deckchair and bikini.

'What exactly did you tell Margaret Creasy about this avenue, Brian?'

'Nothing.'

'About the fire?'

'Nothing.' He dared to take another glance. 'She knew everything about it already.'

'Did she now. So someone has opened their mouth, then.'

'They might not have done.' Brian automatically reached into the back of his jeans. 'She went to the library a lot. They've got copies of the *Gazette* in there going back years.'

He had started to carry the library ticket around with him. He was sure his mother had been searching through his pockets. Whenever she became bored of her own life, she would rummage around in someone else's to help pass the time. He'd thought about trying to sneak the card back somehow. Maybe go round to John's and leave it between the pages of a book, or under a table mat, but he was bound to be caught. He always was.

'What are you messing around in your back pocket for?' said Sheila.

He could never get away with anything. 'No reason,' he said.

'Old copies of the *Gazette* be buggered,' said Sheila. 'She's been told what happened. That's why she's gone missing. Someone needed to keep her quiet.'

'She talked to everyone. Not just me.' Brian went to check his back pocket again, but he stopped himself just in time.

'That's the bloody problem, Brian. She did talk to everybody. She knows everything there is to know about all of us.'

He hugged the record closer to his chest. 'What is there to know?' he said. 'We're just like any other avenue, aren't we?'

Sheila narrowed her lips and her eyes, and everything else on her face which could be narrowed, all at the same time. 'And if anyone's been opening their mouths, my money's on you,' she said.

He stared at her.

Sheila reached over and floundered around in the grass, knocking over a glass and sending a crisp packet tumbling on to the path, until her hands found the newspaper. 'Read it,' she said, 'go on.'

He felt very thirsty. He could sense it, that familiar feeling. The slow, dry crackle in the back of his throat, the ringing in his ears. 'I don't want to,' he said.

'Go on.' Sheila was waving the paper around in front of him. 'Read it.'

'I don't need to,' he said.

'Well, I'll read it, then.' She snapped her glasses on to her face. 'Let me see.'

Local woman still missing, she said. *Police are keen to trace the whereabouts of local woman Mrs Margaret Creasy, who went missing from her home on The Avenue on June 21st.*

Sheila traced the words as she read. *Out of character, no contact, no reason for her disappearance, etc, etc, etc.* She brought the newspaper a little closer to her face. 'Here we are,' she said, 'this is it.' *Mr Brian Roper (43).* She looked at Brian over the top of her glasses and looked down again. *(43), also of The Avenue said, 'We're all worried that someone's done her in, there are some really odd people around this place.'*

Sheila took off her glasses and stared at Brian. 'What on earth are you doing, talking to newspaper reporters?'

'I thought they were just being friendly,' he said.

'Newspaper reporters? Being friendly?' She stabbed at the newspaper article with the arm of her glasses. 'You're forty-three, Brian.'

He scratched the end of his nose. His mother had said the same thing.

'You've got to stop opening that big trap of yours. Newspaper journalists, Margaret Creasy, Grace and Tilly.'

'I didn't say anything to Grace and Tilly.'

'And stop picking your nose.'

'You can ask them if you want, they're only just up there.'

He turned to look at the avenue, but it was deserted. Not even Mrs Forbes' sweeping brush or Eric Lamb's lawn-mower, just the baked, hot silence of a July afternoon. 'They've disappeared now,' he said.

Sheila leaned forward in her deckchair. 'Who's disappeared?'

'Grace and Tilly. They were there a minute ago.'

Sheila put down her newspaper and her glasses. 'Where?'

'At the top of the road.' He looked back and pointed.

'For God's sake, Brian. Where at the top of the road?'

'Just outside number eleven.'

He turned to look at Sheila, but she was already on her feet.

Number Eleven, The Avenue

15 July 1976

Walter Bishop's soap was green and cracked, and so stuck down I had to prise it off the corner of the basin with my nails.

Tilly and I stood next to each other, washing our hands. I knew Tilly was looking at me, but I stared at the long, orange stain in the sink instead, because my eyes hadn't decided what they wanted to say to her.

'That's right.' Walter stood behind us. 'Make sure they're nice and clean, ladies.'

It didn't make us smile. Somehow, the words didn't sound the same as when Sheila Dakin said them.

He handed us a tea towel and we dried our hands, and then I folded it up and put it on the draining board.

'Oh no, no, no.' He tutted as he spoke. 'We never, ever fold tea towels.'

'We don't?' I said.

'They need air, you see. Or all the germs will be trapped. It always belongs on the little peg over there.'

I followed his gaze, and took the tea towel to a hook on the side of the cupboard.

'Much better,' he said. 'We never fold tea towels in this house. It was one of my mother's rules.'

'Did she have many rules, Mr Bishop?' I slid on to one of the kitchen chairs. Tilly put her cardigan on her knee and slid next to me, although every few seconds I could see her look towards the back door.

'Oh yes. Lots of rules,' said Walter. 'Never whistle after dark. No new shoes on the table. Stand in a circle to ward off the devil.'

He put two glasses on the table. They were clouded with dust.

'One for sorrow, two for joy.' He smiled. 'Would you like some lemonade?'

'We really should be going.' Underneath her cardigan, Tilly pulled herself to the edge of her seat. 'It's nearly tea time.'

'Oh, surely not yet. You've only just got here.' Walter poured the lemonade. 'Since Margaret Creasy left, I get so few visitors, you see.'

He turned back to the cupboard, and I looked at Tilly and shrugged my shoulders.

'A few minutes won't hurt,' I whispered.

I looked around the kitchen. It seemed dark and unhappy,

259

and even in the heat of the afternoon, it was strangely cool. The cupboards were all painted green, and in the corners of the room the floorboards peeped through, where the lino had curled up and surrendered.

'Do you still keep all your mother's rules?' I said.

Walter sat opposite. He laced his fingers together as though he was about to pray. 'Some of them,' he said. 'But not all of them.'

'Even though they were your mother's?' said Tilly.

Walter leaned forward and prayed a little harder. 'Even though they were my mother's,' he said. 'It is a wise man who makes his own decisions. It's very important to remember that, especially if you're looking for God.'

'What do you mean?' I said.

'People tend to believe things just because everyone else does.' Walter looked at his hands and began biting into the skin next to his fingernails. 'They don't search for proof, they just search for approval from everyone else.'

I had to sit back in my chair to think about it. Sometimes adults said things which made sense, even if you weren't exactly sure what the sense was.

'So if you've decided to look for God,' he said, 'the first thing you have to do is decide exactly what it is that you're looking for.'

I wasn't even sure. I thought I might recognize God once I saw Him, but the only thing I could be certain of now was that even though everyone said He existed, God didn't seem to be anywhere on the avenue.

'People believe in things without even knowing if they're actually true,' I said.

'Because if everyone believes the same thing, it makes them feel as though they belong,' said Walter.

'Like a flock of sheep.' Tilly picked up the glass of lemonade and put it down again. 'Perhaps that's the only thing people really need. Something they can all believe in.'

Walter stopped biting his nails and looked at us both. 'And that something might not always be God. Which is why it's important to be wise.'

'And make our own decisions,' I said.

Walter Bishop smiled. 'Exactly.'

I had a lot of questions for Walter Bishop, and I was just about to start on the first one when footsteps marched into my thinking and disturbed it. They snapped on the gravel outside and we all moved to the window to see who owned them.

Sheila Dakin. Her pink slippers sent sprays of little pebbles diving for cover.

Within seconds she was in the doorway, her bikini top heaving with the effort. We stood like figurines at the windowsill.

'What the hell do you think you're doing?' she said, her arms folded across her chest and air leaving her body in tiny, angry pockets.

Words came out of Walter Bishop's mouth, but they were jumbled and twisted, and left in the wrong order. I watched sweat creep on to his terracotta forehead. There was silence, but it was a different kind of silence.

'We were just talking,' I said.

'No, you most certainly were not.' Sheila Dakin went to grab our collars, but neither of us were in possession of them, and so she steered us both with mahogany wings instead.

'We weren't doing anything wrong,' I said.

'No, you weren't.' She answered me, but looked at Walter Bishop.

'We were looking for God,' I said.

'Well, you certainly won't find Him here.'

I wanted Walter to explain. To explain that God was everywhere, in the pigeon and the cedar tree and the brass crucifix that stood on the mantelpiece, but Walter was held by Sheila Dakin's stare as easily as if he'd been handcuffed to her.

'We're going,' said Mrs Dakin, and she pulled us out of the kitchen and along the gravel drive.

I turned and looked at Walter.

He stood in the doorway watching us leave, his terracotta arms by his side, but when he saw me turn, he shouted, 'Grace, don't forget this.'

It was Tilly's cardigan. I broke free from Sheila Dakin and went back.

'Remember,' he said, as he put the cardigan into my hands. 'Always be a wise man.'

I smiled and nodded, and he smiled and nodded back.

And in that moment I wondered if sometimes, you only really need two people to believe in the same thing, to feel as though you just might belong.

*

Sheila Dakin paraded us back down the road, and along the way she exhibited our safety to the rest of the avenue, who seemed to have been alerted to the problem by her slippers.

'How did you know we were there?' I said.

'Thin Brian saw you loitering outside number eleven and notified me.' Sheila Dakin spoke as if she had suddenly become a member of the police force. 'He hasn't got many uses, but at least he's good for something.'

Eric Lamb nodded as we went past. He stood in his front garden, a rake in one hand and a trowel in the other, like a giant garden gnome. Dorothy Forbes paused on her chippings with her hand to her mouth, and Thin Brian stood in the doorway of his garage, searching for something in the back pocket of his jeans.

'Where's your mother?' Sheila Dakin said, as we reached the end of the road.

I looked up at the bedroom curtains. 'I think she's having a little lie-down,' I said.

'Then I suppose you'd better come to my house.'

Tilly looked at me and sighed.

Not even Sheila Dakin asked about Tilly's mother.

*

We were placed on chairs, with Elvis and the ironing board, and the whole of Mrs Dakin's kitchen seemed to take on the air of a courtroom.

Has your mother never explained anything to you?

What did you think you were doing?

Did he say anything to upset you?

'Well, did he?'

'We talked about God and pigeons,' I said.

'And believing in things,' added Tilly.

Mrs Dakin watched us, waiting for more words. We watched back in silence.

'Nothing else?' she said eventually.

'Nothing else,' I said. Even though I didn't know what the nothing else was supposed to be, and I was waiting for her to give me a clue.

Her shoulders lowered a good two inches.

'Why does everyone hate him?' I said. 'What did he do wrong?'

'Nothing,' she said. 'Apparently.'

'Then why aren't we allowed to talk to him?'

She sat down. I could see the frustration in her eyes. Sheila Dakin, who would normally allow words to spill freely from her mouth, was suddenly faced with the edited vocabulary of a child.

'People said he did a very bad thing.' She shuffled a cigarette packet whilst she spoke.

'And did he?' I said.

'The police said he didn't, but there's no smoke without fire.'

'Sometimes there is,' said Tilly.

I nodded and we both stared at Mrs Dakin.

'I was accused of copying homework once,' I said, 'but it was a lie, and my mother made Mr Nesbitt apologize.'

I saw Tilly looking at me from the corners of her eyes. 'That's not a very good example,' she said quietly.

'There are lots of other examples,' I said. 'Your Lisa's always being accused of things, and she can't possibly do every single one of them.'

Mrs Dakin frowned and lit a cigarette.

'What did Walter Bishop do?' I said. 'What didn't he do?'

'It doesn't matter. It's not important.'

It was actually the most important thing I had ever come across in my entire life.

'What is important', she said, 'is that you keep away from him. He's not like us, whatever he did or didn't do.' She drew smoke into her lungs and held it there as she spoke. 'He's a bad man.'

I opened my mouth to speak, but changed my mind. Mrs Dakin didn't look like someone who particularly wanted to hear anyone else's interesting viewpoint.

'Is it something to do with his mother?' said Tilly.

Mrs Dakin froze.

She looked like a musical statue with no music. She didn't appear to blink or breathe, and the only thing that wasn't still was the cigarette, which swayed and wavered between her lips.

'What do you mean?' She spoke very quietly, through the cigarette.

'Mr Bishop told us about his mother,' I said, and watched the cigarette waver even more. 'In fact, we had a very long conversation about her.'

The cigarette was wavering so violently, I wondered if it might drop from her mouth, but Mrs Dakin was a seasoned professional and managed to hold it in place.

'Don't take any notice of anything Walter Bishop tells you,' she said. 'He's just as barmy as his mother was.'

'She had a lot of rules,' Tilly said.

'Such as?'

'No shoes on the table, never fold tea towels,' I said.

Mrs Dakin took the cigarette from her mouth and ash drifted on to the kitchen table. 'Tea towels?'

'Walter never folds tea towels.' I watched the ash settle into a place mat. 'Folded tea towels harbour germs.'

Mrs Dakin stared into the distance and frowned. When she had finished frowning, she looked at us and said, 'Do they now?'

We nodded.

'They do,' I said.

Sheila Dakin stubbed the remains of the cigarette into an ashtray and immediately lit another one.

'And did Walter Bishop say anything about Margaret Creasy?'

'Not really,' said Tilly.

I looked at Tilly. 'Loads actually,' I said.

Mrs Dakin's gaze darted between us. 'Does he know where she is? Does he know if she's coming back?'

'He said that if she does come back, she'll be telling everybody everything.' Tilly tried to swing her legs under the table, but they became caught in a washing basket and a gathering of Keithie's toys. 'He said she'll have an awful lot to say.'

Sheila Dakin's mouth dropped open, and her cigarette fell to the floor.

'Be careful, Mrs Dakin.' I handed the cigarette back to her. 'That's how fires start.'

*

It was a good job my mother's bedroom curtains were drawn back at that point, because Mrs Dakin began to feel suddenly unwell and thought she might like to sit by herself for a bit.

We walked down Mrs Dakin's patchwork path, past unfolded deckchairs and a pile of Lisa's magazines.

'I liked Mr Bishop,' I said.

'Me too,' Tilly said.

'You pissed my mam off?' Keithie stood by the bottom gate, trailing his football with the tip of his boot.

'No,' we both answered at the same time.

'You've been to that bloody weirdo's house, haven't you?'

'He's not a weirdo,' I said, 'he just doesn't mix well.'

'Well, you two would know,' said Keithie.

We watched him bounce the football along the avenue, until it hit the kerb and disappeared over Mrs Forbes' garden wall.

'So what do we do now?' said Tilly. 'We can't go back to Walter Bishop's, we'd be grounded for the rest of our lives.'

I looked over at number eleven. 'No, I don't suppose we can.'

'So how can we find out if God is really here?'

We walked down the path at the side of my house, and I could see my mother measuring out her afternoon at the kitchen sink.

'We can do what Walter Bishop told us to do,' I said. 'We can examine the evidence. We can be wise men.'

As we walked through the back door, Tilly took off her sou'wester and stamped out the dust from her sandals. 'Will we be like the wise men who visited Baby Jesus?' she said.

'Yes,' I said. 'Exactly like them.'

Number Twelve, The Avenue

15 July 1976

From her kitchen window, Sheila Dakin watched Grace and Tilly all the way to the back door of number four.

It was a habit, watching children. Even after the fire. Even after they'd all agreed that Walter Bishop had been punished enough and they should leave him well alone, she still watched the kids.

As soon as Grace and Tilly disappeared, she went to the pantry. Lisa and Keithie weren't around, but she didn't switch the light on. It made her feel better somehow, if she couldn't even see herself, if she couldn't see her hands shake and the straight, cold liquid hit the bottom of the glass.

It hadn't always been this way.

She could remember, just about remember, a time when there was a choice about it. She'd said to Margaret Creasy, if she could just get back to those days. Not give up, just take it or leave it. But perhaps Margaret was right, perhaps the days of take it or leave it were gone forever. She'd even got as far as standing over the sink with a bottle, but she hadn't quite got the nerve to go through with it. Funny really, she didn't believe she had many qualities in life, but nerve was something Sheila Dakin didn't think she'd ever be short of.

She took another mouthful. It folded itself into her like an embrace.

*

It had been such an ordinary-looking front door.

She said to Margaret, you never would have thought it from the outside, just what went on in there. A girl from work had given her the address. Not the kind of girl you'd expect, either. Pale and skinny, very quiet, always wiping her nose on the sleeve of her overall. She'd written it on a serviette in the canteen, and put it in Sheila's pocket without saying a word. She'd never spoken to the girl before or since.

She poured another drink. The floor of the pantry was cold and uneasy, but she curled her legs and leaned back into the shelves, and after a while it didn't seem too bad.

She'd kept the serviette in the back of her knicker drawer for three weeks.

It's not like anyone would have noticed anything. Her dad was in a world of his own, and her mam had long since gone. Her brothers treated her as they always had, like another boy, except she was the one who cooked and cleaned and put a fresh shirt out for them each morning. But she worried. She worried about work. If the pale, skinny girl had noticed, it might not be long before the rest of the factory noticed as well.

It took her three hours to knock on that ordinary-looking front door. She'd walked the street, waiting for women to stop whitening doorsteps and for kids to stop playing in chalked-out squares. It was late November, a sharp, raw Saturday afternoon of football matches and shopping trips, with a wind that bit scarlet into faces. Not Sheila's, though. Sheila's stayed pale and watery and lost.

As she knocked on the door, she imagined the woman who might be behind it. She wanted her to be plump and kind, to understand. To have her hair pinned in waves and a stout, flowery apron, like her mother used to wear. But the woman who opened the door was narrow and stern. She looked at Sheila from the ground upwards, and stood to one side without saying a word.

The woman only asked three questions: her name, her address and her age. She lied about all three.

Sheila spoke to the woman in a voice she didn't even recognize. 'Twenty-one,' she said, because she was worried it might make a difference.

Her eyes were beginning to adjust to the light in the pantry. She could see the curved edges of the glass in her hand, and the neck of the bottle as it tilted. She might as well have another now she was here.

She had lain on the bed, with the narrow, stern woman standing over her. Thin, curtained daylight pushed into the room, and she could still hear the outside creeping through the glass. The sound of children's footsteps running on pavements, and pieces of conversation as people walked along the street below. She didn't smoke then, so she'd talked instead to try and unstitch her nerves. She talked about anything – the weather, Christmas, the colour of the wallpaper.

The narrow woman didn't talk back. Sheila wasn't even sure if she was listening.

'You know, I'm not that kind of girl,' Sheila said, as it began.

She'd said the same words to the man a few weeks before.

Then stop dressing like one, he'd said.

Sheila looked up at the narrow woman. 'Sometimes it's easier, isn't it, to not fight back? Sometimes, people don't really have any choices, do they?'

It was her last chance for absolution. Her last chance to rescue the rest of her life.

The narrow woman let her fall.

She had never replied.

Sheila had to tell her father that she'd lost her pay packet.

When he'd finished growling and criticizing, she went into the front room and drank mouthfuls of his brandy. It was hot and bitter, and she heaved it into the bathroom sink a few minutes later. But she went back. And this time the brandy stayed where it was. It wrapped itself around her thoughts and stopped them from moving around the inside of her head, and it sent her misery to sleep, even if it was only for a few hours.

A coping strategy, Margaret Creasy had called it. The only problem was, when your whole existence is something you have to cope with, you look back one day and find that your strategy has become a way of life.

*

'Mam?'

It was Lisa. Sheila could hear her moving around the kitchen, shouting into the sitting room. Sheila heaved herself from the pantry floor, but she must have got up too quickly, because everything seemed to slide sideways and she had to hold on to one of the shelves to steady herself.

'I'm in here,' she shouted. 'I'm just finding something for our tea.'

Her hands grabbed at the first tin she could find, and she felt her way around the walls, looking for the door handle.

The kitchen seemed bright and unfriendly after the darkness of the pantry.

'Peach slices?' Lisa was standing right in front of her.

Sheila looked down at the tin. 'For afterwards,' she said.

Lisa frowned at her and turned away. For the rest of the conversation, Sheila only saw Lisa's back, and the curtain of hair which fell over her face as she bent down and took off her boots.

'I heard about the little girls.' Lisa pulled at the buckles. 'You saved them, Mam. You're a real hero. Everyone's talking about it.'

'Daft little buggers to go over there in the first place,' Sheila said.

She could still taste the brandy. There was some chewing gum in one of the drawers, but she couldn't find it and nothing seemed to be in the right place.

'He needs sorting out. The lads at school think so too. Evil bastard.'

'Lisa, don't say bastard. Or at least, don't say it so much.'

'He is, though,' Lisa said. 'He's a pervert, that's what he is. A bloody pervert.'

Sheila turned to the room, but she still held on to the edge of the sink. The walls sloped and shifted around her, and the light pulled the headache to the corners of her skull.

'I mean,' Lisa kicked her boots into the corner of the room, 'what kind of monster would ever harm a child?'

'I don't know, Lisa.'

Sheila watched her daughter. She was older now, capable. Not really a little girl to be told not to swear.

'Sometimes, though,' Sheila said, 'sometimes, things aren't always so clear cut, are they? Sometimes people don't really have any choices?'

'Of course they do.' Lisa turned around for the first time and stared at her. 'People always have bloody choices.'

Sheila looked down at her hands. They were white and shaking, and liver-spotted from a lifetime of falling.

Number Four, The Avenue

18 July 1976

The removal van sat on the avenue, its diesel engine turning over, and black smoke coughed into a watchful silence. I could hear blurred music coming from the cab, and a spire of cigarette smoke trailed from the open window.

Whilst we were sleeping, the airless July night had tipped into a perfect morning, seamless and still. Tiny clouds danced at the edges of the sky and, above our heads, a blackbird sang with such a beautiful heart I couldn't understand why the whole world hadn't stopped to listen to him.

Tilly and I sat on the wall outside my house, like a cinema audience, with sherbet dips and a sense of anticipation. The sun made slices into our bare legs and we stretched them out into the day.

'Can you see anything?' she said.

'No.' I dipped my liquorice, and the sherbet fizzed on my tongue. 'Can't be much longer, though.'

The removal van had sat outside number fourteen for forty-five minutes, and for the whole of that time my mother had been at the kitchen window, pretending to wash up.

I asked her if she wanted to sit with us on the wall outside, but she said, 'I'm far too busy for that,' and went back to pretending.

'Do you think there'll be children?' said Tilly.

I had told her I didn't know four times already, so I just sucked on my liquorice and kicked my heels against the bricks. Mrs Dakin was sunbathing with her eyes open and Mr Forbes had been to his dustbin six times in the last half an hour. The avenue was delirious with expectation.

The car arrived at either 11.08 or 11.09 (my watch had one of the lines missing, so I couldn't be sure). It was a large, metallic saloon, so large it had to have two goes at getting on to number fourteen's drive. The passenger door opened, and then the driver's door, and then one of the doors in the back. I was concentrating so hard I forgot I had a piece of liquorice in my mouth.

At first, I thought something was being lifted out, something gold and green and sapphire-blue. Then I realized it was material, and not only was it material, it was someone's clothes. And they were folded and wrapped and decorated around the most beautiful lady I had ever seen. She smiled at us and waved, and the man who had got out of the driver's door (and who was dressed in a white shirt and ordinary trousers), smiled and waved too, and a little boy shot from the back seat like a bullet, and began running around the front lawn.

'Oh my goodness,' said Tilly, 'they're Indian!'

I took the liquorice from my mouth, 'Isn't it brilliant?'

Across the fence, Mr Forbes' dustbin toppled over on his driveway and behind my shoulder, I heard the sound of falling crockery.

*

'It's not that,' said my mother (I would tell you how many times she'd said it, but I had lost count).

'Well, what is it, then?' I said.

'They might not want us calling round. They might have their own ways.'

'Because they're Indian?'

'It's not that.'

'But you've baked a cake,' I said.

'Oh that. That's for anybody.'

'It says "Welcome" on the top in blue icing.'

My mother became very interested in the *TV Times*.

'Well, I'll go round on my own,' I said.

'You can't do that!' My mother put the *TV Times* back down the side of the chair. 'Tell her, Derek.'

My father had so far escaped the conversation by reading his book on the outskirts of the settee and being ignored.

He said *well* and *perhaps* and *if*, and then his voice petered out into nothing.

My mother looked at him and did loud staring.

Thankfully, the sound of her loud staring was interrupted by the front doorbell. We never used our front door, it was ornamental. No one was even sure if it worked any more, and, for a moment, we all just looked at each other.

My father jumped up, and we all jumped up with him. He pulled and argued with the front door, and told us to step back, and we waited until it finally shuddered open. The beautiful lady and her husband in ordinary clothes, and the boy who ran like a bullet, all stood on our doorstep.

'Hello,' I said.

My mother smoothed down her hair and her trousers. My father just grinned.

'Hello, back,' said the beautiful lady.

'I'm really glad you're Indian,' I said (I meant to say, would you like to come in, but the words changed their mind on the way up). The beautiful lady and her husband just laughed and within five minutes, they were all sitting in a row on our settee.

The beautiful lady was called Aneesha Kapoor, her husband was Amit Kapoor, and the little boy was called Shahid. Their names were exotic and precious, like jewellery, and I said them over and over in my head.

'Well, that's very kind of you,' said my mother. She had been given a tin of sweets. Aneesha Kapoor called them sweets, but they looked more like biscuits, interesting biscuits.

'I baked you a cake,' my mother added.

'But it's for anyone,' I said.

My mother cornered her eyes.

'It's so nice of you to drop by, we were going to pop round and see you anyway.'

I cornered my eyes back.

'We wanted to get to know everyone,' said Amit. 'It's important, isn't it, to have a sense of community?'

'Yes, yes,' said my parents.

'And to feel part of the neighbourhood, to have an identity?' said Amit.

'Definitely, yes, definitely,' said my parents.

I wondered where this sense of community was. If it was waiting at the back of Sheila Dakin's pantry, or hidden in the loneliness of Eric Lamb's shed. I wondered if it sat with May Roper on her crocheted settee, or scratched itself into the paintwork of Walter Bishop's rotten windows. Perhaps it was in all of those places, but I had yet to find it.

'Well, it's lovely that you're now part of our neighbourhood,' said my mother. 'It will bring a bit of colour to the place.'

My father choked on his biscuit.

'I didn't mean that,' my mother said, 'I mean it will be more colourful now you're here. I mean—'

Aneesha laughed. 'I know what you mean,' she said.

I could hear my father still coughing up crumbs in the kitchen as he made a pot of tea.

He brought it in on a tray. The milk was in a milk jug. I didn't even know we owned a milk jug. People shuffled cups and side plates and elbows, and my mother cut into the 'W' of 'Welcome'.

'So, where are you from?' my mother said.

Amit was moulded into the end of the settee, his arms pressed to his sides, like a soldier.

'Birmingham,' he said. He sliced into the cake and his fork cracked against the plate.

My mother leaned forward, in a conspiracy. 'Yes, but where are you really from?' she said.

Amit leaned forward as well. 'Edgbaston,' he said, and everyone laughed.

My mother's laugh was a few seconds behind.

'Why don't you have some of these?' Aneesha said. She passed the sweets over. 'They're called *mithai.*'

'Pardon?' said my mother.

'Mitheyes, Sylvia,' said my father. He nudged Amit with his elbow and winked. 'Have you never heard of them?'

My mother frowned into the box. 'No,' she said, 'I can't say as I have.'

'Of course, I almost went to India,' said my father.

We all stared at him. Especially my mother. My father didn't even like taking the 107 bus to Nottingham. He said it made him feel queasy.

'You did?' said Amit.

'Oh yes,' my father said. 'I had to give up on the idea in the end, though. Couldn't face the sewerage system.' He patted his insides. 'And the poverty, of course.'

'Ah yes,' Amit said. 'The poverty.'

'We still enjoy a good curry, though, and we always listen to your music.' My father opened another pale ale. 'Love a bit of Demis Roussos, don't we, Sylve?'

We all stared.

'I think he might be Greek, Derek,' said my mother.

'Greek, Indian, what's the difference? The world's a big place these days.'

Aneesha Kapoor looked over at me and smiled. Then she gave a little wink that only she and I could see. I think she probably knew that a very large part of me wanted to die.

My father reached over for another biscuit. 'Help yourself to a beer, Amit,' he said. 'Don't be shy, lad, there's plenty to go round.'

*

After they had left, I sat in the kitchen and watched my parents rattle around against each other and tidy up the plates.

'Well, that went well,' said my father.

'Did it?' My mother stared at the biscuits. 'I'm still not sure how they'll fit in.'

'You've got to learn to move with the times,' my father said. 'There's another Indian family moved into Pine

Crescent. You might have to start asking yourself whether you're the one who needs to fit in.'

My mother examined one of the sweets, then changed her mind and put it back again.

On his way into the hall, my father picked up a newspaper. His voice carried back into the kitchen. 'As Elvis Presley once said, Sylvia, all the world's a stage and each must play his part.'

And he closed the living-room door and switched on the evening news.

'I think I've forgotten what my part's supposed to be,' said my mother.

She put the sweets right at the bottom of the biscuit tin – underneath a packet of fig rolls, and half a Jamaica Ginger Cake.

Number Six, The Avenue

18 July 1976

'What are they up to now?' Harold was calling out instructions from the settee. 'If you pull the curtain back properly, you might see a bit better.'

'They've just gone next door with a tin of some sort. Grace let them in. It doesn't matter how far back I pull the curtain, Harold. They've gone inside now.'

'Beggars belief,' he said. 'You think they might have issued us with some kind of warning.'

'Who?' Dorothy let the curtain fall back.

'The council. To let us know these people had prepared themselves.'

'How exactly should they have prepared themselves?'

'Got used to our customs.' Harold pulled at his shoelace. 'Learned a bit of our language, you know.'

'I'm fairly sure they speak English, Harold.'

'Well, if they do, it's only thanks to the Raj. You can't just go marching into somebody else's country and expect them to follow all your rules, you know.'

'India?' said Dorothy.

'No, Britain.' Harold tutted and began on his other shoe. 'It isn't cricket.'

Harold stood up. Dorothy couldn't prove it, but she could have sworn he was shrinking.

'I'll take a closer look on my way past. I'm just nipping to the Legion.'

'Again?' said Dorothy. 'You were only there last night.'

'I promised Clive I'd pop my head in. See if he needs a hand.'

She stared him out, and he returned to laces which had already been laced.

*

Dorothy watched from the living-room window. Harold narrowed his eyes at number four and glanced over at number eleven, and then he disappeared round the corner with his hands in the pockets of his shorts.

The house always felt more relaxed without Harold inside it. It was almost as if the walls breathed out, and the floors and the ceilings stretched and yawned, and everybody made themselves more comfortable. This was when she missed Whiskey the most – when they would sit together, feeding on the silence.

She sat back in Harold's chair. She had finished today's

list hours ago, and it lay folded in the pocket of her apron, crossed and ticked and satisfied. If Harold had realized, he would have added to it. A woman's work is never done, he would have said. Especially a woman who dawdles and daydreams, and gets herself confused over everything. But she needed the afternoon to herself. She needed to think.

The box was where it had always been, secreted away in the back of Harold's cupboard, behind the folders of paperwork and sheaves of bank statements, and all the other very important documents Dorothy wasn't considered responsible enough to be involved with.

She had discovered it only by accident.

It was after the fire. Dorothy had begun whittling about their home insurance and what would happen if number six mysteriously burned to the ground. It was keeping her awake at night. She couldn't talk to Harold about it because he found her worrying disagreeable. It shortened his temper and made the whites of his eyes even whiter, and so she had decided to check through the policy herself. To use the initiative that Harold said she was never in possession of.

And that's how she'd found it.

Over the years, every so often, she would wait for Harold to leave the house, and then she would remove the little box and take out all the contents, and sit very quietly and worry to herself.

Today was a day when she felt like worrying. She blamed Margaret Creasy and the endless heat, and watching Sheila

Dakin march across the avenue yesterday with those two little girls in tow.

She sat in the kitchen and spread the contents of the box out on to the table. The windows and the door were all open, but there wasn't even a touch of breeze in the air. It felt as though everything had stopped, even the weather, and the whole world was vanishing in a gasping, final pause.

She ran her fingers over the cardboard, looking for scorch marks, a trace of smoke, an answer to a worry which had stretched itself out over the years. She was so lost in her own thoughts, she didn't hear the footsteps, or notice the shadow in the doorway. She didn't realize anything at all, until she heard his voice.

'Dorothy, what in God's name are you doing?'

Eric Lamb.

He walked over to the table and stared. 'What on earth are you doing with Walter Bishop's camera?' he said.

*

Dorothy filled the kettle and lit a gas ring.

'Harold must have taken it,' she said. 'After the fire. When you went to look round number eleven.'

Eric dragged his fingers through his hair. He left them there, static and staring.

'We didn't take anything,' he said.

'He must have done it when you weren't looking. When your back was turned.'

287

He looked up at Dorothy. 'We didn't take anything,' he said again.

'Perhaps it's just slipped your mind? People get confused, don't they? Harold says I get confused all the time.'

'I remember everything.' Eric sat back and folded his arms, and took a long, deep breath. 'The smell of the smoke, the blackened walls. The way the kitchen was untouched, even the ticking clock and the tea towel folded up on the draining board. I haven't forgotten a thing.'

He picked up the camera and turned it over in his hands. 'And why would Harold take this?'

'For safekeeping,' Dorothy said, 'in case of looters?'

'So why did he never give it back?'

They sat in silence. The only sound was the kettle, tapping and spitting in the corner.

'It's boiling,' Eric said, and nodded at the cooker.

Dorothy reached her hand to her throat. 'Did you put it on?' she said.

'No, Dot, you did.'

Eric reached over and switched off the gas. He picked up one of the envelopes.

'There's nothing interesting in there,' Dorothy said. 'I've already looked through. Pigeons. Clouds. One of a blackbird sitting on a milk bottle.'

'He took a lot of photographs.' Eric picked up another envelope. 'What's in this one?'

Dorothy glanced at it. 'I can't remember. Brian emptying

an ashtray into his dustbin, I think. Beatrice Morton tying her shoelaces. Nothing very interesting.'

'I used to see him when I walked back from the Legion,' said Eric. 'Wandering around in the dark with his camera.'

Dorothy sat very still. 'I know,' she said.

Eric shuffled through the photographs. 'Heaven knows what he saw out there.'

'I know,' Dorothy said again.

He stopped shuffling and looked up. For a moment, their eyes matched in the silence.

'Put it back where you found it, Dot.'

'I just want answers.' Dorothy took a tissue from the sleeve of her cardigan. 'I just need to know how it came to be here. I don't understand any of it.'

'Sometimes all answers do is fill you up with more questions. It's a long time ago now. Just let it lie.'

'But Margaret Creasy's brought it all back up, hasn't she? I swear she knew something, Eric. I swear she knew all our secrets.'

Dorothy began folding the tissue into a square. Over and over, until it became so small, it would stand no more folding.

Eric Lamb put his hands over hers. 'Stop it, Dorothy. Stop whittling over something you can't change. Put it all back where you found it. Hide it away.'

'I'm going to have to, aren't I?' She began straightening the pictures and sliding them into the envelopes. 'I just wish I knew why Harold stole it.'

'What difference does it make, Dot? What does it matter?'

'It matters,' she said.

Eric stood up and pushed the chair back under the table.

'My advice to you', he said, 'is to forget that you ever saw it.'

'I can't.' She held on to the box. It felt heavy and difficult. 'You can't ever forget what you've seen, can you? You don't even need photographs. You can just pull it out of your mind whenever it might be useful to you.'

Number Ten, The Avenue

18 July 1976

Eric Lamb walked across a deserted avenue, although he was swimming so deep in his own thoughts, he probably wouldn't have noticed if someone had stood on the pavement right in front of him.

He knew he was right about number eleven. They'd walked around it, looking at the damage. He hadn't wanted to, but Harold had seen him and shouted him over.

'Check the place is safe,' he'd said. 'Don't want it falling down on one of us.'

A dozen firemen and half the police force had already done that, but there was no point in arguing with Harold. It was much easier to agree with him in the first place, rather than spend the next few days batting him away.

They had walked around number eleven with their hands

in their pockets, staring at the walls and the ceilings, and repeating to themselves how awful it was.

They had taken nothing. They hadn't even touched anything.

And then they had left everything as it was, and told the rest of the avenue what they'd found.

But Dot was right about one thing. She was usually confused and neurotic and irrational, and sometimes her whittling could make you want to tear flesh from your own skull, but on this occasion she was spot on. You could always pull things from your mind when you needed them. The only problem was, they sometimes pulled free all by themselves. Things you would rather forget; things that shifted your view and made an uncertainty creep into your head, no matter how hard you might try to push them away.

23 November 1967

Elsie is upstairs in bed. She has spent more time sleeping lately, although Eric tries not to think about how much, because if he does, he knows he will have to come up with a reason for her tiredness. Something to explain it away, other than her health. It's colder now. The cold makes people more tired, doesn't it? Or perhaps it's because the days are shorter, or because they have been backwards and forwards to the hospital so much just lately. He seems to spend his days searching for explanations and evidence, and reassurance. Rummaging through Elsie's life for a straw he can cling to.

While Elsie sleeps, he has made a very quiet lunch, and now he sits at the very quiet table in the very quiet living room and stares out into the avenue and tries to distract himself.

They have agreed to watch Walter Bishop, each of them in turn. Since the baby went missing, there has been a soundless panic in the street. He has seen it in people's eyes. In the way they hurry themselves indoors. No one passes the time of day any more. No one stands on the corner of the road or leans against a garden fence. Whenever he sees anyone, they are always on their way to somewhere else, and even though they're all watching Walter, it feels as though it's everyone else who has become the prisoner.

Sheila's little girl is in the middle of the avenue, unlacing her roller skates. He's sure Sheila must be watching with him from her own window. The child has been skating across the pavements, stealing handfuls of fences and walls to steady herself, circling the abandoned coat in the middle of the tarmac as her confidence increased. He has listened to the wheels grow with assurance, cutting across the concrete in slow, steady pushes. Now she sits on the edge of the kerb, pulling her feet from the skates, the wheels still spinning, reaching for her coat and dragging it across her shoulders.

There is a noise from upstairs. He wonders if Elsie is waking, and he wants to march up the stairs and help her. Lift her out of bed, find her slippers, button her cardigan. But he knows, deep in the corners of his mind, that there will be many days ahead of doing these things. There will be no wanting or wondering then, only inevitability, and if he starts to do these things now, he will take away the very last slice Elsie seems to have left of herself.

This is when Eric sees him – when he looks back into the avenue.

He can't have been there more than a minute.

Walter Bishop.

He has the child's arm. Pulling it, forcing her backwards.

Lisa is crying, shouting. Trying to get away from him.

As Eric pulls open the front door, he hears his cup smash to the living-room floor.

'What on earth do you think you're doing?' Harold is there a few seconds before. He's pulling the little girl away, loosening Walter Bishop's grip.

The child is screaming now. 'You're a bad man. A bad man. My mam says you steal children.'

Walter jumps back. He loses his footing and stumbles against the kerb. Eric has to stop himself from reaching out to help.

'It was a simple misunderstanding. That's all it was.' Walter's voice can barely be heard above the child's crying. 'I was trying to help.'

'Help?' Eric can hear himself shouting. 'How in God's name were you trying to help?'

'Her coat,' Walter says. 'She was struggling to put it on. It's too tight, you see. I stopped to help.'

He points to the pink duffel coat, which lies at the side of the kerb. Harold snatches it up, as though it might need protecting from Walter as well. As he does, the door of number twelve pulls open and Sheila Dakin rushes across the avenue, her arms trying to fight through the distance more quickly.

When Sheila reaches them, Lisa pins herself to her mother, hiding her tears in the folds of Sheila's sweater.

'How dare you,' says Sheila, 'how very bloody dare you.'

The child acts as a shield, Eric thinks, because without her, he was sure Sheila would take a swing at Walter Bishop.

'I was trying to help, that's all. I'd never hurt a child. I love children.'

'Just go. Get out.' Harold's words spit from his mouth. 'Leave us all in peace.'

Walter Bishop is gone. He picks up his bag from the side of the road and hurries away. His head down, his hair stroking at the collar of his coat. Even as he rushes away, he still seems to shuffle. Rounding his shoulders and pulling in his arms, as though he's trying to take up the smallest amount of room he can manage within the world.

Eric turns to Sheila. He asks if she's all right, and when she replies, the sentence has to fight its way out of her mouth.

'I'm fine. I'm just not feeling too well. It's been a bad day.' She falters, steadying herself against Lisa.

'A bad day?' he says.

'An anniversary – of sorts.'

He can smell it – the brandy – wrapped around each word.

'You should get home,' Harold says. 'Try to get some rest.'

'How can I rest?' Sheila holds on to Lisa a little more tightly. 'How can I rest when that monster is living a few feet away from my child?'

They all look over at number eleven. Walter has disappeared, vanishing his life back inside its walls.

'We've got to get rid of him, Harold,' Sheila says. 'We can't live like this. I'll be damned if that bastard's going to drive me out of my own house.'

She turns away and Eric watches as she walks back with Lisa to number twelve, their arms wrapped around each other for support.

And he wonders which of them needs it the most.

*

After that day, Walter is never left in peace. It moves quickly, the news that he had tried to take another child. With each speaker, it grows in force and fury, gathering hatred as it travels through the estate.

Eric watches it, but says nothing. People ask him about what happened. They try to edge his opinion into the conversation, but he refuses to be trapped. If they want to execute Walter Bishop, then so be it, but he isn't going to provide the ammunition. Harold Forbes, however, seems happy to fashion as many bullets as they might require.

In broad daylight, he hears him say. *Oh yes, pulling her across the road to his house. No child is safe while that man is around.*

The bullets are fired. Eric sees the evidence. The contents of Walter Bishop's dustbin, scattered around his garden each morning. Clothes taken from his washing line and dragged across the mud. Everyone watches, follows, waiting for the slightest stumble, the faintest permission that the trapdoors can be opened.

*

Eric is in the corner shop, a few days after the incident with Lisa. He's trying to find something that might tempt Elsie into eating, custard creams perhaps, or some tinned fruit. She seems to have completely lost interest in food, which is understandable really. The weather has turned, and the nights are long and miserable. It doesn't do much for your appetite, this kind of weather. Everyone says so. He scans the shelves. Cyril doesn't stock much, but you can generally find something amongst the tins of custard powder and boxes of Cornflakes. Behind a pyramid of vegetable soup, Eric can hear a group at the counter. He can make out Sheila Dakin and Harold Forbes, and other voices he doesn't recognize.

They're discussing Walter Bishop. Eric wonders what people talked about before Walter Bishop came along.

'Of course, if it was up to me, he would have been gone

the minute all this started. He wouldn't have had a chance to do anything else.'

It was Harold's voice, asserting itself over the loose-leaf tea.

'The police are next to useless. If he touches my Lisa again, I'm going to be the one they'll have to arrest.'

Sheila Dakin.

Eric walks to the till. There are two others there, men he recognizes from the British Legion, and Lisa, buttoned into her coat. It looks as though they've been putting Walter to rights for a while, because the child has sunk to the floor in order to bite her nails in peace.

'We're just discussing Bishop,' Harold says.

'So I hear.' Eric puts his biscuits down and nods to Cyril behind the counter.

'Terrible business, isn't it?' Sheila says.

Eric knows this is an invitation to dance. 'It is,' he says.

'We were talking about getting up a petition,' says Harold, 'handing it into the council.' The words are delivered as a question.

Eric counts out his coins.

'I don't think a petition will get that man moved,' Sheila says. 'The only thing that's going to shift him out is brute force.'

The child looks at Eric with listening eyes, and he smiles down at her.

Sheila is talking about brute force and considering the appeal of its many flavours, when the little bell on the door interrupts her with a whispered chime of apology. When they turn, it's clear they expect to see someone with an opinion to underpin their own, a fellow supporter of brute force and neighbourhood petitions, but standing in the doorway of the corner shop is Walter Bishop, his coat wet from the rain, the steam already creeping across the surface of his glasses. Their words die in the silence.

Sheila lifts Lisa from the floor, and she takes the child's breath with the force of her grip.

Walter Bishop walks the length of the shop. His shoes squeal across the lino, his bag knocks against tins on the bottom shelves. When he reaches the counter, he takes off his glasses and wipes them on a stained, grey handkerchief. Eric can see the tremor in his hands, the gathering of sweat on leathered skin.

'I wonder,' says Walter Bishop, 'I wonder if I could trouble you for a pint of milk?'

No one speaks.

Behind the counter, Cyril folds his arms, setting his jaw in a line of battle.

Walter Bishop waits. He smiles. It's a faded smile. One fashioned out of optimism rather than happiness, but it's a smile nonetheless. Eric can't decide if Walter Bishop is foolish or just plain stupid.

'We don't have any milk,' Cyril says.

They watch in silence, the others, the conversation ticking in their eyes.

'Just the one pint.' Walter points to a row of milk bottles in the fridge behind the counter.

'We don't have any milk,' Cyril repeats his words. 'In fact, I don't believe we have anything for sale at all in this shop right now.'

Walter holds the shopkeeper's gaze, the smile still hanging on his mouth, but very slowly it begins to drain away, until all that is left in its place is an emptiness. A face looking for a way out, an expression with which it might be able to save itself.

Walter hesitates. Eric can hear the fold of Harold's arms and the tap of Sheila's fingers on the counter.

'Will that be all?' Cyril says.

Walter turns. There are murmured apologies and thank yous, and sentiments so whispered Eric can't even tell if they are real words or just the sound of a man's defeat. After the door has closed, and the little bell has quietened, they all stand together in the silence.

Sheila bangs her fist down on the counter.

'That's what we need,' she says, 'someone to show Walter Bishop what being civil bloody looks like.'

*

They walk back through the estate. Harold is talking, and Sheila is taking in his words, together with lungfuls of Park Drive.

Eric is trying not to listen.

They are weaving plans and petitions, talking about meetings in the Legion, phone calls to the council. Eric has more important things to think about, bigger worries he can use to paper the inside of his head.

He stares ahead. Lisa is climbing on the walls that run alongside the pavement. She's reaching up, trying to touch the lower branches of the trees, stretching to find the twigs with the ends of her fingers. She can't quite manage it, always falling an inch or two short. He watches her. Strange, really. She's a tall girl, you'd think she'd have no problem.

Then he realizes why she's struggling. The reason she can never quite reach. The pink material pulls across her shoulders, holding her back, stopping her from lifting her hands into the branches.

This is the reason she's struggling. It's her duffel coat. It's far too tight.

Number Fourteen, The Avenue

20 July 1976

'I suppose it doesn't really bother you?' said Mr Forbes.

We were all watching Mr Kapoor clean his very big car. I was sitting on the grass, next to Mr Forbes' feet.

Mr Kapoor looked up from his bonnet.

'Doesn't bother me?' he said.

'The heat.' Mr Forbes pointed at the sky, and I watched his heels lifting up from the back of his sandals. 'I don't suppose it gets you down? Like the rest of us?'

Mr Kapoor frowned and rubbed his cloth at a circle of bird poo. He wasn't using any water, or Mrs Morton would have been on to him in seconds.

'Harold means that where you're from, it must be like this all the time.' May Roper was leaning against the fence behind me. I could hear the wood quarrelling with her bosom every time she spoke.

'Birmingham?' said Mr Kapoor.

'Is there a Birmingham in Pakistan as well?' said Mrs Forbes.

Mr Forbes looked at his wife and frowned, and turned back to Mr Kapoor. 'It's in the genes, though, isn't it? They can withstand the heat, the Indians. Hardy race. Put up with a lot.'

'Well, we can agree on that much,' said Mr Kapoor. He was still rubbing very hard at the bird poo, although I couldn't see that there was any left.

'Not that I'm racist.' Mr Forbes' feet rocked backwards and forwards in his sandals. 'Not at all.'

'Not in the slightest,' said Mrs Forbes.

'Not one little bit,' said May Roper.

'I'm just *patriotic*.' He said the word very slowly. 'I want to keep Britain great. It's like an exclusive club, isn't it? You can't go letting any old Tom, Dick or Harry in.'

'Quite right, Harold,' said Mrs Forbes.

Mr Kapoor crouched down and began cleaning the number plate. The heat had brought with it a layer of dust. It was everywhere. It settled on the cars and the pavements and the houses. It even found its way into your skin and your hair. You couldn't get rid of it, no matter how much you washed and cleaned and tried to scrub it away. It made everything seem grubby and disguised.

'In fact, I'm quite multicultural,' Mr Forbes was saying.

Mr Kapoor looked up from his number plate. 'Multicultural?'

'Oh yes.' Mr Forbes feet did some more rocking. 'Definitely multicultural. I'm a big fan of Sidney Poitier, for example.'

'He is,' said Mrs Forbes.

'And Louis Armstrong. Coloured people have got such a good sense of rhythm, haven't they?'

I thought I heard Mr Kapoor say something, but I couldn't quite make out what it was.

'Being patriotic doesn't mean you're not open to new ideas, though. We just need to remember that Britannia rules the waves.' Mr Forbes smiled and agreed with himself.

'You'll be celebrating the Jubilee next year, then?' said Mr Kapoor.

'Celebrating?' Mr Forbes' toes did excited tapping. 'We're going to have the best street party on the estate. I've formed a committee, haven't I, Dorothy?'

'You have, dear,' said Mrs Forbes. She smiled at Mr Kapoor. 'I'm secretary.'

'Well, we've still got to finalize a few things.' Mr Forbes tapped the side of his head, and winked at Mr Kapoor. 'But we're going to put all the other streets to shame.'

'I've heard Pine Crescent are hiring a bouncy castle,' said May Roper, 'a red, white and blue one.' The fence began to creak. 'And Poplar Drive has a conjuror.'

'Do they?' Mr Forbes spun around to look at Mrs Roper. There were little beads of spit in the corners of his mouth. 'Where do they get the money from? We've only got a certain budget, you know.'

Mrs Roper and the fence shrugged their shoulders.

Mr Kapoor stood up and shook the dust from his cloth. 'Perhaps I could help?' he said.

'Oh, I don't think so,' Mr Forbes turned back. 'I'm not sure it's your sort of thing.'

'But I have a friend,' said Mr Kapoor, 'in catering. He'd provide a banquet for you for a very small fee if I had a word with him.'

'He would?' said Mr Forbes.

'Oh yes. Show all the other streets how it's done.'

'Well,' Mr Forbes smiled, and the little beads of spit stretched across his gums, 'that would be very decent of you, if you wouldn't mind.'

'Very decent,' said Mrs Forbes.

'Considering it's for our queen,' said Mrs Roper.

'I'll get on to him right away.' Mr Kapoor opened his front door. 'He makes the best curries this side of Bradford. Very multicultural. You'll love them, Harold.'

The front door closed.

Mrs Kapoor must have said something funny, because as soon as Mr Kapoor disappeared, I heard him start to laugh.

I looked down at Mr Forbes' feet.

His toes were doing a little dance in his sandals. Like piano keys.

Number Four, The Avenue

26 July 1976

I decided that Detective Inspector Hislop must be a much more important policeman than PC Green or PC Hay, because he always travelled in the back of a car, and they allowed him to wear his own clothes.

'He must be from the Serious Crimes Squad,' said Mrs Morton.

'Aren't all crimes serious?' said Tilly, but none of us answered her.

He didn't talk about *Tiswas*, or smell of material, or creak at the knees. Instead, he had long, quiet conversations behind tightly shut doors, and when people finished these conversations, they always looked shiny and slightly bewildered. When it was my father's turn to have a conversation, my mother paced around the house with her arms folded across her chest, and she made three cups of tea, which still sat on the draining board two hours later. Tilly and I stood on the landing, hanging over the banister, watching the top of my mother's head travel up and down the hall.

When my father emerged from his conversation, my mother opened her mouth to let all the questions out, but before they could appear my father held his hand up and shook his head, and disappeared into the front room. He was still in there when I went to bed. For a long time, my mother sat at the bottom of the stairs, her arms wrapped around her knees and her head pressed into her chest. I was beginning to wonder if she'd ever move again, but then she tightened her arms even more, lifted her head and shouted, I don't know about you, Derek, but I can't stand much more of this bloody heat.

The words seemed to swing around in the air afterwards, as if they really didn't want to leave. I turned to Tilly, because I felt as though I needed a smile. But Tilly didn't smile back. Instead, she put her head down and bit her lip, and didn't meet my eyes.

*

On the Monday morning, Detective Inspector Hislop decided to ask the television to bring Mrs Creasy back.

This was to be in the form of an Outside Broadcast, or an Oh Bee, according to Mrs Morton (who, all of a sudden, had become very knowledgeable about these things). Tilly and I decided to wear our best outfits for the Oh Bee, because you never know when you might be called upon to appear on the local news at the very last minute. Sheila Dakin dragged her deckchair to the front end of the lawn for a better view, and Mrs Forbes took off her apron and put on an extra layer of lipstick. Everyone came out into the avenue, including my parents (even though they did stand at different ends of a wall). The only person missing was Mr Creasy. He had just had another conversation with Detective Inspector Hislop and it made him come over all funny, so he was lying on Sheila Dakin's settee, with the curtains drawn and a cold flannel.

The avenue was filled with vans and cables, and people walking about with clipboards and their hands on their hips. There were two reporters from the local newspapers, and they watched Detective Inspector Hislop whilst he paced around in front of Mr Creasy's house with a piece of paper, learning his lines.

'I think I should quite like to be in the local newspaper,' said Tilly.

We were sitting on Mrs Forbes' wall. Normally, Mrs Forbes would have had something to say about this, but she was too busy trying to persuade information out of one of the clipboards.

'Why do you want to be in the local paper?' I said.

Tilly was sitting on her hands. She stretched her legs out and bounced them into the sunshine. 'People would see me,' she said.

I waited.

She bounced her legs a little more.

'Anyone in particular?' I said.

'Well,' she continued to bounce, 'if I was in the local paper, my dad might see. And he might be so proud, he'd get in touch, because he'd want to talk to me about it.'

'Your dad lives in Bournemouth,' I said. 'I don't think they have our local paper in Bournemouth.'

She stopped bouncing and looked at me. 'You just never know, though, do you?' she said.

And I realized she was giving me the words. So I took them and held on for a moment, and then I handed them back. 'No,' I said, 'you just never know.'

And she smiled and went back to her bouncing.

*

When Detective Hislop was ready, PC Green and PC Hay made sure everyone was quiet and well behaved, and knew not to run in front of the camera or bump into the man with the big fluffy microphone. They didn't turn back to Detective Hislop, but stayed watching us all instead, like the policemen at a football match.

The man behind the camera made numbers with his fingers and then pointed at Detective Inspector Hislop, who began to speak.

We all listened.

Concerns are growing for the welfare of a local woman, he said. *Mrs Margaret Creasy was last seen on the night of the 20th of June at her home address.*

He pointed behind, to Mr Creasy's house, and we all stared, as if we had never noticed it was there before.

Mrs Creasy's family and friends state that her disappearance is completely out of character.

He looked down at his notes. When he looked up again, he started to frown very hard, and his face became even more unhappy.

In addition to this, a recent discovery has caused us to become very keen to locate Mrs Creasy and, indeed, to speak to anyone who might have knowledge of her whereabouts.

Everyone on the avenue seemed to lift themselves up a few inches.

Mrs Forbes put down her knitting and strained her neck to listen. Sheila Dakin edged forwards in her deckchair. My father stood up a little straighter, and my mother laced her fingers behind her head. Even Tilly stopped bouncing.

Detective Hislop carried on. *At approximately eleven o'clock yesterday morning, a vigilant member of the public found a pair of shoes which have now been identified as belonging to Mrs Margaret Creasy.*

There was a single breath. It was drawn into our lungs from a thick mask of heat, suspending each of us in the turn of a moment. Sometimes life gave you these moments, I thought. And it always happens when you least expect it.

The shoes, he said, *were found by the side of the canal.*

It was just a tick of silence before the avenue began to unravel.

Mrs Forbes' was the first voice. 'I knew it. Someone's

done her in. I knew it. I knew it.' She began pacing up and down the pavement, like a metronome. Even Mr Forbes taking hold of her shoulders couldn't stop the beat of her anxiety on the concrete. He was hissing words at his wife, trying to pull her into a silence, but anyone watching could see that he was completely wasting his time.

Sheila Dakin launched herself from the deckchair. 'It's Bishop,' she said. 'It's got to be. Who else would do something like that?'

'For Christ's sake, Sheila, we don't even know that she's dead.' It was my father.

Since Detective Hislop had finished speaking, my father had continued to lean against the wall with his palms pressed into his face. Now he shouted across the avenue, and he shouted with such force, my mother laced her fingers even more tightly at the back of her neck and started breathing very quickly through her mouth.

'Of course she's dead.' Sheila had reached the pavement. She was trying to march across the road, but her legs didn't seem to want to do as they were told and she stumbled against the kerb. 'What else would she be?'

'She might have jumped.' May Roper was waddling across her lawn. Brian tried to stop her, but he tangled himself up in the washing line and his attempt was foiled by three tea towels and an extra-long vest. 'She could have thrown herself in. They'll have to dredge it if we're going to have a funeral.'

'For God's sake, May, don't be so bloody morbid,' my father said.

'She's right, though.' Mr Forbes had abandoned Mrs Forbes to her metronoming and was staring into the pavement. 'They'll have to send the divers down.'

'That's what you get,' said Mrs Forbes, as she brushed past him, 'that's what you get for knowing too much about other people's business.'

Everyone began shouting at the same time. Their voices all crowded into one big noise, and it was impossible to hear what anyone was saying. I watched Detective Hislop, who was still standing in front of the camera, his notes folded and pressed into his pocket, and a look of deep satisfaction on his face. I saw him nod very slowly at PC Green and PC Hay, and I saw them nod very slowly back again.

I turned to Tilly, to see if she'd noticed too, but she was staring at Sheila Dakin's lawn. I stared as well, but it took me a moment to see him.

Mr Creasy was lying in the grass. It seemed as though he was curled up asleep, but his eyes were open and his arms were folded around his chest. It looked very much as though he was counting something.

'I don't like this any more,' said Tilly. 'Shall we go inside?'

I said I didn't like it either (even though I did). Quite a bit of me would like to have stayed to see what happened next, but I slid off Mrs Forbes' wall and on to the pavement.

Before I went inside, I turned back to look at number eleven. The curtains in one of the bedrooms were open just a fraction, and Walter Bishop's face was pressed against the glass.

I couldn't be absolutely certain, but I was almost sure I saw him smiling.

*

After Detective Hislop had told us about the shoes, the avenue became very quiet. It was as though everyone had got all their shouting out in one go, and there was nothing left for the rest of the week. Even my parents became quiet, and instead of slamming and screaming and marching, they just slid around the house trying to avoid each other.

I asked several different people if Mrs Creasy was dead now, but no one seemed able to give me a proper answer. My mother switched the television on, my father said *well, now, well*, and suddenly found something important to do in the front room, and Mrs Morton just said *nobody really knows* and stared into space.

For people who didn't really know, everyone was acting very strangely.

Number Four, The Avenue

30 July 1976

It was a Friday morning. Tilly and I sat in the front room with the Kays catalogue and a bottle of Dandelion and Burdock. The curtains were drawn to keep the heat out, but it still managed to get in somehow, and every time I turned a page, the shiny paper stuck to my fingers and didn't want to let go.

'I like this,' I said and pointed to a denim jacket.

Tilly just put her chin into her hands. I knew she was waiting for me to get to the Whimsies.

'Or these,' I said and pointed to a pair of mules.

I circled both of them in green felt tip. I had planned to leave the catalogue and all my circles in a helpful place for people to be interested in them.

'They're very expensive.' Tilly peered at the page in the semi-darkness.

'Only twenty-five pence a week in forty-eight easy instalments,' I said. I underlined *easy*.

'How will you get twenty-five pence a week?'

'I can get a paper round. Lisa Dakin has one.'

'Lisa Dakin is a lot older than us, Gracie. We're too
young to do a paper round.'

I circled a tartan scarf. Sometimes, I could hear Tilly say
something before she even let the words go.

'She's not that much older,' I said.

'Do you want a game of Monopoly?'

'Not really.'

'Do you want to go round to Mrs Morton's?'

'Not really.'

We sat in silence while I circled.

'Why are you circling all of Lisa Dakin's clothes?'

I stopped circling Lisa Dakin's clothes. 'I'm not,'
I said.

'Yes you are. Why do you want her to like you so
much?'

I looked at all my circles. Sometimes Tilly said questions
that were already in your head, but you didn't especially
want them to be asked.

'If Lisa Dakin likes me, then the rest of the school might
like me as well,' I said.

Tilly took her chin out of her hands. 'I don't think
people like that really matter, Gracie. We've got each
other, haven't we?'

'Of course they matter. Everyone wants to be popular.

Everyone needs people to like them, don't they?' I turned the catalogue pages over and stared at pictures of models with their hands on their hips, laughing at each other. 'It's normal, isn't it?'

'I only want you and Mrs Morton, and my mum and dad to like me,' said Tilly. 'Anyone else is a bonus.'

'Then you're not really normal, are you?' I picked up my felt tip again. 'Not like Lisa Dakin.'

I knew Tilly was staring at me, but I didn't look. If I looked, it would mean I'd see her face, and if I saw her face, I knew I would have to say sorry.

'I might go home for a bit,' she said.

I heard her standing up and leaving the room, but I kept my eyes on the circles.

'Bye then,' I shouted.

But she had already gone.

*

The house was very quiet. I could hear my felt tip sliding over the catalogue pages, but there wasn't anything else I really wanted to circle.

I went into the sitting room, but that was very quiet as well, and the only sound in the kitchen was Remington, snoring under the table. It was strange, but the only thing I really felt like doing right at that moment was having a game of Monopoly.

I needed Tilly to come back.

I knew she'd come back eventually. Perhaps that was half the problem.

I put my head in the fridge to cool down.

*

They were a few minutes later than I thought they would be, but I caught them above the whirr of the refrigerator – Tilly's sandals, slapping on the path that reached around the side of the house.

The sandals were very fast and very loud, and before I had a chance to take my head out of the ice box, she was flinging the back door open with such force, the glass rattled against the wood.

'Gracie!' she shouted.

Tilly never shouted. Once, she was stung by a wasp, and it took ten minutes for any of us to realize.

'Why are you shouting?' My head was back in the kitchen, and I could feel the heat creep into my face.

'You've got to come now,' she said. Her face was tomato red, and the words struggled to leave her mouth with all the breath in there. 'Now,' she said again.

'Why?'

I wrapped my arms around my chest and leaned against the fridge door, so I wouldn't look interested.

'You'll never guess who's at the end of the avenue. You'll never guess.'

She repeated 'you'll never guess' a few more times, just

in case I was under the ridiculous impression that I might be able to guess.

I leaned a bit more. 'Who?' I said, and looked at my fingernails.

Tilly took another deep breath, and when she spoke, she made sure the words came out with as much force as her lungs could possibly muster. 'It's Jesus!'

The Drainpipe

30 July 1976

I think we might have left the back door open, but I couldn't be certain.

We fell out of the kitchen in a tangle of questions and Tilly's cardigan got caught on the door handle. Remington woke up to see what all the noise was about, and was nearly fallen over as we tried to get outside.

'I don't understand,' I said.

We tipped out on to the path. I realized I wasn't wearing any shoes, but it didn't matter. The concrete was as warm as carpet.

'You'll see,' she said, and her excitement pulled me along the side of the house and down the avenue.

We passed Mr Forbes, who watched us from his lawn.

'Jesus is here,' I said, by way of an explanation. He continued to stare, but a touch of a frown wandered into his eyebrows.

Sheila Dakin looked up from cooking herself and rested on her elbows. She screened her eyes from the sun and waved, and I slowed down to wave back.

'Come on,' said Tilly. 'He might leave!'

We reached the far end of the avenue, where a small patch of grass blended into a spray of chippings. Tilly stopped very suddenly and held on to my elbow. There were two council garages there, but both of them were empty and their shutters had long since disappeared. Shells of cool, dark concrete stared back at us, but no Jesus – just rainbow pools of spilled oil and the soft conversation of leaves in dusty corners.

'Where did he go?' I said.

Tilly made a strange squeak and nodded towards the nearest garage. I took a few steps forward, followed by Tilly, who still held on to my elbow.

The little white stones bit into my feet.

'There,' she said, 'look.'

I looked. There wasn't anything. 'There isn't anything,' I said.

I had expected Jesus to be waiting for me, wearing a clean, white robe with deep sleeves, and a neat beard, and possibly a generous smile. Instead, there was a torn bin liner and a rotten tyre, and where I expected Jesus to be standing were lines of thirsty weeds, marking the place where paving slabs had once sat.

'There,' Tilly said and nodded into fresh air.

I didn't move. She gave a small sigh and pulled me towards the outside wall of the garage. 'There,' she said.

I looked again. Nothing. 'All I see is a drainpipe.'

'Grace, look at the drainpipe!'

I looked at the drainpipe. It was made of some kind of ceramic. I thought it must have been white at some point, but now it was peeled and chipped and there was a large brown stain near the bottom, where something had been spilled.

I looked at the stain again.

'Do you see it?' Tilly said.

I crouched down to get a better look. There were swirls of paint or creosote. Patchy marks of brown where the tip of someone's brush had grazed the pipe. But there was something odd about it, something almost familiar.

I sat back and made my eyes very narrow.

And then I saw Him – as plain as anything. So obvious that I couldn't imagine why I hadn't noticed Him in the first place.

'Jesus!' I shouted.

And Tilly began to squeal.

*

Tilly's squealing brought Mr Forbes out of his garden, and because Sheila Dakin had seen him leave, she felt obliged to leave too, in case she missed out on a situation which required her presence.

They crouched next to us in front of the drainpipe. I could smell sun cream and tobacco.

Mr Forbes turned his head this way and that. He took

his glasses off and moved them backwards and forwards between his face and the drainpipe.

'Do you see?' I said.

He moved his glasses a bit more, and then all of a sudden he fell back into his shorts.

'Jesus Christ!' he said.

'Exactly!' said Tilly.

Sheila Dakin saw Him at the same time, and said *bloody hell* and blew Lambert & Butler all over the Son of God.

Mr Forbes told her to be careful, and we all waved our arms around, and everyone started coughing (except Mrs Dakin, who seemed to have done all her coughing on the way over).

'I'm going to get Dorothy,' said Mr Forbes. 'This will perk her up no end.'

Sheila Dakin ground her cigarette into the chippings with the tip of her slipper. She peered in at Jesus.

'He looks bloody miserable, though, doesn't he?' she said.

'I always imagined that when I met Jesus, he'd be quite cheerful,' said Tilly. 'I thought he'd wear a long smock and look people in the eye.'

'Me too,' I said.

We both stared at the drainpipe.

I tilted my head to one side. 'Perhaps he's having an off day.'

*

'I haven't finished my list yet, Harold.'

I could hear Mrs Forbes being led along the pavement. When she appeared, she had a duster tucked into the waist-band of her apron, and Mr Forbes' arms around her shoulders, as though he were guiding the blind through traffic.

'Harold, you're confusing me again.'

'Just open your eyes and look,' he said.

She stood very still and stared at the garage, and her hand went straight to her mouth.

I wondered which words were trying to escape.

'Jesus,' she said. 'Jesus is in the . . .'

'Drainpipe,' said Mr Forbes.

'Well, I never did.'

She saw Him straight away.

*

By lunchtime, Drainpipe Jesus had caused quite a commotion.

Mr Forbes fetched a selection of deckchairs, and Mrs Forbes insisted on sitting as close as possible to Jesus, without blocking His view of anyone. She took a tissue from her sleeve and dabbed her nose with it.

Every so often she said, 'It's a sign.'

'Of what?' I whispered.

But no one answered.

At one point, Sheila Dakin said *God knows* under her breath, but she nipped home for a T-shirt to cover herself up, just in case.

Under the circumstances, she said.

After half an hour, Eric Lamb appeared, in thick wellington boots covered in soil. He left a trail right up to Jesus, where he bent down and stared at Him straight in the eyes.

'I don't see it,' he said.

'How can you not see it?' Mrs Forbes stopped at dabbing her nose. 'It's as plain as a . . . as a . . .'

'Pikestaff,' shouted Mr Forbes.

'It's just a creosote stain, Dot.' Eric stood back and folded his arms. 'Just a regular, everyday creosote stain. The heat must have brought it out.'

Mrs Forbes tightened her eyes and arched an eyebrow. 'Well, I suppose it's a question of faith, Eric, isn't it?' she said.

And strangely, when Eric Lamb stepped back and squinted, and stared at the drainpipe from a different angle, he did in fact find that it was Jesus after all. 'I'll be damned,' he said.

Mrs Forbes just nodded and told Mr Forbes to fetch people a glass of lemonade.

Sheila Dakin said, *a glass of sherry might be nice*, but everyone ignored her.

Mr Forbes returned with lemonade and more deckchairs, and we all sat in the shade of the garages, with the rotten tyre and the dusty leaves and Jesus.

'What do you think it means?' said Sheila Dakin.

Thin Brian sat on the grass in his plastic jacket. He'd

started off in a deckchair, but it had to be abandoned because, every time he moved, it tried to fold him up.

'I reckon it's a warning,' he said. 'Like when you see a magpie or break a mirror. I reckon it means there's trouble coming.'

'Don't be ridiculous, lad.' Harold Forbes took out his pipe. 'They're just superstitions. This is religion.'

'Well, he's obviously here to tell us something.' Mrs Forbes disappeared the tissue again and sipped at her lemonade. 'He must have a message.'

'What kind of message?' said Tilly.

'I'm not sure.' Mrs Forbes bit into her top lip. 'But that's what Jesus does, isn't it? He brings messages.'

People shifted on canvas seats and Tilly drew her knees up to her chest. 'What could Jesus have to say to any of us?' she whispered.

Harold Forbes coughed, and everyone else just shuffled their feet in the chippings.

'Do you think Jesus is trying to tell us Margaret Creasy is still alive?' said Mrs Dakin. 'That she didn't fall in the canal after all?'

'Don't be so ridiculous, Sheila. Of course she's not alive.' Harold Forbes rearranged his shorts on the deckchair. 'People's shoes don't turn up at the side of a canal without good reason.'

Mrs Forbes crossed herself and looked at the drainpipe out of the corner of her eye.

'We need the vicar,' she mouthed, 'to translate.'

*

It was about half past three when Mrs Morton appeared. She had been alerted by a telephone call just after *The Archers*, and had brought her reading glasses along especially.

'I didn't know how tall He'd be,' she said.

She peered and frowned like everyone else had, then Mrs Forbes told her to step back a bit, and when she did, the shock of seeing Jesus sent her straight into a deckchair.

'Isn't it exciting?' I said.

'Who found him?' said Mrs Morton.

Tilly shuffled along the grass until she was level. 'I did,' she said. 'I was hanging around here, trying to decide whether to go home or go back to Grace's and say sorry.'

Mrs Morton looked at me, but didn't comment. 'Well, you should be very proud,' she said to Tilly. 'He wasn't easy to spot. It was obviously meant to be.'

Tilly turned to me. 'Perhaps the newspaper will want to interview us,' she said. 'Perhaps people all over the place will see us. Even people from Bournemouth.'

'Perhaps,' I said.

'I wonder if I should wear a dress.' She scratched at a stain on her cardigan sleeve. 'Although perhaps people won't recognize me if I don't wear a cardigan. I want to make sure people recognize me, don't I, Gracie?'

'Definitely,' I said.

'You were the one who found Him, though, Tilly, not Grace,' said Mrs Morton.

'But we're friends.' Tilly looked at me. 'We go halves on everything. Even Jesus.'

We both stared at the drainpipe and smiled.

Number Two, The Avenue

30 July 1976

'What do you mean, Jesus?' May Roper pulled the crocheted sea a little further up her legs.

'On the drainpipe. I've seen Him with my own eyes.'

'Have you been in the sun again, Brian?'

'Sheila Dakin thinks it's a sign.'

'A sign she's been at the sherry.'

Brian turned back to the window. There was quite a crowd now, and he could see Harold Forbes, marching around in the middle of it all in his shorts. 'Everyone's out there, Mam. They reckon it's something to do with Margaret Creasy going missing.'

'You don't need to be Jesus to work out what's happened there. You've only got to look at number eleven.'

Brian frowned, but said nothing. 'They reckon the vicar from St Anthony's is coming later,' he said.

'The vicar?'

'Maybe even a bishop. You know, to give it the green light. As a miracle.'

'Why on earth would the Lord God Almighty choose to perform a miracle on this avenue?' said his mother. 'I doubt very much the vicar will even give Jesus the time of day.'

'I think he will.' Brian took one more look and straightened the curtain. 'Dorothy Forbes is in charge of it all.'

'Dorothy Forbes? In charge?'

'Oh, yes. Definitely in charge.' He turned from the window. 'What are you doing?'

His mother had unwrapped herself from the crochet and was on her feet. 'I'm going over there, of course,' she said. 'If anyone's in charge of Jesus, it's going to be me.'

The Drainpipe

30 July 1976

The afternoon passed by and we passed by along with it.

Mrs Forbes refused to leave the Son of God, for fear
of Him disappearing on us, and May Roper refused to
leave Mrs Forbes. Eric Lamb said it was quite relaxing,
sitting in the sunshine, and Sheila Dakin kept dozing off,
so we all sat together, fanning ourselves with the backs
of our hands and talking about nothing in particular. Other
people came and went – people who didn't live on the
avenue, but had heard about Jesus in the corner shop, or
over a washing line. They admired Jesus from a safe
distance, designated by Mrs Forbes as being just beyond
Sheila Dakin's left foot. She wasn't taking any chances,
she said. They were tolerated interlopers in our small
corner of the world. We were kindred, locked together

330

by Jesus, and sitting in a circle around Him, like pieces of a jigsaw, waiting to fit.

*

When I returned from having my tea, I brought my mother and father back with me.

My mother was easy to persuade, because it was a choice between Jesus and the washing-up, but my father had to be talked into it.

'Are you serious?' he said.

I said that I was, and he picked at his teeth and said the heat must have affected us all.

'At least give it a look, Derek.' My mother put the unopened Fairy Liquid back on the window ledge. 'It won't do any harm.'

And so we waited for him to finish getting round all his teeth, and pull his shirt sleeves down and button the cuffs, and put a lead around Remington (who didn't really need a lead, but everyone played along with it), and we walked to the end of the avenue in thick evening sunshine, through clouds of anxious midges, accompanied by my father's sighing and smirking, and saying that the whole world had gone bloody mad.

Mr and Mrs Forbes had been persuaded to go inside and have their dinner, and Mrs Forbes had nominated Mrs Morton to be left in charge of Jesus. She had taken up her post on Mrs Forbes' vacant deckchair and was being very serious about everything, although she was also involving herself in some knitting at the same time. Eric Lamb sat in the next deckchair, unwinding wool for her from a thick, blue skein.

My father raised his eyebrows. 'Busy?' he said.

Eric Lamb smiled. 'Makes a change,' he said, 'brings back a few nice memories.'

My father tried to peer around them. 'Well, where is He, then?' He looked up and down the garage wall. 'Grace says you've got Jesus stuck in a drainpipe.'

My mother clasped her hands and leaned forward as far as she could without falling over.

'He's there.' Mrs Morton pointed with a size 7 needle. 'But be careful you don't breathe on Him, we're not sure how resilient He is yet.'

My parents shuffled forward, to stand before the Son of God and Mrs Morton's rows of stocking stitch.

I could tell the moment my mother saw Him, because she gave a little squeak and jumped backwards. 'He doesn't look very happy, though, does He?' she said, leaning in again.

My father took a step closer and squinted, and pulled a face so all his teeth were showing. He turned his head to the left, and then to the right, and then he stood back and frowned. 'It looks more like Brian Clough to me,' he said.

Mrs Morton took a shocked breath.

My father started turning his head again. 'It does, though, doesn't it? Do you not see there?' (He started to point, but Mrs Morton's knitting needle interrupted him.) 'It's the eyebrows.'

'No, it's definitely Jesus,' said Mrs Morton. 'It's the nose, you see. Couldn't possibly be anyone else.'

'Shame, though.' Sheila Dakin leaned back in her deck-chair. 'Our Keithie would be down like a shot if he thought we'd got Cloughie here instead.'

Number Eight, The Avenue

30 July 1976

There were eleven of them now.

John could see it all from the front-room window, although the piles of letters and photographs had become so high, he had to squeeze between them to peer through the glass. There were a lot of comings and goings: Sheila rushing around with a T-shirt, Harold fetching a stack of deckchairs. A few hours ago, he'd watched May Roper roll up her sleeves and march over there as if she was going into battle.

He wanted to go and see for himself what was going on, but he couldn't face the questions. He'd managed to avoid everyone since they'd found Margaret's shoes. Sheila had knocked on the door a couple of times and he'd seen Brian skulking around outside, looking up at the windows, but he'd generally done quite a successful job of hiding himself away.

PC Green had been a little more persistent, but then policemen always were. He'd knocked at the front and at the back, but it was only when he started shouting through the letterbox that John thought he'd better answer before PC Green summoned up the entire avenue with the racket he was making.

He wanted to know if John would like a liaison officer.

John explained, very politely he thought, that he didn't liaise with anyone, least of all policemen.

PC Green had told him to try and stay calm, and John said, how was he supposed to do that with DI Hislop rushing around suggesting all sorts of ridiculous things about what might have happened to Margaret. It was obvious she'd be back when she was good and ready. It was their wedding anniversary soon, she'd definitely return for that, and he didn't care what PC Green, PC Hay or even Detective Hislop had to say about it.

PC Green had just stared at him and breathed with an open mouth, which – as John had pointed out to him quite correctly – was a principal cause of halitosis and proven to lead to a more than significant increase in the risk of oral cavities.

Since then, PC Green had left him alone. He knew he should ring DI Hislop and tell the truth, but there was no way any of them would understand. He'd only get himself into a whole lot of trouble.

It was actually just as well if he didn't ring. John didn't trust himself with policemen. He really didn't trust himself with anyone, because his mouth always seemed to run away with him. He always ended up saying something he wished he hadn't, and if he hadn't rabbited on to Brian when he was twelve years old, he wouldn't be in the mess he was in now.

16 November 1967

There is a darkness on the avenue.

Long shadows creep over silent, frosted lawns and heavy skies press into the slate-grey roofs. John Creasy watches through the glass. He stirs his tea very carefully, keeping the edge of the spoon away from the china, worried that the noise might somehow wake the darkness and allow it to roam free.

The tea is too hot and too sweet. Since his father died, his mother has filled his life with starch and sugar. He wonders if it's a way to keep him here, to slow him down with so much butter and cream, so that he will be too full and too drowsy to ever consider the idea of leaving her.

We've got to keep our strength up, she says.

Although he isn't entirely sure what for.

He can hear her now, kneading stoicism into a thick pastry, and measuring out spoonfuls of endurance for the mixing bowl.

He wipes the rim of the cup with a clean handkerchief and looks back at the window.

Since last week, the avenue has turned in on itself. He has watched it happen. He has watched Eric Lamb lift the collar on his coat, and Sheila Dakin tighten a cardigan around her shoulders and bury her thoughts into the wool. He has watched milk bottles snatched from doorsteps and the snap of curtains as they are pulled to in the earliest dusk of a November evening. He has watched the silence grow. He has watched it creep into every corner of the street, and now the avenue seems to have drifted into one long silence, stitched together only by nods and stares and wordless eyes.

He watches Brian cross the street and stand in front of number eleven. Most days, he sees Brian do this.

Sometimes Harold Forbes wanders across and joins Brian, his arms folded, his gaze set on the dusty quiet of Walter Bishop's front door. John has seen Sheila do the same, too. He has seen her put bags of shopping down in the middle of the road and look up at the windows of number eleven, and pinch her lips into a thin streak of loathing.

They seem to take it in turns, John thinks. Brian, Harold, Sheila, Derek. A clockwork of people, a timetable of staring and watching, of trying to pull Walter Bishop out into an well-lit arena where he can be prodded and examined, and assessed.

Despite their best efforts, Walter has stayed in the shadows. No one has seen him.

John wonders if Walter only comes out at night, if he finds a reassurance somewhere within the darkness, a beat of comfort from footsteps echoing on a blackened pavement, and although he would never admit it to Brian or Harold or Sheila, John can understand how that feels.

He wipes the cup again and places it in the middle of the table, away from the edge, an edge where it might be in danger from a careless elbow or the brush of a newspaper. The movement seems to catch Brian's attention and John finds himself waving back through the glass, even though he does his very best to disappear behind an artificial Paradise Palm his mother has placed in the centre of the windowsill.

Unbelievably realistic — you will fool everyone! The ticket still hangs from one of the stalks.

John disengages himself from a frond and makes his way outside.

*

Brian has moved a few steps back and is leaning against the fence which runs between Harold Forbes' house and the Bennetts'. John leans against the fence as well. He doesn't even want to think about how many germs are on there, but he's discovered over the years that it's sometimes less trouble to go along with what everyone else wants you to do.

When he asks Brian what's going on, Brian's reply is a nod at Walter Bishop's house.

John stares over at Walter's house as well, because this is what Brian is doing and it seems to be expected of him. John has done this since school, this watching and copying of Brian. Brian was his reconnaissance, his only template for what the world might eventually require of him.

They continue to stare at number eleven, although John isn't sure what it's achieving.

'He'll get what's coming,' Brian says eventually.

The fence is uncomfortable. John can feel the wood scuff and scratch his legs, even through the material of his trousers.

'You really think Walter took the baby?' he says.

Brian folds his arms. 'Who else would it be?'

John glances around the avenue, but says nothing.

There are forty-seven bricks in Sheila Dakin's garden wall – more if you add up the half bricks, but they could falsify the result, so he decides to ignore them.

Sylvia Bennett is walking up the avenue with bags of shopping pulling at her arms, and they move their legs to allow her past. She notices, but keeps her eyes to the pavement. As she walks next to them, John can smell her perfume. It's heavy and dark, and it clings to the air long after she has disappeared. Brian is still looking at the space she has moved through.

'You're still sweet on her, aren't you?' says John.

A flush creeps across Brian's face. 'Don't be so bloody daft,' he says. 'She's married.'

'You've always been sweet on her. Since school.'

John knows Brian used to wait in corridors, planning his day so he could steal awkward stares. A congested child-hood, stuffed with a quiet desperation and not knowing where to stand. Neither of them had a template for girls. They still didn't.

John nods back at number four. 'She looks a bit like Julie Christie.'

'Julie Christie my arse,' says Brian.

They go back to staring at Walter Bishop's. The afternoon is edging away, taking the silhouettes of the trees and the wet, grey streak of distant rooftops. The streetlight clicks and buzzes and starts to glow pink.

'How long are you going to keep this up?' John says.

'As long as it takes to flush him out. Harold's taking over at four.'

'And then what? What are you going to do once you've got him?'

Brian just stares.

'You can't be serious?'

'He's a nonce, John, a bloody pervert. He doesn't belong on this avenue. Everyone wants him gone.'

Brian shifts his weight against the wall. 'I would have thought you'd be the first to want to see the back of him.'

John feels a twist of anxiety find its way into the bottom of his throat. 'I don't understand,' he says.

'You know. What with your dad.'

For once, John is glad he is leaning against something,

because he can feel his legs pull away from him in waves. 'I don't know what you mean,' he says.

Brian stares at him and looks back at number eleven. 'Yes, you do.'

Yes, he does.

He can remember the conversation, rushed and whispered, in the school changing rooms after everyone had left. He was only looking for another template, for reassurance – for someone to tell him that this happened to everybody. He should have done what his dad told him to and kept it to himself.

He doesn't look at Brian as he speaks. 'You got it wrong. I was confused,' he says. 'It was just a misunderstanding.'

Brian's eyes are still on Walter's house. 'No, it wasn't, John.'

If you count the half bricks, there are sixty. Sixty seconds in a minute, sixty minutes in an hour. It's a good number is sixty – safe and reliable. You can't really go wrong with sixty.

The sound of a front door makes them both look across the avenue. Harold is walking along the pavement, in a pool of orange streetlight, his hands behind his back, his spine as straight as time will allow. He looks like an old soldier, although John knows Harold has never served even a minute for his country.

His country didn't want him, apparently. Touchy subject, Dorothy always says, whenever anyone mentions it.

'Reporting for duty, sixteen hundred hours,' says Harold, as he reaches them. 'Any movement?'

Brian pushes himself back off the fence. 'Nothing,' he says. 'John and I were just saying how much we want this pervert out of here, weren't we, John?'

Brian stares at him, but John says nothing.

There are thirteen tiles on top of Sheila Dakin's wall.

John starts to walk away. Away from the stares and the questions, and the past creeping its way into his present.

Thirteen has always been a bad number for him. There were thirteen steps, but there were only twelve if you didn't count the one just before you reached upstairs, because that was more of a mini landing.

He closes the gate behind him, and starts to walk back up the garden path.

He was confused. It was just a misunderstanding. His mother had said so.

The Drainpipe

31 July 1976

It was before ten, but Jesus had already pulled quite a crowd.

Mr and Mrs Forbes were sitting at a fold-up card table which Mr Forbes had carried over from their garage, and they were teaching Sheila Dakin and Eric Lamb how to play Canasta.

No, eleven cards, Sheila. The pile is frozen now, do you see?

A river of ants poured themselves over Mrs Forbes' discarded cereal bowl, which lay at her feet on the grass, and a rogue wasp lazed around Eric Lamb's head.

But I don't understand why I can't take a card. You just took a card.

Mrs Morton stood before Jesus with a glass of orange juice and the *Daily Telegraph* wedged under her arm.

'What I don't understand', she said to no one in particular, 'is why we didn't notice Him in the first place.'

343

Eric Lamb leaned back in his deckchair, and it gave a growl of discomfort. 'We don't always see things, though, do we?' he said. 'We walk past the same scenes every day without ever looking at them properly.'

'I suppose so.' She walked a few paces to the left, stared at Jesus and sipped some more orange juice. 'He's just so obvious, though, isn't He?'

Eric Lamb's deckchair growled again. 'It's often the most obvious things that we miss.'

'Plus,' said Mr Forbes, 'it might be the heat.'

Mrs Morton turned around and her shoes shuffled around in the chippings. 'The heat?'

'The heat might have brought Him out,' said Mr Forbes. 'It does strange things, does the heat.'

Sheila Dakin readjusted her T-shirt, and Mrs Morton walked around the duster, which had fallen from Mrs Forbes' waistband the previous day and had never been picked up.

'It does indeed,' she said.

'It brings you out in a rash, doesn't it, Mam?' said Thin Brian.

'Does it?' May Roper lifted her face to the sky and smiled. 'I can't say that I've ever noticed.'

*

It was mid-morning. Mrs Morton had decided to take a nap and Eric Lamb had rolled his trouser legs up a little more, and Mrs Forbes went to fetch some biscuits, *to keep everyone going.* My father sat staring at a newspaper and my mother sat staring at my father, and Mrs Dakin had positioned Keithie at a safe distance. I could hear him, kicking the ball against the far wall of the garages and rummaging around for it in the hedge bottom a few minutes later.

Tilly had arrived with a packed lunch and a clean cardigan, in case the newspaper reporters turned up, and we sat on the grass reading an old copy of *Jackie* I'd found under the settee. Tilly didn't read as quickly as I did, and every few minutes I was forced to stare at the page and pretend, whilst I ate the packed lunch and waited for her to catch up. Sometimes, I made her wait instead, so she would never suspect.

I was just in the middle of pretending, when I heard footsteps.

'Well, I never did,' said the footsteps. 'This is where you all are.'

It was Mr Kapoor. He walked over to the drainpipe, bent down and stared at it. 'Whatever do we have here?'

Mr Forbes got up from his deckchair and joined him. 'This is Jesus,' he said, and jabbed his finger towards the wall. 'From the Bible.'

Tilly looked up. 'Is Mr Kapoor deaf?' she said.

I frowned. 'I don't think so.'

My father stood up as well, and all three of them gathered in front of the drainpipe.

'He's the Son of God.' My father smiled and nodded

345

at Mr Kapoor. 'I know it's a bit confusing to an outsider.' He kept smiling and nodding, even after his words had finished.

Mr Kapoor bent down a little further and squinted. He moved around the drainpipe and leaned in a little further, and then he straightened up and turned to my father and said, 'To be honest, I think it looks more like Brian Clough.'

My father said, *Ha!* and laughed, and slapped Mr Kapoor on the back.

It was a bit unfortunate, but in fairness, my father doesn't always know his own strength.

*

The vicar arrived at four o'clock, just in time for macaroons, which Mr Forbes passed around, along with some milky tea and half a packet of Malted Milks. Mrs Forbes stood up from her deckchair, to give the vicar a better view, and he paced around Jesus with his hands behind his back. Every so often, he rocked backwards on his heels and nodded. He was wearing ordinary trousers and an ordinary shirt. I could still smell candles.

'Where's his cloak?' whispered Tilly.

I shrugged my shoulders. 'Dunno,' I said, 'perhaps he only wears it for God.'

Someone coughed and I heard chippings move beneath people's feet. Mrs Forbes said *Well*?

The vicar frowned and drew air in through his teeth. 'I

don't think Jesus has ever dropped in on the East Midlands before,' he said eventually.

May Roper beamed, as though she were personally responsible for arranging the visit.

'But you see Him, don't you?' Sheila Dakin took a step forward. The vicar drew more air between his teeth and she stepped back again.

'The thing is,' he began to say. And then he stopped and looked at everyone.

Mr Forbes was handing the macaroons around. Eric Lamb had taken off his wellington boots and was lying on the grass in rolled-up trouser legs. Sheila Dakin was pouring him another glass of lemonade. Mr Kapoor and my father were playing Canasta, and Mrs Forbes was smiling. Everyone was smiling.

The vicar frowned, but his face became softer. 'I think it's a very special thing you have here,' he said eventually.

Mrs Forbes applauded.

After a few seconds, she stopped very abruptly. 'I do hope we're not going to be overrun with pilgrims,' she said. 'They'll make a terrible mess.'

*

Jesus gave us all a routine.

Mrs Forbes would always be there first, to claim her deckchair next to the drainpipe, although one day Mrs Roper almost beat her to it and they had a race in their slippers along the pavement. Mrs Kapoor taught my mother how to make Indian biscuits, and Sheila Dakin became a champion at Canasta. Eric Lamb brought us all tomatoes and sweet peas from his garden, and Clive from the British Legion walked down with his dog and handed out pork scratchings. Keithie played football with Shahid. It was better for him, really. He didn't lose the ball so often, because whenever he kicked it away, there was always someone there to kick it back to him. When my father and Mr Kapoor got home from work, they would sit in the corner on their deckchairs, and Mr Kapoor would tell my father all about India. Not about the poverty and the squalor, but about the temples and the gardens, and about a country filled with so much colour and light and music, we all said we would like to visit one day. Of course, everyone knew we never would, but that wasn't really the point.

Tilly said everyone was happy because of the weather. She said it was the warmth of the sun on people's faces and the whispery breeze that came through the leaves of the alder trees. She said it was the smell of summer that made people smile, as it pushed out of the flowers and the grass, and Eric Lamb's bags of tomatoes. I didn't think it was, though. I thought it was something else. I liked to think Walter Bishop was right, that it was because everyone had found something they could believe in. I watched them from time to time, when they thought no one was looking – they would each glance across at the drainpipe and smile, as if they had made an arrangement with Jesus, as if they had all suddenly found another way of seeing everything.

Looking back, I can't remember when it all started to go wrong. It was difficult to tell, but I know that you could smell it travelling through the air. Like rain.

The Drainpipe

2 August 1976

'It's been six weeks,' said Sheila Dakin.

Mrs Forbes looked up from her puzzle book. 'Since what?' she said.

'Since Margaret Creasy went missing.'

Tilly and I were lying on the grass under the alder tree. I nudged her with my spare elbow.

Mrs Forbes didn't reply. She returned to her puzzle book. For someone who always looked very puzzled, she didn't seem to be doing much puzzling.

'I mean, it makes you wonder, doesn't it?' said Mrs Dakin.

'It makes you wonder what?' said Mrs Forbes.

'It makes you wonder if she's ever coming back.'

'Of course she's not.' Harold Forbes stood up from his deckchair and began patrolling the length of the drainpipe wall. 'Lying at the bottom of that canal, that woman. As sure as eggs is eggs.'

Mrs Dakin looked over at me and Tilly.

We had anticipated this and were feigning sleep.

'So why haven't they dredged it, Harold?' Sheila Dakin took off her sunglasses and squinted over at him. 'I thought they would have sent the divers down there by now.'

'It's all about this.' Mr Forbes made money signs with his hands. 'They don't want to spend the cash.'

'He's right, you know,' said May Roper. 'Everything's run on money these days.'

Mrs Roper and Mr Forbes nodded approval at each other.

'I promise you she's down there, though.' Mr Forbes stopped patrolling. He rocked on his heels with his hands behind his back, staring at Jesus. 'Bottom of that canal. As dead as a dodo.'

'She's not dead.'

We all turned.

It was John Creasy. He stood at the edge of the pavement. I could see his shirt drifting from his trousers, and his eyes heavy and unsure.

'John!' Mr Forbes clapped his hands together and did a little bounce with his knees. 'We were wondering when you'd turn up. Come and sit down. Come and meet Christ.'

Mr Forbes ushered him past the drainpipe and into a deckchair.

'She's not dead.' John Creasy stared at Jesus as he walked past. 'She really isn't.'

Mr Forbes said, *No, no, of course*, and *Sit yourself down, John*, and *Have a glass of Dorothy's lemonade*.

Mr Creasy had the glass put into his hands. 'She really isn't dead, Harold,' he said.

Mr Forbes crouched next to the deckchair. 'I think we have to be like good sailors, John. Hope for the best, prepare for the worst. It's the shoes, you see. There's no denying the shoes.'

'The shoes don't matter.' Mr Creasy still held on to the lemonade. 'They really don't.'

Harold Forbes looked over at Mrs Dakin, and I saw him raise his eyebrows for support.

'They wouldn't be next to the canal, though, would they, John,' she said, 'if Margaret was all right?'

'I've told you.' Mr Creasy put the glass down with such force, lemonade slipped over the edges and spilled on to the grass. 'The shoes don't mean anything.'

Mrs Dakin frowned at him. 'How can you be so sure, John?' she said.

He folded his arms and looked up at her. 'Because I put them there.'

*

'What the hell do you mean, you put them there?' Harold Forbes stood up and dusted chippings from his hands.

'She forgot them, you see.' Mr Creasy leaned forward in the deckchair and hugged at his chest. 'She left without taking any shoes.'

He began to rock, very slowly.

'Oh, God.' Sheila Dakin sat back and pinched the top of her nose.

I looked round at everyone. They all watched with open mouths, and May Roper had a Quality Street paused exactly halfway between the tin and her face.

'I still don't understand,' said Mr Forbes. 'Why, for heaven's sake, would you leave a pair of shoes by the side of a canal?'

'Margaret was always walking along the towpath. She used to sit and have her lunch down there, and I left them next to the little seat so she'd find them. You can't manage all this time without a pair of shoes.'

'Like the gloves by the door, and the umbrella at the bottom of the stairs,' said Mrs Dakin, who was still pinching at her nose.

'Yes!' Mr Creasy smiled. 'You understand, don't you?'

'Bloody hell, John.' Mrs Dakin covered her face with her hands. 'Why on earth didn't you say anything?'

'I didn't think anyone would bother. I didn't realize the cobbler's ticket was still stuck to the bottom of them.'

'Jesus Christ, John,' said Mr Forbes.

Mrs Forbes glanced at the drainpipe.

'So she'll be back, you see,' said Mr Creasy. 'And she'll be back very soon, because it's our wedding anniversary.'

Everyone stared in silence. I thought I could hear someone swallowing. Mrs Morton had woken up and was looking very confused.

'When is your anniversary, John?' said Mrs Roper. Her voice sounded very small.

'The twenty-first.' John Creasy smiled. 'And Margaret wouldn't miss it for the world.'

Mrs Dakin dug around in her handbag and handed him a two-pence piece.

'What's that for?' he said.

She held her head in her hands and sighed. 'To ring the bloody police.'

*

They dropped Mr Creasy off in a panda car two hours later. Mr Forbes said he was lucky not to be charged with wasting police time. I didn't realize you could be arrested for wasting someone's time, but Mrs Morton said it only applied to policemen, which was probably just as well.

Everyone still sat with Jesus, and we watched as Mr Creasy trailed up his garden path and through the front door of number eight.

Tilly pulled at my sleeve. 'Does that mean Mrs Creasy is still alive?' she whispered.

'I think so,' I said.

We looked around at all the faces.

'Then why does everyone look so worried?'

Number Four, The Avenue

2 August 1976

'I suppose you're glad, are you?'

I could just about see my mother through the banisters. She was standing in the kitchen with her hands fixed to her hips.

My father sat at the table. He looked crumpled, as though someone had let all the air out of him. 'What do you mean, glad? Glad about what?' he said.

'That she's alive.'

'Well, of course I'm glad that she's alive. What kind of a question is that?'

'Glad about your fancy woman,' said my mother. Her voice was at least an octave higher than usual.

'For God's sake, Sylvia. How many times? She's not my fancy woman.'

My mother picked up a mug, just so she could put it back down again. 'I saw your face,' she said, 'when John

Creasy said he'd put those bloody shoes there himself. You looked relieved, Derek. Relieved.'

For once, I was glad that Tilly wasn't with me, that it was just me and Remington on the stairs. Remington didn't like my parents' arguments any more than I did. He would curl his tail around my toes and look up at me with confused, Labrador eyes.

'Don't tell me you weren't relieved, because I could see it in your face,' my mother was saying.

'Well, of course I was. Wouldn't any decent person feel relieved to hear one of their neighbours isn't lying at the bottom of a canal?'

'Especially if you were the last one to see them alive.'

I heard a small cough. 'Well, there is that.'

'So you admit it, then? You admit she was at the office with you, when you should have been at a Round Table in the British Legion?'

My father was quiet for a moment. When he spoke, the words sounded tired and beaten. 'Yes, Sylvia. I admit it.'

'Finally,' my mother said. Her hands left her hips and sailed into the air. She sounded like someone who had won a competition that she had never really wanted to enter in the first place.

'It's not what you think,' my father said.

'Oh no, Derek, it never is, is it?' My mother started marching around the kitchen, but she came into view from time to time, and her hands were still swimming through the air. 'It never is what people think.'

'I mean it, Sylvia. It really isn't.'

My father reached out for my mother's arm as she passed, and she allowed herself to be stopped. 'Please sit down. If I'm going to tell you this, I need you to sit down.'

My mother sat down.

'She was helping me,' he said. 'Margaret Creasy was doing me a favour.'

'Helping you? What on earth was she helping you with?'

My father sat back. I could hear the chair scrape against the lino and his hands rest on the table.

'She used to do a bit of accounting before she married John,' he said.

My father paused, but my mother stayed silent.

'She was helping me with the books, Sylvia. She was helping me sort out the finances.'

'Sort what out with the finances? I don't understand.'

I heard my father take a breath. 'We're broke, Sylvia. We're in a mess. I'm struggling to pay the wages, let alone keep up with the rent on the office.'

He took another breath. 'We're going under,' he said.

No one spoke for a very long time. I must have made a noise, because I felt Remington beat his tail against my feet.

'Why didn't you say anything?' My mother's voice disappeared into almost nothing.

'I was trying to protect you. I have only ever tried to protect you and Grace.'

I thought I heard my father sob, but my father never cried at anything, so I must have misheard.

'What am I going to do, Sylve? I'm a businessman. I'm successful. People can't find out the truth.'

'We'll get through it, Derek. We've always got through things.'

'But it's the shame,' said my father, 'I couldn't stand it. I couldn't stand the shame of people finding out I'm something that I'm not.'

I felt Remington push his head into my lap. He wanted me to keep stroking his ears, even though I didn't realize I was doing it.

'It's all right, Remington, don't worry,' I said. 'Nothing's going to change. Everything is going to be exactly the same as it's always been.'

Dogs were like that sometimes. They needed reassurance.

Number Three, Rowan Tree Croft

3 August 1976

'But why isn't she coming?'

Mrs Morton was closing the back door.

The perfume Tilly's mother wore still hung in the air. It smelled like wet soil.

'Her mother thinks it best if she has a rest today. She's looking a bit peaky.'

'Peaky?'

'Tilly's a delicate child, Grace. You know that.'

I thought about the way Tilly opened marmalade jars when I couldn't manage it, and how she carried my mother's shopping bags in when my mother ran out of hands.

'She's not that delicate,' I said.

Mrs Morton frowned and wiped her hands on a tea towel. 'It was good of her mother to let us know,' she said. 'She looked very worried.'

Tilly's mother always looked very worried. I had learned not to take any notice, because she carried worrying around with her at all times, like a spare cardigan.

'Tilly's mother always looks worried,' I said. 'She's very good at it.'

Mrs Morton sat across from me at the kitchen table. 'That's how it is when you care about someone.' She smoothed down the plastic tablecloth. 'You worry.'

I made a wrinkle in the tablecloth with my elbow. 'Like I worried about Remington when he was poorly last summer?'

'I suppose so. Although I'm not sure how appropriate it is to equate Tilly to a yellow Labrador.'

'Oh don't worry, it's more than appropriate,' I said.

I watched Mrs Morton's eyes. They looked very busy.

'She will be all right, though, won't she?'

'Of course.'

'She's always all right, isn't she?'

'She is.'

Sometimes, with grown-ups, the gap between your question and their answer is too big, and it always seems like the best place to put all your worrying into.

*

I was disappointed, because I wanted to talk to Tilly about the conversation I had accidentally overheard the night before. Mrs Morton said I could talk to her about anything, but Mrs Morton's life was quiet and carpeted, and her clocks always told the right time. I didn't think she would know very much about being poor. Tilly, on the other hand, used to live in a hotel where everyone had to share a bathroom, and all the ornaments were glued to the windowsills, so she might have had a better idea.

Mrs Morton and I decided to have a game of Monopoly instead.

Tilly was always the boot and I was always the racing car, so Mrs Morton decided she would have to be the top hat.

I threw the dice and moved along the squares.

'Don't we have to throw a six to start?' said Mrs Morton.

'Only Tilly bothers with that nonsense,' I said, and landed on Whitechapel.

'Are you going to buy it?' she said.

I looked at the board. Tilly always bought Whitechapel and the Old Kent Road. She said she felt sorry for them, because they were brown and uninteresting, and the people who lived on them probably didn't have very much money.

'Do you think the people who live on the Old Kent Road are happy?' I said.

'I expect so.' Mrs Morton stopped shuffling the Community Chest and frowned. 'Or, at least, as happy as everyone else is.'

I looked across the board. 'As happy as the people who live on Mayfair or Park Lane?'

'Of course.'

'Or Pall Mall?'

'Naturally.'

'Do you think lots of people on the Old Kent Road get divorced?'

Mrs Morton put down the cards. 'Grace, what is this conversation about?'

'I'm just taking an interest in things,' I said. 'Well, do you?'

'I shouldn't think so. No more people than anywhere else.'

'Even though they're poor?'

Mrs Morton was in the middle of buying King's Cross Station, and it took her a minute to reply. 'I think only having a little money puts people under stress, but it doesn't stop them loving each other,' she said.

'Or caring about each other? Or worrying about each other?'

She smiled.

'Do you worry about me?' I said.

'All the time.' She put down the dice and looked right into my eyes. 'Every day since you were a little baby.'

The Drainpipe

6 August 1976

My parents sat together, next to Jesus. From time to time, my mother squeezed my father's hand, and gave him the same smile she gave to me when I was on my way to the dentist's. My father just stared at his shoes. Mr Forbes sat on his deckchair with his arms folded, and, in the corner, Clive fed his dog left-over pork scratchings and wiped his fingers on his trousers.

The playing cards sat quietly on the fold-out table, except for the King of Hearts, which turned in Eric Lamb's hand as he lost himself in thinking. May Roper was rubbing her feet and waiting for Brian to fetch her ointment, and the only sound I could hear, as I lay on the grass, was Mrs Morton's knitting needles tutting against each other in disapproval.

Tilly smoothed out her dress.

'Are you feeling less peaky?' I said.

'Much less, thank you. I think my mum worries about me.'

'Worrying is a good thing,' I said. 'Worrying means someone cares about you.'

'Then I think my mum must care very much.'

I watched my parents. My mother was still holding my father's hand, but I couldn't tell if he was holding hers back.

'Do you think the newspapers might come today?' said Tilly.

I looked around at everyone's faces. 'I don't think they're going to get much of an interview if they do.'

'I hope they turn up,' said Tilly. 'It would be a shame not to have a photograph of Jesus.'

Mrs Forbes looked up from her deckchair. 'We could take one ourselves – if we had a camera.' She looked at Mr Forbes and then she looked at Clive. 'Couldn't we, Eric?' she said.

Eric Lamb looked at all of them, and brushed dried mud from his wellingtons.

'Why is everyone so quiet?' Tilly did a bit more smoothing. 'And where's Mrs Dakin?'

'She nipped home for something,' I said, 'again.'

We were all drifting in a wide ocean of silence, when Mrs Forbes stood up out of nowhere and clapped. The King of Hearts fell to the grass and May Roper looked up from her rubbing.

'I know what everybody needs,' said Mrs Forbes. 'We all

need a little pick-me-up. I'm going to fetch a board game and some custard creams.

Everyone's gaze returned to the ground.

I pointed to the drainpipe. 'Look at Jesus,' I said to Tilly, 'even He seems even more unhappy than he did before.'

'Perhaps it's the heat,' said Tilly.

July had been hot, but August seemed even more brutal. The heat poured itself over the country, swallowing rivers and streams, emptying reservoirs and burning through forests. 'People are dying,' my mother said, as we watched the news. 'Human beings aren't made to tolerate this kind of heat. It's not normal, Derek.' As though my father could somehow control it. I had stared at the coat on the back of my bedroom door that morning, and couldn't imagine ever wearing it again.

A few minutes later, Mrs Forbes returned with three packets of biscuits and a box of Scrabble. Whilst she was gone, Mrs Roper had somehow slid unnoticed into Mrs Forbes' deckchair, and was sitting next to Jesus with a box of Cadbury's Roses on her knee and her eyes shut.

'Oh,' said Mrs Forbes.

It was a very small *Oh*, but I had learned from my mother that words didn't necessarily have to be big to make a good impression on people.

'I thought it was time for a little change around,' said Mrs Roper.

'I see.' Mrs Forbes put down the biscuits and the game of Scrabble. She stood over the deckchair and the shadow she cast covered the whole of Mrs Roper and most of my father's left leg.

There was a silence, and we all stared into it and waited.

'You're obviously not aware', said Mrs Forbes, 'that I'm the one who sits in the deckchair next to Jesus.'

Mrs Roper didn't open her eyes. 'That's not a rule I've agreed to,' she said.

Mrs Forbes forced a small cough. 'I am the most logical choice. Not only am I in charge of the altar flowers, I also polish the brass every other Thursday. I'm the closest to God out of all of us.'

Mrs Roper opened one eye. 'It takes more than a duster and a can of Pledge to make somebody respectable,' she said, and closed it again.

Mrs Forbes took in a large amount of air between very pursed lips, and we all sat forwards in our deckchairs.

'Of everybody here,' she said, 'I am the most entitled to sit next to Jesus.'

Mrs Roper opened both of her eyes and shuffled herself higher in her seat. 'I think you'll find if anyone is entitled to sit next to Jesus, then it's me.'

'I think you'll find', said Mrs Forbes, 'that I was sitting next to Jesus first.'

'*Anyone who has two coats should share with the one who has none.*' May Roper folded her arms.

'Luke, Chapter 3, Verse 11,' said Mrs Forbes, and folded her arms back again.

Mrs Dakin criss-crossed her way over the road and tipped

herself into a deckchair next to me. 'What are those two arguing about?'

'Who deserves Jesus more,' I said.

Tilly sat up and lifted the brim of her sou'wester. 'I thought God was supposed to bring people together.'

'I have not "stolen" your seat. It wasn't yours to begin with,' Mrs Roper was saying.

'*As a thief is ashamed when he is caught*,' said Mrs Forbes.

'Jeremiah, Chapter 2, Verse 26. And don't you start with your lies, Dorothy Forbes. *Each of you must put off falsehood and speak truthfully to your neighbour.*'

'Ephesians, Chapter 4, Verse 25.'

John Creasy began to rock in the corner. 'I can't deal with all the numbers,' he said.

'I came over here for a bit of peace and quiet,' said Eric Lamb. 'Not to listen to a bloody argument about which one of you is the most respectable.' And he started to pull on his wellington boots.

'No, Dorothy. Jesus Christ wasn't crucified just so you could get to choose your own deckchair.' May Roper's voice lifted itself higher into the air. 'He was crucified so we can all make our own bloody decisions about where we want to bloody sit.'

I was in the middle of enjoying Mrs Forbes and Mrs Roper having their argument, when I realized that everyone else was turning round and staring. Even the argument stopped, when Mrs Forbes tapped Mrs Roper on the elbow and pointed to the pavement.

It was Walter Bishop.

He stood watching us all from the edge of the kerb, a loaf of bread in one hand and two boxes of fish fingers in the other.

'I was just on my way back from the shops,' he said. 'I heard about Jesus, and I wondered if I might take a look.'

'I don't think so.' Mrs Roper leapt from the deckchair and stood shoulder to shoulder with Mrs Forbes in front of the drainpipe. 'This is private property.'

Walter Bishop looked at the council garages. 'Is it?' he said.

Mr Forbes marched over to the little gap between the alder trees and the chippings, to where Walter stood and waited with his shopping.

'There's nothing to see here,' he said. 'Nothing you'd be interested in. I'd get off home if I were you.'

He pointed to the top of the road, and I could see the tip of his finger shaking very slightly as I watched.

I wondered if Mr Bishop might try to argue, or at least say that he was as entitled to look as anyone else, but he didn't. He just nodded at Mr Forbes, and then he turned away and started to walk.

Mrs Roper spread her arms and covered the drainpipe with her dimples. 'Jesus isn't here for just anyone, you know,' she shouted.

As Mr Bishop walked away, Eric Lamb turned to me and Tilly, and he smiled.

'Take no notice,' he said. 'Grown-ups sometimes say confusing things.'

Tilly sighed. I knew there was a question coming, because whenever she wanted to ask one, Tilly had to do a very big sigh first in order to prepare for it.

'Can I ask a question?' she said.

Eric Lamb said yes, and we all waited.

'You know what Mrs Roper said about why Jesus was crucified?'

We watched Walter Bishop walk up the pavement into the sunshine.

'He wasn't crucified over deckchairs, Tilly,' I said.

'I know that.' She did another sigh. 'But why was he really crucified, Mr Lamb? Why did they have to kill Him?'

Walter Bishop paused by Mrs Forbes' wall and looked across the avenue.

'It's complicated,' said Eric Lamb. 'It's because He had different beliefs, different views on life. In those days, people were very hard on anyone who didn't think the way they did.'

I could hear Walter Bishop's shoes as they ate into the gravel on his driveway.

'He was an outsider, Tilly.' Eric Lamb looked down at us both. 'An unbelonger. That's why they crucified Him.'

'So really,' said Tilly, 'if that's the case, then Jesus was a goat as well, wasn't He?'

'I suppose He was,' said Eric Lamb.

'In fact,' said Tilly, 'He was probably the biggest goat of them all.'

We stared up the road and watched Walter Bishop disappear into number eleven.

'Perhaps you're right,' said Eric Lamb. 'Perhaps He really was.'

*

We all settled down after the excitement of Walter Bishop and the argument. Tilly smoothed her dress a little more and Mrs Morton sorted out Tilly's bobbles. Eric Lamb was persuaded to take his wellington boots off again, and Mrs Forbes appeared to have renegotiated her deckchair, although every half an hour Mrs Roper walked up and down in front of Jesus and got in everyone's way.

I was just thinking about having a little doze, when Lisa Dakin stamped across the chippings in her mules.

'Finally,' said Mrs Dakin, 'you've decided to come to see Jesus. Did curiosity get the better of you?'

Lisa Dakin circled her mother like a wasp. 'I haven't come to see Jesus,' she said, glancing over at the drainpipe. 'I've come to let you know that we've run out of milk.'

Mrs Dakin tried to find her purse. It was actually on the grass, right between her feet, but she didn't seem to be able to see it properly until I passed it to her.

'At least go and have a look, Lisa, while you're here,' said her mother.

I watched Lisa Dakin trail across the grass. She stood in front of the drainpipe with her hands on her hips, sending out little tutting noises and kicking at the chippings with her mules.

'I just don't get it,' she said. 'Why are you all so interested in a stain on a garage wall?'

Tilly looked at me and traced a pattern in the grass with the tip of her finger.

I pretended not to notice.

Lisa kicked at a few more chippings. 'I mean, why would anyone bother?'

I got up and walked over to the drainpipe. 'If you stand back a bit and squint,' I said, 'you'll be able to see Him.'

'I don't want to see Him.' She said the words like they belonged to someone else. 'It's just a bloody creosote stain, Grace. It's a joke.'

'Well,' I said, 'it is only a creosote stain, I suppose.' My words faded in my mouth, because they couldn't decide if they wanted to be true.

*

'So this is where Jesus is hanging out these days?'

The voice was loud and unfamiliar, and it stretched out its vowels, as though it would like to be American but hadn't quite worked out how to go about it.

We all turned to see a small man in a big suit. It hung in folds around his frame, and there were dusty marks on the hems where the stitches had escaped. Around his neck was a giant camera on a thick strap, and the weight of it pulled his neck forward and made him look slightly uneasy.

'Andy Kilner-localpaper.' He said it all at the same time, as if it had become part of his name. He nodded at everyone and at no one, and then he smiled at me and Lisa Dakin. 'And you must be the two girls who found Him. Brilliant. If you just stay where you are, I'll take a few shots now if that's all right? Fantastic, great, brilliant.'

I could see Tilly. She had stopped tracing patterns and was looking straight at my face. Mrs Morton sat forward and started to say something, but her voice disappeared into a frown, and instead she just stared with heavy eyes.

When my gaze found Tilly again, she looked pale and alone, and although we were only a few feet apart, she seemed to be very far away.

I tried to hold on to her, I tried to keep her with me, but she became lost in Lisa Dakin's smile.

*

Lisa Dakin and I made various poses around Jesus, guided by Andy Kilner and a ribbon of *fantastic, great, brilliants.*

All the time, Tilly watched from the grass.

'Quite a find, eh?' said Andy Kilner.

'Yes.' Lisa Dakin flicked her Quatro flicks and pressed ChapStick into her lips. 'Quite a find.'

Lisa Dakin's smile switched on and off with the click of the camera. She put her hand on her hip and pointed her knees together, and got lots of *fantastic, great, brilliants.*

And I just stared across the grass at Tilly.

*

Afterwards, I only saw the photographs once. My mother always cut out the important bits from the local paper – the top of my head on the carnival float and half of my face at the Jubilee party the following year. She even cut my father out when the police pulled him up for speeding. But she didn't save any of me and the drainpipe. I saw them in the window of the local newspaper offices a few weeks later. Lisa Dakin switching on her smile and Jesus sitting in between us looking disappointed, and me staring into the distance, searching for Tilly. And losing her.

The newspaper quoted Eric Lamb and Mrs Forbes, and spelt both of their names wrong. And *'quite a find' said Lisa Dakin (15) who discovered Jesus with her friend Grace Bennett (10). 'The Second Plumbing'* the headline read.

*

By the time Andy Kilner had finished taking his photographs, Tilly had disappeared. I searched the faces in the crowd, but I couldn't find her, and so I looked over at Mrs Morton instead.

She stared back at me, but something had left her eyes.

Number Ten, The Avenue

6 August 1976

Harold and Clive stood at the far end of the avenue.

Eric Lamb could see them at the edges of his view, but he made the mistake of thinking if they didn't find his eyes, then he wouldn't have to stop and talk to them.

'Eric, just the man!'

With Harold, life was never that simple.

'Rum business, eh?' Harold dipped his head towards the bottom of the avenue.

Eric wasn't sure if Harold meant Jesus, Walter Bishop or Dorothy's theatricals over the deckchair, so he gave a general smile of agreement to cover all three.

'Don't know quite what to make of it all, do we, Clive?' said Harold.

Clive didn't reply, but made a noise which could have

been a no, but which could equally have been the start of clearing his throat.

'New family seem nice?' said Harold.

Eric said that they did.

'Doesn't look like this weather's going to break?'

Eric said that it didn't.

'Garden's not doing too bad, considering.'

Eric said that it wasn't, and that, as it was nearly tea time, if Harold and Clive would excuse him, he was just—

'The thing is.' Harold's feet took a step closer and the tone of his voice took a step lower. 'Dorothy and that comment about photographs. What did she mean exactly?'

Harold and Clive were looking straight into Eric's eyes. He didn't think it was possible to slide even a small lie in between them.

'I think you're better asking Dorothy, rather than me,' he said. 'It's really none of my business.'

Eric tried to walk away, but Harold's gaze wouldn't let him. Despite the curve of Harold's spine, despite the peppered hair of an old man that pushed from Harold's pale flesh and peered through the gap in his shirt, he was as stubborn and as sharp as a teenager.

'She found the camera, didn't she?' said Harold.

Eric didn't reply. It was an answer all in itself.

'Jesus Christ,' Clive said, and leaned back against the wall.

Harold put his hand up. 'No need for panicking, Clive. We did nothing wrong.'

Eric raised an eyebrow.

'We didn't, Eric. It was a public service. We had every right to take it.' Harold glanced over at Clive. 'God alone knows what he had on film.'

'A blackbird on a milk bottle?' Eric could hear his voice becoming louder, but he couldn't help himself. 'Beatrice Morton tying her shoelaces?'

'Dorothy doesn't think we had anything to do with the fire?' said Clive. 'We took the camera hours before that started.'

'I'm not sure what she thinks, but she's not as daft as you make out, Harold.'

'She probably thought we were rescuing it from looters,' Harold said.

'Looters?' Eric raked his fingers through his hair. 'You mean people who break into empty houses and steal other people's property?'

Clive began walking down the avenue, a firm, brisk walk. A walk that took him away from blame and accusation.

'You've got to understand,' Harold turned back from watching Clive, 'we didn't know what was on there. We had to be sure, and Bishop was on holiday. It seemed like the perfect opportunity.'

'You can't just take someone else's belongings because it suits you, Harold.'

'It would have been destroyed in the fire anyway,' Harold

said. 'If we'd known that, we could have saved ourselves the bother, and left it where it was.'

Eric didn't reply.

'We couldn't take the risk, Eric.' Suddenly, Harold looked very old and very tired. 'If people found out,' he said. 'If people knew,' Harold's voice had faded to a whisper, 'I couldn't stand the shame.'

*

Eric closed the back door behind him and dropped the catch. He walked over to the kitchen window and snatched the curtains closed, pulling them so tight, not even a cutting of sunlight could manage to break through.

If he had been a drinker, he would have drunk. Instead he stared at Elsie's chair, smooth and unfilled, and tried to imagine what she would have said had she been here.

But the chair remained silent.

It was strange how the past often broke into the present like an intruder, dangerous and unwanted. Yet whenever the past was invited in, whenever its presence was requested, it seemed to fade into nothing, and made you wonder if it had ever really existed in the first place.

It had all started with the past. It had all started with Walter Bishop stealing the baby, and everything that happened afterwards unravelled from that very first moment. Even now, the memory of that moment travelled around the avenue. No matter how much they all wanted to escape it, no matter how many other memories they tried to put in its way, it was still there. Creeping into the present; shading and colouring everything that happened afterwards, until the present was so disturbed by the past, no one could really decide where one ended and the other began.

Eric sat back in his chair and bit at his nails. He hadn't bitten his nails since he was a boy. Perhaps the past was shaded too, he thought. Perhaps it worked both ways. Everyone was so certain of what had happened, but maybe the present crawled into our memories and disturbed them as well, and perhaps the past wasn't quite as certain as we would like it to be.

7 November 1967

It takes three buses to get to the hospital. None of the journeys is long enough to get comfortable, either. They are short and winding, and filled with traffic lights and roundabouts and sharp corners. Eric Lamb sits with the little case on his knee, swaying this way and that, trying not to sway into the person next to him or fall into the aisle, or get his feet in anyone's way. By the time he arrives to the hospital, he is exhausted just from the effort of not being a nuisance.

Other passengers move on and off the bus, and he watches

windows of people's lives as they pass through: the couples who wind and whisper around each other; the mothers, fighting wars with prams and shopping bags; the young man with a book, whose pages lean in time with the tarmac. As they near the hospital, there are uniforms, porter grey and staff-nurse blue. Shoes designed for corridors. Ankles rubbed. Necks stretched out. The uniforms are hidden under anoraks and coats, secreted away beneath cardigans, but they break through from time to time, as though the wearer will never be free of who they are, no matter how many layers of another life they try to put on top.

He has been to visit Elsie. He visits each afternoon and each evening, and in between visits he returns home to watch the floor and the walls, and the empty seat where Elsie always sits. Staring at the seat always makes her seem even more missing, as though he's found the very centre of her not being there and set it free to take over the whole house.

Tests, they said. *We just need to run a few tests. We need to find out why you're tired and pale and thin.*

'I'm getting old,' she'd said, and laughed, but the doctor didn't laugh with her. Instead he smiled very quietly and wrote in the notes, and the sound of the nib scratching on the sheets of paper had filled the whole room. The hospital had called for her a week later, and she'd packed her best nightie and a pair of slippers, and the book she was reading, as well as the little sachet of lavender that Eric could never understand the point of, because it always made him sneeze.

'Because it will help me to relax,' she'd said.

He'd tried to fish out what she needed to relax about, but she'd shaken her head and squeezed his hand, and said it was a strange bed and different food, and sitting about all day waiting for doctors to appear.

'Calm down. Don't look so worried, Eric.'

And so he'd tried very hard not to look worried, and the effort he had to put in to manage it made him worry even more.

Today, he had tried not to look worried all the way down the long, grey corridor. It was always cluttered with relatives waiting for the doors to open, and he moved slowly, past obstetrics and paediatrics and orthopaedics, the heavy, swinging doors which led to theatres, and the hushed importance of the cardiology suite. It was like a path of life, stretching out in front of him, and in the distance he could see the oncology wards and the palliative care unit. At the end of the corridor were the biggest queues – knots of people, all waiting for the click of two o'clock, measuring every second.

Elsie's ward was three quarters of the way along. *Ward 11, Female Surgical*, it said over the blue doors.

'Not everyone on a surgical ward ends up having surgery.' The nurse who admitted Elsie saw their faces. 'There's no need to be anxious.'

There was every need to be anxious, but Eric was becoming more practised at sweeping it from his face.

*

Today, Elsie had looked very small. The hospital and the ward and the bed seemed to swallow her up, and she gripped the sheets as though she were afraid she might disappear altogether into the stiff white pillows. They had talked about the book she was reading and how the garden was doing, and when the weather might change – very small, ordinary conversations, conversations that they might have had without a second thought over the break-fast table, but over a hospital bed, they seemed like forgery. The doctors had already been on their ward round, she said, a whole collection of them in white coats. They look like bakers, she said. Perhaps they might offer her a tin loaf and half a dozen teacakes, and she'd laughed. No, she hadn't asked about the test results. They were busy. She didn't want to bother them. She would ask tomorrow. Eric had stared into his hands. Has he been eating properly, she asked? Not just tomato soup? And they swam back into shallow waters and counterfeit words.

He sways this way and that on the journey home, trying to sieve reassurance from his thoughts. Through the windows, watercolour streets pass by, nothing sharp enough to focus on, nothing clear enough for distraction. Around him, the seats empty and fill, but he simply sees the outlines, shapes moving at the edges of his worrying, all their detail eaten away. It's only when the bus turns into the estate, when his eyes find a pattern in the rooftops, and the brakes hiss and spit out a familiar song, that he is pulled away from

Elsie and how the skin draws on her bones, and how the wedding ring turns on her finger.

He walks slowly, marking out time on the pavement. Four hours, and he will make the trip back, four hours of staring and thinking and trying to find the map to chart this journey of his life. He doesn't see Sylvia at first. She seems to appear in front of him, spinning from nowhere, white with anxiety, a tremor around her lips, even though no words appear. He hasn't seen that kind of fear for twenty-five years. Not since the telegrams. *We deeply regret to inform you.*

Eric puts the little suitcase down on the pavement and places his hands on her shoulders. The fear has carved into her, and she barely moves. Very slowly, he asks her what's wrong, and he repeats it over and over, until she finds his eyes. She whispers in the beginning, so quietly he can barely hear, and he needs to lean towards her to listen. Then the words become louder, more desperate. She shouts them across the avenue, again and again, until Eric wonders if there was anyone left in the world who couldn't help but take notice.

'Grace has disappeared,' and then she covers her ears with her hands, as if she can't bear to hear the words said out loud.

Number Four, The Avenue

7 August 1976

The next day, Tilly didn't appear at the drainpipe.

She would usually be there by ten, but even as Mr Creasy waited for the five to eleven bus, and even as he walked back up the avenue with his hands deep in his pockets, she still hadn't appeared. There was only Mrs Forbes, shouting out clues from her crossword, and Sheila Dakin, sunbathing and pretending not to hear.

I decided to go home. Jesus wasn't as much fun without Tilly.

*

My mother sat in the kitchen, sewing buttons on my father's shirts. She looked at me as I walked in.

'Has anyone called?' I said.

She shook her head and went back to the shirts.

My mother had been very quiet since Andy Kilner took the photographs. When Tilly left without saying goodbye, I thought my mother might have given me one of her dentist's smiles, or told me Tilly was just being ridiculous, but she hadn't. Instead, she had just looked at me wordlessly from time to time, and then gone back to whatever it was she was doing. I would normally have given up. I would normally have gone round to Mrs Morton's, but Mrs Morton said she would be especially busy that day and she wouldn't have time to sit with me or make any Angel Delight. She said I should stay at home instead, and have a really good think about things.

I went up to my room and tried to choose what I should be doing to look very busy and unconcerned when Tilly finally did decide to turn up, only I couldn't really find anything to do. Instead, I listened for her sandals, but all I could hear was a burned, measureless silence. It was too hot even for the birds to sing.

It was three o'clock when our telephone rang. I was sitting on my bed, rearranging all the Whimsies and then arranging them back to exactly how they were before. Our telephone didn't ring very often, so whenever it did, I always felt obliged to go on to the landing and involve myself in listening.

'If that's Tilly, tell her I'm very busy,' I shouted over the banister and sat down.

I stood up again. 'Well, not so busy that I can't speak to her. Just really quite busy,' I said.

I heard my mother waiting for the pips.

I tried to listen to what she was saying, but as soon as the conversation started, she turned her face to the wall and spoke too quietly for me to hear. When she finished talking, my mother put the receiver down very slowly and went into the sitting room, where my father was doing his paperwork, and she shut the door behind her.

I felt as though I had been sitting on the landing for a very long time. My back ached, and my legs started to tingle, but I couldn't stop watching the door of the sitting room and wishing it would open.

It was only when it did open that I realized I actually didn't want it to open after all.

My mother shouted up, 'Grace, come downstairs for a minute. We need to talk to you.'

I didn't answer.

After a moment, her face appeared at the bottom of the stairs.

'I'm really quite busy, you know.' My words only came out as a whisper.

'It's important,' she said. She gave me one of her smiles.

When I stood up, my legs felt so watery, I wasn't even sure they could take me all the way to the hall.

*

I sat on the chair next to the fireplace.

My parents sat opposite, on the settee, and my father

put his arm around my mother. They looked pale and strange, as though they might break at any moment.

'We need to talk to you,' said my father.

I tried to stand up. 'Actually,' I said, 'I'm supposed to be going to Mrs Morton's, so you're going to have to speak to me later. Or perhaps tomorrow.'

My father leaned forward and made me sit down again. 'Grace, I need you to listen,' he said. 'There's something we have to tell you.'

My mother began to cry.

And when I looked down at my hands, I saw they had started to shake.

7 November 1967

Sylvia Bennett's shouts force people out from their houses.

Sheila Dakin appears first. She's wiping her hands on a tea towel, frowning, angry. She's asking what all the shouting is about. Her slippers thump along the garden path.

'It's Grace.' Eric still holds Sylvia's shoulders. He's worried that if he lets go, she will slip through his hands. 'She says Grace has disappeared.'

Sheila rushes through the gate and across the street. The tea towel falls to the pavement.

'Disappeared?'

Sylvia's hands tighten against her head.

'People don't just disappear.' Sheila edges Eric away and takes Sylvia's wrists, pulling her hands away from her ears. 'Listen to me,' she says.

Eric lets Sheila take over. He has never been very good with upset. He's always the one putting the kettle on and making phone calls, and giving directions. It's not that he doesn't care, it's just that he can't help himself getting upset as well, which only seems to grow everyone else's upset even more.

Sylvia begins to moan and stumble, as though all the fear has exhausted her.

'Listen to me,' Sheila says again, and Sylvia becomes quiet and looks up at her like a child.

Sheila asks a run of questions, each one tipping into the next. She pauses for Sylvia to speak, but it only delays her a beat, before the next one arrives. When Sylvia replies, the answers are fragments, swaying words that lurch and stagger, fear stealing away the shape of the sentences.

Grace was in the kitchen, she said, in her pushchair. They were going out. Sylvia went upstairs to change her shoes, and when she came back, Grace and the pushchair had gone.

'How long were you upstairs?' Sheila says. Sylvia is looking at the pavement, and Sheila moves her head to find Sylvia's gaze. 'How long?'

'Not long,' she says. 'Not that long.'

Eric puts his hand back on Sylvia's shoulder. 'Yes, but how long, love? It could be important.'

Sylvia's fingers rake through her hair. It seems to pull her eyes even wider, even whiter. 'I sat on the bed. I think I might have fallen asleep,' she says. 'Not for long. Just for a minute. I don't know.'

Eric looks at Sheila. Their eyes partner for just a brief moment, but Sylvia sees it.

'It's not my fault!' She is shouting again now. 'No one understands what it's like. No one.'

More people have come into the street. May Roper stands at the edge of her garden, listening, her eyes saucered with curiosity. She is eating, and her chewing slows with each sentence, as though she needs her entire face to be still in order to concentrate properly. Brian appears at her left shoulder, but she holds out a hand to prevent him from disturbing the view.

'Have you checked all over the house?' Sheila is saying. 'Every room?'

Sylvia nods. She is crying now, purging herself with deep, torturous sobs that echo through her entire body.

Sheila looks around and sees May. 'Check the house again,' she says, 'just to be sure.'

May's hand presses to her chest. 'Me?' she mouths.

'Just do it, May. Hurry up.'

May scuttles across the road, like an over-ripe insect, and Sheila turns back to Sylvia. There is a crowd now. Harold and Dorothy Forbes, John Creasy, Thin Brian. They make a circle around Sylvia, holding in the hysteria, containing it within a space, as though it were a wild animal that needed to be trapped.

'Tell us what happened this morning,' Sheila says. 'Everything. Did you see anyone? Speak to anyone unusual?'

Eric listens as Sylvia runs through her day. It's a very ordinary day. It's strange how the worst day of your life often starts just like any other. You might even complain very quietly to yourself about its ordinariness. You might wish for something more interesting to happen, something to break the back of your routine, and just when you think you can't bear the monotony any longer, something comes along that shatters your life to such a degree, you wish with every cell in your body that your day hadn't become so unordinary.

'We walked to the corner shop, this morning,' Sylvia is holding her head in her hands, as though the weight of thinking is too much to bear, 'for milk.'

'Was there anyone in the shop? Anyone you didn't recognize?' Sheila says. 'Did anyone follow you?'

'We didn't see anyone. No one except the postman. We walked out of the shop, down Lime Crescent and through the alleyway. It was warm. I was telling Grace she didn't really need her cardigan.' Sylvia stops speaking and looks up at Sheila.

'What? What have you remembered?'

'We saw someone else,' Sylvia says. 'Someone stopped to speak to us on the way home.'

'Who was it?' Eric says. 'Anyone you know?'

Sylvia looks at each of the faces surrounding her before she speaks. The words are tissue-paper quiet, almost nothing more than a breath. 'It was Walter Bishop,' she says.

'We spoke to Walter Bishop.'

They all look across at number eleven, each of them holding the house in their gaze for a brief moment before they turn back to Sylvia.

'What did he say to you?' Sheila says.

'He said—' The sobbing has started again, and Sylvia has to fit her words around jagged breaths. '—he said how beautiful Grace was. He said how much he loved children.'

Brian turns back to number eleven. 'Well,' he says, 'there's your answer.'

*

'Let's not jump to conclusions.' Eric feels he should make the effort to calm things down. There are more people now, people who don't live on the avenue, but have floated towards a crisis like driftwood. John Creasy is organizing them into groups to search the estate. The police have been called. Someone has gone to the phone box to ring Derek.

'There's only one conclusion you can jump to.' Brian stares over at Walter's house. 'We should go over there. Confront him.'

'You can't just march over there and accuse him of taking

390

a child.' Sheila is speaking now. She keeps her back to Sylvia, trying to shield her from the conversation.

'The police will be here soon,' Eric says, 'let them deal with it.'

Brian punches his hands into his pockets. 'He sits in that park all day, you know. Up in the bandstand. Staring at children. He's a bloody pervert.'

'Brian's right, he does. I've seen him.' Dorothy Forbes has picked up Sheila's tea towel, and she is folding it and unfolding it as she speaks. 'He's always in that bandstand. He just sits there and watches all the kiddies.'

There is a slip of unquiet. Eric can feel it. It snakes around the group, lifting voices and brightening eyes. He tries to tell them to calm down, to think about it, but Harold is drumming through the crowd, grabbing the restlessness and sharing it out.

'Well, I'm going over there,' he says. 'Everyone else is out here, trying to help. Where's Bishop? Where is he?'

Harold starts walking towards number eleven. Brian is right on his heels. Eric shouts to stop them, but he knows it's pointless. The crowd are trailing across the avenue, moving with the story, not wanting to miss a chapter. Eric follows them. It's all he can do.

Walter Bishop's house has the kind of front door that looks as though no one has opened it in the last ten years. A skin of paint peels around the frame, and dust has turned the black into a quiet, deadened grey.

Harold bangs on the wood with the heel of his hand.

Nothing.

He bangs again. Shouts. Tries to rattle the handle of the letterbox, but the rust has eaten its way into the hinges.

He shouts again.

Through the window in the door, behind the bubbled glass, Eric can see a shadow of movement, a brief change in the light. A chain shakes and slides, and the door opens a few inches. Just enough to catch the pale, stubbled skin, the reflection of a pair of spectacles.

'Yes?' Walter Bishop's voice is soft and unclear. There is a faint lisp, which stretches the word into a whisper.

'There's a child missing. Grace Bennett.' Harold's words are like needles by comparison. 'Did you know?'

Walter shakes his head. Eric can see the edge of the man's clothes. They are grey too. He looks washed through and faded, as though he has given up trying to make any sort of imprint on the world.

'You spoke to her mother this morning,' Harold says, 'in the alley next to Lime Crescent.'

'I did?'

'You did. You told her how much you liked children.' Harold's temper is roped in, but it pushes against every syllable.

Walter shifts behind the chain, and Eric sees the gap narrow just a fraction.

'I was making conversation,' he says, 'being friendly.'

'Friendly?'

'It's what people do, isn't it?' There is a glaze of sweat on Walter's forehead. 'They pass the time of day, they admire someone's child.'

'Not if that child goes missing a few hours later.'

Eric can feel the weight of people behind him. He can feel them tighten and wind. There are a few voices at the back, low and rumbling for now, but Eric knows it would only take one of those voices to strengthen and speak up for the entire group to unravel.

'Have you any idea where Grace might be?' Harold is saying. His voice is slow and deliberate.

'I really couldn't say.'

Walter tries to shut the door, but Harold's foot is too quick.

'The thing is, everyone is out here searching for her. Will you be joining us?'

'I wouldn't know where to start.' A faint tremor floods Walter's voice. 'I have no idea where she is.'

'Perhaps, then, you wouldn't mind if we take a look around the house?'

With Harold's foot blocking the door, Eric can see Walter's face slightly better. His skin is a little too milky, his hair is a little too long. Discomfort gathers in beads around the edge of his glasses, and Eric looks for a splinter of concern behind the lenses. He finds nothing. Only an unease, a layer of self-preservation.

'This is private property,' Walter says. 'I'm going to have to ask you to leave.'

'We're not leaving until we find Grace. So you'd better open this door and let us get on with it.'

Eric can hear boots scuff and drag on the path. The voices are building, feeding from each other. He feels an elbow dig in his back, pushing him forward.

'I must insist.' Walter's breathing is shallow, rapid. 'I must insist that you go.'

Thin Brian is at Eric's shoulder. There is a young man's rage there, Eric can feel it, the kind of rage that smoulders and spits, and looks around for a place to land. He remembers being the owner of that kind of rage, before time sandpapered it down into something he could hold on to.

The crowd is about to break. He can feel it in the voices, in the push of bodies behind him. He looks at the doorway.

Walter Bishop doesn't stand a chance.

Just as he thinks it will happen, just as he braces himself for the surge, Eric hears a shout from the back of the crowd.

'Police,' it says.

And it's like loosening a knot. The crowd unfastens, men walk back across the avenue, along pavements, down alleys.

Harold Forbes turns and, as he does, Walter Bishop's front door slams shut.

'That was close,' Eric Lamb says. 'I was getting worried there.'

'Worried? He took a baby, Eric. He took a bloody child.'
Harold looked back at the door.

'At least the police came before it got nasty.'

Harold looks back as he walks away. 'This time,' he says.

Number Four, The Avenue

13 August 1976

'I want to go to the hospital.'

I said it to my mother and my father, I said it to Mrs Morton, and I said it into the darkness each night, as I lay in bed trying to find my sleep.

No one gave me an answer. They just smiled or hugged my shoulders instead, as though I hadn't said a real sentence. Sometimes, they tried to distract me with sweets or magazines, and every time my father spoke, it started with *Let's*.

Let's watch the television.

Let's go to the park.

Let's have a game of Monopoly, Grace. You can teach me.

I didn't want to do any of his *Let's*, I just wanted to see Tilly.

My mother circled rooms, containing her worrying at the edges of the house. She tried to hide it behind wide, shiny eyes, and a smile so tight and untruthful, I wondered if I would be able to trust her smiling ever again.

Mrs Morton came round a lot. She sat in the kitchen with my parents, and drank tea and ate biscuits. I wasn't sure why I hadn't noticed before, but just when I wasn't looking, Mrs Morton had become old. It must have been when I was eating my tea or reading my book, or when I had turned away to watch the television, but I could see that she had changed. Her face had been tugged into creases, and her jaw quarrelled with itself as she ate.

I decided to confront them all, as they sat in the kitchen one day, passing quiet words around the table between themselves.

I stood in the doorway, and the quiet words stopped. My mother stretched a smile across her face and Mrs Morton tried to reorganize the sadness in her eyes.

'I want to go to the hospital,' I said.

My father stood up. 'Let's get you something to eat, shall we? Do you fancy a bowl of Angel Delight? Or some crisps?'

'I want to go to the hospital,' I said.

My father sat down again.

'A hospital isn't a place for children.' My mother stretched her smile even more.

'Tilly is there,' I said. 'Tilly is a child.'

My father leaned forward. 'Tilly is feeling very poorly, Grace. She has to stay there until she's well again.'

I saw my mother look at my father.

'She's been in hospital before,' I said. 'The nurses wore

tinsel in their hair. She got better.' I felt a ball of tears move into my throat. 'She came home.'

'I think we should leave the nurses and the doctors to look after her.' My mother weighed out her words. 'They need to work out what the matter is.'

'She had something wrong with her blood.' I knew my voice must be getting louder, because Remington walked over and sat by my feet. 'We need to go and tell them. Perhaps the nurses and doctors don't know.'

'They know that, Grace,' said Mrs Morton. 'They're just trying to find out how to stop it.'

I stared at the three of them, and they stared back, a wall of grown-ups.

'I want to go to the hospital. She's my friend, and I have a present for her. If your friend was in hospital, you would want to go and visit them as well.'

Mrs Morton put her cup on to her saucer very slowly, and looked at my parents. 'I think,' she said, 'it's sometimes better for children to see for themselves. Otherwise, they fill the gaps with all sorts of things.'

My father nodded, and looked at my mother.

Everyone was looking at my mother.

'Fine,' she said, after a moment. 'Don't mind me. You do whatever you think is best.'

'Fine,' said my father. 'We'll go.'

My mother looked disappointed. She was used to her words being escorted by a translation.

The Drainpipe

13 August 1976

'Post!' Keithie dropped a pile of letters on to Sheila Dakin's knee, and his bike disappeared around the corner of the garages.

'Jesus Christ, Keithie,' Sheila snapped open her eyes and sat forwards in the deckchair, 'you'll give me a bloody heart attack.'

There was one interesting typed, white envelope. She held on to it and let the brown envelopes slide to the grass. Brian reached down to pick them up.

'Don't bother, Brian,' she said, 'if I lose them, the electricity board are always kind enough to send me another one.'

She looked at the empty deckchairs. 'Quiet, isn't it?'

Brian sat back again. 'Harold's gone. He says he's not even sure it's Jesus any more. He says we've probably all been fooling ourselves.'

Sheila looked over at Jesus and squinted. 'Where's everyone else?'

'Dorothy was here a while ago, but then she said she was too upset about Tilly. She said she couldn't face Jesus any more, and she went home to lie down.'

'Any news?'

Brian shook his head and stared at the ground.

'Poor little bugger.' Sheila sat up straighter and put her legs on the tyre, which she'd reinvented as a footstool. 'It breaks my heart, it does. You'll understand when you've got kids of your own.'

'Not much chance of that.' Brian laughed, but his eyes didn't go along with it.

She watched him. Skinny and unsure, a man who had never shed the awkward skin of adolescence. Even Keithie had more confidence.

'You want to move out of number two before it's too late. Cut those apron strings, Brian.'

'She's tied the knots too tight,' he said. 'Not much chance of that either.'

Sheila shook her head and looked back at the envelope. 'I think this is from the council,' she said. 'About voluntary work. Margaret said I'd enjoy it.' She held it out to Brian. 'Read it to me, would you. I haven't got my glasses down here.'

The envelope stayed in her hand.

She looked over at him. 'Brian?'

'You don't have to read it now,' he said. 'It's not going anywhere, is it? Read it later.'

'But I want to know what they say.' She held the letter out a little further. 'I want to know if they'll have me.'

He looked at her. 'I can't, Sheila,' he said.

'What do you mean, you can't?' She watched a flush crawl from Brian's neck and on to his face. He looked at the deckchairs, the drainpipe, his feet – anywhere but her eyes.

'Brian?'

'I mean I can't,' he said. 'I just can't.'

*

'You daft sod, why didn't you say something?'

Brian was standing by the drainpipe, smoking one of Sheila's cigarettes, even though he didn't smoke any more and hadn't been able to speak for the first ten minutes for the coughing.

'How could I?' he said. 'How could I tell people that?'

'They'd understand, Brian.'

'They'd understand I was thick,' he said. 'They'd understand I was bloody stupid.'

'You're not bloody stupid. And you must be able to read a bit? Some of the words?'

'Some of them.' He took another drag on the cigarette. 'But the letters all swim around on the page, and I can't get them in the right order. They get mixed up.'

He looked at her, and she realized she was staring at him. 'You see, even you don't understand. Even you think I'm thick.'

'I don't, Brian.' She could see his frustration twisting itself into anger. 'I'm trying to understand, really I am.'

'Margaret Creasy understood.' He pulled a last lungful out of the cigarette. 'She was helping me.'

'How was she helping you?'

'That appointment,' he said, 'she was teaching me to read. She told me to get a book out of the library. Something I liked the look of.'

'Oh, Brian.' Sheila put the letter down and stood up. 'Why did you leave it so late? Why on earth didn't you tell one of us sooner?'

'My mam. She said it didn't matter.' He looked at Sheila. A child's look, a look that didn't question. 'She said if I needed to read anything, she'd always be there to read it for me.'

He dropped the cigarette and pushed it into the chippings with his boot. 'Anyway,' he said, 'how could I tell anyone? How could I face that kind of shame?' He started to walk away. 'You'd all think I was weird.'

Number Four, The Avenue

15 August 1976

'You know that you won't be able to go into the room?' my father said.

I told him that yes, I knew this, because I had already been told four times.

'Because they don't want Tilly catching any of your germs,' he said. 'They have to keep everything really clean.'

'I am clean,' I said.

'Extra clean.' He picked up the car keys.

My mother stood in the doorway, tapping her fingers against the wood. 'Let's just get this over with,' she said.

*

I had never been to the hospital before, except when I was born, which I decided didn't really count. It was a long, snaking building right at the edge of the town, and you could see where other buildings had been added on to the snake, as more and more people became poorly and they had to find somewhere to put them all.

We had to park the car a long way from the entrance and trail across the car park, my mother folded into her arms and my father pushing his thoughts into his pockets. When we did finally get to the main corridor, we had no idea where to go. When you visit a hospital, I think you can always tell the people who work there, because they have very quiet shoes and always look straight ahead when they're walking. Everyone else stares at up the signs hanging over the corridors and points at maps, and follows little arrows painted into the floor.

'It's this way,' said my father, and we walked to the end of a very long hall, filled with pictures of flowers and very quiet shoes. At the end of a corridor was the Children's Ward. There was a painting of Tigger on the wall outside.

'Well, Tilly won't enjoy that at all,' I said. 'She doesn't even like Tigger. She thinks he's too noisy.'

*

My father spoke to the nurse at the desk, and the nurse at the desk looked at me over my father's shoulder, and she smiled into a nod.

While they were talking, I wandered around. I couldn't see Tilly anywhere.

I expected it to be louder on a children's ward. I thought there would be games and felt tips and cartoons.

I thought there would be shouting. Like school, but with nurses instead of teachers. There was none of these things. Children lay on narrow mattresses, parents' chairs were pulled close to beds, and sleeping mothers lay with their hands reached into cots. Only one little girl sat at a table, painting. When she turned to me and smiled, I saw a tube coming out of her nose, which looped and twisted around one of her ears.

I went back to my mother and pushed into her legs.

She put her arm around my shoulder, and said 'I knew it,' and glared at my father's back.

*

The nurse led us down another corridor, past more paintings and giant sink units, and stacks of towels in metal cages.

I saw my father look at my mother.

'It's this way,' said the nurse. 'Tilly's mum has just gone to the canteen.'

I took more steps to catch up with her.

'I know I'm not allowed to go in,' I said, 'but I have a present for Tilly.'

We stopped outside a door. The door said 'WASH YOUR HANDS' in loud capitals, as though it was shouting at everybody.

'We can't take anything in there,' said the nurse. 'It's an infection risk.'

'But it's important.' My words came out all tall and shaky.

'Perhaps,' my father said to the nurse, 'perhaps you can give it to Tilly when she's better?'

I saw the nurse look at my father. 'Okay,' she said, without taking her eyes from him. 'We'll do that then.'

I handed it to her, and she slipped it into her pocket.

*

There was a big window at the side of the door, and the blind was open. It was too high, and my father had to lift me so I could look through.

The room wasn't lit, and I couldn't make sense of very much to start with. There was the edge of a bed and the corner of a sink unit, but everything else seemed to disappear into darkness. It was only when my eyes got used to it, only when the shapes began to join together and make a room that I realized I was staring straight at Tilly.

She hadn't got her glasses, or her bobbles, and she looked tiny and pale. The bed seemed to overwhelm her. Her head was too small for the pillows, and her hands were gripping the blankets, as though she was trying her very best to keep holding on to the world.

Even though her eyes were closed, I waved at her. I waved harder and harder, because it felt as though, if I waved hard enough, she was bound to hear and open her eyes.

I shouted her name.

'Don't shout, Grace,' my father said.

I shouted again. And again.

Wake up, I shouted, *wake up, wake up, wake up.*

'Grace!' My father let me slide to the floor. 'This is a hospital, you can't shout!' He was shouting.

'It's not Tilly,' I said. 'If it was Tilly, she'd know it was me and wake up.'

The nurse crouched down to me. 'She's very poorly, Grace. She's too poorly to wake up right now.'

'And what do you bloody know?' I shouted.

I got to my feet and started running. I ran past the pictures and the sinks and the towels, and my mother and father ran after me, and out on to the corridor.

'Tilly can't disappear,' I shouted. 'You can't let Tilly disappear.'

My mother stopped running. I could hear her voice echoing down the corridor.

'I told you this was a bad idea, Derek,' she shouted. 'I bloody damned well told you.'

All the quiet shoes turned around and stared.

The Drainpipe

15 August 1976

I sat on the chippings in front of Jesus.

When we got home, I went straight back out again. My mother wanted me to stay in, but my father said it was better for me to *get it out of my system*.

I didn't know what was in my system, but I thought it might help if I went to see Jesus, although I had been talking to Him for ten minutes now, and I still didn't feel any different.

Mr Forbes had taken all the deckchairs away, and the card table, and the only thing that said any of us had ever been there in the first place was one of Sheila Dakin's slippers, propped up against the far garage wall.

I stared at Jesus. 'Why are you making Tilly disappear?' I said.

He looked back at me with creosote eyes.

'I thought if I found you, it would keep everyone safe. I thought if you were here, it meant we could all stay where we belong?'

An afternoon sun crept up the side of the garage. It rolled over Jesus and the drainpipe, and lifted itself up to the top of the wall, where it found a spider, weaving and plotting and planning out its web.

Tilly loved spiders. She said they were clever and patient and gentle. She couldn't understand why everyone was so afraid of them, and I wanted her to see it. But Tilly wasn't there.

The only thing that was there was the emptiness, the space in my life where Tilly used to be.

Jesus just watched. His corners had started to blur, and the edges of his face had begun to flake and crumble.

'Please don't let her go,' I said.

But it seemed, along with everybody else, Jesus would quite like to disappear as well.

Number Four, The Avenue

17 August 1976

We sat in the front room. Me, my parents, and the bowl of Angel Delight my mother had made for me.

'Don't you want it?' she said.

I stared out of the window. 'I'm not really hungry.'

I could see Mrs Dakin on her deckchair and Eric Lamb pruning something in his front garden, and Mrs Forbes wandering up and down her chippings with a sweeping brush. It felt as though nothing had changed, as though the world was just carrying on, even though a piece of it was fading away.

'Why don't we look through the catalogue?' my mother said. 'That always cheers you up.'

She tried very hard. She turned the pages, pointing and trying to make fun of the models, and choosing imaginary presents for all of us.

We got to one of my green circles, and she looked at

my father. 'You can have those mules, Grace, if you want them,' she said.

I stared up at her. 'We can't afford them,' I said. 'We're poor.'

'We can afford twenty-five pence a week in forty-eight easy instalments.' She hugged my shoulder, and pointed to the green lines.

I looked at the mules. 'Actually,' I said, 'I don't think they'd suit me after all. I think I'd rather just stick with my sandals.'

My mother brushed the hair from my face and did a shiny smile.

*

'It's a police car,' my father said.

We had heard the shudder of an engine and the thud of closing doors, and my father had gone to the window to investigate.

'Inspector Hislop and that other copper,' said my father. 'What's his name?'

'Green?' said my mother.

'That's it. Green.'

My mother looked up. 'Do you think they've found Margaret?' she said.

'I don't know.' My father pulled the curtain back a little more. 'But everyone's out there.'

The Kays catalogue fell to the carpet as my mother got to her feet.

*

By the time we got outside, Detective Hislop was surrounded.

Everyone seemed to be shouting questions at him, Mr Forbes and May Roper, Thin Brian in his plastic jacket, and Dorothy Forbes waving her arms around and becoming quite hysterical. PC Green was trying to keep everyone quiet, and Detective Hislop was holding his palms out and refusing to open his eyes until they'd all bloody shut up. Mr and Mrs Kapoor stood on their doorstep looking completely bewildered.

'I need to go inside and have a word with Mr Creasy, if you would all just step out of the way,' said Detective Hislop. He tried to walk towards number eight, but the crowd moved with him, like a lake of curiosity.

John Creasy stood at the edge of the pavement. He was the only one not making any noise.

'Anything you want to tell me, you can tell me out here,' he said, 'in front of everyone else.'

His words seemed to have much more of an effect than either Detective Hislop's or PC Green's, and the crowd became very quiet.

The detective looked around at all the faces. He turned to PC Green, who just shrugged his shoulders and took a notebook from his top pocket. 'Very well,' he said.

He paused for a moment, and we all paused with him, holding our breath. 'I came here today, to tell you that your wife has reported to one of our police stations to confirm that she is, indeed, safe and well.'

Everyone in the crowd seemed to breathe again at the same time, although it did sound as though all the breath was going in, rather than coming out.

'I knew it,' said Mr Creasy. 'I told you all, didn't I? I told you she was alive.'

No one replied. All the faces were silent, but I did think I heard someone at the back say *Oh my God*.

'Where has she been?' John Creasy said. 'Did she tell you why she left?'

'I believe she said she'd had a lot on her mind,' said Detective Hislop. 'She used one of these new-fangled expressions women seem to be fond of these days. What was it again, PC Green?'

PC Green studied his notebook. 'She said she needed to "work things out", sir,' he said.

'That's it.' Detective Hislop shook his head. 'Work things out.'

I definitely heard someone say *Oh my God* this time.

'Oh, and she asked us to pass this on to you,' said Detective Hislop.

PC Green handed Mr Creasy an envelope.

The detective looked at the crowd. 'She said you'd all understand.'

John Creasy stared at the envelope, and we all stared with him. Detective Hislop and PC Green walked back towards the police car.

'Is she coming home?' shouted Mr Creasy. 'Did she say?'

'Oh, I do believe so, sir.' The detective opened the back door of the panda car and heaved himself inside.

PC Green turned the ignition, and Detective Hislop wound down the window and looked out at us all. 'But she did say she'd like to pop into the station and have a little chat with us first,' he said.

*

We watched the police car drive down the avenue and disappear around the corner. It was so quiet, you could hear the engine for ages afterwards.

Mr Creasy still stood with the letter in his outstretched hands.

'Aren't you going to open it, John?' said Mr Forbes.

Mr Creasy turned the envelope over. 'It says "The Avenue" on the front,' he said.

'So it's to all of us?' said Sheila Dakin.

Mr Creasy nodded. He ripped open the edge and took out a piece of paper. When he'd read it, he looked up and frowned and read it again.

'Well?' said Sheila. 'What does it say?'

'I don't understand.' He looked at it again.

'For God's sake, man, spit it out,' said Harold.

John Creasy cleared his throat and began to read. 'It says Matthew, Chapter 7, Verses 1 to 3.'

We all waited.

'Is that it?' said Sheila Dakin.

'What in hell does that mean?' Mr Forbes threw his arms

into the air. 'Has the woman gone completely bloody crackers?'

Mrs Forbes and Mrs Roper stared at each other. When they spoke, their words came out at exactly the same time.

'*Judge not, that ye be not judged,*' they said. Like a duet.

Number Twelve, The Avenue

17 August 1976

Sheila Dakin snatched open the pantry door, and started pulling tins from the shelves.

'Mam? What are you doing?'

She knew the bottle was finished, but it was worth looking again. It was always worth looking again. Sometimes she forgot where she'd put them. There was always a chance.

Pasta shells spat on to the floor.

'Mam?' Lisa stood in the doorway, her hair in a towel.

'I'm looking for something, Lisa.'

Perhaps there was one under the sink. She could remember leaving something there a while ago. Perhaps. She pushed past Lisa and the ironing board.

'Eighty-two degrees.' Sheila pointed at the thermometer on the windowsill. 'Eighty-two bloody degrees. How is anyone supposed to function in this bloody heat?'

She crouched on the floor and reached into the cupboard. Tins of polish and bottles of window cleaner fell like skittles.

'Mam, what the hell's happened?'

Sheila looked over her shoulder. 'Margaret Creasy, that's what's happened. Margaret Creasy is coming back.'

'Isn't that a good thing?' said Lisa.

'No, it isn't a good thing. It isn't a good thing at all.' Sheila went back to the cupboard. 'Because she's not coming back on her own, is she?'

'She isn't?'

'No, Lisa, she isn't.' A can of Mr Sheen span across the lino. 'She's coming back with all our secrets. She's got a bagful of them. She knows everything.'

*

'That's it. We're all done for.' Dorothy Forbes appeared in the doorway, her arms raised to heaven. She billowed with hysteria in the centre of a cloud of taupe.

'Oh Jesus, Dot. That's all I need.'

Dorothy must have followed her across the avenue.

'I'm telling you, Sheila. I've said it from the beginning. That woman's worked it out. It's going to be the end of all of us.'

'Don't be so melodramatic, Dot.' Sheila sat back on a Brillo pad. 'We just need to think, we just need to get our stories straight.'

'I don't even know what my story is any more. Every time I try to think of it, I just get in a muddle.'

417

Lisa pulled the towel from her hair and stared at them both. 'You've both gone bloody mad,' she said, and turned on her heels. Her footsteps thudded up the stairs and across the ceiling.

Sheila swayed to her feet and reached for the cigarettes. When she looked back, Dorothy was collecting all the cans and packets from the floor and rearranging them in the cupboard.

'Would you stop tidying up other people's houses, Dot. It drives me crazy.'

'I can't help it.' Dorothy reached for a bottle of bleach under the kitchen table. 'It's my nerves,' she said.

'We've got to stay calm.' Sheila began pacing the lino with her cigarette. 'We've got to put the pieces together. What did you say to Margaret? What *exactly* did you say to her?'

Sheila waited. She could feel her heart, throwing its pulse into her neck.

Dot stared at her and blinked.

'Dorothy?'

'What was the question again, Sheila?'

The pulse seemed to fill Sheila Dakin's whole body, turning her stomach and pulling her chest, and hammering at the sides of her skull. She watched Dot folding the tea towel.

This way, then that. Squares of material, backwards and forwards in her hands.

'Would you stop folding that bloody tea towel.'

'I can't help it. It's a habit,' said Dorothy. 'I don't even know I'm doing it.'

Sheila took a drag on her cigarette. 'You're not supposed to fold tea towels, anyway. Not according to Walter Bishop. They harbour germs.'

The folding stopped and she put the tea towel on the draining board.

Sheila stared at it. The kitchen was silent, but the clock ticked away at her thinking. She stared at the tea towel again. Folded. On the draining board.

'Walter Bishop doesn't fold tea towels,' she said.

Dorothy blinked.

'But you do, Dot. Don't you?'

There was no reply.

'Dorothy?' she said.

Dorothy Forbes looked at the tea towel, and looked back at Sheila. Her eyes were very wide and very blue.

'The whole avenue wanted him gone, Sheila. You all said so. It was doing everybody a favour.'

She hadn't got a reply. For the first time in her life, Sheila Dakin had run out of words.

Number Three, Rowan Tree Croft

17 August 1976

Mrs Morton replaced the receiver.

She thought it might have been about Tilly, but it was May Roper, standing in a phone box with a pile of two-pence pieces, dispensing news about Margaret Creasy. She had a feeling her telephone call may have been one on a long list.

The estate had always been this way. A parade of people, joined together by tedium and curiosity, passing other people's misery around between themselves like a parcel. It had been the same when Ernest died. It had been the same after the funeral.

She went back to the sitting room and returned to her chair and her knitting, but even though the wool was waiting for her, wound around the needles in the middle of a stitch, she couldn't quite settle back into it. She stood up and rearranged the cushions. She opened the window a little more, and moved the footstool further away, but it was no good. The feeling of quietness had left, and in its place was a wash of unease. She wasn't sure if it was because of the breathless anticipation in May Roper's voice, or the sense that, every day recently, the past seemed to be drawing up alongside the present, or perhaps it was neither of those things. Perhaps it was the feeling that there was something she had missed – something about that day which lay paused and expectant in her memory, waiting for her to discover it and remember.

7 November 1967

There are twenty-two cards on the mantelpiece.

Mrs Morton counts them, although she knows the number hasn't changed from three hours ago. They run in diagonals between the plate she brought back from Llandudno last year and their wedding photograph, joining her life together with sincere sympathy.

There are more cards on the kitchen table, and a few on the telephone stand in the hall, but she hasn't got the heart to open them. They just repeat themselves, over and over, an endless stream of meaningful waterfalls swimming with deep condolence. You can tell a lot about a person by the card they choose. There are the safe ones, the lilies and the butterflies, with straightforward messages in a simple text. Then there are the ones that hint at a bigger force at work, the sunsets and the rainbows, and whole ranges of mountains with interesting rock formations. And of course, the religious ones – the ones that suggest you're suffering for a very good reason, the ones that tell you the Lord is supervising your misery, in swirling, gold letters, because when God speaks, he appears to speak only in a decorated font.

Call upon me in the day of trouble. I will deliver thee, says one.

Beatrice Morton isn't sure she will ever be delivered – not from the despair and the sorrow, but from the shame.

*

She sits in curtained daylight, although the weak November sun is pressing through the material and cleaning away the shadows. The curtains have been drawn for two weeks, holding the house in a pause between loss and acceptance. She had drawn them as soon as the policeman left, watching him walk down the path as she pulled them to. He had been a self-conscious young man, and clearly unsure of the etiquette of informing someone their now-dead husband had acquired a female passenger somewhere between the Chiswick Flyover and Reading Services. She had wanted to make it more comfortable for him, to tell him that she had long since known about the passenger, that the last fifteen years had been spent living in her shadow, and about the enormous amount of effort it had taken to shape a life around her existence. She wanted to offer the policeman another cup of tea, and smooth down the edges of the conversation, so they could journey across the awkwardness together. But the policeman had an inventory to get through, a list he had to tick off before he was allowed to leave the untouched cup and the edge of his seat.

Ernest doesn't even like the New Seekers, she'd said, looking for a loophole that might bring him back from the dead.

The policeman had fashioned a group of small coughs at the back of his throat, and explained that the female passenger had survived. More than survived, she was right at that moment sitting in the Emergency Department of the Royal Berkshire Hospital, drinking tea from a plastic beaker and explaining everything to one of his colleagues.

I'm sorry, he'd said, although she wasn't entirely sure if he was apologizing for her husband's death, or apologizing because her husband's mistress had survived.

As she watched him leave, she knew. She knew he would talk to his wife that evening as they ate their meal, leaning back in his seat, chewing the details of her life along with each mouthful. And the next day, his wife would sit in a hairdresser's chair and say you mustn't tell anyone, and the hairdresser would hold a comb between her teeth and pull hair around blue plastic curlers, and wonder which anyone she was going to tell first. And how very easily everyone would know the secret she had worked so hard to keep airtight.

*

The warmth of the sunlight finds the windowsill and carries the smell of decomposing flowers into the room. The house has been taken over by Ernest's death. There are flowers hiding everywhere, in vases and jam jars and earthenware jugs. Their leaves are eaten into frail skeletons, and the petals crowd on to the carpet in solemn clusters. She should really sort them out, deal with the slurry of stagnant water which fills the air with a slow, quiet decay, but she hasn't got the energy to clean it all away and start again. It was a mess she had never asked for to begin with.

The flowers were left on the doorstep, or delivered by a pleasant young woman in a red van. No one has been inside the house. Sheila and May did make it to the doorstep, three days after the accident, fuelled by curiosity and half a bottle of sherry, but even they disappeared when they realized that widowhood wore a beige cardigan and said very little. It certainly said nothing about dead husbands – or dead husbands' mistresses. They wanted to know how she was getting on *under the circumstances*, but they were circumstances she couldn't even discuss with herself, let alone with Sheila's hopeful eyebrows and the rise and fall of May's larynx, as it travelled within the folds of her throat.

Instead, the funeral had fed them on her behalf. The funeral had provided a feast. It had spread out her foolishness for everyone to see, unrolling each thread of misery, each word of deceit, and she knows that whatever she chooses to do in the future, it will always be played out on a background of her own stupidity. She hadn't turned around when the sobbing began. She had spent fifteen years facing the front, and she wasn't about to look away now.

*

She needs to go shopping, but each journey from the house is a difficult one. She tries to take the least crowded pavement, the quietest time of day, but she still feels like an exhibit, a curiosity. She knows that her presence on the street will switch conversations on like a string of fairy lights. As soon as she has moved beyond hearing, they will begin dissecting her misery and her ridiculousness, and dish it out between themselves in manageable bites.

She moves from shop to shop, as quietly as she can, like prey.

The hands of the woman in the greengrocer's clasp around hers. 'And how are you feeling?' she says, tilting her head to one side, and frowning, as though Mrs Morton were a riddle that needed to be solved.

'I'm feeling like a pound of tomatoes,' says Mrs Morton, 'and one of your best cabbages.'

She isn't sure how she feels. Or how she is supposed to feel. Are her feelings normal? Appropriate? She has never lost a husband before. There is a part of her that thinks she should be more upset, and she waits each morning, bracing herself for the sorrow. But it never arrives. Instead, she feels an unpleasant sensation of disruption. As though, in the journey she had planned for herself, she has been forced to take an alternative route, and she isn't sure if the shock she feels is the result of losing Ernest, or the surprise of having to change her travel arrangements.

She crosses the High Street, to the side with fewer shops. The stares still find her, but they seem easier to manage if she can put a road between them. On this side, there are a couple of banks and a hairdresser, and a shop selling baby clothes. The sales have started, and there are red and white banners shouting at her from every window.

'Beatrice!'

She is too busy looking at the Unbeatable Sale in the shoe shop opposite, and almost walks into Dorothy Forbes.

'How are you?' Dorothy drags the words out to fill the whole pavement.

'Mustn't grumble,' she says.

'Mustn't you?' Dorothy looks openly disappointed.

'Doesn't do any good, does it?' Mrs Morton tries to

smile, but she isn't sure if smiling widows are appropriate, so it evolves into a strange grimace that smothers half of her face.

'Yes, but in the circumstances,' says Dorothy. The end of the sentence floats for a while before it dissolves. Everyone talks about the circumstances, but no one really wants to say exactly what they are.

Mrs Morton makes 'if you'll excuse me' sounds, and tries to edge around the large, tartan flap on Dorothy's shopping trolley.

'It was a beautiful funeral,' Dorothy shifts very slightly to her left, 'for the most part.'

There is a smear of tangerine lipstick on Dorothy's front teeth. Her mouth is moving around the words too quickly, leaving a blur of orange.

'Dreadful business between Psalm 23 and the organ starting up, mind you.'

She is trapped – trapped between the wheels of the cart and a shop doorway, and Dorothy Forbes' tangerined sympathy.

Shocking. Alarming. Embarrassing, Dorothy says.

'If you'll excuse me.'

Did you know her?

'I just need to.'

Harold says she isn't local.

'I should really.'

She must have been very close to Ernest? To get so upset?

'There's something I need,' she says, 'from here.' And

she slips through the doorway, closing the questions on the other side, watching through the glass, as defeat spreads across Dorothy's face in small bites of disappointment.

It's the baby shop.

She has never been in here before. It smells of wool and towelling – a clean, undamaged, unspoiled smell that only children seem able to produce. The girl behind the counter looks up and smiles. She's very young, surely too young to have a baby, but Mrs Morton knows she has lost the ability to judge someone's age. Her barometer has become broken with time, calibrated only by the stubborn perception she keeps of herself. The girl goes back to her folding. She doesn't look at Mrs Morton with interested eyes. There is no appraisal, no opinion. Perhaps she's far away. Or perhaps the whispering has yet to push itself through the nappies and the swaddling.

Her gaze wanders over the shelves. Each one is filled with comfort. Everything is intended to soothe or blanket or cradle. Even the colours are restful: Alice blue and powder pink, and soft, watery apricot. Here there is a pocket of relief from the noise of other people, a feeling that all things will eventually pass; a sense of calm folded into the shawls and the quilting, and hidden between the pleats of silent crochet.

'You have a beautiful shop,' she says. It's the first time she has spoken about a subject other than death for the past two weeks.

The girl looks up and smiles again.

'It's so peaceful,' says Mrs Morton. 'Calming.'

The girl keeps folding. She is putting blankets into polythene bags, and the wrapping makes a soft crackle as she works. 'Sure, babies can be the most calming people on this earth, as long as they're not crying.'

The sentence is pinned and tucked with an Irish accent.

'You're not from round here?'

The girl smiles into the folds. It was a practised smile. 'No,' she said, 'I'm an outsider.'

'I wouldn't say outsider.'

The girl looks up. There is a dance of mischief in her eyes. 'Oh, I would. This town is always a little flustered by anything outside the ordinary. It doesn't cope well with a varied diet.'

'Well, that's true enough.' Mrs Morton wanders into the next aisle. It's filled with balls of wool, towered into pyramids, and rows of knitting patterns. Knitting patterns for every conceivable item of clothing a baby could ever have a need for.

'That's why I like being around children,' the girl says. 'They just see you. They don't see all the things you carry in your pockets.'

Mrs Morton doesn't know many children. There's Lisa Dakin, of course, but she's at school all day now, being fashioned into a small-scale version of Sheila. Grace Bennett must be nearly one. She often sees Grace and her mother on the estate, and they stop and pass the time of day, but Sylvia always looks exhausted, as if she's just woken from a nap. Mrs Morton stares at the pictures on the knitting patterns. A choir of babies look back at her. Heads round and smooth like eggs, and deep, clear irises filled with nothing but simplicity. This is what she needs. Eyes with no verdict. A person who doesn't see the pockets. Perhaps if she could spend just a little time with someone who didn't look at her and see only a foolish old woman, perhaps then she might start to remember who she used to be.

'Were you looking for something in particular?' the girl is asking. 'A gift, perhaps?'

Mrs Morton looks back at the photographs. 'Yes,' she says, 'that's it. A gift.'

'Boy or girl? How old?'

'A girl. She's nearly one.' She walks to the counter, past shelves of quiet reprieve. 'Her name is Grace.'

*

She leaves with a soft toy – an elephant. He has large, cream ears lined with velvet and very solemn, stitched eyes. She tucks him into her bag, underneath the cabbage and the pound of tomatoes, for fear of anyone spotting him and assuming that she has finally gone completely and irretrievably mad.

The bell above the door chimes as she leaves.

'Goodbye, Mrs Morton. Take care of yourself,' says the girl behind the counter.

She frowns and starts to reply, but the girl is already back to her folding.

*

The estate sleeps in a lunch-time quiet. She meets no one. The solitude is a blessing, and it allows her to look ahead, in place of watching the constant setting of her feet on a pavement. She stares at the trees, brushed with November paint, gripping the last of their leaves like children's hands. These are the last few days before winter gathers her skirts and wraps the evenings in darkness; the last looks at chalked clouds and apple-green lawns, until the frost rushes in and hurries them away.

The avenue is silent, the windows blank and impassive. People are working or eating, or travelling elsewhere through their day. Mrs Morton moves past the houses undisturbed. She walks past Sheila Dakin's, Lisa's toys scattered on the grass like wounded infantry, the breeze clicking at the latch of an indecisive gate. Across the road, Dorothy and Harold's driveway sits tidied and soundless, its chippings almost certainly surrendered to a sweeping brush, before it has even begun to break light.

She stops, just outside Grace's house, and ties her shoelace. As she does, she glances up at the rest of the avenue. She wonders if she is being observed, if somewhere behind the shadowy glass a person is watching, but when she turns, each house holds its contents with a poker face, giving nothing away.

431

Grace's house stands a touch further back from Dorothy's. It has a swish of neat lawn, and carefully managed flower beds, but next to the Forbeses', any garden would look a little inconvenienced. Mrs Morton walks through the space where Derek would ordinarily leave his car, past the bubbled glass of the pantry and the hall, and the row of plants on the kitchen windowsill, to the back door, its paint blistered and torn from the previous summer.

The door is slightly ajar. When she knocks, it creeps open a touch more, and she can see the wheels of a pushchair and Grace's stout little legs kicking from its seat.

She shouts hello.

She pushes the door further.

She shouts hello again.

She walks inside.

The kitchen has captured the early afternoon sun, and it smells of warmth and eaten meals. There is a slow, steady drip of water from one of the taps, beating time into the sink, and crumbs of music drift from a radio sitting on the window ledge.

Grace is alone.

When she sees Mrs Morton, she laughs and throws her fists at the air, and kicks her stout little legs even more. You can't help but laugh back. There is an inevitability about it. Grace seems to realize she is entertaining, and laughs again, crinkling her face and flapping her arms, until the whole pushchair shakes with amusement. Mrs Morton feels her spine unfold and her shoulders untighten, and a flood of relief so deep and so mighty, it steals the breath from inside of her lungs.

She reaches over to the sink and tightens the tap.

When she looks back, Grace is leaning in her seat, trying to shuffle herself towards the open door.

'What's the matter?' says Mrs Morton. 'Do you want to look at the garden?'

She opens the door a little further, and pushes Grace forward, into a pocket of frail November sunlight which has stretched itself over the kitchen floor. Grace would be fine there, just for a moment.

She walks into the carpeted silence of the hall, and there is a rustle of fear at an uninvited journey into someone else's life. The front room and the sitting room are both ticking-clock empty, and she stands at the bottom of the stairs, straining her neck towards the landing. She chances another hello.

Still nothing.

When she returns to the kitchen, Grace wriggles in her seat and throws pudding-fists at the open door. She tries to explain what she wants in burbles and bubbles and a number of looks filled with varying degrees of concentration.

'Shall we wait for Mummy in the garden?' says Mrs Morton.

She moves Grace on to the patio, beneath the branches of a cherry blossom tree, although its petals have long since been taken by a summer breeze. A quarrel of sparrows skitters and tips between the branches, and they watch –

Grace and Mrs Morton — as the birds chatter and bargain and try to find their title.

'Can you see, Grace?' says Mrs Morton, but Grace is leaning towards the path at the side of the house, and stretching her fingers towards Mrs Forbes' cat.

'Whiskey?' she says. 'Do you want to look at Whiskey?'

And so they follow the cat, along the path, down the side of the house — and past the row of plant pots in the kitchen window and the bubbled glass of the hall and the pantry, and through the space where Grace's father would ordinarily park his car.

'Just to the end of the drive,' says Mrs Morton. 'We'll go to the end of the drive, and then we'll come back and wait for your mummy.'

The cat inches against the brickwork and the sparrows squabble in the branches of the cherry tree. The wheels of the pushchair rattle and shudder on the concrete.

They wait at the end of the drive, looking out on to an empty avenue. Through the little plastic window of the pushchair, Mrs Morton can see Grace turning and leaning and addressing everything she sees with equal importance: the yellow beak of a blackbird, the papery whisper of fallen leaves, the silver curve of the dustbin lid. They are all treated with the same degree of gravity.

She looks back at the house. It waits for them with a quiet patience.

In a few minutes, it will still be there, unchanged.

'We'll just go as far as the postbox,' says Mrs Morton.

But the postbox becomes the end of the road, and the end of the road becomes the fire station, and the fire station becomes the gates of the park. The handles of the pushchair feel like a float, keeping her above the misery and the shame, and she allows herself, just for these moments, to imagine how life might have been, if it had permitted Mrs Morton a float of her own. She doesn't think of the walking. She doesn't notice the trees or the pavements, or the lamp posts. They all sit in the margins of her mind as she moves through the estate, skirting the borders of other people's lives, the fences and the walls and the precisely cut hedgerows. Instead of walking, her travelling is made up of a sequence of thoughts. A ball of feelings, as tight as a marble, which appear to move her from one place and on to the next.

When she looks back, the journeys she takes do not seem like journeys at all. They seem like a series of small decisions, one placed thoughtlessly upon the next. It's only when she stops and turns, and realizes she has reached a destination, that the importance of the decisions become clear. They stack behind her, the perhaps and the another-times, and the one-day-soons, and they hold her in a place she never meant to be held. The choices she has made are now a part of her. They have stitched themselves into the person she has become, and when she stops to see who that is, she finds that the cloth from which she is cut has begun to suffocate her.

*

When they reach the park, Mrs Morton decides they should sit in the bandstand, away from the tail of autumn, the single ice-cream seller, and the apron of leaves on the surface of a forgotten paddling pool. There are benches nearby, but they are all empty, except for a seat at the very end of the path, where an old man dozes into the pages of a newspaper and his Yorkshire Terrier listens in defeat to the sound of his master's snoring. As they walk towards the bandstand, Mrs Morton wonders if Walter Bishop might be in his usual place – if he would be sitting in a neat square, eating sandwiches from the plastic box on his knee, and stealing helpings of other people's lives as they passed by in front of him. But the bandstand was empty save for a pigeon scratching out the passage of time between last night's chip wrapper and today's morning headlines.

Mrs Morton turns Grace's pushchair towards the seat, and the child looks at her with wet, blue eyes. 'We'll go home soon,' she says. 'We'll get back and see what's happened to your mummy.'

Grace smiles. It fills her whole face.

'We'll sit for a moment first, though. Just until we get our breath back.'

She watches as Grace copies her expressions, like a mirror, her mouth trying to find its way around the words, her eyes making cartoon saucers. She plays to her audience, and when Mrs Morton laughs, Grace squeals and wiggles with achievement. As she does, there is the sense of a greater power, the spark of a beginning. It's a beginning she hasn't found in the rainbows and the sunsets and the rock formations, or gathered in the petals on the sitting-room carpet. It is a beginning not to be heard in shallow words, or seen in the stares which travel from the other side of a road. She wasn't even sure there was a beginning, until now, and having found it, she can't imagine how she hadn't seen it in the first place.

'Perhaps your mummy might like my help from time to time? Perhaps you and I can be friends?'

The pigeon flaps and blusters its way past the railings of the bandstand, and the commotion makes Grace turn in alarm.

'Don't worry.' Mrs Morton leans forward and links Grace's fingers around her own. 'As long as you are with me, nothing bad will ever happen to you, because I will guard you like a little tin soldier.'

*

They sit and watch the last light of an afternoon stretch over the park, picking out the grey of the flower beds, where the strict council loops of reds and blues and whites once grew. It follows the criss and cross of the paths and the lines of empty benches, all the way to the fishpond, where it trips and flickers on the surface of the water and dissolves into nothing. It is only when the light becomes richer, when the deep orange of afternoon fills the park, that Mrs Morton thinks they should really be on their way. She remembers the elephant.

'When we get home,' she says, 'I have a little present for you. But first I need to check if it's all right. It's good manners to ask your mummy first.'

She wheels Grace down to the pond, to the shaky, wooden footbridge and the dark columns of reeds, but the sun is trimming the rooftops and starting to unbutton the day. She stops and looks up, and turns the wheels back towards the pavement.

'Perhaps,' she says, 'perhaps we should take the shorter route home.'

They meet no one. Even if they had, Mrs Morton wouldn't have noticed. She is too busy talking to Grace about what they might do, and where they might visit on their next day out. The zoo, perhaps. Although she does think that zoos are rather cruel, so maybe they could go to the river gardens or take a picnic to the woods at the edge of the town. When Grace is a little older, they could even catch a bus and travel to the seaside for the afternoon. Has Grace ever been to the seaside? It would be an adventure for them both. When Grace starts school, they would be more limited of course, but there are always weekends and long summer holidays. There will always be something to do, somewhere to go, something to get up for.

Mrs Morton is still talking when she turns the corner of the avenue. She is explaining to Grace that one of her cousins has a friend with a caravan in Cromer. The site stands right by the coastal path. You can watch the seagulls plunge and soar, carried in ribbons of salty air, and all the little caravans look like scattered paper, littered along the grass at the top of the cliffs. She doesn't see people gathered in the street, or the eggshell-pale of Grace's mother, or Grace's father sitting on the edge of the pavement with his hands plated to his skull. She only looks up when she hears the cry of Eric Lamb's voice.

You've found her, you've found her! he says.

And then she sees the crowd, and the anger which digs into their faces. She sees Derek's car spanning the kerb, its door stretched open; Harold Forbes and Sheila Dakin, standing on the path and staring up at number eleven, the curtains drawn in all the windows, as though the house were shutting its eyes against the shouting; John Creasy rushing across the road towards her; Dorothy Forbes folding and unfolding a tea towel, her face stitched with worry. Everything is in chaos. The avenue looks as if someone has shaken all the contents and tipped them back out on to the street.

The dark, angry faces all surge forward and Grace begins to cry. As she does, Sylvia stumbles free of the crowd, the relief pulling at her legs until she can barely walk. She drops in front of the pushchair and folds herself into the child, whispering into her ear. The only tears belong to Grace. Sylvia looks like someone who has had all the crying wrung out of her.

'Where was she?' Derek is standing in front of Mrs Morton, his hands laced on the top of his head. She looks

439

for a mention of mistrust in his eyes, but they are so crowded with relief, she struggles to see.

She stares at the other faces. Her fingers make fists around the handles of the pushchair. 'I found her,' she says.

Sylvia lifts Grace from her seat and the child locks into her mother, like pieces of puzzle. The pushchair feels too light now, weightless almost. As if it might drift away and disappear, and take Mrs Morton with it.

'Where?' Derek says. 'Where did you find her?'

She can feel it. The big decision, attempting to be nothing, hiding amongst all the small decisions, hoping it will be unseen and unimportant. It's making its way to the front of the queue, carrying everything in its pockets.

'Beatrice, where was she?' Eric Lamb is speaking now, but they are all listening. Everyone stares. Everyone waits for her answer.

She looks across at number eleven. The curtains are still tight to the glass, but at one of the upstairs windows she thinks she sees the edge of a figure.

'The bandstand,' she says. She doesn't take her eyes from the window. 'I found her in the bandstand.'

'I fucking knew it.' Thin Brian pushes out of the crowd, and marches back across the avenue, towards number eleven. He stops by Dorothy and Harold's and lifts a piece of Yorkshire stone from the rockery.

'That's not the answer.' Eric Lamb was shouting, but words are not powerful enough to pull Brian back. He is fired from a barrel of his own anger and he launches himself towards Walter Bishop's, arms raised, temper lit.

Mrs Morton looks at the faces around her. She feels the feeding of a forbidden hunger – the stealth of approval. It's in the quickness of the breaths and the width of the stares. She sees it in the wetness of Sheila Dakin's lips, the tightness of Derek's fist, the spark that moves between them all, building up its charge. She knows it's been there all along, but now it can find its way out. Now it has an escape.

The crack of the stone on the glass seems to fill the whole avenue. The window splinters and splits. It holds for a fraction of a second, but then it falls in a sheet, smashing on to the concrete. It's the kind of noise that makes your ears ring and your pulse march through your neck. But it's not so much the noise, it's the silence afterwards which is the most shocking.

'Pervert,' Brian screams towards the shards of glass. 'Fucking pervert.'

The wind takes the hem of the curtains. They break free of the window frame and the material begins to beat against the brickwork, as though it's trying to escape.

They all watch, stilled by the idea that what they had just witnessed could go unanswered.

Eric walks over to Thin Brian and stands a few feet short of him. 'Come on, lad. Let's leave it. There are other ways.'

Mrs Morton pulls the cardigan around her shoulders.

The edges of the day are beginning to fade and the light is changing into the soft purple-blue of dusk, leaving them standing beneath a bruised sky. Derek takes the pushchair from her. As he does, he nods. It's wrapped in a brief smile, but it is a nod all the same.

Her hands feel very empty.

Sylvia is still holding Grace, cradling the child's head against her body. 'How can we ever repay you?' she says.

She holds on to the smell for as long as she can. 'She's a beautiful baby,' says Mrs Morton. 'Perhaps I'll be able to spend some more time with her.'

Sylvia leans forward and kisses Mrs Morton on the cheek. There's the smell. The smell of the undamaged and the unspoiled.

As she walks away, they are still gathered around number eleven – watching and waiting. She feels it again, the sense of a beginning, but this one is injured and fearful. This is a beginning she wants no part of. She walks home along empty pavements, carrying the weight of her shopping, past houses filled with the joined-up lives of other people. It's the small decisions, the ones that slip themselves into your day unnoticed, the ones that wrap their weight in insignificance. These are the decisions that will bury you.

She thinks of the elephant, lying beneath the tomatoes and the cabbage. Grace will never remember. She will grow up and go to school, and make friends. She will find a joined-up life of her own, and one day, perhaps, she will hold a child in her arms and breathe the same smell and feel the same pull, and she will understand the need for a beginning. Grace will remember nothing.

But an elephant, an elephant never forgets.

The Drainpipe

21 August 1976

Jesus didn't really look like Jesus, even when I squinted and sat back on my heels and tilted my head.

I wondered if He ever really had. The garages were empty shells again, and the pool of oil and the rotten tyre were silent and ignored. Even the leaves didn't talk in the corners any more.

I put my face right up to the drainpipe. 'Was it really you?' I whispered.

I pulled my knees to my chest and listened.

I heard it – a few minutes after I thought it would be, but it was there: Tilly's sandals slapping against the path, slower and softer than before. But I heard them.

She appeared a few seconds later, all smiles and carrying her sou'wester. She had taken the bobbles out of her hair, but it stayed in exactly the same position as if they were still there.

444

'My mum says I can't stay long,' she said.

I moved across on the grass and she sat down next to me. 'I thought you were only going to be ten minutes?' I said.

'I had to go back.' She reached into her pocket. 'I forgot to bring it with me.'

I looked at the bushbaby. 'I can't believe you carry a Whimsy around with you,' I said.

'Of course I do. You gave it to me. It's important.' She turned it over in her hands. 'I thought you said they couldn't be separated, though. I thought you said they were a pair.'

'They are,' I said. And I decided it really was true after all. You only really need two people to believe in the same thing, to feel as though you just might belong.

'I was thinking,' I sat back on the grass. 'I don't know if it really was Jesus after all.'

Tilly squinted and tilted her head to one side. 'Perhaps not,' she said. 'But it doesn't actually matter, does it?'

'How do you mean?'

'Well,' Tilly stretched her legs into the sunshine, 'it doesn't actually matter if it was Jesus or Brian Clough, or just a stain on a garage wall. For a while, it brought us all together, didn't it?'

'For a while,' I said.

'It just shows, though,' she said, 'doesn't it?'

'I suppose it does,' I said.

'And, after all, Jesus is definitely in the drainpipe. He always has been.'

I sat up a bit straighter. 'How do you mean?'

'God is everywhere, Grace,' she said. 'Everybody knows that.'

And she waved her arms about, and I laughed, and waved my arms back.

*

We sat in silence. Everything was different somehow. I wasn't sure what it was at first, but it felt as though the day had turned and shifted, as though something in the avenue had gone missing. It was only when I looked at the sky that I realized what it was.

'Oh my goodness,' I said.

We both stared up.

'The sun has disappeared,' said Tilly. 'Where did it go?'

The sky was an iron-grey, blackened and angry. It grew darker as we watched, anchoring itself to the rooftops and forcing the daylight back under the ground.

'It's still hot, though,' said Tilly. 'How can it be so hot when there isn't any sun?'

'It's because it's still there.' I pointed into nothing. 'It hasn't disappeared. It can't just disappear. It's impossible. It's only that we can't see it any more.'

We were both still thinking about this when I remembered the time.

'Quick, we've got to go, Tilly. It's almost here.'

'What's almost here?' she said.

'The bus. Today is the day.'

'The day for what?' She pulled her sou'wester down and dusted the chippings from her socks.

'The day we've all been waiting for,' I said. 'The day Mrs Creasy comes home.'

The Avenue

21 August 1976

When we turned the corner, everyone was already gathered in the middle of the avenue.

Mr Forbes in his shorts, standing next to Clive. Dorothy Forbes gripping the edge of a duster, and Sheila Dakin watching her and frowning. Thin Brian in his plastic jacket, waiting by the side of his mother and a bag of sherbet lemons; and Eric Lamb next to them, leaning against the wall. His wellington boots had left a trail of mud all the way from his front door. My parents were there as well. I checked to see if they looked worried about each other, and I decided that they did. One of my father's hands rested on my mother's shoulder, and his other hand sank into his face. I decided that it didn't really matter if we were poor, because as long as we all worried about each other, everything would always be all right. Even Mrs Morton was there.

She looked strange and distant, not like Mrs Morton at all, and in her hands was a soft toy. I wasn't really sure, but I think it looked like an elephant. In the middle of everything was Mr Creasy. The lapels of his suit had begun to curl against his shirt, and in his hands was a bunch of flowers, which gasped and wilted in the heat.

'It's nearly time,' I said and looked at my watch.

*

We didn't notice to begin with. It was Thin Brian who saw it first.

'Look at that cat,' he said.

We all stared at the bottom of the avenue.

Dorothy Forbes dropped her duster. 'Whiskey?'

'Well, I'll be buggered,' said Mr Forbes, 'after all this time.'

The cat padded along the pavement, each careful paw placed on the concrete, edging its way past the fences and the walls. It looked as though it knew exactly where it was going.

It reached Mrs Forbes and jumped into her arms.

'Whiskey,' she said again and kissed the top of its head. 'You didn't disappear after all.'

'I told you so,' said my father. 'I told you it would come back.'

Brian peered around his mother's shoulder. 'How long has it been missing, Dot?'

'Since the night of the fire,' said Mrs Forbes. 'Haven't you, my darling?'

The cat purred and rubbed, and kneaded its paws into Mrs Forbes' cardigan.

'Nasty taxi, scaring you off like that.'

Mrs Forbes kneaded whiskey back again.

Sheila Dakin was frowning at her. 'What taxi was that, Dot?'

'The one that brought Walter and his mother home.' Mrs Forbes carried on kneading, and gave more kisses to the top of Whiskey's head. 'I said to Margaret, it's no wonder he ran off. Big, scary car like that, pulling up in the avenue in the middle of the night.'

'You knew she was in the house?' said Mrs Dakin.

Mrs Forbes smiled. 'I thought they both were,' she said.

Mrs Dakin's mouth fell open, but no words seemed to want to come out of it.

'It's a wonder you recognized it,' said Brian, 'after all this time.'

When Mrs Forbes answered, she didn't look at Brian. She looked at Sheila Dakin instead. 'That's the thing, though, isn't it? You can't ever forget what you've seen,' she said. 'Even if your photographs have gone, you can just pull it out of your mind whenever it might be useful to you. Memories are only forgotten when someone dies. It's a dangerous thing. Worth remembering, that is.'

And she carried on staring at Mrs Dakin, even after the words had disappeared.

I looked at Tilly and shrugged, and Tilly looked at me and shrugged back again.

*

We could hear the bus from miles away. We could hear it push around the estate, stopping and starting on corners, hissing its brakes, and coughing and spluttering in the heat. The sky seemed to become even darker, and the air even thinner, and I watched Mr Forbes take a handkerchief from his pocket and wipe at his forehead.

'She's nearly here,' said Mr Creasy.

Sheila Dakin lit a cigarette, but she didn't smoke it. Instead, it just rested between her fingers, burning itself into a thread of ash, as she stared at Dorothy Forbes.

We were standing like that, all of us watching the bottom of the avenue, when he turned the corner.

Walter Bishop.

He carried an umbrella and had his coat over his arm, and instead of shuffling and staring at the pavement, he looked straight at all of us as he walked past everyone's houses.

'Well,' he said, when he reached our little collection. 'This is quite a welcoming committee, isn't it?'

'Mrs Creasy is coming home,' I said.

'So I hear.' He put down his umbrella and his coat, and reached over to stroke the top of Whiskey's head.

'We're all very excited,' said Tilly.

'So I see,' he said. 'Although for people who are very excited, none of you look especially happy about it.' He laughed.

I had never seen Walter Bishop laugh before. He looked like a completely new person.

Walter stood for a moment and stared at the sky. When he had finished staring, he picked up his umbrella and his coat, and his eyes met everyone in turn.

There was silence – the kind of silence that only Walter Bishop was comfortable with.

After a few minutes, he turned to Mrs Forbes. 'I'd get that cat inside if I were you,' he said, 'it looks like rain.'

As he spoke, there was a rumble in the distance. At first, I thought it was still the sound of the bus, but then I realized it wasn't. It was thunder. Creeping across the horizon and cutting into the dark, slate-grey of the sky. It was quiet and indifferent at the beginning, but then it grew louder, joining in with the sound of the engine, until the whole avenue started to snarl and growl, and all the little houses seemed to shake in their gardens.

The brakes hissed and the engine spat, and the bus pulled up at the bottom of the road.

It was then that the first drops began to hit the pavement. There were just a few at first, smacking the concrete as though they had been thrown at us, but then there were more, lots more. And they raced and gathered until there was no space in between the sounds, just the unbroken, unquiet noise of rain, carrying off the heat and the dust and washing away Jesus as if he had never been there in the first place.

The bus still waited. And we stared.

And we watched Mrs Creasy's feet appear on the platform. 'She's here,' said Mr Creasy.

'Oh Jesus Christ.'

I turned around to see who had spoken. I looked at all their faces. Mr and Mrs Forbes, and Clive from the British Legion. Thin Brian and his mother, and Sheila Dakin, who hadn't taken her eyes from Dorothy Forbes. Eric Lamb and my parents, and Mrs Morton, who still held on to the elephant.

Walter Bishop stood underneath his umbrella and watched everyone with me.

I knew I'd heard the words, but I couldn't decide who it was.

I turned back to wait for Mrs Creasy.

It didn't really matter. It could have been any one of them.

We all stood in the middle of the avenue, watching. The rain dripped from our hair and from our noses, and it pushed through our clothes and soaked itself into our skin.

I looked at Tilly, and she smiled at me from under her sou'wester.

And it felt like the end of summer.

Acknowledgments

To list all the people who have cheered for *Goats and Sheep* would be impossible, so I would just like to say a huge thank you to the writing community as a whole for the most incredible support and encouragement, with an especially big thank you to Kerry Hudson and Tom Bromley. A huge debt of gratitude to my amazing agent Sue Armstrong, and all the team at Conville & Walsh, and to the very lovely and very talented Katie Espiner, and everyone at The Borough Press and HarperCollins. Thank you also to the staff at The George Bryan Centre in Tamworth and ECW at the Radbourne Unit in Derby, for teaching me to understand the importance of a narrative, and for caring for the goats as well as the sheep. Lastly, thank you to the patients I have had the privilege to meet. Our paths may have only crossed for a short time, but your courage, wisdom and humour will stay with me forever.